A LIVING GRAVE

A Katrina Williams Novel

ROBERT E. DUNN

LYRICAL UNDERGROUND
Kensington Publishing Corp.
www.kensingtonbooks.com

LYRICAL UNDERGROUND BOOKS are published by

Kensington Publishing Corp.
119 West 40th Street
New York, NY 10018

All Kensington titles, imprints, and distributed lines are available at special quantity discounts for bulk purchases for sales promotion, premiums, fund-raising, educational, or institutional use.

Special book excerpts or customized printings can also be created to fit specific needs. For details, write or phone the office of the Kensington Sales Manager: Kensington Publishing Corp., 119 West 40th Street, New York, NY 10018. Attn. Sales Department. Phone: 1-800-221-2647.

Lyrical Underground and Lyrical Underground logo Reg. US Pat. & TM Off.

First Electronic Edition: September 2016
eISBN-13: 978-1-60183-807-0
eISBN-10: 1-60183-807-7

First Print Edition: September 2016
ISBN-13: 978-1-60183-808-7
ISBN-10: 1-60183-808-5

Printed in the United States of America

This is for my father. Robert W. Dunn served his country and his family in two branches of the military during three wars. He believed in a better world for me. I think he would have liked this book if he'd ever had the chance to read it. I know he would be glad I wrote it.

Chapter 1

Therapy is not for the weak. It is spine-ripping, devastatingly hard work that shines a light on all the secret parts of your soul. We are all vampires at the center of ourselves, I think. Those bits of ourselves, the secrets that are protected by ego and self-delusion, burn like phosphorus flames when the light finally pins them down.

I didn't choose therapy. The sessions were a requirement of keeping my job with the Taney County Sheriff's Department. I'm the only female detective in the department and the only one required to attend counseling.

There had been an incident—

There had been incidents—

I guess the final straw that I had tossed onto the sheriff's back was what I called a "justified adjustment of attitude." It wasn't that I minded so much the trouble setting the wife-beater straight got me into. What really got to me was that the wife, with her two raccoon eyes and broken nose, picked him up at the hospital and took him right back to the familial double-wide. Some things no amount of adjustment can fix.

My therapist said that I was violent toward the man but exhibited more anger at the woman. Those were the kinds of things she said and I had to listen to. That was easy to blow off, but sometimes she said something that stuck like a bit of glass in my eye. That morning she had mentioned my clothes in the way only a woman in pencil skirts and strappy shoes can bring up another woman's choice of jeans and boots. I work for a living and being pretty isn't part of the job. Sometimes her questions and observations made me want to grab a fistful of perfect hair and adjust her attitude a little.

I didn't, though, because sometimes—just sometimes—she shines a light that I guess I really need to see. Maybe I need the burning away.

Sessions were over at ten, but I took the mornings off until noon. The doctor was in Springfield and the Taney County seat was Forsyth. It was close to an hour drive each way the best of times. Post-session was never the best of times, so I usually went through home. Nixa, Missouri has little to distinguish itself to the rest of the world, but it was my hometown. It was where I went after the Army, and it's where I return every few days just to touch something that was gone. There really aren't words for what was gone. I didn't know the thing, just the absence of it. That's the kind of crap you learn in therapy. Home didn't fill the hole, it just let me walk the edges without falling in. I learned that on my own. Something else it did for me—it let me eat without feeling like a complete carb whore. Sometimes I would pick up Dad and take him to the Drop Inn Café for a late breakfast of biscuits and gravy. If it was a bad day, I had the big plate of eggs, runny over medium, with sides of grits and bacon and toast. Therapy to get over therapy. That morning Dad was gone, off again to D.C., where he still did consulting work for the government twenty years after retiring from the Army. He never told me anything but happy stories about his time in the service and I never told him anything but happy stories about mine. My therapist says we're both lying to ourselves and each other, but honestly I think I'm the only one with lies to tell. I missed him as I sat alone in the café and had the eggs and bacon with extra grits.

Missouri roads are some of the worst in the country but have some of the best curves. There is so much up-thrust sandstone and limestone karst topography that straight lines had been impossible for anything but federal road projects. I would have made better time on Highway 65. It was a bland seam of government concrete, no joy at all. But I wasn't looking for progress. I was looking to grind time under my wheels and kill it with horsepower and dangerous turns. Going through Nixa kept me on 160 the whole way. The long way back to Forsyth, but even in a truck, the curved path is more fun.

Already the sun was high and burning languid heat into the day. I like to drive with the windows down on the pickup. Nixa is my hometown, but the entire Ozarks region is home. And I like the feel of home on my skin as I drive. The moving air smelled of cut grass and horse manure. Despite the heat, it was heavy with humidity.

When the cell phone vibrated on the console I stared at it hard, hoping it might back down. It didn't. I put the windows up and turned on the air before answering. I needed to hear clearly. The only calls I ever got were from the office and never casual.

"Yeah," I answered. I wanted her to know how I felt about the intrusion. Not that it would do any good.

"Hurricane. It's Darlene."

I gritted my teeth at the sound of the nickname and took my calming breath. I always imagined every woman named Katrina picked up the same extra baggage after 2005. It sounded kind of action-movie lame to me, but I knew a lot of male cops who would love to be tagged with it. Just another of the things that make me different.

"Yes, Darlene. It's always you," I said back into the phone. Darlene was the most professional dispatcher on the planet. Nothing much seemed to ruffle her panties, which means people like me feel almost all right dumping our moods on her. "What have you got for me?"

She gave the location of a call out to a farm road south of Walnut Shade and on the south side of Bear Creek.

"What's the call?" I asked.

"Just see-the-man. No name. No complaint. He said it was an emergency but didn't need EMTs."

"Did his information show up on the computer?"

"He didn't call 9-1-1. Used the office number."

That told me he was one of the longtime residents. A lot of people around here remembered party lines and there were more than a few left who could tell you what it was like to walk miles to the only phone that you had to crank. They were the ones who remembered the sheriff's department office number but never seemed to get comfortable with 9-1-1.

"I'm on one-sixty coming up on the Reeds Spring cutoff," I told Darlene. I had passed the cutoff at least a mile back. "Don't you have anyone closer?"

"Closer but not available. Almost everyone else is up at Walnut Shade looking for that Briscoe girl."

"Briscoe girl?"

"Thirteen years old, reported missing when she didn't come home for dinner last night. Sheriff has everyone not already tied up and about forty volunteers checking the dirt roads and late night dirty-tango spots."

"I've got it then. It gives me an excuse to drive fast."

"You need an excuse?" Darlene asked before hanging up.

Walnut Shade was one of those towns that had been something less than a town for a hundred years until the lake region exploded along with Branson in the 1990s. Now it was what we called an *unincorporated community*, subdivided and paved, but remaining something less than a town. The old-timers don't want change and the new-timers want the illusion of rural life. What that means for us is the sheriff's office getting called every time a mobile home with a leaking septic system floods the yard of the McMansion next door. Still, a call is a call and I had a job to do.

There was no direct route to where I needed to be. If I stayed on 160 it would take me right into Walnut Shade. But since I needed to be below there and on the far side of Bear Creek, I had to take 65 where the two highways crossed. After that, it was mostly hunt through the unmarked farm tracks and fishing paths until I found someone who looked like they'd been waiting an hour.

It didn't take an hour; it only took about forty minutes. The old guy was sitting on the open tailgate of an early-sixties GMC pickup that looked like it had once been painted Forest Service green. When I pulled up and parked he waved a fishing pole in greeting. He was polite but unenthusiastic about dealing with the cops. We get that a lot.

When I introduced myself, he looked me up and down without trying to hide the appraisal. Since he didn't leer, it wasn't clear if he was checking me out as a woman or as a cop. He was pretty old and since he didn't make any comment, I gave him the benefit of the doubt and assumed it was cop first, female second.

"You want to let me in on why you called?" I asked him.

He looked at his feet and spit a stream of tobacco into the weeds. It wasn't me bothering him. You get to know, as a cop, when you're the problem with someone. When you're a woman cop you get to know a few extra problems.

"I'll show you," he said before dropping off the tailgate. His name was Clarence Bolin. Everyone called him Clare, he told me as we walked. He was the kind of old-timer who the Ozarks had been both commercializing and trying to live down for a generation. Hillbilly. Of course, nowadays that was an epithet to be avoided. Like being drunk and slovenly was the role an oppressive government forced on him. He wore a T-shirt that had once been white under overalls that were un-buttoned at the side to provide room for his huge belly. If it weren't for the belly anyone would have thought the man had no weight on him at all. He had thin arms and legs that flapped like wings in the big legs of the overalls when he walked.

Clare led the way as we tromped over the fallow field. When we got to the border of overgrowth that bounded the cultivated land and separated it from the creek, he held back and waited for me to take the lead.

He walked behind me on the narrow path of crushed foliage for a few yards before he said, "You're the one they call Hurricane, ain't you?"

"Why do you say that?" I asked without looking at him. I was curious to see where this would go.

"People talk about the big-ass female deputy."

I turned around then and gave him a look with crosshairs in it.

"I don't mean to say you got a big ass . . . I mean—it's just a way of talking . . . Oh hell, you know what I mean—there just aren't that many six-foot-tall women that pile on boots with a cowboy heel."

Just to keep him squirming, I kept the look locked on the old man for a long time, then I said, "Detective."

"Huh?"

"Detective. Not Deputy." Clare relaxed a bit, his shoulders coming down to their usual slump. "Are you sure you don't want to make a comment about my boobs now?" I asked.

His shoulders tensed again and his eyes remained aimed exactly at mine. He didn't answer. It was obviously all he could do to keep his eyes off my chest.

"Good man, Clare. There might be hope for you yet," I told him and then turned away, not caring where his look wandered.

From behind me I heard him say, quietly, "No need to bite a man's head off." Then Clare started walking. He kept muttering to himself and it was like Popeye in the old cartoons; you knew he was saying something—you just couldn't understand it. I stopped and in the quiet I heard him say, ". . . not like I had a very good day myself."

I understood why. There was a girl on the ground in front of me. She was dead. I looked at Clare and he wasn't looking. Not at the girl, not at me. He had turned to look into the high branches of the covering trees, but I got the feeling he wasn't seeing leaves.

There wasn't any doubt in my mind who she was. It had to be the

Briscoe girl. Death—this kind of death—just wasn't common here. The chances we would have one missing girl and one, unrelated dead girl within a few miles were nonexistent.

I took another look at her but didn't linger. Something that felt like fear, a hot wave of nausea, and a pounding drumbeat signal to run boiled from my stomach into my throat. It lingered as a flush on my face, but made my feet feel as though they were growing roots into cold ground. This was the abyss the philosopher Nietzsche talked about. The one that stares back if you stare too long into it. A girl left dead and alone. For an instant, the forest floor was desert dust and the girl was me. Just for an instant. Then I regained control.

This is my job. I can do this.

She was flat on her back with her hands up and to the side. Down below her legs were together and her feet splayed. Death was always pigeon-toed. Her shoes were well-worn flats and her skirt a medium-length denim that covered her knees. The knees were scratched and scraped with old injuries and new wounds. Those that looked old also looked normal, benign. One expects kids to have scrapes on knees and elbows. Scabs are the hard-earned badges of youth. Those other marks, though—the ones on the lower part of the knees—were ripped skin with the ground-in detritus of the woods. Black soil and flecks of bark were embedded in the wounds. Bits of leaves glued with the girl's blood were clinging to her limbs. I checked her hands. They were scratched and caked with black soil as well. She had crawled before she was put on her back.

I tried. I worked very hard to focus on her knees. It was important to see those wounds and keep them in my mind. I needed to remember those knees because if I didn't, the image I would always recall was that of her face. It was all but gone.

"Stay here with her," I told Clare. "But stay back where you are. And don't touch anything. I have to make a call."

Making a call required walking back to the high ground at the edge of the woods and fishing the air for a signal. I was glad for the distance. I needed it to pull myself back into myself and focus on the job. As soon as I got a couple of bars, I called Darlene for a description of the girl. She read what she had and told me the name was Angela Briscoe. Then I told her Angela was here, and dead. I asked her to call the sheriff to get help out to me. After hanging up, I stood there for a few moments and waited for the tears that, as always, hit a road-block and piled up just behind my eyes.

At that point I was mostly waiting for the system to get in motion. It's like a living thing: Something lumbering and brutish that has to un-limber itself, have coffee, and work its way up to a task. You needed to overcome its inertia, get it moving with enough energy to carry it to the end. The sheriff would make calls, talk with the family, the press. Deputies would secure the scene. Investigators would help collect evidence and the ME team would collect the body. I was part of the system too. Because I was first on scene and had awakened the death system, I would be responsible for finding who did this. The trick with this system was to move it without getting it stuck on the wrong paths. There were always more wrong paths than right ones.

How many paths were there that lead to murdered little girls?

I sucked it up. There had been more than a few dead bodies in my life. Some even children. I had been on the investigative team in Iraq when those soldiers—Americans—had killed a family, then raped, killed, and burned the body of a fourteen-year-old girl. People talk about the stress of war driving good soldiers to do bad things. It's crap. It drives bad soldiers to do terrible things. That's what happened to this girl, Angela Briscoe. Someone bad did something horrible to her. I could make it stop.

A few minutes later I was standing over her body again. This time I looked at her, really looked. I had no camera with me so I pulled out my pad and pen and started writing and making a diagram. Photos fix things in the mind; the notes and drawings I make for myself keep things more fluid. They let me recall what I felt at the time, the truth of the moment more than the truth of the scene.

I had noted before that her legs were together, but this time I took note there were no clothes separate from the body. Specifically under-clothes.

"Look away," I told Clare. He did, and I noticed he turned completely away without making any attempt to see what I was doing.

What I did was to grab a fallen branch and break off the smaller twigs and leaves until I had a long, crooked stick. I used the stick so I could stay back from the body and lift the girl's skirt. Her panties were where they should be. She probably hadn't been raped. She was wearing a white T-shirt printed with the phrase *All Girl All Awesome*.

The blood covering the top half of the shirt showed clearly the outline of a bra that was in place.

I wrote in my book some more, telling myself all the whys about my belief that there was no sexual assault. Scribbling quickly, I drew out her hand and noted where something had been chewing at her fingers. There were tracks of bird's feet on the arm too. Probably a crow had walked through her blood and then perched on the arm to peck at the fingers.

"You can turn around if you want," I told Clare.

"I'd just as soon not," he answered. When he spoke you could hear a thickness to his voice that had not been there before. My estimation of him went up a few points.

"I have a granddaughter about her age," he added.

I wrote it down that he said *her* and not *that*. Then I noted he had no visible blood and he had called it in and waited maybe an hour for someone to show up. At the bottom of that little column I wrote, *Clarence Bolin, not very likely.*

"When I get home, I'm gonna call her. I get annoyed sometimes, thinkin' that she oughta call me. I'm her grandpa, after all. I don't think I'll worry much about that anymore."

He still had his back to me and I heard him blow his nose. I'm pretty sure he didn't have a handkerchief. In my little notebook I circled the word *not* in the last sentence I had written.

"I know your Uncle Orson," he said. "Been fishing with him more times than I can remember."

I crouched to be close to the ground and kept poking around the body with my stick, then sketching things in the pad. Clare's talk was actually soothing to hear. Normal, even though he was doing it to keep his mind off of something not normal in his life at all.

"Your daddy too. Way back when."

I think I nodded, reacting more to the sound than his words. Tossing my stick aside, I stood, then circled the body. Each time I stopped I added to my sketches. I had to force myself to look into the face. Into where the face had been. I sketched. Then I looked away. I sketched her hair. Then I looked away.

"There are monsters in the woods," Clare said, his back still to me. I was listening then. "It used to be a joke. When I was a kid, people talked about Momo, the Missouri monster. It was like a local Bigfoot. But the real monsters are people, aren't they?"

I didn't answer him.

"Perverts." He spit the word out. "Monsters that do that to children. There isn't hate big enough for them nor a hell deep enough. This will rile some people up. He lives in one of those piece-of-crap mobile homes in that big development off of F Highway. You know, over by the McKenna farm."

"Who does?" I had stopped writing and was paying very close attention to Mr. Bolin at that point.

"The guy. The rapist."

"Turn around and look at me, Clare." He did. "Tell me what, and who, you are talking about."

"He's on the sex-offender site."

I let my breath out slowly.

Clare went on talking. "One of those Web sites with the names and addresses of all the kiddie guys. He's listed on it. Lives just a few miles from here."

I hated those listings. Someone thought it would be a good idea to let everyone know where the sex offenders lived. Problem was in some places you were prosecuted as a sex offender if you stepped into the woods to urinate because toilets in the park were broken. Most of the bad ones, the ones you really had to worry about, didn't hang around with a big neon sign pointing at them. I'd check the guy out but it already felt like a waste of time.

"Clare," I said, "I don't think this girl has been sexually assaulted."

"No?" he asked. I could see the certainty drain out of his face. It wasn't pretty. That's the thing about certainty: It makes everything easier. When it goes, you're left with a wide-open landscape of horrible possibilities and it's hard to find any comfort in doubt. It seemed to hit Clare pretty hard. "Who . . ." he started, then faded out. Then he drew up his breath again. "Who would do something like this unless it was for . . . ?"

"I don't know," I told him. "I'm going to find out." I tried to sound certain.

"I hope so," he said. "But I don't see how."

"There's always something. Evidence or witnesses. Usually criminals do something stupid or they'll be like your sex offender. Part of the system. I'll check him out and anyone else in the area who stands apart from the crowd. Anyone new who might have been hanging around the girl or even around here."

Clare was starting to look a little deflated and sick. He swallowed hard and looked back off into the green again. The grip on his fishing pole had turned to a hard white. As much as I wanted to ask him what was wrong, I didn't. He wanted to say something; that was clear. I wasn't going to push.

Just let it come.

I looked away to give him some thinking room. When I did, I noticed something that had escaped me before.

Leech.

The word was freshly carved in ragged letters on the trunk of a white oak.

"This mean anything to you?" I asked.

Clare came closer but kept a wary distance. He had changed in the last few moments. Change was something good in witnesses; it means a connection; it means they know something or they think they know something. Whatever it was that Clare knew bothered him. I didn't have any doubt it bothered him enough to spill it. The question was how much line he would take before letting himself be reeled in.

He was looking hard at the carving. Harder than it probably deserved. I almost asked him if it was my badge or my big ass that was making him uneasy. He wasn't ready to have the mood lightened up.

"No. Kids carve all kinds of shit on the trees around here," he said.

"Sure," I agreed and I ran my fingers over the lettering. "But why *Leech*?"

"Who knows?"

"It's an odd word. Capitalized like a name."

"What about bikers?" he asked.

"What about them?" I kept my gaze and my fingers on the carved letters.

"You think bikers could do something like this? If there were any around?"

"Oh, there're always some around. Some good ones and some bad ones—mostly they all try to look bad. Makes them hard to weed out, but if I have a reason, I'll sure look into anyone who needs looking into."

Clare looked away, casting his gaze to the creek bank and up the little trail that ran alongside it. Then he looked at me and quickly looked back to his feet. "Okay if I get on out of here?"

"Thought you were going fishing." I nodded to the rod he still carried in his hand.

"Not with all the cops that'll be around here. Who needs that?"

I almost said "the little girl there," but stopped myself. It would have been needlessly cruel in more than one way. Shaking my head, I went back to stand close to the body, maybe a little possessively. "No. I'll need you to stick around for a while."

The girl was close enough to me now that I could feel her presence without looking. Death has a gravity and Angela Briscoe was pulling at me. Even so, I didn't move any closer. I didn't want to cause any contamination to the scene. Each step I took in proximity to the girl was where I had carefully stepped before.

I looked at Clare and caught him looking at the girl. He was trying to see a face where there was just red and splinters of white. Even her corn-silk hair was fanned out away from the face as though in surprise at the violence that had erased it.

Clare walked toward the creek bank and the sound of running water.

I had to pull myself away from the girl too, or orbit her tragedy forever.

It was full summer and everything along the riverbank was green and dappled yellow with sunlight. Within the banks were flat stones and smooth-tumbled gravel from black to white with colorful scatterings of pink and molted greens. The water that ran over it was so clear, if it were not for the ripples, it would be invisible. There was an empty space in the mud where a stone had lain, half in and half out of the water. At the edge of the space were the marks of fingers where the stone had been lifted. Small fingers.

A woman's? Or could Angela have been forced to choose her own murder weapon?

Water tinkled where the shallow flow ran over stones.

"Why were you up here?" I asked Clare.

"Like I said," he raised up his pole to reinforce his point. "I was sucker grabbin'."

I nodded and then reached up to push aside a strand of hair that had fallen with the movement. For the sake of my pale skin, I usually keep my hair under a hat when outdoors. No matter how hard I try though, every summer my nose burns and my hair goes from a deep reddish brown to summer red. Unconsciously, my finger found the scar that started in my left eyebrow and followed the crescent of the orbital bone. It was a small scar. Small wasn't the same as meaning-less. As soon as I realized, I pulled my hand away. It was a bad habit. The slight discoloration barely showed to anyone but me. When I touched it, though, when I was aware of touching it, the ridge of skin seemed like a jagged, red wall I had yet to climb over. No one else has climbed over it, either. A couple have tried. Only a couple. Both had made the mistake of saying it gave me "character." It was as much of my character as they ever got to see.

When I lost myself in thought, or when there was a puzzle, I had the habit of touching the scar like a little talisman. Just then I was puzzling about sucker grabbing. Sucker were big, carp-like fish. Bot-tom feeders, they were hard to catch on a bait hook. They're mostly caught by weighting a line with a big treble hook and dropping it into a congregation of fish. Then you jerk the line and grab them with the naked hook.

I carefully stepped back from the water, checking the ground for any other evidence of the girl's last moments, and then started hiking downstream.

"Follow me," I told the old man. He did, but he set his own path and pace. Slow.

The woods were thick with wild grapevine and poison ivy run-ning under the mantle of oak, walnut, and hawthorn. The ground was lumpy with softball-sized hedge apples. Along the bank, just skirting its edge, was a path. Bare dirt littered with cigarette butts, beer, and soda cans.

Kids come to party and drink.

Down in the streambed, the water deepened. Here it had eroded more than gravel. Large, flat slabs of sandstone were all along and under the water. They were the remains of an ancient shallow sea that now defined the shape of a spring-fed stream. Here the water was silent. Another two hundred yards down, the cold flow dumped into the deeper, swifter water of Bear Creek.

"I mean, why were you up there?" I almost had to shout to be heard, Clare had fallen so far behind.

"What?" he hollered back.

As I stood waiting on the old guy, I caught myself fingering the scar again. There's another reason it's a bad habit. Every time I touch it, even when I don't realize it at the time—*especially* if I don't realize it—I get pissed off. That little scar is kind of a trigger. When things don't add up or they start to churn in my head just a little too much, I reach up and pull it.

"Get your old ass down here, Clare." This time I did shout. I was getting tired of the waiting game with him. And I'm usually such a patient person.

As he picked his way through the path, I was rubbing the rubbery pucker of skin around my eye and thinking, not for the first time, how everyone seemed to have lies that had to be worked out of them. Watching Clare work his way forward, like if he moved slowly enough I would forget about him, made my dark mood churn.

"Now, I want to know why you were up there," I said emphatically, "where the water's way too shallow for sucker grabbing. And not down here at this pool, where I can see at least thirty fish just waiting on you to pull them out."

Clare opened his mouth to speak, then seemed to think better of it. There was something there. It was impossible to miss. I decided he just needed a little more pressure at his back.

"That's good, Clare. Saying nothing is better than lying. But saying nothing won't let me know you had nothing to do with this."

"I called ya, didn't I? I brought you out here. Why would I do that if it was me that hurt the girl?"

"Happens all the time. Lots of people get the bright idea to throw off our scent by being the first to report. It pays to consider the motives of the person that calls. Especially when that person is not completely forthcoming."

"I don't know what you're talking about." His words said one thing but everything else about him said another. It was an interesting change. I wondered what he was protecting.

Who?

For a long moment I stared at him and then turned away to point downstream. "I bet the kids have a name for their little party spot, don't they? That clearing by the fork."

"Whiskey Bend."

That says something.

"When I was seventeen we called it Budweiser Corner." Clare

looked like he was trying hard to remember seventeen. "Kids been coming here for years. For a while I heard they were calling it Coors Corner. Course, back when I was a kid, you couldn't get Coors this far east. You ever see *Smokey and the Bandit*?"

"Why whiskey, Clare?"

He stopped smiling and his eyes got that same caught-in-the-crosshairs look. "Huh?" was all he managed to get out.

"Whiskey. Kids like beer. It's what they usually start with. What they can get away with. My old man kept a refrigerator in the garage filled with the stuff. He never noticed when a couple disappeared."

"So?"

"So, now they call it Whiskey Bend. I have to wonder where the whiskey comes from."

Clare was thinking. He had the look of a man weighing options. Heavy ones. I kept watch on him from the corner of my vision as his face squirreled around itself. He had nothing to do with killing the girl; I was sure of that. But the girl was dead and that left no room for anyone's secrets in my tally.

Leech.

There it was again, carved into another tree. This time the word was more than written, it was stylized like a logo or brand. The capital L was formed with arrow points at each termination and the rest of the word inset within the angle.

"I don't want no trouble," Clare said. "And I don't want to start nothin' where there ain't nothin'."

I just looked at the man and nodded. He needed to know I was listening, but interruptions had a way of derailing even the smallest of confessions. To give him a little thinking room, I turned away again to examine the carved graffiti. This time I pulled a pen and notebook. Both the word and the style went onto the paper.

"I don't give it to 'em or sell it, either. But they're kids. Kids get into things."

When I finished my rendering of the carved mark, I wrote the word *whiskey* beside it. I added the phrase *kids get into things* as well. Then I lowered the pad and looked right at him again. I didn't speak; silence did the talking.

"It ain't me you gotta worry about anyway. I just make a little for fun. For me and friends and I only sell to the old-timers."

"I think it's time you spit it out, Clare. This is one of those only-the-truth-will-set-you-free moments."

"My mama used to say, 'It's time to come to Jesus.' You kind of remind me of her."

The old man's eyes wandered down and, for a second, I wasn't sure if he was falling into memory or checking out my shape again.

"Clare!"

"There's another guy that's been coming around here. He busted up my rig and he's been telling me to shut it down. A real badass-biker type."

"By rig, you mean a still?"

He nodded. "Small-time. Just for fun and to make a few extra bucks. I never believed it could cause things like this."

"What are you talking about, Clare?"

"The biker. He said if I didn't stop, someone was going to get hurt."

Chapter 2

"**B**ootleg whiskey?" the sheriff asked me. "You think that's what the girl was killed for?"

Sheriff Charles Benson—Chuck to his friends, and everyone in the county seemed to be his friend—was an elected official. Like a lot of elected sheriffs, he was better at what he considered his real job—making the citizens feel confident in the department—than he was at actual law enforcement. In his favor, though, was his own understanding of the two roles. He was a Vietnam veteran, a former farm insurance agent, and a Mason, but he hired people with training and experience and listened to them. He was a good man and I tried not to roll my eyes at him when he tried to fill in the blanks with obvious answers.

"Who knows?" I asked him. "I'm just telling you what the old guy told me. Still, we have bikers, bootlegging, and a dead girl. There's probably some connection, even if it's bad luck."

"Why would bikers try to muscle into a small-time still operator? Where's the money in that?" the sheriff asked. It sounded like a conversational averting of the eyes. Easier to talk about the bikers than the girl. "Besides," he went on, "bikers run more to meth these days. It's a lot more money and easier to transport. Whiskey just seems too much work."

"And killing, this kind of killing, doesn't make sense. Yet."

The sheriff nodded like he was agreeing, then said, "Clare's not so old. He was a grade behind me in school."

"You know him?"

"Of course I know him. Known him all my life. We're in the same lodge. If he said there was a biker snooping around I believe him."

"I believe him too and I'll check it out. I'm just letting you know there's no one waiting, all trussed up in a bow, to be our killer."

"Yeah," he said, waving his hand like he could clear some horrible thoughts. "I get it. No easy answers. And almost as bad, nothing to tell the parents when I go back to see them."

"Sorry, Sheriff."

"Me too," he answered sounding tired. "But you understand, easy or not, there will be answers. We won't have an unsolved child murder in my county—on my watch. You get what I'm saying?"

I got it. I nodded.

"People forget sometimes, they think we live in the modern age. This part of the world just kind of wears its civilization like a Sunday suit. Once church is over it comes off easy. Last thing we need is a reason for them to take off the suit and go looking for their own answers."

Despite the folksy delivery, the threat was real. The Ozarks had a long history of citizen justice.

"I'm going to need to talk to the parents," I told him.

"I know." He sighed as he said it. "Make it tomorrow. Let me talk to them again first—ease them into it."

"Sheriff, that's—"

"I know. It's not the way to do things. But it's the way I want it done this time."

"Fair enough," I said. "I have plenty to occupy me."

I left his office fuming a little. The sheriff was no professional, but he knew enough to understand this probably had more to do with either family or people known to the family than it did to any stranger. Even a stranger that was a booze-running biker.

Failing an interview with the parents, the next best thing was to talk to close contacts. Kids the age of Angela were in many ways more deeply connected to friends than to their family. That was where I wanted to start. I wasn't going to ignore the other issue, either. I had asked Clare to come in and look at some booking photos. The biker was our only lead so far and I wanted a name to go along with it. I asked the desk to set that up for me and I headed out to the Briscoe address. I had a feeling there would be some kids hanging around.

The windows were down on the departmental SUV I had taken. At lake level the air was relatively cool. I liked the feel as it kicked my hair. Leaving Forsyth, the roads snaked under green cover following ancient animal and Indian trails. Sunlight shooting through the gaps in leaves stuttered across my windshield. Both temperature and elevation rose as I moved away from Lake Taneycomo.

The roads in the county were my thinking spaces. They were just right for splitting my concentration. One part of my mind drove, watching the road and controlling my hands and feet, and by extension the vehicle. Another deeper part of my brain was freed to gnaw over problems like a dog working an old bone. I didn't even need a specific problem. Sometimes you let the mind free and it takes you to places you never planned.

I had just started to relax into my own thoughts when the cell phone rang. So much for mental freedom. It wasn't Darlene. Everyone from the sheriff's department had the same ring tone and it wasn't playing. I took a quick look at the number, then set the cell down and let it ring. Five-seven-one area code, that's Quantico, Virginia. You say *Quantico* and most people have the same first thought: FBI. That wasn't who I thought of. Quantico is also the home of the U.S. Army Criminal Investigative Division Headquarters. It would be Major John Reach calling and being ignored again. I didn't know what he wanted. The one message I had listened to said only that he wanted to speak with me. I didn't want to speak with him. The call went to voice mail and I tried to get my mind free again.

Freedom wouldn't come. I knew I had fallen blindly into one of those cases that had no good ending. It would end. There would be a time that it was no longer at the forefront of anyone's mind but the parents of the dead child. But it would pass without grace. The best that could be hoped for would be a clean-lined, official stamp of finality. Answers and consequences. Not that either would really matter. This girl's death would be a landmark in the lives of an innocent family. Like a strip mine sunk into the private landscape of their life, it would exist as a huge, horrendous wound that would never heal. People like to talk about closure. They especially like to say it to cops. They *need* closure. They *want* closure. There would be no closing the pit for these people. For the moment I was glad the sheriff would be talking with the parents. It was a brave and honest thing for him to deliver the news himself. He deserved respect.

That's what the drive does for me, perspective. I had gotten on the road thinking only of how Sheriff Benson had slowed me down and gotten in my way. I need a lot more perspective in my life.

I wasn't going to get it on that drive, it seemed. At the same time, the cell rang again and I came around a bend to see a man fire up a loud pipe Harley and tear ass away from an older crew-cab pickup on the side of the road. That wasn't so alarming, but the body lying in front of the truck was.

The phone call was the same one I had ignored before, and it was easy to ignore again. I crossed over the highway and parked facing traffic in the same dirt cutout as the pickup truck. Before leaving the SUV I called in the location and requested an ambulance. I also asked for a BOLO—*be on the lookout*—for the Harley and the biker. I didn't see the patch on his vest, but that's the nice thing about club bikers. Even if you don't see the colors their look is like a uniform. If he stays on the road we'll get him.

When I stepped from my vehicle the man on the ground grunted a hard, achy-sounding breath into the dirt. He followed with a series of hacking coughs coming up from deep in his chest. Once the coughing passed, his hands scrabbled out in the dirt, rocks, and trash looking for a place to land before pushing his body up. His shaved head was smeared with blood running from a wound in his scalp. It was ugly and there was no telling if he had any damage to his neck.

"I don't think you should try getting up just yet, sir," I told him.

He ignored me long enough to push up onto his hands and knees. His head remained dangling from his shoulders like it weighed just too much to lift. Then he spit a bloody glob into the dirt.

"Who the hell are you?" he asked, still without looking up.

I told him and he nodded his head in a vague waggle. "Nice boots," he said. "Lady cop?"

"I'm a cop."

He laughed a little, but it turned into coughing. He looked like he was fighting to control that as well as to keep his head still. When it passed, he asked, "That mean you're not a lady?"

"It means I'm a cop and it's all that matters in this situation."

Once again he spit out the blood pooling in his mouth. There wasn't as much this time. "Only reason I ask was, the footwear didn't seem to match the voice. You're Hurricane, aren't you?"

"My name is Detective Katrina Williams."

"Hurricane," he said bluntly. "I've heard of you. I don't suppose you got them?"

"The guy got away on his bike but I got a call out. We'll find him. EMTs are on their way too. You just relax."

"Guy?"

"Excuse me?"

"You said guy. There was only one?"

"That's all I saw."

"Me too, but it felt like a whole herd."

"Herd?"

This time when he laughed he put a little more head into it. Before he spoke again he spit out another mouthful of blood. "Collective noun," he said. "You know how a group of crows is a murder. A flock of ravens isn't a flock. It's an unkindness. Then there's a shrewdness of apes. When I was lying here I decided that I had been kicked to pieces by a herd of bastards."

"Well, aren't you the interesting one?"

"I know," he said and I could hear the smile in his voice now. "Why would anyone want to give me a beatdown? I'm just a harmless, interesting guy." He lifted his head and looked up at me for the first time. As soon as he did he winced at the pain and started coughing again.

"Take it slow and easy," I cautioned.

In answer he nodded, grimacing with the effort. Even with the pained look it was a nice face. Under the blood was a square jaw that managed to be masculine without getting into lantern shaped. His eyes were a rich hazel-brown that could have been chosen from a color chart to match perfectly with his sun-darkened skin. There was one incongruity. His head was bald and it looked like a recent development. The scalp was still paler than the rest of him and made him look maybe a bit older than I thought he was. If I had met him someplace else I would have looked twice and thought three times. Even here, on the side of the road, with blood running down his cheek and his lip swelling, I liked what I saw. Or maybe it was just that I would like any man that took an ass-kicking and got up laughing instead of whining and cursing.

"What's your name?" I asked.

While looking up at me he ran his tongue around his mouth,

probably looking for missing or broken teeth. A couple of times he winced when he found something, the sources of the blood he spit out one more time. The look on his face was the down-but-not-out of a fighter, a crooked smile that broke into a bent grin as he offered up his hand to me.

I took it and helped him up.

"I'm Nelson Solomon," he said.

"Like the painter?"

The grin that had shaped his lips made its way to his eyes and then it was a genuine smile. "Exactly like the painter," he told me. For a moment he stood there holding onto my hand and steadying himself. When he was confident enough in his footing he let go and waved me over toward the barbed-wire fence and the pasture beyond. "Give me a hand with the rest of my stuff?"

"I really don't think you should be climbing fences or tramping through fields right now, Mr. Solomon."

He waved my concern off. "I was never unconscious, just took a few shots and got the wind knocked out of me." Before I could say anything more he went for the fence and ducked through the sagging, rusted strands of tetanus waiting to happen.

"You mind telling me what happened here?" I asked as he came up on the other side. In his hand was a stained rag and a couple of tubes that looked like toothpaste.

"I was over there." He pointed off to a tree line. "There's a good view of the lake and I was painting." As he talked, he walked, picking up more tubes and adding brushes. The tubes were paint.

I had thought he was kidding after I said his name was like the painter. I didn't know much about art, but his was all over the place—posters, coffee-table books, calendars. He was a merchandising gold mine. I couldn't afford even a decent print and couldn't imagine the cost of one of the originals. I had heard there was a place selling them down on the Branson Landing, a shopping development for tourists. Other than loitering teens, locals don't spend much time there.

While I was thinking, he kept gathering. Working his way down a trail trampled in the grass, he pulled up a box with legs on it. When he set it upright it was a little fold-up easel and compartment for supplies. After dumping everything else he had picked up inside, he collapsed the whole thing and held it up by a handle. He was grinning even bigger than before, pointing to a stain on one corner.

"I got him with this," he called out. "See? Blood."

"So he attacked you?"

Walking back along the trail, he nodded at me as he kept an eye out for any other pieces of his kit. "He was just trying to scare me, probably."

"Why would he do that?" I asked. "Did you know him?"

"Nope," he answered, still smiling. This time, though, his eyes didn't quite look at mine.

"So why'd he come mess with you?"

"I don't know. Some people are just general, all-around assholes." That time he was looking at me, but there was something more than the conversation at hand in his gaze. He looked like a man having a good time. He added, "You know?" And then he looked from my face down my body. He wasn't rude or trying to be obvious about it; just a little more honest than I was used to.

"Yeah," I said. "I know what you mean."

Nelson Solomon, the famous painter, looked back at me then. He pursed his lips and looked like a schoolboy caught checking out the new teacher. I thought I should keep things on track, so I said, "Things don't usually happen that way."

"What do you mean?"

"People, even asshole bikers, don't usually start in with random strangers. Especially not when they have to get off their bike, climb a fence, and cross a field to do it. Must have been some reason."

"Maybe he doesn't like art?"

"Do all your critics work so hard to make their point?"

"Sometimes it feels like it," he said, smiling again.

"Could this have been his property?"

"No," Nelson said, and it was the first time he sounded absolutely certain. "Bank owns it."

"Did the bank give you permission to be here?" I asked as I put a foot on the center strand of wire and pulled up on the top strand.

Just before ducking through he nodded again. Once back on the road side of the fence he said, "I'm a good customer."

I didn't doubt that.

"So, you don't know what the guy wanted?"

"He wanted to kick my ass and he mostly did." He said that with a self-deprecating smile that, if I'm honest with myself, I enjoyed.

Then he added, "I think he wanted me to be scared a little bit too." That was the truest thing he'd said to me about the fight.

"But you didn't just leave and call the sheriff's department?"

"I've had enough scares in my life."

That's when I looked at his eyes and saw the kind of resolve that can make a cop's life both easier and more difficult. You want to root for the good people who stand up for themselves, but at the same time you see the consequences of that every day.

"You decided you just had to fight him, then?"

That grin again.

"There was no fight. Mostly it was just me getting beat up. I was already finished up and packed, but I learned a long time ago, if you let the bastards take, they never stop. He started pushing me around when I told him to kiss my ass. Then he took hold of my painting and said he was keeping it, and I was leaving. That's when I swung the field kit at him."

I looked again out to the trees he had pointed to earlier. "Out there?" I asked. "Then how did all the mess get strewn around up here?"

I looked away and watched the big cube-shaped ambulance pull up behind my SUV.

"No," he said. "That was where he left me on the ground. There, where everything spilled out, was where I caught up to him."

"And I found you *here* because . . ."

"I caught up to him again at his bike. He must have gotten a good one in to my ribs, because I went down. Then the kicking started. That's why I thought maybe there were more of them. It felt like I was being trampled."

One of the EMT's, an older man named Lawrence trotted up to me at the fence with his big kit.

"What's up, Hurricane?" he asked.

I pointed over to Solomon.

"I don't need an ambulance," he said, waving both hands in front of himself.

"Go with Lawrence," I told him. "If nothing else, he'll wipe some of that blood off your face."

Solomon hit me with a look that said something there were no words for, but women always recognize. The surprising thing about it was that I didn't mind. Then the look blossomed into that grin again. "Pretty delicate for a hurricane, aren't you?" he asked and it wasn't just teasing, it was flirting. Real flirting, not just banter. It had been a long time, but not so long that I completely missed it.

I smiled. I couldn't help it; the expression took over my face so quickly I was unprepared. Then I touched the scar beside my eye and let the smile fall off my face before I said, "Believe me, Mr. Solomon, delicate is not one of my stronger qualities."

Who knows what thoughts that put into his head, but he was smiling like he had just caught me naked and liked what he saw, before hefting the painting kit into the bed of his truck. Something happened then and Solomon fell against the truck, coughing deeply. When he turned back around there was fresh blood spattered his lips and on the back of his hand. None of it killed the gleam in his eyes.

As he let Lawrence take him to the back of the ambulance I heard Solomon say, "I think she likes me, don't you?" Lawrence laughed and muttered something I couldn't hear, but Solomon laughed until he was coughing again. I went through the fence to see what was in the trees, but I'll admit I was smiling.

It was an amazing view, but not what I had expected. From what I had seen of the guy's paintings, Solomon painted landscapes that were more natural than nature. He was famous for capturing scenes of light and shadow crafted by sun and mountains. Like Ansel Adams in color. I had never seen one that had man-made features in it. The view from the tree-lined bluff showed the lake with part of the town of Forsyth and the serpentine asphalt wending through canyons of cut-away stone. In the faces of the rock cuts were still the precise vertical lines put there by steam drills two generations ago. Over everything were dancing shades of green, billions upon billions of leaves topping a million trees.

Somehow I didn't think the biker was possessive of his favorite view. Still, the only thing that seemed even remotely odd about the scene to me was a single wisp of white smoke curling up from the trees below.

Backtracking the trail, I stopped to pick up a rolled-up, half-empty tube of paint from the field grass. Cobalt green. When I looked up I saw the light bar on the ambulance flash. It whooped once and U-turned into the road going the way it had come. The driver kept the light bar spinning. Solomon was being taken to the hospital.

Damn it.

I was kicking myself for being caught up in the man's charm. He must have been hurt more than he seemed and I should have made sure he stayed down until help got there. For a moment I stood in the middle of the empty field. Inside my gut there was a weird twinge, like a small slip in a tight knot.

How bad was he? And how much was my fault?

It was just for a moment, though. You can't last long as any kind of cop dwelling on the things that you have no control over and anything past is completely out of your control. I could best help Mr. Solomon by catching the guy who gave him the beating. And just maybe finding out the truth behind it.

Once my feet started moving again a deputy's car pulled up with his lights on. I let him call a tow truck for Solomon's vehicle and wait for it.

I got back on the road to my original destination, wishing the drive was longer. My head needed a little clearing.

Chapter 3

B ecause the day was already wearing thin, I kept my mind in one place and focused on the road in front of me. I wanted to watch the steady whip of the yellow line as it passed under the SUV and think of other things. There was work to do and my thoughts were needed there. Besides, there was something else. . . .

I touched at the scar and, despite my resolve, wondered about the man. Nelson Solomon was different from anyone I had met in a long time. Different was good. But thinking about him made me feel guilty, both because I thought I should have been firmer about his waiting for the ambulance and because a girl was dead. Each time I caught myself thinking about anything other than her I felt like a failure.

While I was thinking about what I should or should not be thinking about, the twisting miles disappeared. I was at Angela's home. The sheriff's car was parked outside and I felt pride in the man. No one likes family notification visits, least of all someone who relies on elections for his job. The fact that Sheriff Benson made it a personal responsibility told all of us just what kind of man we were working for.

I didn't stop at the house. I went to the end of the street, where it dead-ended in a steel barrier and bare dirt. Parked there was a twenty-year-old Chevy Beretta. The old car looked burdened by the mass of kids sitting in and on it. Behind the wheel was a pockmarked boy with a sneer and a bad haircut smoking like he was the first person to come up with the idea of cigarettes. All the other kids looked younger. One girl, probably fifteen or sixteen, baby-fat pretty with straight hair and bangs dyed blue-black, had the look of queen to the pimply-faced king. Kids always run in groups and someone is always the first among equals.

I pulled up and parked. Immediately the grumbling started. The half-loud smart remarks of kids showing off but not brave enough to go all the way. A couple of them faded back and started wandering off toward sagging homes with trash and toys littering the lawns.

The girl stayed put on the car's fender, her short skirt showing far too much leg for her age. Probably for any age, I thought, and wondered when I had become my mother. She didn't say anything, but she didn't look away, either.

"Hi," I said.

Suddenly she changed and it was the second time that day I was struck by a smile. She had dimples and blue eyes that looked icy under all the black hair.

"Hi," she said right back, like she was actually glad to talk. Her eyes drifted from my face down to my hips and I knew what she was looking for, but my weapon was holstered at my back just so it wouldn't be that obvious.

"I bet you guys knew Angela, didn't you?"

All the other kids looked at the ground. The girl looked back at my face. She let go of the smile, but something of it remained in her eyes. It was a strange look.

"She was our friend," she said. "That's why we're here."

The kid behind the wheel leaned out the window, whispering something to another boy. They both covered their mouths and snorted behind their hands. They bobbed their heads like something was amazingly funny and the best secret in the world. Even before that I was ready to dislike them. It's good to have an excuse, though.

"You boys have something to say?"

They straightened up but didn't bother to look contrite. Obviously they spent time in front of mirrors mastering their smug looks.

"Are you really a cop?" the girl asked.

I dropped my glare and nodded at her. "Detective," I told her. "Detective Williams, with the sheriff's department. What's your name?"

Pimple Face behind the wheel stuck his head out the window again and said, "Hey. Aren't you supposed to show your badge or something?"

I looked over my shoulder at the departmental SUV with the star on the side and *Sheriff Taney County*, in big, reflective letters. Then I turned back to him. "You think I drive that thing because I like the style?"

"Can I see it?" the girl asked excitedly. I couldn't tell if she was ignoring the boy's rudeness or was just oblivious to it.

"You want to see my badge?"

She nodded with a smile, then said, "I'm Carrie Owens." As I pulled my badge she leaned closer and whispered, "Just ignore Danny. He's mad because he got a ticket yesterday."

"Danny?"

"Uh-huh. Danny Barnes." She reached out to touch my star without asking and ran her fingertip over each point. "He lives over there." She nodded over at a mobile home on blocks with no skirting that sat centered on a thickly treed, acre-sized lot.

"And where do you live?"

Carrie pulled her fingers off the badge and looked at me. She wanted to lie. I could see that. She decided not to, either because she didn't have one ready or just decided it wasn't worth the effort. "Over there, the big one."

The big one was a white, vinyl-clad two-story with a deep portico and four vinyl-wrapped columns. It was also sitting on the largest lot in the division and right across the street from Angela Briscoe's home.

Tucking away my badge, I said, "Tell me about Angela."

"She was okay," Carrie said quickly. She leaned again as if offering a confidence. "Not very mature."

"She was a couple of years younger than you?"

"No. I just turned fourteen. Angela's birthday was next month."

I felt a little sick.

Looking around, I noticed for the first time the kids around the car were all boys, except Carrie. The skirt that I had thought too short for a girl of sixteen seemed suddenly less like a skirt and more like a terrible mistake. I pictured the girl in the woods with her skirt discreetly covering her knees. I had the feeling Angela and Carrie were two very different girls. This one was pushing at maturity, trying so hard to make herself a woman. I imagined Angela Briscoe had not been in such a hurry.

"Were you with Angela at all yesterday?"

"Sure," Carrie answered. Before she could say more, the engine of the car started up.

"Come on, Carrie," Danny shouted out the window. When I gave him a look, he tried to stare me down through his dirty window, but gave up after a second and lit a fresh cigarette.

"Maybe you would like to come talk at the sheriff's office," I said to Carrie.

"Could I?" She surprised me again with her enthusiasm for the idea.

"I'll talk to your parents. Maybe you can ride down with me. We'll put the lights on and drive fast."

That was the first time she looked uncomfortable. "Do you have to ask her?" She didn't wait for an answer. Her feet kicked out and she hopped off the fender, circling behind me to go for the passenger door. "I have to go."

"Hang on," I told her as I pulled a card from my pocket. "You can call me if you want. About anything."

Carrie reached for the card, but as soon as her fingers touched it her eyes flicked toward home. "I guess," she said.

"One other thing. Have you ever heard of anything or anyone called Leech?"

Her eyes widened. This time I had surprised her. When her eyes looked away they went to Danny, gripping the wheel of the car.

"No."

It was a lie. A bad one. Danny honked the car horn. At the sound Carrie jumped, then darted for the door. At the same time, the other kids, the lingering boys, all bolted. Rather than trying to catch anyone, I turned and put my hands on the car's hood. Danny revved the engine and tried again to look like the tough guy, but I looked right back.

"Shut it off!" I shouted at him.

He did, twisting the key, then looking away, trying to show contempt even in his compliance. I stepped around to his window and looked in. Up close, Danny wouldn't meet my eyes at all. He kept staring at some point past my shoulder.

"Leech," I said, taking both of them into my view. Danny kept staring off and Carrie looked at her feet. "Tell me who it is."

From behind me came a popping roar, the sound of open pipes

winding down. Carrie looked up and Danny's eyes widened. All of his tough pretense was gone.

I turned to look at what they were seeing. It was another biker, not the same one I had seen rushing off from assaulting Nelson Solomon. This one was bigger, but lean. Tough and wiry-looking with greasy hair and no helmet. His bike was an old Sportster that looked to be as greasy as the rider. It was now idling up to a stop in the middle of the street. The rider was watching me just as much as I was watching him.

"Who's this?" I asked the question to myself, expecting no answer, but I got one.

"That's him," Carrie said. Then, louder, she added, "Leech. That's him."

The biker twisted the throttle and turned the bike as soon as I stood and stepped in his direction.

When I ran for my vehicle, Danny started his engine again. As soon as it caught, he spun his tires in the dirt and bumped the car up onto the road just as a news van showed up from the other direction.

I didn't catch the biker.

They say that epileptics feel an aura of impending seizure. I've read descriptions of a lightness, both in sensation and vision that surrounds them, or of an embrace that is more known than felt, which signals to them an event is coming. People like me, survivors whose experience of trauma never really leaves, are hung with the diagnosis of PTSD, post-traumatic stress disorder. We can feel an aura too, although it is different and our events are much different.

An event for me is an actual transportation back to a time and place that I've never actually left. Ghosts of a terrible moment continue to live in my mind. Most days I go on with them haunting from the edges of my thoughts. Some days I feel my own aura—a dark sense of impending transition, like a series of small black stones dropped on me until their weight drags me to that other place.

As I drove, at first chasing the biker—then, once I admitted that I'd lost him, chasing the hope—I felt the weight settling. Anyone that tells you a child's death doesn't put a weight on a cop, on every cop, doesn't know us. I'd called in, asking for assistance from any units in the area. But it's a big area with lots of twisting roads and crossing dirt tracks to get lost in. Telling yourself, or anyone else, that you did it right, did everything you could, feels as much a failure as the failure itself. Another weight.

Along with it came the usual craving to drink. There's a strange illusion in the mind of someone like me—something else you learn in therapy—the belief that being drunk will blunt the pain of that moment you're running from. Maybe it does in a way, but it's like digging a grave and crawling inside because the sun is too bright. Nothing is easy about any of it. There is just the unending pain and fear and the whisper of the alcohol, saying it can help. I can't explain it well enough to find an answer. I've never met anyone who could. You just have to know it's a lie.

There have been many times I've given in to it. But never while working. I can say that with a little pride. But the black pressure makes for a black mood. I was feeling them both and sinking even deeper into it when I pulled up outside the sheriff's office. News vans were packing the street. Law enforcement and journalists, we're the carrion eaters cleaning the bad meat of death from the nation. Sanitizing.

I need a drink.

Inside, I ended what had turned into a long day by leaving a few messages and checking on my own. Routine and work are the best things to lift the weight. I asked the deputy on the desk to find out for me who had written Danny Barnes a ticket. On a yellow legal pad I wrote a long note filling the sheriff in on my investigation. He would be sure to read a handwritten note on his desk. From experience, I knew an e-mail would just be skimmed and he would come ask questions I'd already answered.

On my desk was a note telling me Clarence Bolin had come in and identified the man he had seen in the area where Angela Briscoe was found. It was written on the back of a photocopy. When I turned it over I got my first really good look at Cotton James Lambert. My first look at him had been when he sped away after leaving Nelson Solomon in the dirt by the side of the road.

At least we had a string to begin pulling, but not much of one. Lambert's rap sheet had his affiliations, but nothing about being part of an organized gang. He could have been recruited since he was last arrested or during his last stay in jail. There wasn't any doubt in my mind that he ran with the same group as the guy I'd seen on Angela Briscoe's street. I searched the system for a name on anyone using the alias Leech. Nothing.

I hadn't heard anything on that BOLO, so I left myself a reminder to check on it in the morning. After that I went through voice mail. I should have been more careful.

The first message was from Major John Reach. I didn't catch what he was saying; in fact I hit the *delete* button as quickly as I could. It didn't matter. His voice fell over me, a heavy blanket of darkness that brought the fear with it. I had to get out of there.

As I went for my truck, I folded up and tucked the photocopy of Cotton Lambert's intake photos in my pocket. I felt like I was dragging a train of fear behind me. Searching my mind for a handle that offered a little control, I found instead a bright smile and shining eyes: Nelson Solomon. It was a surprise, but a nice one and I held it as I drove out of Forsyth to Rockaway Beach.

My eggs and grits seemed like a million years ago and I hadn't eaten anything since. I lied to myself that I would feel better if I ate something. It was an easy lie because I would feel better seeing Uncle Orson and he had the food.

There was a military tradition in my family. It went beyond the Army into which I had been born. On my father's side, his father and uncles had all served in World War II. They had been Army, Army Air Corps, regular Navy, and the Seabees. My father followed his father into the Army, but Uncle Orson, a man who said he wanted nothing to do with following, chose to enlist in the Marines in 1964. He was on the northern perimeter when the NVA hit Con Thien. Every sunrise after that night of flamethrowers and knife fighting was a gift he made the most of. Orson retired as a master gunnery sergeant and never put the uniform on again. Every year, though, he has his dress uniform cleaned and altered if needed. It's always ready for a call to duty or his funeral. He won't be buried in anything else.

Both my father and his brother had seen combat and come back grateful but changed. My father romanticized and surrounded himself with the best of that world. He went to reunions and visited the wall. His dreams were a darkness buried so deep he convinced most of the daytime world they did not exist. Uncle Orson wore his dreams of elephant grass bent by helicopter wash and burning hooches billowing with the smoke of rice and human bodies on his skin. They were scars cut into his skull by Zippo tracks and young boys with AK-47s screaming their death in black pajamas. All of it was lit up by the muzzle flash of M16s in a nighttime ambush. He didn't romanticize; he drank. I come by it naturally.

Uncle Orson loved the corps but he understood the spine of the thing was violence and raw force. It had no real ethics and it had no regrets. There were just the dreams of veterans. I could tell him things that would have shattered my father. And I did.

That was why on nights like that one, when the fading blue of a summer sky burned red ocher on the underside of high clouds, when I see the color bleed and the air fill with blowing dust, I go to Uncle Orson. He sees his own ghosts.

Like so many times before, I didn't remember driving to Rockaway Beach or walking up the swaying suspension walkway of the dock. One moment I was in the truck trying to hold on to the smile of someone I didn't know; the next moment I was there. On one level, I know the in-between was a brown wash of dirt and the grinding roll of Humvees on patrol. I know that the passing time carried a horrific sense of loss and anger so blinding it colored the entirety of my life. I know. I know, but I don't really remember.

"Wondered if I'd see you tonight," Uncle Orson said from behind the counter. He was a big man who filled the space, any space, he was in. This space was his. After retiring, he had purchased the dock and floating general store/bait shop. He lived in an apartment on the second level never more than ten feet from the minnows and night crawlers or the humming machines that kept them alive. Over the years, inventory in the shop moved so slowly the place looked as much like a museum of lake life as it did a gas station and store. On the wall behind him was a rack of Zippo lighters with transparent cases within which were feathered fishing flies. They had been there when he bought the place and were probably twenty years old then. The one modern look to the place was provided by the large art calendar on the wall at a right angle from the lighters. That month was a high view of a river bottom that had been harvested for a first growth of hay. The bales were sitting in golden squares on a verdant green second growth. A snaking river caught the light of the sun just breaking from dark clouds in a somber sky. Sunlight hit the water and broke into shards of silver-gold. It was an image that made you proud to be a part of life and in awe of it at the same time. In the border between the picture and the stapled seam under which the calendar page dangled, was the name Nelson Solomon.

"Katrina," he said. I heard him but it was as if from a distance. "Katrina," he called again softly, "come back, Katrina."

"I'm here," I reassured both of us.

"Yeah. Like I said, I wondered if I would see you tonight."

"Why's that?" I asked.

"People talk," he answered. "A friend of mine called. Said you both had a bad day." He watched, waiting for me to tell him. I didn't, so he went on. "I've got brats and chicken on the grill. You want one? Or for you, I might throw on a T-bone."

As soon as he mentioned it I smelled the smoke of the grill. It was a 55-gallon drum that had been cut in half along the length and hinged together, with legs welded on. It burned and rusted constantly until the bottom fell out and the drum was replaced.

"Brats would be wonderful."

"You want a beer?" he asked me, but it wasn't exactly a question. "I was afraid you would get the case. The girl. I know things like that get to you."

"They get to everyone."

"So you don't want a beer?"

"You know I want a beer."

He pointed to the table in the corner, right under the calendar, and pulled a bottle from a packed cooler. Brushing away the flecks of ice and clinging moisture before opening it, he set the bottle on the table in front of me.

"I talked to your dad today," he said over his shoulder as he went out to the smoking grill.

"About what?"

"This an' that."

I watched him through the screen as he moved meat around on the grill. Grinning like he had just won the lottery, he held up four fat brats skewered on a bit of tree limb he had whittled the bark from.

"I told him he needed a girlfriend."

That made me smile. It was a common discussion between the two of them and always ended up circling back to me.

"And he said you needed one more than he did."

"Yeah, he did. But I told him I had more women than I could shake a stick at."

"And he said, Why would you shake a stick at women?"

"Yup." He put brats and buns and paper plates on the table and sat down across from me. "But we both agreed what we really needed was to get you a man."

"I just bet you did. But I'd just as soon you keep out of my sex life."

"No one said anything about sex. You stay away from that. It's bad stuff. You just need a boyfriend to do things with, like . . ." Waving a hand in front of his face, he searched for something a woman might possibly want to do.

"Like dinner?" I helped him. "Dancing? Going to movies or shows?"

"Fishing."

I loaded up a brat and took a bite, then washed it down with a long drink of cold beer. I felt so good I almost forgot why I felt so bad. We talked and ate for over an hour, luxuriating in the feel of family, spicy sausage, and beer.

Finally, in a quiet moment, I said, "I kind of met a man."

Uncle Orson scooted his chair up close and took a swallow that emptied the last half of his second beer. It struck me how odd this was, but how natural. I had no idea how it would have worked to have this discussion with another woman. In a way, my tough-as-old-callous, sixty-eight-year-old uncle was my best girlfriend.

"Well, come on. Tell me," he said as soon as the bottle was drained and a new one opened. "Are you going to bring him around?"

"Slow down. I just met him. I don't know him, but he seems pretty nice. I don't think I'd mind getting to know him."

"Just met him? Is he a perp?"

"You need to stop trying to talk like cop shows. No one says *perp*."

"Sure they do. It's short for *perpetrator*."

"I know what it means, and no, he was not a suspect. He was jumped by a biker."

"Sounds like a weenie." Uncle Orson let his face tell me what he thought of weenies. And I knew for a fact that wasn't the word he would have used if he wasn't talking to me or any other woman.

"The biker tried to back him down, but he went down swinging. Went down and got back up three times."

He grunted, but it was a grudging sound of reconsideration. Orson liked men who won their fights but he gave respect to any man who lost with honor. "You should have brought him with you. I'd have thrown on steaks." Throwing on a steak was my family's idea of slaughtering the fatted calf.

"I told you, I don't know him. I just met him. Besides, the ambulance took him to the hospital."

"Hospital? Was he hurt that bad?"

"I don't think so, just stiches. They probably took him for observation. He might have had a concussion."

"How'd he get into it with a biker?"

I told him about Nelson Solomon and how we met earlier that day. Added to that, I told him how it intersected with the murder of Angela. He pulled down the calendar from the wall behind him and examined each page as I talked.

"You know," he said, folding the pages back to the current month, "I'd actually looked forward to turning the page each month. Now I've flipped through it, I ask myself why I waited on things so amazing."

I had the definite feel that he was trying to tell me something more than he liked the pictures.

"So was Clarence Bolin the friend that called you about me?"

"I guess you *were* listening," he said. "Clare's a good guy. Makes good whiskey."

"You know about the whiskey?"

"I sell it. Off the books, of course."

To say my jaw hit the table and bounced would not be much of an exaggeration.

"Don't look so surprised, Katrina. Homemade whiskey has a long history around here. My granddaddy sold a few jugs to Pretty Boy Floyd himself."

"I've heard the story, Uncle Orson. That was in the depression. Why do it now?"

"It's a fad. Like cigar bars and microbrews. Whiskey is hipster cool."

"Hipster? Do you even know what that means?"

"Honey, I'm a hepcat from way back. Besides, I read it online."

"Uh-huh. It's still a crime."

"Yeah, but there are crimes and there are *crimes*. This is basically tax evasion."

"I'm a cop. And we don't get to pick and choose the laws we follow."

"Don't we?" His question was like a hard foot on the brakes. I felt the burn of a flush creeping up my face. Orson knew me and he knew there have been times in my life I had opted for justice over law. He wasn't throwing it in my face, though. It was my own guilty conscience doing that. "Ever heard of the Whiskey Rebellion? Ever know anyone who didn't play a little loose with their tax return?"

"I don't make enough to worry about my taxes."

"You should worry more. You know that since the 1950s—America's most prosperous years, I might add—the tax burden has been methodically shifted from corporations to the individual?"

I pressed my fingers to my temples and massaged the ache that bloomed there every time he got started on these things.

"Uncle Orson, I'm talking about law, not taxes."

"There is no way to disentangle the two. But I'll tell you this: The mark of a good government is how it chooses to apply law."

"I don't need a lecture on good government."

That stopped him. He let out a big breath of air, deflating slowly. "I know you don't, sweetheart. I guess we've both seen the best and the worst of that."

"Just tell me about the whiskey."

"What's to tell? He sells it to me for five dollars a jar and I sell it to fishermen with more money than sense for twenty. No taxes, all profit."

"It sounds like good money, but is it worth violence?"

"What violence? Those are the old days, tommy guns and speak-easies. Nobody's fighting over this anymore."

"Maybe . . . Can I stay in the boat tonight?"

"You never have to ask."

Uncle Orson had a huge houseboat that stayed parked at the dock. For a long time it had been his home. Now it was my home away from everything and I always asked before I took it over. I told him thanks and stood to head to the hard bed that would rock me gently. Before I made it through the door, he said, "Hang on." Then he reached behind the counter and tossed over a canning jar filled with clear liquid. "For your *professional* interest."

In Uncle Orson's defense, he didn't know how deep my relationship with whiskey went. In my defense I resisted. Darkness, a hazy blowing of memory that sucked up all light, was already enveloping me. My body began trembling and my eyes began crying, but those things were happening without me. I was somewhere else.

Chapter 4

I felt like it was the end of summer. Not that there was a hint of green or the creeping red-oranges of leaves turning. In Iraq, everything was brownish. Not even a good, earthy brown. Instead, everything within my view was a uniform, wasted, dun color. It was easy to imagine the creator ending up here on the seventh day, out of energy and out of ideas after spending his palate in the joy of painting the rest of the world. This spit of earth, the dirty asshole of creation we called the Triangle of Death, didn't even rate a decent brown.

I had been in country for eight months. I had been First Lieutenant Katrina Williams, Military Police, attached to the 502nd Infantry Regiment, 101st Airborne Division for a little over a year. Pride and love had brought me here. Proud to be American and just as proud to have come from a military family, I was in love with what the ROTC at Southwest Missouri State University had shown me about my country's military. I fell in love with the thought of the woman I would become serving my nation. I wanted to echo the men my father and my uncle were and add my own tone to the family history. Iraq bled that all out of me. Just like it was bleeding my color out into the dust. Bright red draining into shit brown.

It was the impending weight of change that made me feel like the end of summer. As a girl, back home in the Ozarks, the summers seemed to last forever. It wasn't until the final days, carried over even into a new school year, when the air cooled and the oaks rusted, that I could feel them ending. Their endings were like the descent of ice ages, the shifting of epochs. That was exactly how I felt bleeding into the dirt. The difference was that I felt an impending death rather than transition. The terminus of an epoch. In Iraq though, nothing was as clear as that. It was death; but it wasn't.

Lying on my back, I wished I could see blue sky, but not here. The air was hazed with dust so used up it became a part of the atmosphere. There was no more of the earth in it. Grit, like bad memories and regret, hanging over an entire nation. I coughed hard and it hurt. A bubbly thickness slithered up my throat. Using my tongue and what breath I had, I got the slimy mass up to my lips. I just didn't have it in me to spit. Instead, I turned my head to the side and let the bloody phlegm slide down my cheek.

Dying is hard.

Wind, hot and cradling the homeland sand so many factions were willing to kill for, ran over the wall I was hidden behind. It eddied there, slowing and swirling and then dumping the dirt on my naked skin. A slow-motion burial. Even the land here hated naked women.

I stayed there without moving, but slipping in and out of consciousness for a long time. It seemed long, anyway. I dreamed. Dreamed or remembered so well they seemed like perfect dreams of—everything.

Green.

We played baseball. Just like in old movies with kids turning a lot into a diamond. No one does that anymore, but we did. My grandfather played minor league ball years ago and I had a cousin who was a Cardinals fan. Everyone was a Cardinals fan, so I loved the Royals. When the games were over and it was hotter than the batter's box when I was pitching—I had a wild arm—my father would take me to the river. Later when we had cars, I was drawn there every summer to swim and swing from the ropes. We floated on old, patched inner tubes and teased boys. That was where I learned to drink beer. My father would take me fishing on the river. My grandfather would take me on the lakes. I used the same cane pole my father had when Granddad taught him about fishing. Both of the men used to say to the girl who complained about not catching anything, "It's not about the catching, it's about the fishing." I don't think I ever understood until a good portion of my blood was spilled on the dirt of a world that hated me.

My head spun back to the moment and back to Iraq. If I was going to die, I would have done it already, I figured. At least my body. That physical part of me would live on. That other part of me, the girl who loved summer . . . I think she was already dead. Death and transition.

It was a huge effort to roll to my side and when I did, I saw the stain of my blood. It was already mixed with the dirt, surrendering its color. Everything becoming something less than brown. I wondered about the rest of my color: the auburn of my hair, turned redder in the sunlight; the pale green of my eyes; and the almost-peach–toned spray of freckles that trickled from my nose to the tops of my breasts. Was it going too? All that color, all that life—wasted here.

The worst wound was in my back, below the shoulder blade. The knife had been thrust straight down and hard. There was no telling how bad it was, but it was bad. I had been left for dead, after all. Or at least to die. And I'd been left with no weapons. My uniform had been cut and stripped away. If soldiers had found me dead, they would assume I was abducted and raped by insurgents. If insurgents found me, they would assume another faction was responsible. If I was found alive by any insurgent, I would be raped some more and condemned to die for the sins of being female and American.

The men who had raped me first, who had killed the girl that loved summer, were Americans too. Hating women crosses all borders and faiths. Something all the boys could agree on. They thought they were careful, but I knew who they were. I had seen their hands.

Another gust rippled over the wall, dumping a handful of grave dirt over me.

It took a while, but I finally rolled completely over and rose to my hands and knees. Every part of me was shaking with the effort. My head throbbed a golden flash of spinning pain and then I vomited.

Concussion.

The word was part of the catalogue I began writing in my mind. An inventory was needed to assess chances and options. Concussion. Hole in my back. My rib might be broken.

When my gut seemed ready, I opened my eyes again. The puddle of puke under my face had lost its color to the Iraqi dust, making a mottled mud. Careful not to put my hands in the mess, I backed away. That was when I felt the cuts in my backside. I remembered the captain slapping and cutting my ass with the knife as he sodomized me. When he bucked up against me, moaning with his release, he had stabbed, thrusting the blade deep into my right buttock.

The effort of turning my head back to look only made the world spin again. I let my head sag so I could look down the length of my body. More blood and more cuts. Both of my breasts were tracked with bruises, black finger marks on pale skin. The right one, though, had a long gash starting high on my chest and running under the soft flesh, causing it to hang lower and at an impossible angle. On my left, the nipple was sliced and twisted.

Scars. So many scars.

The freckles that had been a part of my identity since I knew to think of myself as separate from my mother were faded out.

I'm becoming the color of bone.

There was another laceration in the pubic hair, a violent, jagged gash, and a bare strip where the darker red curls had been stripped away.

The lieutenant's souvenir.

Blood was flowing, a fresh rush over the sticky, semidry coating between my legs. The fresh fluid cut a new path that trickled right down dead-white thighs with dark galaxies of bruising. Most of the blood seemed to be coming from my vagina. I recalled the lieutenant punching between my legs several times before he shoved his fist inside. That ring raking me. Afterward, he said he wanted a lock of hair, like a lover might. He used the Ka-Bar to cut away the strip. With one hand he pulled the hairs tight. With the other, the one with the ring, he cut.

Both of the men had rings. Different years and different designs, but the rings came from the same school. They had the good sense not to wear them during patrols, but around base the rings were always on display. Everyone knew those rings.

Everything hurts.

I cried. For a short time or a long one, I wasn't sure. Maybe it was a short time that only seemed equal to all the time I had lived so far. I stayed there on my hands and knees because it hurt too much to move, and I cried. It poured from my frothy lungs, a quiet, keening wail that sounded almost like a meadowlark, but there was no answering call.

They were supposed to be on my side. My people. I'll never know how anyone can survive feeling as alone as I did then. When the tears and the pitiful wailing dried up, I was left with just the silence. Eventually even the silence was too great a weight to bear. I started gathering clothes and doing what I could to cover myself. The only thing worse than being raped and left naked behind some mud wall and shack in Iraq, was being found naked in any condition by the local faithful. A naked woman in this part of the world was a whore and whores got no sympathy.

My bra was cut in two and my uniform shirt was just gone. The T-shirt was there. More brown. I found my panties down by my feet, but someone—the lieutenant, I assumed—had ejaculated in them. I wouldn't put those on for anything. I could reach my pants, but only found one boot. It didn't matter; I had to get moving.

The clothes went on slowly. When I pulled the shirt over my head I almost screamed. Fresh blood streaked the cotton.

More color stolen.

It took another five minutes to get pants on.

When I stood, my head lurched again and the guts followed. There was no fighting it. I draped my body over the low wall and puked in hard spasms. Gold starbursts patterned my vision. I smelled bile and copper.

I didn't remember rising again. Nor did I remember walking from the wall. There is a gap in time and place that left me staggering toward a road, but away from the village in the distance. If I was anywhere near where I thought I was, there would be a traffic checkpoint in about three kilometers. It could just as well have been a million. Before I made it a hundred yards down the road, a white dot appeared on the horizon. A vehicle.

If it wasn't green it wasn't safe.

There was a depression in the dirt alongside the road that was almost deep enough to pass for a ditch. It was mostly bare dirt but here and there were bits of trash. No cover.

No choice. I dropped into the dirt. When I hit, something popped in my chest. It was physical and audible and started a cascade of wrenching pain. A doctor told me later a nick in my lung must have torn through. Air was escaping into the chest cavity at the same time that blood was running into the lung. Each breath was a loud, gasping rattle that brought in little air and almost as much dust.

The white pickup truck slowed on shrieking brakes, and then wheeled around after passing. They had seen me. I had seen them. It was a small truck, but it carried three men up front and six in the back. All were armed.

Even over the old engine and bad brakes, even over my own ragged breathing, I could hear the excited shouts of the men.

Summer's over.

I said good-bye, in quiet thoughts, to my mother and father. All thoughts had become prayers. Everyone who had ever done me harm, I forgave, except the men who had put me where I was. Then I waited for the real death.

One man jumped down from the truck bed and the others stayed behind, shouting. I couldn't tell if the shouts were instruction or encouragement. The bolt on an AK-47 was pulled. All the shouting stopped.

I'm not ready.

The shouting started up again, but it was different in tone and urgency. The man with the AK ran back to the truck. He sprayed a wash of rounds at me without aiming as the truck left the road and took off across open ground.

A moment later, I watched as a column of Humvees stopped short of my position. A squad of men piled out and formed a perimeter. A sergeant I had never seen before stalked up to me with his weapon at the ready. He looked close and long before calling back, "We need a medic and a litter up here."

I rose early in the damp chill of sunrise on the lake. Every breath captured the full life smell of watery fecundity and the slow decay of deadwood. Carried across the width of deep liquid green was the sound of a woodpecker hammering his way into the carcass of a standing, dead cedar. I noticed all of it, but appreciated nothing as I skulked from the houseboat to my truck. The beauty of the world around me felt like something to hide from after a night spent reliving what I had come to think of as my first death. Closing the truck door shut it all out. It failed to shut out the shame I felt. It might have helped if I hadn't carried the jar of whiskey with me.

At home I cleaned up and caffeinated. I did it all like someone trying to ignore a camera in their bedroom. I kept all my thoughts behind a veil of normalcy. Then I caught myself looking out from the mirror. So much of me was gone from what I was.

"It wasn't your fault," I said to myself. I looked back with sad eyes and scars that seemed to disagree. It was an odd sort of shame that I felt; I was ashamed of what others had done to me. I was ashamed of the flashbacks that made me relive it. Both seemed like a kind of weakness. I kept staring at myself, the short hair with the red summer cooked into a burnished penny color, the scars that tracked my skin, the pale skin and faded freckles that spoke of hiding under mannish clothing for so long. All those things carried an accusation that I had been facing for a decade.

While I stared I saw the girl, Angela Briscoe. Finding her, seeing her body in the woods, had pulled the hammer back on me, then pulled a slow-motion trigger. The thought and self-knowledge that came with it did nothing to lessen any of the effects of the flashback. But they did serve to make me mad. It was the anger about her that got me out of the bathroom.

Powder fresh and dressed for work, I carried a thermos full of hot, black coffee out into the world, resolved—once again—to keep my ghosts behind me. When I climbed into the truck, I saw myself in the mirror again. This time I tried something the therapist had told me. I tried to visualize what others saw rather than my own judgment. What I visualized was Nelson Solomon looking at me, more than what I imagined he saw. But it made me smile. Smiling changed the image and I brushed the hair back from the scar beside my eye. That was the woman I wanted him to see.

I felt a little hope and then I felt a little shame. Story of my life, really. Suddenly I thought of the night before, with my uncle, and regretted telling him about Nelson. It was a mixture of wishful thinking on my part and the desire to seem normal to my family. Uncle Orson would tell my father. For a while Dad would be hopeful that his daughter had finally walked away from the damage in her life. I looked away from the rearview mirror and tucked it all away. I had work to do.

My official day began when I called in and let Darlene know I would take my own vehicle to make a couple of calls following up on the murder of Angela Briscoe.

First, I went to the murder scene. I stopped at the convenience store for a soda. Thirty-two ounces was 99 cents and twice that much was $1.19. I got the giant size. It was an offering of thanks for a long, boring job. I passed it through the window on the cruiser posted on the road where I had first met Clare. The deputy was William Blevins by his nameplate, but everyone called him Billy. It wasn't just an affectionate nickname; it was because he looked to be twelve years old. He was short and pudgy with wire glasses and a kid's haircut. The hair came courtesy of a barber named Finas Gold who was half blind and, it's said, learned his trade snipping hair under bowls before

sending boys off to Korea. Billy was
never imagined in uniform. Funny ar
imagine him being bully bait in scho
ing him for a few minutes everyon
know how he became a deputy, bu
one else wanted. Honestly, I thin
and out of harm's way. But he
plaint.

"How'd you know?" he asked me with ⌐ ⌐
the soda. He took a big drink with his eyes closed. ⌐⌐
needed that."

"Your vices are open secrets, Billy. They aren't really vices, either."

"Caffeine."

I watched him take another long drink. "Anything happen overnight?"

"News trucks all left by eleven. I heard some noise out that way." He pointed north with the soda cup. "And probably a truck driving around. It was up the road a ways. I called it in, then went to keep an eye on the scene just in case someone was trying to get around me."

I was impressed. Any other deputy would have been bored and happy to go check on the noise. When I said that to Billy, he shrugged and said, "I wasn't told to check out noises or cars. I was told to make sure no one went past that tape."

It was good to know there was still someone who did his job, even a small one, with respect and pride. Someday he'd probably be the sheriff, and I would be working for him.

"Did they find anything?"

"It was quiet by the time anyone got here. I called it in at . . ." he checked a notebook even though it should have been recorded at the station. "Four-twenty-eight."

"Okay. I'm going to have a look around. What time are you being relieved?"

"Don't know that I am." He read the look on my face. "Something wrong?"

"Probably nothing," I told him. "This killing is going to get a lot of attention. I'm afraid our scene will get a lot as well."

"Kind you want it to get or the kind you *don't* want it to get?"

"What are you asking, Billy?"

"If you just want the scene kept clean, I can hang around and bvious. Looky-loos won't stop if cops are here. If you who comes in for a closer look . . . well, I can bring a pole k. There's a nice spot close by."

ver said I was above taking advantage of someone's good na-Billy had to return the cruiser and pick up his truck, but he'd be ck within the hour to set up his off-the-clock surveillance. Until he was back I planned to stick around and check some things out.

The field and trail showed new wear from all the activity of the previous day. In the wooded area the ground was pinned in places by wires with little plastic flags. They marked where evidence had been taken. In a wide, rough circle crime-scene tape was strung from tree to tree centered on a blank spot where Angela had died. The only remaining evidence of her presence was blood spatter that haloed a void where her face had been crushed.

There was no new evidence and no startling revelations waiting. That was for television. Real police work was based on logging hours of repetitive tasks and questions. Very often the job isn't finding out who did the crime. It's more about proving the case against the person you already know to be guilty. Most murders are committed by someone known to the victim. That only holds truer with the murder of a child.

Along the stream bank there were a few more flags where rocks had been moved and the one marking where a roundish stone had been found with blood and hair on it. Beyond that I headed north, the opposite direction I had taken with Clare the day before.

Everything yesterday had been about the girl and my supposition that Clare and his whiskey were only coincidentally involved. The biker—make it *bikers* now—had taken a run right up to the top of the suspect ladder. That meant their interests had to be examined. One was seen here near the murder scene. The day of or day after the murder, he was kicking an artist around. That same day, another one was seen close to the dead girl's home.

Connections.

Upstream and on a bend where the bank was shallow I found what I was looking for. Across the water, around a black burn mark, was a pile of cinder blocks, a pile of firewood, and a few old pallets tucked within a copse of trees. I crossed the stream for a closer look. The ground was clean, surprisingly so. There were parallel lines where a rake had been dragged through the grass and bare dirt. Even so, whomever had tidied up had left behind several bits of broken glass from canning jars and tatters of brown paper. The paper was the same tough, thick stuff feed sacks are made from. It wasn't until I saw the paper that I noticed the kernels of corn scattered around.

There was still a surprise waiting and I found it by smell, not by sight. It was a rich, yeasty smell but sweet as well, like a bakery gone bad. I followed my nose outside the main circle and, under an old hedge apple tree, found a compost bin cobbled from the wood of more pallets. It looked like Clarence Bolin was a green bootlegger. Inside the bin were the solid sediment of the missing still along with food scraps, hedge apples dropped from the tree, and a dead armadillo. I had no idea if you could compost the leavings of your still, but I had to give the guy points for trying.

For a while I poked around, partially just killing time. I found fresh tire tracks in a rutted path where the still had been carried out the night before. How long did it take to set up in a new spot and begin a new batch? How long did a batch take from start to finish? I didn't know anything about moonshine. I decided to make Clare my personal mentor on the subject as soon as I got hold of him.

Billy came back in less than an hour. Even at that he'd already drained and refilled his soda cup.

Chapter 5

The home of Nelson Solomon was one of those best-of-both-worlds places only the wealthy ever seem to manage. It was close to town, in this case Branson. And it was still secluded, tucked into a cliff top lot with a view of the lake. It was my second stop of the morning. Solomon's assault looked even less random now that I knew Cotton Lambert had been at both crime scenes. That raised questions, serious questions that needed better answers than I'd gotten yesterday.

The only approach to the house was a meandering gravel drive that switched back on itself a couple of times before dumping out on a large, paved parking area. As soon as I pulled onto the concrete pad I heard a motorcycle start. It was a big Harley V-twin with loud pipes that roared as the engine revved up. A familiar sound. When it ran by me like a scalded cat it carried the smell of hot exhaust. Even over that, I swear I could smell the rider, a raw mix of sweat, grease, old beer, and tobacco. He was a big man with long, ratty hair and a beard to match. His head was bare but his eyes were covered by dark sunglasses.

He was not Lambert, the man whose picture I carried in my pocket. It was the one Carrie had identified as Leech. He was the same type, though. And I was willing to bet the pair of them belonged to the same club. This time I got a look at the patch.

When I saw Lambert running from the scene of Solomon's beating he was wearing a leather vest with his colors. This guy, Leech, was wearing a cut, the traditional denim jacket with sleeves sliced off, but the patches on the back were the same. This time I was close enough to see them clearly. There was a center image of a masked Bald Knobber, with a rocker patch above that read *Ozarks Nightriders*, and one below that read *Missouri*. To the side was a smaller white patch that had the

MC for "motorcycle club." I had heard of them; nothing good. Missouri had been open ground for a while and several clubs had formed or chapters of established clubs moved in. They were all tangling over turf and trade. From what we'd been hearing, these guys were big into meth.

They had to be local. No one else would use a Bald Knobber mask in their colors. Bald Knobbers were a violent vigilante group in the Ozarks, mostly in the late 1800s. In night rides, they ran off blacks or burned out white farmers they didn't like, using the whip and the torch to enforce their will on the region. Like the Klan would wear peaked hoods and white robes to hide their identity, the Bald Knobbers wore masks made from flour sacks with embroidered eyeholes and tasseled horns. They took their name from the bare tops of hills called *bald knobs* where they held their secret meetings. There was a time in these hills when night riders inspired a level of dread to which their modern imitators could never aspire. That, I think, is because of the collusion of the citizenry. Bikers wallow in the idea of being outsiders living apart from society. The Bald Knobbers, and all of the other various night-riding groups that our nation spawned between the Civil War and the First World War, were not outsiders. They were what masks allowed citizens to become.

There was no damage to the house that I could see. I had either caught the biker just as he arrived or he was waiting for someone. Nelson, I would guess. I would guess also that he hadn't been there to have a quiet chat about art. Nelson Solomon was a target of some nasty people. The questions were why and did he know more than he claimed?

I left the house under the care of a deputy named Calvin Walker.

"So you're gonna just stick me with babysitting a rich guy's house?" Calvin asked me after I explained the situation to him.

Calvin was not my best friend in the department. In fact, he didn't like me very much at all. I resisted the urge to tell him how useless he was. Something I didn't always do, to tell the truth. Another benefit of therapy.

"You're not babysitting the house," I told him, quite patiently, again. "The man who lives here was assaulted by one of these bikers yesterday. I don't know where he is or why this is happening. You are here to make sure the bikers don't come back before he does so they can try again."

"Babysitting," he said.

"Call it what you want, Calvin. Just do it."

"You know what your problem is, Hurricane?"

"I'm sure you're dying to tell me, but you need to know something first." I looked him hard in the eyes and took a step closer. "If you even think the word—period—I swear to God it'll be the last thought you have."

"You know, sexual harassment works both ways. You're making a very uncomfortable work environment for me." He presented me with the kind of grin Uncle Orson always referred to as *shit-eating*.

That was the kind of thing I've had to deal with every day of my working life: Boys getting petty and wanting to test you every moment. There's no way to pass, but every failure is tallied up and held against you. If I don't play along, I'm a bitch. If I do, I'm a dyke. Go through channels and complain—well, that's just something I'll never do again.

After a few more words I left Calvin and headed back to Forsyth to check in with the notes and calls I left the day before. On 160 I had passed the water tower and was coming up on Forsyth Hardware when I saw a familiar car. The girl sitting on the hood was familiar as well. Carrie Owens.

I pulled in and parked alongside the same Chevy I had first seen her on.

When she saw me she smiled, but it was a cautious smile.

"Hi, Carrie," I said through my open window.

She glanced at the storefront trying to see through the glass before she looked back at me and said, "Hello. I'm just waitin' on Danny."

"That's fine," I told her. "There's no law against waiting."

Her smile eased up a bit and she said, "You're not in the cop car."

"No, not today. Does that mean I should show you my badge?"

"No," she laughed. "I'll trust you."

"I'm glad to hear it. Trust is important." Then in a quieter, conspiratorial tone I said, "Especially between us girls."

She smiled again, but something about it was broken. Like she hadn't gotten that it was a joke. Her body tensed and her lips froze, but her eyes were someplace else. I had said something wrong but I had no idea what. The faraway look in her eyes, though—that I had ideas about.

"Are you all right, Carrie?" I asked her.

"Sure," she said quickly. Her eyes came back with a new hardness to them. "Why wouldn't I be?"

"You kind of went away for a second, there. I wondered—"

"I should go inside. I need to see what's taking Danny so long."

"Okay, Carrie. If you think you should. But I wanted to ask you something first."

She had scooted down off the hood of the car and I noticed how low her jeans were riding on her bony little hips. The panties that peeked out of the waistband had cartoon bears on them. A little girl trying so hard to be a woman; or a girl, older than she should be, reaching back for childhood?

I stepped out of the truck to show I would follow her if she tried to go into the store. She got the message and stood beside the car.

"I need you to tell me about the man called Leech."

"My mother told me not to talk to you about things. She said I didn't have to unless she was around." She spit the words out quickly and without thought. She had practiced saying them, I was sure.

"It's true," I told her. "You don't have to talk unless we make it all official and bring you in and call your parents." I let that sink in a moment before continuing. "Is that what you want? Or would you like to help me find out what happened to your friend?"

Carrie crossed her arms and looked back at the storefront, then to the sky and back to the ground. "She wasn't my friend, okay?"

I wondered if her surliness was about guilt or fear. "Even if she wasn't, wouldn't you want to help find her killer?"

"What would I know about it?"

"I'm not saying you know anything about it. But you know something about that man, Leech."

"So?"

"So it might help me to understand what happened if I knew something about him."

Her arms were crossed over her chest and she kept looking off into the street or into the store window, avoiding me and the word. Afraid of being caught talking or hoping for rescue? "Carrie—"

"I don't know."

"Remember what I said about trust, Carrie. You can trust me. I just want to help you."

"No one helps anybody. I've got my own help and it's none of your business."

"What help, Carrie?" No answer. "Can you tell me why you need help?" She looked ready to cry. "Does it have something to do with this Leech?"

Carrie reached down to the car hood and, with a finger, wrote the name in the grime. Leech. As soon as it was complete she swept away most of the word with the palm of her hand. "You don't understand anything," she said.

"Help me to understand, Carrie. I've been looking for him. Can you tell me his real name?"

She grinned like she knew a secret but only for a second before she dropped it and said, "No."

"Are you afraid of him?"

She nodded, then quickly said, "That's not why I can't tell you. I don't know."

"Is Danny afraid of him too?"

Carrie nodded again.

"Has he threatened you?"

"Why can't you just catch him and put him in jail?"

"Because I need information. I don't know if he did anything. I don't even know his name."

"He killed Angela."

I looked at her and she turned away to look at the dirty car hood again.

"Do you know that for sure? Did you see it?"

Still looking down, she shook her head.

"Do you know anything I can use in court?" I asked.

"I know he's bad. I know he did it."

"How?"

"I just do. Because I hate him." Then she looked up and past me. Danny had just come out of the hardware store with a bag. She leaped at him.

"What's going on?" he asked. The question was quiet and addressed to Carrie, but he wasn't taking his gaze off of me. Carrie whispered something to him and his eyes turned down to look at the hood of his car. The L was still there with the lower point wiped away. "We have to go," he said.

I didn't stop them.

* * *

Nelson Solomon was still in the hospital. A nurse at the third-floor desk pointed to an open door at the end of a long hall. As I approached I heard a raised voice coming from inside saying, "You act like everything's a big joke. I'm tellin' you this guy will gut you like a fish and smile the whole time." The voice was thick with a meaty sound that matched the accent that sounded halfway between Brooklyn and New Orleans. I stopped in the hall and listened at the door.

"What?" Nelson asked. "Are you trying to do me a favor?"

"Someone needs to. But I ain't doin' it."

"You aren't living up to your reputation," Nelson said and I could hear the humor in his voice.

"That's business. This ain't."

That's when I walked into the room expecting to see someone more in line with the biker look. I was surprised to see someone who looked like a fireplug with a gin-blossom nose and wearing an expensive suit.

"Hello," I said, more as an announcement than a greeting.

Nelson smiled. The other guy looked like some men I had seen when something explodes nearby. Instantly ready to fight.

"Hurricane," Nelson said. "I mean, Detective Williams."

"Whatever," the other guy said. Then he brushed past me leaving the room.

"What was that?" I asked.

"Nothing," Nelson answered. "Some people want to buy something from me. I'm not in the mood to sell."

"Not enough money?"

"More than enough money. But money isn't everything, is it?" He asked the question with the kind of tone that implied humor, but there was nothing funny about it.

He turned to look out the window. The view was mostly of a parking lot and traffic, but beyond that were trees whose green heads looked like a sea spreading out to the horizon. He was like a sailor watching the sea move, but caught between memories of journeys taken and dreams of those that would never be. "Mr. Interesting," I said to his back.

He didn't turn right away, but in the faint reflection on the glass I saw him smile.

"I've been waiting for the nurse," he said.

"Time for your sponge bath?" That time it was me trying to be funny and not quite getting it right. Hospitals always put me in a weird state of mind, but I was in a proper enough state to instantly regret the joke.

"Only if you're offering," he answered and when he turned there was anything but regret on his face. "But mostly I was wanting to get out of here."

"I just came from your house, Mr. Solomon," I said, trying to bring it back to business. "There was another biker there."

"Did you like it?"

"What?"

"The house. I had it built a couple of years ago. It's one of those semi-prefab things, a log cabin with all the logs cut in a factory and delivered on a truck. I don't know what I was thinking."

"It's a beautiful home but I didn't go inside. There was no break-in. But it concerns me that two club bikers have turned up with you apparently in their sights."

"You're bound and determined to make this official, aren't you?" He stepped away from the window and turned to face me. For the first time I noticed the pole and the bag it was holding that dripped clear fluid through a needle into his arm. Nelson saw me looking. "This," he said, showing off the arm with the IV needle taped over his vein, "has nothing to do with yesterday." The thought made him smile at something. I couldn't see what it was but I could see the way his gaze focused elsewhere. "But it seems to have everything to do with tomorrow."

"Tomorrow?" I asked before my mental train pulled into the station.

Understanding must have shown on my face because he didn't explain and I didn't say anything. Still, he nodded, a silent acknowledgement. Mr. Solomon had been sick before the biker got hold of him. Everything fell into its unpleasant but inevitable place as I looked him over again. Loss of weight. Newly bald head. Blood. And worst of all, the look of resignation in his eyes. It wasn't pitiful at all, just kind of sad, like someone who has to leave home for a place and a duty he can't get out of.

If I had to guess, I would have said that the medicine in the IV was some kind of chemotherapy. I didn't want to guess.

Before I could say I was sorry or think of any other words to hide behind, he said, "Now. About that sponge bath . . ."

We laughed together, but it was short-lived. Nelson covered his mouth and hurried into the bathroom. Even though he took the extra time to close the door, I could hear him vomiting. When it was over I heard water running and the brushing of teeth before the door opened again.

"I thought you would be gone," he said as soon as he came out.

"Told you, I'm not very delicate."

"Well, that makes one of us." He smiled again and it was a wounded look, the kind to follow a shameful confession. "I would have been here today anyway getting the drip. Because I was unconscious yesterday they wanted to keep me overnight. Two birds, one insurance bill."

"You got your ass kicked yesterday and spent today on chemo."

He nodded and the shame was lingering.

"Then you hit me up for a sponge bath almost as soon as I walked in the door. I'd say you don't have a delicate bone in your body."

His smile then was genuine. He grinned as a matter of fact. It was the kind of a look that sits well on a man and that makes a woman proud to have put it there. I had to remind myself that his smile was not the reason I was there.

"Can you tell me about the bikers?"

"I would if I had anything to tell. I've seen some around but my first conversation with one was yesterday."

"And that little spot of land you were on?" I asked.

"Like I said, the bank owns that and I had permission from Jack Elliot, the manager, to be there."

I pulled the folded paper from my pocket, the one with Cotton Lambert's picture on it, and handed it over.

Nelson held it up in the light from the window. As he did, the short sleeve of his hospital gown rode up and revealed a tattoo on his shoulder. It was a small EGA—eagle, globe, and anchor. Marine.

"That's the guy," he said, handing the picture back. "You get him?"

"No. But I expect to run him down pretty quick. Are there any other areas that you've been painting lately?"

He hesitated and thought. I could see a question in his eyes and thought for a second that something had sparked a connection that would make sense. I was wrong.

"Is there a Mr. Hurricane at home?" he asked me.

My answer was no answer. "Other places you've been painting?" I reminded him.

Either I was completely transparent—and that I doubted—or my face gave away something without the rest of me knowing it. Nelson nodded again. This time it was a knowing, satisfied bob of the head. "All over," he said. "Pretty much anyplace I can get interesting views of the lake. I've been doing a lot of painting."

"Do you know anything about bootlegging?"

"Bootlegging?" He sounded completely surprised by the question. "Do they still do that?"

I nodded.

"Why? You can go into any liquor store and buy whatever you want." I was about to answer but the aspect of his face changed. He looked like he was concentrating hard on something. For a moment I thought he was going to admit something or give up a piece of information. Instead, he put a hand over his mouth. His concentration was all in keeping himself from throwing up again. After a moment, he said, "I have a friend that might know something."

That's something cops hear a lot. Not just, *I have a friend* but *I know someone who knows someone* or *I read about this one crime . . .* It's the flip side of what Clare Bolin had said when he was pointing the finger at the sex offender in the neighborhood. People want to help and they always try to fill in the gaps when they don't have actual information. It's a weakness we exploit in interrogation, but in the initial questioning phase it tends to produce useless information.

So instead of asking about his friend, I described the area where Angela had been found and asked if he had been painting around there. It was a question that had to be asked because of the overlap of the cases more than any thought he was involved. He answered no. When I asked if he knew Angela Briscoe he said the same. His negative responses were believable more because of how he looked than what he said. It would take a strong person to lie that well when he was looking like he had to puke again.

"I'll let you get back to resting," I said and folded the picture back up to tuck it into my pocket. "I'm sorry to bother you."

"What? No sponge bath?"

Again, I almost put my foot, boot and all, in my mouth. I started to say that he might not be up for it. The unintentional double entendre caught my attention just in time. Instead, I told him that his truck was impounded and where it could be picked up.

"I'll need a ride," he told me. There was nothing coy about the statement. It was both fact and hope. "I get out of here this afternoon."

"Maybe you'd rather—"

"No. I wouldn't."

"The impound closes at five."

"Then maybe I'll need a ride home."

Chapter 6

Sheriff Benson had told Mr. and Mrs. Briscoe to expect me. They were grief-stricken but gracious, offering tea while we sat in the small family room stuffed with matching floral sofa and love seat. The walls were cluttered with family pictures that showed Angela's entire life from birth to just weeks before her death at thirteen.

I was there for most of an hour with the meat of the time spent in long pauses and painful inward-pointing blame. Parents who lose children violently rarely remain married. The loss is a hard wind on a strong tree. At first they cling, needing the comfort of each other, but slowly seams appear that no one ever suspected. The only thing stronger than the guilt is the need to blame. Even when the person responsible is caught and punished, it's not enough. It's almost as if love demands personal responsibility. Either one partner blames the other or one, or both blame themselves. The truth is that their love for each other becomes the mirror of loss and no one can look into that for very long.

As I sat with the parents of Angela Briscoe I was witness to the opening of the first seams. Mary Briscoe was holding a photo of her daughter. Whenever her husband, David, leaned her way or put an arm around her, she protected the picture. In private, he had probably told her to put it down. I imagined he thought it was unhealthy for her and she wondered why he wasn't showing more pain.

David Briscoe turned from his wife and looked right into my eyes and asked me, "Was she raped?"

I shook my head and dropped my eyes to his hands. They were twisted into each other like knots. "We don't think so," I said as I brought my gaze back up to his.

"Don't think?"

"There will have to be lab work, medical inspection. That happens up in Springfield. But there are normal indications we look for. There was nothing like that."

"I was just . . . thinking . . ." he said, picking through his word choices carefully. "Wondering . . . maybe if she had . . . If it had happened . . . there might be DNA. If there was, then you would catch him for sure, wouldn't you? Now there's a chance you won't. The sheriff said things. He wouldn't promise us. He said things like, *do our best* and *never stop trying*, but that's not the same as saying the bastard will be caught. Not the same as saying the man that killed my daughter will pay."

In his face I could see both the fire that burned and the need he had to throw on more fuel. David Briscoe believed—had to believe, I guess—that the fire could be stoked high enough to consume the pain, then die. He didn't understand that it would linger within him forever, a furnace within his heart.

"Kill him," he said.

"Sir?"

"If you find him. If you get the chance. Think of my baby girl and pull the trigger on the son of a bitch. It would be the right thing."

"I understand, sir," I told him. "But you need to put those thoughts out of your head. They won't help anything."

For the first time Mary looked me in the eyes. "Can you promise?" she asked.

"Ma'am?"

"Promise that you will catch this man."

I wondered about the strength of Chuck Benson, an elected sheriff who wanted everyone to be happy and like him. He looked into those same eyes and refused to promise. It was the right thing, but it had to be hard. I know how hard it was for me. I changed the subject.

"Do you know anything about the motorcycle club called the Nightriders?"

"Motorcycle club?" Mr. Briscoe asked, and it was more than a question.

"What would we know about a motorcycle club?" Mrs. Briscoe said with almost no meaning or inflection. She was looking at Angela's picture again.

"You mean bikers," he said. "There's been one around. I've seen him. Is that the one that did this?"

"We don't know, Mr. Briscoe," I told him. "We have to look at everything."

"I should have known," he said. "A man should know when things are wrong. When people like that show up, nothing is ever the same."

"When have you seen a biker, Mr. Briscoe?" I asked.

He looked down at his wife, who seemed to still be ignoring us in favor of the photograph. "Sometimes at night," he said. "You can hear the engine at all hours, fast and loud. She didn't hear it. She sleeps—heavy." There was a note of accusation in his voice and on his face.

I wondered if by *heavy*, he wanted to say "sedated." Pills or drink? Either way, it was a source of friction that was only going to heat up between them.

"What nights did you hear it?"

"I don't know," he said, finally looking up but not at me. He was looking out the window to the front yard and street. It was easy to imagine him, in the middle of the night, watching for a noisy motorcycle. It was easy to imagine that he was wishing he knew then what he thought he knew now. "All hours. Any night. Whenever. I heard it several times but only saw him once."

"Can you describe him?"

"Big guy. About all I can say. Even at night his arms were bare. He wore one of those biker vests with patches all over it."

"Is there anything else you can tell me about him?"

He shook his head and simply said, "They're all criminals. Sons a' bitches."

I asked him some more questions about bikers and moonshine and the name Leech. I asked about the kids that I had seen the day before and Carrie Owens. He had nothing good to say. He seemed to feel about teenagers the same way he felt about bikers. In all, I was there a couple of hard hours asking intrusive questions about their life and their daughter. In the end, I got what you usually get in these situations: Angela was well liked and friendly; she had no known connection to criminals or drugs; she took cookies to a retirement home at least once a month and sang songs to the residents. A perfect daughter.

At the bottom on my notes I again wrote the name Leech then underlined it with thick black marks. The biker was the only connection I was finding.

"I'll be in touch as soon as I have any information," I told them as I set my card on the coffee table between us. "You can reach me here if you think of anything."

"Can I have her crucifix?" Mrs. Briscoe asked my back. It was the first thing she'd said in half an hour.

I turned to look at her. "Ma'am?"

"Her crucifix. I want it. What good would it be to the police? I want it."

"Ma'am, we didn't find a crucifix."

Mary burst into fresh tears and turned away from her husband to cry against the couch cushions. David Briscoe looked embarrassed but didn't seem to have the strength for it anymore.

"It was a big silver cross," he said. "Plain silver. It was a present. On the back it was engraved *All Our Faith in You*."

I nodded and told him that if it was found they could have it back as long as it was not evidence. They stayed on the love seat as I let myself out.

Before I got into my truck I stopped to take a breath and I cursed my Uncle Orson. I was taking his name in vain because he had given me that jar of whiskey. I hadn't opened it last night, but I had taken it with me and it was sitting in the console of my truck. I wanted it. I wanted it badly.

I wouldn't have admitted to a problem, but I would admit that I liked the separation from my thoughts that a few good, long swallows could give. Never had I drank on duty, but honestly, I was tempted at that moment. Instead of opening my door and locking myself inside with Clare Bolin's best, I crossed the road and knocked on the door at Carrie Owens's home.

There was no answer, but I could hear movement within. I knocked again more firmly, like I meant business. Muffled giggles came through the door and more movement. Carrie was in there and she wasn't alone. I couldn't help but picture the Barnes kid in there with her, but I was afraid to imagine what that really meant.

After knocking one more time I pulled another business card and wrote *Please call* on the back. I wedged the card into the door crack and remained on the porch long enough to jot in my notebook the time and what I suspected. As an afterthought, I wrote down the information about Angela Briscoe's crucifix as well.

* * *

The moment of need and self-pity had passed, replaced by a simmering anger at the Owens family. Where were her parents? What was she doing spending all her time with that older boy? It was probably the anger that allowed the jar of whiskey to remain untouched within the box between my truck's seats.

At the sheriff's office I shot off e-mails and made notes. One of the e-mails went to Michael Hamm, the detective who sat two desks away from me. He was our gang unit. I needed a meeting to find out all I could about the Ozarks Nightriders. Another e-mail went to our juvenile case officer for any information on Carrie Owens, Danny Barnes, or any of the other kids that might be in the same group. I had also asked the Division of Family Services for any information they might have that never made it to our files on the Owens family. There are a lot of confidentiality issues about queries like that, but if there is an obvious problem someone will find a way to let me know.

It's funny, but in TV shows and movies you always hear cops talk about the difference between street cops and desk cops. It makes a good image: the solitary detective, out in the field finding clues and tracking suspects. The sad truth for most of us is that the tracking is often done from the desk. We investigators secure the crime scene and then delegate, delegate, delegate. We gather information and sort it out, looking for the things that don't fit or for the information that holds all your ideas together.

That's what I did for the next couple of hours. I made more calls and searched every database available for Leech. I learned the Nightriders were a new club limited to southwest Missouri and northwest Arkansas. There had been an arrest in Oklahoma, but the warrant was for domestic violence out of Arkansas. I developed a list of last known addresses for eight men known to ride with the club. The next step was door-knocking.

I had just picked up my phone to call Billy and check on his day at the crime scene when a shadow moved across my open door. I looked up to find the shadow had solidified, if not gotten any lighter. A tall black man, erect of bearing with coffee-colored eyes that never smiled, leaned against the door frame without slouching. He wore Army class A's and a rod permanently up his ass.

Billy answered his phone and I said, "I'll call you back," before hanging up. "Major Reach" was all the greeting I gave.

"Hurricane Katrina," he said, taking his shoulder off the door frame. "I've been trying to get hold of you."

"I'm sorry," I said. "I was ignoring you. Was I being too subtle?"

He laughed, but it was just for show. "It wasn't social. It's all business."

"Oh? Let me guess: After all these years the Army is actually interested in what happened?"

"A lot of things happen. The happening to which you refer was investigated. And by the way, I'm not Criminal Investigations Division anymore. I'm with the Inspector General's office working with the DOD."

He stopped there and watched me, goading me with silence, inviting argument. I didn't rise to that bait anymore. In fact, I gave as good as I got, sitting silently and waiting for him to go on. He did, dropping the false smile.

"There was another thing that happened, which is not to say that all things that happen involve you, but . . ."

He spread his hands wide and open in a presenting gesture. I leaned back in my chair and tried to make myself look as comfortable as possible. Neither of us even glanced at the two visitor's seats in front of my desk.

"This one does," he finally went on.

I answered with a nod.

"You're not going to make this easy, are you?"

"I don't owe you anything," I told him.

"Fine," he said. "Major Rice was killed in Iraq."

"It couldn't happen to a nicer guy," I said.

"You're not surprised," he noted.

"It's been almost seven years. Word gets around."

"I bet it does. What else do you know about it?"

I knew enough not to tell him what I knew. I asked, "It happened . . . how many years ago?"

"A long time ago. Long enough you were still holding a grudge and making a lot of noise."

"*Major* Rice. I was still lieutenant. I remained lieutenant. My noise and grudge hurt only me. Isn't that true?"

"That's what I'm wondering. See, his death was written off as duty related. There were so many things going on in the conflict at the time, and he was killed working local tribal contacts. Funny thing, though . . ."

I kept listening without saying anything or even acknowledging his words.

"Your name came up."

"My name came up in what *official* investigation?" I asked.

He smiled his shark smile again. "Homeland Security," he said. "It seems a man named Sala Bayoumi applied for a special immigration visa based on his employment by the U.S. Army and intelligence services. Certain things about his story didn't add up and State called Homeland. Turns out, Sala Bayoumi was the contact that Major Rice met with before he was killed."

Reach paused and watched me. He was waiting for a reaction or for me to try to explain something I hadn't been asked. I gave him nothing. I didn't move forward or back, neither opened or narrowed my eyes, and controlled my breathing. He was fishing with the right bait but I'd spent years expecting someone to dangle this in front of me.

"You remember Sala Bayoumi. He mentioned that he'd had contact with you before he ever met with Rice."

"No," I said and let my response sit there between us. I knew about interrogation too.

"How is that?" he asked. "He remembers you so well."

"I, and every other MP officer involved in information gathering, met with dozens of contacts. We worked tribal leaders, nationalists, Ba'athists, Sunni and Shia militias, smugglers and arms dealers, and criminals of every type, including U.S.-government sanctioned contractors. There are more of them I don't recall than those I do."

"Hurricane Katrina," he said, dragging the phrase out and letting it drip with spite. Then, stepping back from my door, he spread his hands like he was displaying a title and said again, "*Hurricane*. That's a good name for you because you're a dangerous lady. I was just stopping in to give you a heads-up, a courtesy call, you know. I have an appointment to talk with Sheriff Benson and didn't want you feeling . . . inappropriately targeted."

Reach walked out. I put the tips of two fingers on my scar, then closed my eyes. There was no darkness behind my lids. It was all dirty haze and old blood drying in fine, dead soil.

It was my father who pulled me out this time. His call came through to my desk after only a few minutes. The sharp trill of the phone echoed at first like the fast thunder of an M240 machine gun. On the third ring the illusion of war and violence faded and I opened my eyes.

"You don't sound right," was the first thing he said after my hello.

"Busy day," I said, trying to sound bright and lively.

"Is there anything you want to tell me?"

There were a million things I wanted to tell him, but I said, "No."

"Okay." The sound of his voice said it was not okay at all but he would live with it. "Your uncle said he saw you last night."

I smiled. Everything was sane and proper again. Home and green. We talked for a few minutes, family stuff and a little cooking. He wanted to cook a pot of chicken and dumplings for Sunday dinner if I would promise to come up to Nixa. My favorite, but I didn't feel like I could promise. There were too many swords hanging over my head. I didn't mention to him the one sword that dangled with a honed edge or the major who was hoping to cut the string.

"Are you busy with the man you met?" Dad asked.

I don't care how much I expect these questions, they always catch me a little off guard. It was taking me a few moments to compose a response, so Dad jumped back in.

"Your uncle told me," he said needlessly.

At least it was needless to me. I knew where he'd gotten his information, but he sometimes feels the need to explain himself when he rummages around in my life. It'd been that way since my mother died. That was while I was in college. Ever since, my father and uncle had been trying to become some kind of weird, manly mother hens. They failed wonderfully and it only made me appreciate them more. *Them*, not the questions or the constant push to become the kind of girl I'll never be, a normal wife and mother.

"I know who told you," I said back, realizing as I did that it was just as needless a comment. "It's not what you think."

"Who says I think anything?"

"You always do, Dad. Nelson is a nice guy, but I'm not sure he's in the right place for romance. Neither am I."

"If the world waited for the right place or time there'd be no people at all."

I guess my answer was the silence he heard on the line as I touched at the scar beside my eye. It wasn't intentional. I just didn't know what to say.

"You know," he said, sounding cautious with his words, "it's okay with me whatever happens. As a matter of fact, it's perfect if I'm the only guy in your life forever."

"Thanks Dad," I said and I meant it. "But Uncle Orson would get jealous. Besides, what would the two of you do if you weren't trying to get me married off?"

Then he asked me a question that set the tiny hairs on my spine up and tingling.

"Are you having problems with the Army?"

"Why would you ask me that?" I didn't even try to keep the suspicion out of my voice. My father's military career had long ago transitioned into a civilian consulting job that had lots of contacts and influence in the intelligence community. This wasn't the first time he'd let me know that he was aware of things he shouldn't be. When he didn't answer, I prodded again. "What do you know?"

"It's just a question."

"Something like that is never just a question."

"I'm guessing from your response that there is something going on with the Army."

My career had not gone well; there was no way of hiding that. He knew that there were legal issues and that I had made enough noise about something that the Army wanted me out as quietly as possible. He knew all that and he knew that I didn't like to talk about it. This was the first time he had ever directly asked me anything about it and it had me on the defensive.

"Nothing I can't handle and nothing I need you to be involved in. There are things we've never discussed, Daddy, and I want you to respect my privacy here. All right?"

In the silence coming from his end of the phone I could feel something like vibrations on a spider's web. After the assault in Iraq, I'd tried hard to keep the details from my father. I'd thought both that he couldn't handle it and that I didn't want to shatter illusions he had about his beloved Army. There were times, though, that I felt like the only illusions were mine.

How much did he know? Had he involved himself? Did I even want to know?

"Daddy?" I pressed again.

"You know you can come to your old man about anything, don't you?" he asked.

"Do you know something?" I asked, suddenly sure that it was another needless question. He didn't respond and I thought he was about to say good-bye, so I said, "Yes, Dad. I do."

Instantly, it was like a curtain had been dropped that separated the man from my dad. It was the same on his end. His voice was much brighter when he said, "I can be pretty helpful at times. And I don't just mean Sunday dinners and picking out your husband for you."

"You wouldn't have picked this guy, Daddy."

"What?" A wave of new concern came through the phone line. "Why? Orson said you acted like he was a scrapper."

"He is, Daddy, but there's something else. Something you wouldn't approve of."

"What are you trying to say, sweetheart?" His voice was so serious and burdened with concern that I almost felt bad for him.

"He was a Marine," I told him and then quickly added, "I have to go."

Chapter 7

Nelson was escorted from the hospital by wheelchair, a fact that seemed to embarrass him no end. When I brought the truck up to the release door he was fussing like an old hen with the woman who had wheeled him out. She seemed to tolerate it well. He was wearing the same clothes that I had first seen him in. They were still bloody and filthy with roadside dirt.

"No one brought you clean clothes?" I asked him as soon as he climbed into my truck.

"I don't know who it would have been," he said, looking at the shirt and pants like he was noticing them for the first time. Then, brushing at dirt on his knee, "Sorry about that."

The short stay in the hospital had diminished him. Instead of being a vigorous, laughing man, he was tired and worn down. He had been bigger lying on the ground.

"Nothing to be sorry about," I said. "Don't you have family around? Friends?"

"I am a man without baggage," he answered, trying to sound glib but not quite managing it. "Without relations baggage, that is. I've been carrying around that thing in my lung for a while."

"I'm sorry."

"Nothing to be sorry about," he echoed my words. "You've heard of government cheese? I have government cancer. I was in the Kuwaiti oil fields when Saddam's boys got all pissy and set the wells on fire. Fat lot of good it did them. We still kicked their asses and went back to finish the job later."

He laughed. Suddenly he seemed to be the man I had first met.

When I didn't laugh with him, he said, "Hey, don't get all gloomy on me."

"Who says I'm gloomy?"

"Look in the mirror."

"Actually, I was feeling like a jerk for thinking what a bad day I'd had."

"Yeah," he said thoughtfully. "Someone else's cancer will do that to you. Perspective. God, I could use a beer."

"No beer," I told him. "But I do have this." Reaching into the console, I pulled out the jar of whiskey Uncle Orson had given me.

"Is that the real stuff?" Nelson asked, grinning at the jar. "Like illegal, cooked in the woods, moonshine?"

"It is."

He started twisting the lid.

"Don't do that," I warned. "I think that's the last thing you need right now."

"Thanks, Mom," Nelson teased. "I'm crazy but not stupid." He lifted the lid slightly and took a whiff from the opening. "Whoa, I think that's better than we make at the restaurant." Sealing the lid back tight, he then shook the jar and watched the bubbles in the light.

"Restaurant?" I asked.

"A guy I went to school with was starting a distillery restaurant and asked me to go in with him. It's been nothing but a pain in the ass and so far bleeds money. He's wanting to buy me out, but at a big loss for me. I figure if I'm taking a loss I may as well do it fighting."

"Distillery restaurant? I've never heard of anything like that."

"It's like a brewpub, only instead of beer you distill whiskey or rye or whatever. It sounded like a good idea but between the city, state, and the feds, there are more regulations than putting a combination strip club and gun shop between an elementary school and church. Remember I told you I knew someone who might know something about bootlegging? Gabe Hoener. He's our master distiller. You should talk to him. We'll go there for dinner."

"Dinner?" I asked. "Are you telling me or inviting me?"

"I'm just hoping."

He seemed to have grown in stature since leaving the hospital.

"And what exactly is it that you're hoping?" It was a teasing question. A flirtation. Nelson was the kind of man who put me at ease and let me think about all the things a man could be in my life. That also makes me incautious to a degree that I'm not used to. My inept flirtation, combined with the dark shadow of the unknown sitting between us, made the moment more than it was supposed to be. The answer I had expected was a laugh or some half-veiled innuendo. What I got was a look that said the question was much harder than he was ready for.

I reached over the compartment between our seats and took his hand. I didn't look at him. I didn't smile. I just held and enjoyed the feeling when his fingers returned my grip.

On the last bend in the road before the turn into Nelson's drive, I noticed a car in the rearview mirror. It was a late-model, midsized sedan, generic and white. Everything about it read *fleet vehicle*. Either it was a rental car or government issue.

Nelson's home was filled with light and art. Saying it was a log cabin was to say it was made of logs, but the accuracy of the description stopped there. We entered through the garage side that faced the road, but he escorted me directly to the front side that was shaped like the prow of a ship made mostly of glass. It looked out over a deck of cedar plank and rail poles onto a VistaVision view of a wooded canyon wall that dropped 200 feet to the lake. The room itself was all wood grain, glass, and art. Some of the art was obviously his own, but most pieces—framed original paintings and bronze statues—were by others and given special treatment. The exception was one corner between a huge river-stone fireplace and the bank of windows. That space was for working. There was an easel with all the tools of his trade on a spattered drop that protected the hard pine floor.

"Would you like something?" he asked.

I shook my head and pointed to the painting sitting on the big easel. "That doesn't look like what you're known for." It was a portrait of a woman wearing a niqab, only her very expressive eyes visible over the dark fabric. "I thought you only painted landscapes."

"Actually, my first big success was a painting of a pair of old cowboy boots. Not so much the painting itself, but the poster, then T-shirts. It was licensed by the boot company for advertising. That let me quit my job and paint full-time."

"And her?" I nodded at the painting of the Muslim woman.

"I saw her once in Iraq. She was just standing there against a wall, watching as we passed."

"You remembered her enough to paint her years later."

"It's all memory, I think. Even if I'm looking at it while I paint. A photograph is perfect memory of one fraction of a second. Painting is like a slow-motion memory and anything but perfect."

He was beginning to sound sad again. Sad or tired or both. I was about to say something about leaving him alone to rest when he asked if I minded waiting a moment while he took a shower.

"Not at all."

For a few minutes I looked at paintings. The landscapes were there, some racked in the work area, some hanging on display. Other paintings were what drew me, though. They were like mile markers in life, a place where a crossroads had been passed or a new destination had been spotted in the distance. Faces and places with people moving, life roiling and active and imposing itself, not just life, but *Life*—capital L—marked the difference between then and now. I liked the new work so much more.

After I had pawed through Nelson's work, uninvited, I went to his bedroom. In the bathroom beyond, he was showering and the water must have been hot. A fog of steam seeped from the cracked door.

I moved close enough to listen to the water splashing against his skin. The same heat that washed over him billowed out to caress me. The scent of soap, simple and strong, carried out on the frothing air.

I want to be in there with him.

Proximity was temptation, I'll admit it. I imagined myself undressing and getting into the water with him. Then I wished I was the kind of woman who would. I had to correct my thinking. I was the kind of woman who would. I was just the kind of woman who couldn't.

Still, the warmth and scent of the air drew me to the door, where I pushed it fully open and let myself bask.

"I'm at the door," I told him and I stopped on the threshold.

He was in a glass shower with every surface fogged. Within, he was a barely darker shade of gray feathered out to white.

"You're not coming in, are you?" he asked, but it was really a statement. The tone was not teasing or disappointed. It was just a fact and understood.

"No. Do you mind that I'm here?"

His hand came up to the glass and wiped away a narrow slice of mist right at eye level. Then he looked out at me. I was reminded of the painting on his easel, the woman in the niqab. Or more accurately, I thought of the lingering memory of the woman's eyes.

Nelson's eyes had a weight to them as well. As quickly as I felt the weight, he let it go and a smile fell into his look. "There is only one other place I would want you to be." There was the tease, the easy good humor.

I want to be naked for those eyes.

"I need to shave. Hand me the razor by the sink?"

That brought me all the way into the room. I'm sure that was his thinking. After handing the razor over the top of the glass, I was tempted to open cabinets and drawers looking for anything feminine. One box of tampons and I would be running. But there was nothing feminine about the room. It wasn't masculine, either; more temporary, like a hotel bathroom.

"How long have you lived in this house?" I asked.

"A year."

I thought of my year. Then I thought of my last decade. It was like this room. Time waiting to be filled in.

My head began swimming in the heat, but a shiver of cold ran down my spine. It settled in between my thighs. I took a step, not to go anywhere but to shift my body. The pants I was wearing felt tight and my hips tingled with an internal blossoming, a waking feeling of both warmth and chill. It was a confusion of needs that walked on tiny feet up my body. Under my bra my nipples hardened and I couldn't pretend ignorance of what I was wanting anymore.

Nelson shut the water off.

I took a long, deep breath of the moist air.

He opened the shower door and then reached through to grab a towel from the bar.

As I stepped back the thought that I should turn away entered my mind. That's all it did: It entered and just waited to be noticed. I took no notice or action.

When he stepped out, the towel was wrapped around his waist. His face and scalp were freshly shaved, pinking his skin and making him look almost boyish. Water was still dripping from his shoulders and running in thick drops down his chest, pulling all the hair and my gaze downward. The center of his body was gaunter than I had expected. He had lost more weight than I had imagined. I could tell by the line of his ribs and the skin of his belly that looked both tight but soft. Even though his stomach was flat, the front of the towel covering his hips wasn't.

He wasn't aroused but he was definitely aware that I was in the room.

I wanted to say something. Nelson stepped forward and put his hands on my face and drew me into the softest, most genuine kiss I had ever experienced.

As soon as our lips parted, though, what he had said about painting and memory passed through my mind. This was a moment just like that. I couldn't help wondering if a year from now, or twenty, this moment would be as static and real as a photograph or painted, filtered through my thoughts until it becomes more than it ever could have been.

That's the funny thing about memory. Everything colors it. Everything that comes after the event and everything that precedes has a say in the remembering. The real irony is that it works the other way around too. All those things in your memory can conspire in delicate, black whispers to color every moment of your life with shades of meaning. My memory paints my life with color, pale and drained of vibrancy until everything is surrounded by a spent and split cocoon. It offers no protection; instead, it seems to confine me within the filmy chamber at the same time as it invites in all the terrors of the world. Inside a dirty translucence with echoes both of color and history, I fight until I have to break away.

It wasn't graceful. I made excuses. At least in my mind they felt like excuses. In word and deed I'm sure they were much less. That's to say, I ran from the room. I ran from Nelson.

I didn't run home. That would have been a sane action. And while I might not have been sane, I wasn't quite insane. I had sense enough to leave the county I was employed in to get drunk. Up in Christian County there was a place I knew but was not known in. It was new and still not quite broken in. The old place was called Wooly's before the fire. The owner had been keeping fireworks in the basement to sell at a summertime roadside stand. When the place went up, everyone within ten miles watched the show.

Wooly's was now Shep's, Wooly having gone up with a bold white chrysanthemum burst. People in the area now call the finale of any fireworks display the big Wooly. Shep had rebuilt a much nicer place, killing the character of the red-painted cinder-block roadhouse. He still served cheap food and beer along with the music of local bands.

It was Friday-night crowded when I got there. Exactly what I needed. Inside, I took the only booth I could get and sagged into red glitter vinyl to hide and drink. After the first beer I had another with a whiskey back. I don't care what anyone says about drinking for pleasure or loving the taste, you don't have a boilermaker unless you mean business. The whiskey was house brand. That meant it was about as strong as hard water. But it was cheap enough to get the job done and enjoy the ride getting there.

I thought about the jar in the console of my truck. Clare Bolin's whiskey. If I needed to get quick about it, that was my hole card. Drinking blew away the dust that always seemed to hang at the edges of my vision. It let the colors come but muted the meanings. For me it was like watching my own life on television with the sound turned off. I knew what was there, but didn't have to listen anymore.

The waitress was a pretty older woman who had been here even when the place was Wooly's. I had heard her name before but didn't know it. Everyone called her Angel, from the song about Angel being a centerfold. She had been a feature in a men's magazine once upon a time and still had the looks to draw men's eyes. The thought occurred to me that I should ask her, but when she came to the booth she carried a highball glass with two fingers of something good.

"Here you go, sugar," she said as she set the glass in front of me.

"I didn't order this," I said, but never looked at the glass. I was looking at her and honestly I was thinking that there was probably not a scar on her body.

"I'm thinking you probably don't need it, either. Fella over the bar ordered it. I'll tell him to take a hike for you, if you want. Maybe call a ride?"

I couldn't think of anything to say. I kept looking into her eyes. They were green. I wanted to ask her what it was like to be beautiful. I imagined the look on a man's face—Nelson Solomon's face—when the last of Angel's clothes hit the floor and she was naked for him. I bet they looked at her with joy.

Since I didn't answer, she said, "Either way, this is your last one, hon."

"Who bought this?" I asked.

"He did." She gestured to the bar where Major Reach was standing with a mug of beer and a lethal smile.

Angel asked if I knew him and I said I did. She looked like she didn't believe me. Then I said that I wished I didn't know him. She believed that. I could tell by the way she looked at me, then over to Reach. Angel nodded at me like she knew everything and nothing more ever needed to be said, then left. Men watched her as she walked. So did I. When I looked away, Reach was sliding into my booth.

"I hated to see you drink alone," he said.

"I hated to see you too," I hit back.

He grinned. "That hurricane's blowing tonight, isn't it?"

I wish I could say I threw the drink in his face and walked away. I can't and it tasted wonderful, despite the company. After a big first swallow I said, "You followed me."

"You killed Rice."

"Are you stupid enough to believe that? And here I thought you were just a pissant, wind-up soldier who got his feelings hurt when I didn't roll over and let you push me out of the service."

"Just doing my job."

"Bullshit," I said and followed it with a long swallow of whiskey. When I sat the glass down it was almost empty. Ice tinkled loudly. "Bullshit," I said again, then closed my eyes and touched the scar. The liquor wasn't working as fast as I had hoped. "You did what you were supposed to do. But you never did your job."

"Yeah? What was I supposed to have done differently?"

"You were supposed to believe me. Even if I couldn't prove it. Even if everyone in the world lined up to lie for the men that did that to me."

"I'll tell you what I believe now. I believe that you're going to face charges for murder."

"What murder?"

"Rice. Probably even Ahrens someday. Whoever I can make the case on."

Hearing those names turned the world upside down. The pair of them had done terrible things to me and never been punished. Now I was being accused—

I remembered what my father had asked me. *Was I having problems with the Army?* Obviously I was, but how did he know? Something else struck me that I'd ignored before. When we'd talked at the office, Reach had made a point of telling me that he was working with the Inspector General and the DoD. That's how my father knew. Those were the people he did consulting work for.

"What's the bigger picture?" I asked Reach. "You're not here for a decade-old murder."

"Maybe I am. Maybe not. But that's what I'm going to put you away on."

Not for the first time I decided that there was no reasoning with this man. I didn't understand him any more than I could understand those who assaulted me. Any more than I could understand myself. But at that point I was past trying to understand. I reached out, sliding the highball glass across the tabletop, then dumped what was left right into Reach's lap. Then I got up to leave.

Reach did just what I expected and wanted: He grabbed my arm and pulled me back. Hard. I was drunk by then. Not so drunk that I would get into a fight with an investigator from the DoD, but I will admit I was drunk enough to be vicious. Even though I knew I wouldn't be proud of it later, I said, "You're hurting me."

That's all it took. A person, especially a cop, should always be aware of his surroundings. Reach was used to being protected by his rank and his position in the Army. But Shep's bar was pretty far from anything to do with Army life. It was actually pretty far from the rest of the country in a lot of ways that he didn't yet understand.

Reach was the only black man in a redneck bar and I had said he was hurting me. Before he could let go of my arm there were three men with huge belt buckles and actual cowshit on their pointy-toe boots standing in front of him. They all kept their gaze locked on him as one asked if he was bothering me.

I said, "This guy's been following me all night. I think he's a stalker. I wanted to go home but I was afraid."

At the same time, I played the damsel-in-distress card and the race card. Not pretty, but there it was. Let Reach deal with it.

He surprised me. He had enough sense to keep his mouth shut when one of the cowboys said, "You can go home now. We'll make sure no one follows you this time."

I left him standing there beside the booth with a wet crotch and clenched jaw, staring hate at me as I walked out to the truck.

It was Billy who found me later that night. After leaving the bar I had made it all the way back to the dirt strip where I first met Clare Bolin and found Angela Briscoe. I can't really say I recall the drive. Only blind luck kept anything memorable from happening. He rolled up behind me with the light bar on. The flashing red, blue, and white lights looked like a low-flying UFO creeping up out of darkness. The light bar died and the spot came on as Billy pulled up alongside. He swept a million candlepower of blue-white pain into my eyes and over the truck for a long moment before killing it and stepping out of the cruiser.

"The hell, Billy," I called out as soon as he was on his feet. "The hell? What the hell? Couldn't you tell it was me?"

"Oh, I knew it was you. I just wanted to be sure you were alone."

"Who would be with me out here?" I asked without thinking. Then I realized what he was suggesting. We catch a lot of kids out parking and sparking on these roads. I laughed.

"What's so funny?" Billy asked.

For a second I thought about that then told him, "I don't really know."

He seemed to do a little thinking of his own before he asked, "Are you armed?"

"Of course I'm armed," I answered. "You know I am."

"Would you give me your weapon and your keys, Katrina?"

That made me smile. "I like it when you call me Katrina."

"I know."

"You do? Then why do you call me Hurricane?"

"*I* like calling you Hurricane. It fits you more than you know."

"Maybe," I said and handed my service pistol and keys through the window. Then I started crying. Started again. My face was wet with tears I didn't remember. With the back of my hand I wiped my eyes. It's one thing to cry, it's another thing entirely to be seen at it. Billy turned and went back to his car in slow, careful steps, giving me privacy and distance. He secured my gun and keys in his car before coming back around to the far side of my truck and climbing into the passenger seat.

It's funny, but the one thing I really noticed when he closed the door behind him was that he had no soda in his hands. Billy sat there for a minute not looking at me. He stared forward out the front glass and into the darkness at nothing that I could see. Two people staring together into nothing will never see the same things. When I looked at him again he had settled more into the seat and closed his eyes.

"You suck at this," I said.

"At what? Sleeping?"

"Talking. Finding out what the problem is."

"Do you want to talk about it?"

"No. But—"

"Then I'd say I'm pretty good at it."

I laughed again. Then wiped my face again. "Gentlemen used to carry handkerchiefs for this sort of thing."

"Thank God we live in an enlightened age."

I laughed again but this time it wasn't a funny laugh. "Do we?"

"I think you need to get laid."

That made me choke and laugh at the same time. A bit of bile and whisky-beer bubbled up in the back of my throat. When I could talk again I asked him, "Is that an offer?"

His silence lasted just long enough to have some meaning behind it, but not long enough to give it away. The smile that followed the silence was the kind you appreciate in the worst times of your life. "I would not embarrass you or me by offering."

"Saying it's not an offer is not the same as saying you don't want to."

"Honey, you're the kind of woman that every man wants even if he doesn't know it."

"Except for the—"

"No excepting, Katrina. You are a beautiful woman."

That statement hung in the air between us like a lead sculpture of an elephant painted red. So heavy and odd, it had to be meaningful.

"But?"

"But you're my friend. You've been drinking. I'm not here to tell you you're pretty, I'm here to keep you out of trouble."

After a few more minutes of quiet, I said, "You're a good friend, Billy."

"Don't I know it," he answered. It was the last either of us said until the sun came up right into my face.

Billy was already up and out of the truck, trudging along the grass edge of the road. His attention was on the line of trees beyond the grass. Behind them was where Angela Briscoe had been killed. The trees were a straight-edged green wall, a clear line between here and there.

Lines. Walls. Separations between one place and another, life and death, being and not—my world seemed to be crossed over with them. Not a gate in sight.

As Billy wandered farther from the vehicles I waited and watched, trying not to think of the conversation we would have to have. Trying not to think of a lot of things, actually. That was almost a full-time job for me.

New sun was bringing in the warmer air. At ground level the cool air, kept chill by the nearby river, was misting into fog. The walking clouds spread out until Billy seemed to be like a kid from a fairy tale walking on them. His feet were hidden and he looked to be gliding more than walking. The cuffs of his pants would be getting wet from the dew forming on the grass. When he was far enough away I slipped out of the truck. The dome light glowed, scattering its yellow aura into the rising mist.

Billy's cruiser was unlocked and my gun and keys were sitting on the passenger seat waiting for me. It came to me that maybe he wasn't just strolling in the mist to take a leak. He was giving me space and making the exit easy. That thought made me feel like a one-night lover sneaking off with her shoes in her hands.

Should I leave a note written in lipstick on his windshield?

I smiled at the idea and wondered how long it had been since I wore lipstick. How long since I had put real effort into my look at all?

That was another line of thought to be left behind. I grabbed what I wanted and walked on my toes back to the truck. The door closed with a soft sound that died quickly in the misty air. That only made the starting of the engine seem that much louder. It could not have made more noise if I had started the engine on a fighter plane.

I couldn't see Billy then and I didn't want to. I backed the truck out until I could cut the wheel and turn around. Billy stayed behind in the mist as I drove home.

Chapter 8

It was a good thing Saturday was my day off because I was useless that morning. It doesn't mean much to have a day off in a small department with a murder to be investigated. It only means that they won't call to see why I haven't signed in yet.

Work was the only call that didn't come. While I was cocooning behind drawn curtains, taking aspirin and flushing things out with sports drinks, Dad and Uncle Orson both called. I felt bad about ignoring them. Reach called several times. I didn't ignore his calls. Each time his number showed up on the display I stared hard at the phone and flipped it off until it went to voice mail.

The last thing I thought I wanted was quiet time to think. That's what I was doing, though. My head was pounding from alcohol and my body was aching from sleeping in the truck. All at the same time I was ashamed, embarrassed, afraid of the past, and—with good reason—afraid of the future. Reach's threats weren't idle. If cops were magnets he and I would be at different poles. That seems to be where most of us are pushed by experience: to the extreme ends. As strange as it sounds to most people, it comes down to faith. A man like Reach maintains his faith in the system and that reinforces his faith in everything he does. He doesn't have a lot of room for questions or gray areas. On the other end is someone like me that is nothing but questions and doubt in the system I serve. My faith—my small, withered, and fragile faith—is in the people within the system. Even though it has let me down far more than it has held me up, I have seen the potential. That is the divide in cops and a lot of people, I guess. It shows up in the big questions, like the death penalty. I can't support it because I know from experience that the system isn't perfect. Reach, I was sure, would be firmly on the side of a terminal penalty. The system must be right for him to be right and he can't function without certainty.

Even with all that churning in my brain, there was room for guilt. I was spending a lot of energy thinking about my problems. Under everything was the knowledge that Angela Briscoe was my responsibility now. All I had there were thoughts and suspicions, none of which made real sense. The kids bothered me. The fact that I had found out nothing about the man called Leech was beyond a bother, it was pissing me off. But, most of all, I had a feeling about Carrie Owens and her home life. I needed to know more but I was hiding in the dark.

Guilty.

All of that aside, when I fell back to sleep on the couch I was thinking about color. When I woke again my first thought was again about color. This time, though, it was a thought that had a handle on it. Something the therapist had said—if I wanted the color to come back into my life, I was going to have to put it there. It wasn't going to come on its own.

Screw feeling sorry for myself. Screw living in the dark haze of other wars. Definitely screw you, Major John Reach. And Nelson Solomon . . .

I didn't finish the thought but I smiled in the gloom at where it was going. In the end it was the romantic thoughts about Nelson that got me up off of the couch, not the guilt. Still, I didn't go to him. I went to work.

With nothing more to go on, I followed my list of known members of the Ozarks Nightriders. Over the next two days I drove about 500 miles checking off the names one by one and adding new ones that I'd gotten from the interrogations. No one talked about Leech. Of course, most of these men wouldn't tell a cop anything on principle. Aside from that, the ones who talked acted like they didn't know anyone called Leech. I was beginning to wonder if Carrie and Danny were wrong about the biker they'd pointed out. Or had they lied?

It was still very possible that Leech was just the kind of guy the rank and file didn't talk about. And I didn't exactly have a significant sample to work from. Out of the handful of names and addresses I had, only five produced a club member. Of those, only three dropped new names and locations. I went from one end of the county to the other and slipped out of my jurisdiction more than once.

While I drove from one biker's trashy hovel to another, wondering what these guys had against taking out the garbage, I worked the phone. Wading through the alphabet soup of government agencies, I requested information from DEA, FBI, ATF, and Bureau of Prisons. I was dreading what my in-box would look like when I got back to the office.

I could say the driving, the phone, and the lowlifes served to keep my mind off of my problems, but I'd be lying. The activity did help me ignore most of them and that was almost as good. Sometimes the mind, maybe even the heart, does its best work when we take off the reins and let it run free. My mind didn't solve any great problems, but when I pulled back into my driveway, stinking and tired, I wasn't entirely afraid of my feelings for Nelson Solomon anymore.

By the time I stepped back out of the house, showered, shaved, and powdered, as my mother used to say, the summer evening was blooming. Since I was taking a chance already, I went all the way and wore a skirt. It was hidden in the back of my closet and took some effort to find. It was long and white, Western-styled with ruffles and turquoise beading. Above it I put on a matching turquoise shirt and a wide brown belt with a big silver buckle. Below, I wore lacer boots. My gun and badge went into a handbag. That part left me feeling naked.

Opting for surprise—and denying him the chance to say no—I didn't call Nelson. If he had company or was mad about how I had left him last time, I had a good-cop-just-checking-up-on-a-crime-victim excuse rattling around in my head. Feeble, I know, but you work with what you have sometimes.

When I stepped out of the truck at Nelson's place I was suddenly self-conscious. Hair, makeup, dress—none of that was how I had seen myself in a long time.

What if he laughed?

Then there were the bigger issues.

What did I hope would happen?

Maybe we were the perfect pair. I was running from life and he could be running out of it. It was a cruel and self-serving thought. But what kind of woman opens herself to a relationship with so many questions? I hated the fear I felt and the indecision. Truth be told, if I wasn't ashamed of myself for wanting to run again, I would have.

Nelson didn't come to the door when I knocked. I rang the bell with the same result. It took a hard conversation with myself to convince me that Nelson was not standing behind a curtain watching me. I tried the knob, sure that nothing would happen. What kind of idiot would leave the door unlocked after being stalked by violent bikers? Apparently an artist and ex-Marine.

One step inside the house I was sure he was here and I was afraid he was dead. It smelled like sweat and old vomit.

"Whoever you are, go away." Nelson's voice came from the couch. "Unless you're finally here to kill me. Then come on in."

I didn't answer. I didn't know how. The thought came to me that I could still leave if I said nothing. My feet never got the message. I kept walking into the room until I stepped around the end of the couch.

Nelson was lying on the leather cushions, shirtless and dripping with sweat. On the floor beside him was a trash can with a frothy, stinking fluid standing in the bottom.

"You're expecting someone to come kill you?" I asked.

"You came back," he said. His voice was flat and tired-sounding. There was no telling from the tone if he was glad I had returned or angry.

"I wanted to see how you were doing," I said. It wasn't a complete lie. "Do you need help?"

"Do I look like I need help?"

"Yes," I said. "You do."

"Well, you look nice."

I was glad he noticed and said it, but immediately I felt bad for feeling good about anything. "Thank you. I thought I should come check up on you."

"I'm sorry about the other day," he said.

"You're sorry?" I asked. "Why? I ran out. I'm sorry about that. All of it."

"Nothing to be sorry about. You were the one put on the spot. That was my fault."

"Not entirely," I said. After that I had nothing to say. I simply looked at Nelson and he looked at me.

He tried to smile but it didn't seem to be in him. Then he said, "It was my fault. But I'd do it again in a heartbeat. Hell, if I didn't stink so bad, I might try to kiss you now."

"If you didn't stink so bad, I might let you," I told him. It was a small confession, but for some reason it must have been important. After that everything seemed okay. If not okay, at least normal. Nelson really did smile and puffed out a rasping laugh that smelled of roadkill.

I went back to the door and pushed it wide open. At the other end of the room I pushed open the door to the deck. Then I went through the room opening up windows. The temperature climbed quickly, but a nice breeze started clearing the house of the sickroom smell.

"Can you get up?" I asked Nelson.

"If I have to," he responded without moving, except to put an arm over his eyes.

"You do." Taking the trash can away, I sat it out on the deck. "That's horrible. What did you eat?"

"Half a beer and some Vienna sausages."

That almost made me throw up.

"If you get clean I'll see what's decent in the refrigerator."

"Good luck with that," he said, still not moving.

He was right. There was nothing in there but condiments and stains. Men always seem to manage to be men.

"How do you live like this?" I asked him. It was the wrong thing to say. I knew it as soon as I said it. Nelson's dry, weak laugh made it even clearer. "I'm going to get some groceries in here."

I started for the door but stopped when Nelson pulled himself up on the back of the couch and said, "Don't. Please. Don't go." He squirreled around, using legs and arms to pull himself upright. When he finished, tired and breathing hard, he patted the cushion beside him. "Sit here, by me," he said. "Just for a minute."

It took a minute for me to make up my mind and move to the couch. When I sat beside him, Nelson didn't reach for me or even look at me. He was staring at the painting in progress that was sitting on his easel.

"I know it doesn't look like it, but I'm better," he said. "Feeling better, stronger."

"I hope so."

"I am. I've turned a corner."

"What corner?"

"See that painting?" he asked me.

I nodded but it didn't matter. His eyes and thoughts were elsewhere.

"*That*—is a desperate painting."

I looked but I didn't understand. It was a lake scene with a small boat in the water. There was something uneasy about the painting, but I couldn't say what. For a long time we stared at it together, and I imagined seeing different things. Just when I stopped thinking about the image and started thinking again about Nelson and how he must feel, something struck me. There were no people in the picture. The boat was by itself in the water. Adrift and untethered.

Small things fell into place. Everywhere, light dappled the water like the sun had been broken into shining pieces and scattered to float on the lake. Everywhere except in the shadow of the boat. It was more than that. The boat itself should have been vibrant in the sunlight, bright red to just above the waterline, stark white above that. The boat was as muted as the dark green water in its shadow just as if the boat were in a shadow itself. If you thought it out, the light didn't work. If you simply saw it, you could understand. The boat carried something invisible.

"I'm not going to die from cancer," Nelson said.

My hair stood on end and something like a wind ran across my skin. Even in the rising heat of the room, I shivered. The sensation spread until it touched me intimately, creeping with airy pleasure across my breasts and down my belly. The last traces of it tingled and faded at the same time like the tiny ghosts of a million ants dancing on my scalp.

"I'm glad," was all I could say.

"I mean it," he told me. "I know how scary the thought can be. Sickness. Lingering. You don't have to be afraid of that."

"Who says I'm afraid?"

"Why wouldn't you be? I am."

Sometimes, I realized, men can surprise the holy hell out of you.

"How about you let me take you to that dinner we talked about?" he asked.

I looked him over, thinking that was the craziest idea I'd ever heard. In a way he looked stronger than I'd seen him in the hospital, even considering that he still looked horrible, but a gown and IV can make any man look worse. In fact, he looked almost exactly the way he had lying in the dirt at the side of the road, like he'd just been beaten.

He must have been reading my thoughts, because as soon as I said, "You're crazy—" he shot back, "This isn't chemo. This isn't even about being sick."

"Then what is it?"

"This is sitting alone and feeling sorry for myself."

"It's a hell of a pity party."

"I've had a lot of practice lately."

Haven't we all? I thought it but I didn't say it. What I did say was, "I'm not so sure you're up to it."

"Getting up's not a problem."

Sometimes men don't surprise you at all.

"Please," he said. "I can't stand sitting alone any more. I can't stand my own company. I just want to get out and be around a little life and I'd love to do it with you."

Sometimes they do surprise you.

"You need a shower," I told him.

"Sponge bath?"

"You couldn't handle a sponge bath." He looked like a kid whose birthday had been cancelled. "Get into the shower." As soon as he started to smile, I said, "Alone."

He went. He was slow and weak, but he went.

This time I stayed out of the room. If I had gone in there I would not have run out again. However, I wasn't ready for what would have happened.

While he showered with the doors open—an invitation if I've ever seen one—I closed the doors and windows I had opened and let the air conditioner bring things back down. For the rest of the time I stared at the painting on the easel. Some of the time I spent trying to understand what Nelson had done. The remainder I spent trying to understand why. When he came back into the room I was still looking at the painting.

"What do you think?" he asked.

I answered with a kiss. It was deep and wonderful. With my arms around his neck I crushed my body against his and felt the heat there. When he breathed I could feel the rise of his chest against my breasts. I didn't let it break until I felt something else begin to rise against my leg. Even then I sucked his tongue into my mouth and nibbled it gently before moving away. It was a good kiss, full of meaning and promise.

* * *

The restaurant was called, predictably enough, Moonshines. It was all kinds of contradictions. Upscale in price and menu with a bar full of house-made micro-spirits, it was paneled with recovered barn wood and clichéd *Li'l Abner* décor. At the center of everything was a glass room that contained the distillery, a stainless-steel, space age–looking stack of plumbing that clashed with both the atmosphere and the clientele. The only place everything seemed to be working right was the patio space. It had a bandstand on one end with a lumber deck that stuck out over the lake waters. Under strings of white lights that were just beginning to show in the fading summer evening, the floor was stuffed with an eclectic mix of people. There were tourists and fishermen, performers from the Branson strip, college kids, and locals of every stripe.

After just a few minutes I had changed my mind about how the space age still clashed with the atmosphere. It was so out of place that the people seemed to be conforming around it. Stick stained-glass windows or expensive art and muted light in a room and people react to the space. You get church whispers and minded manners. Stick a still in the middle of a room and you get the Wild West. Moonshines looked like it was designed by Disney Imagineers, but it felt like a knife fight waiting to happen.

Nelson whispered a few words to the hostess and we were shown to a table that was shielded from most of the room, but next to a window that looked out over the water and patio. The smoked glass of the window muted the already gloaming sky.

"The head chef is Andre," Nelson said once we were seated. "I think the name his mother gave him was Andy, but that wasn't good enough after cooking in New York."

I laughed. "And what is the best that Andre has to offer?" I asked.

"I don't know. I guess it's all all right, just a little fancy for me. With him it's all sauces and reductions and I don't know. I'm more of a steak or fried chicken kind of guy." He looked up and nodded at a man standing at a bar table along with a country western cowboy. The cowboy might have been a performer with one of the Branson music shows or just a snappy dresser. His jacket was suede with Indian beading and fringes. Below that were tooled leather boots with silver toe and heel caps. Between the jacket and boots were jeans whose fading could only come from an acid wash. They used to call them drugstore cowboys. Nowadays it seemed these guys were all rich posers. He was probably a New Yorker who thought all the Branson folk dressed like that.

"That's Johnny Middleton," Nelson said. "Not the fancy cowboy, the other guy. This place is basically his baby."

Johnny was as different from Nelson as I could imagine. He was soft and round but wearing snug black slacks with an untucked black silk shirt that did nothing to hide his shape. He had a desperate smile that looked to be the natural hang of his mouth rather than a projection of any emotion. He left the cowboy and headed our way stopping twice, once to talk to one of the bar girls and once to schmooze with two other out-of-place-looking guys whose faces I couldn't see. There were a couple of fingers pointed and Johnny left them looking nervous.

"Have you ordered anything yet?" he asked as soon as we were introduced.

"We were talking it over," Nelson answered.

"Good. I asked Marsha to bring over our new appetizer. I want you to try it out. Did you think any more about what we discussed?"

Nelson opened his mouth to say something but never got the chance.

Johnny jumped back in, saying, "There's a man here that I really want you to meet. I asked him to come over when I saw you."

"We just want to have a nice dinner, Johnny," Nelson told him. "This isn't the time."

"Just listen for a minute, please, Nelson. These aren't the kind of people you want to offend. Know what I mean?"

"No, I don't," Nelson said, then glanced at me. There was apology in the look. By the time he had shifted his gaze back to his friend, one of the men from the bar was standing beside Johnny. It was the same man I had seen with Nelson at the hospital.

He was a big man. His bulk still looked powerful but without the tone of youth, like a linebacker past his prime. The fat that layered his body gave a solidity. The same fat in his face seemed to have the opposite effect. His countenance was soft and drooping, pulling the bags under his eyes down until the lower lids turned outward. Like an old hound he had jowls that were always in motion. Most striking to me were his hands. They were much too small for all the largeness to which they were attached. Short, little sausages, the fingers were adorned with heavy gold and diamond rings that only made them look stubbier.

Johnny introduced the man as Byron Figorelli.

"I've met Mr. Figorelli," Nelson said, looking at Figorelli, not Johnny.

"You have?" Johnny asked. He was surprised.

"Johnny said we could talk a little business with you," Figorelli said, ignoring Johnny.

"We?" Nelson asked.

That was when I caught a look between Nelson and Figorelli. That was all, a quick look. It wasn't something of great meaning, more of a guy thing. The testosterone of two men sizing each other up. Just for a moment, though, I had the feeling that they knew more about each other than either wanted to let on.

"Beg pardon?" Figorelli asked and the moment passed.

"You said *we*, but I only see you," Nelson said.

The big man's rheumy eyes narrowed. "Johnny said you were a sharp one. Sharp enough to get the point, I figure. I want to purchase your share of this place and I am making the offer on behalf of an investment group. For said group, I have full authority to negotiate. Does that make things clear?"

"Clear as mud on milk glass," Nelson said, then gestured to me. "Now, if you don't mind, we're trying to have a dinner here. Maybe we can do this another time?"

At that moment, a woman came from the bar and slipped a platter of fried appetizers and smaller plates on the table. "Enjoy the Missouri mountain oysters," she said.

Figorelli kept his gaze locked with Nelson's while he jabbed his fat little fingers into the dish. "Oysters, huh?" He tossed a pair of the breaded balls into his mouth and started chewing loudly. Then he stopped, and with his mouth still full, he said, "The fuck?" It was obvious he wanted to spit the food out. At least he grabbed a napkin first and put the mess there. "You eat that shit? It tastes like chewy liver and dirt."

Nelson leaned forward as he pushed his chair back to rise. I beat him to it, placing my hand on his shoulder. "Mr. Figorelli, those are mountain oysters, fried bull testicles. They are a bit of an acquired taste. If you would like to take them with you and go acquire it, I think it would be best."

"What am I, like some kind of phone number on your shithouse wall, Johnny? Everyone keeps trying to get rid of me?"

"Maybe it just isn't the time," Johnny said to him.

Nelson stood slowly beside me and for the first time I noticed that he was shaking and supporting himself on the table. How long had it been since he'd had a meal he'd kept down? The white shirt and khaki pants he wore were both loose on him and his belt was pulled into holes that had never been used before. Still, he wasn't backing down.

"Johnny's right and I've told you the same, Mr. Figorelli. This isn't the time."

Johnny put his hand on the bigger man's arm and tried to urge him from the table. Figorelli jerked away and said, "Get your hands off me. Does everyone here have cornpone in their ears? I have business to do."

"Not with me you don't," Nelson told him. "You need to be going."

"Maybe you got a few oysters of your own, but you look like a piece of toilet paper. The wind would carry you away. Or are you gonna let the bitch off her chain? I could have some fun with a tall drink like her."

He never even glanced at me as he spoke. It was one in a string of mistakes. Nelson was ready to come over the table. That would have been a mistake of a different order altogether. I was going to settle this, but I wasn't going to do it in any way that would put Nelson in the middle. I'm lucky that assholes are so easy to manipulate.

I put my right hand back on Nelson's shoulder, urging restraint and calm. My other hand I reached out to Figorelli. "Mr. Figorelli is going to go over to the bar and have a drink on us, aren't you, sir?" My voice was soothing. Anyone in earshot would have told you how reasonable I sounded. My left hand, however, was digging into the man's meaty trapezius muscle. At the same time I squeezed hard and pushed him away. My gaze was anything but placating. Everyone else saw a woman trying to smooth over a confrontation. Figorelli saw someone taller, manhandling and challenging him.

He swept his arm up to knock my hand away. He was about to say something too. Probably something about a bitch, but he never got the chance. Once his hand struck me I stepped around the table and bumped against him. That's when I said, "Sheriff's Detective Williams." Out of habit I reached for a pocket I didn't have for the badge that was stuffed in the handbag hanging off my chair. The one time I try to dress well.

As I had expected, though, Figorelli didn't listen and he wasn't interested in seeing a badge anyway. He shoved me back first with his chest, then with his hand right in my sternum. That was all I needed. I grabbed the hand on my chest and twisted it hard over and around his back, turning him at the same time. In the same movement I stepped behind him and pushed his bulk over the table.

I thought there was going to be trouble when I heard a man's voice yell, "Hey, Figgs." I caught a glimpse of a man coming our way and was regretting having left my weapon out of reach.

Backup came in the form of Billy. I heard him saying, "Hold on. You don't want to be interfering with the sheriff's department, do you?"

It should have ended there. I wanted to provoke a response that allowed me to end the encounter and send Figorelli on his way. There would have been no charges and we could have had a quiet dinner.

Nothing in my life is ever easy.

There was a short-nosed .38 revolver tucked into the small of Figorelli's back.

"Billy—"

I wanted to tell him that they were armed but I never got the chance.

Billy yelled, "Don't move."

I heard a sharp crackling of electricity, then a grunt, and the man hit the floor. Billy had hit the other guy with a stun gun. At least it wasn't the knife fight I had been afraid of.

Chapter 9

I wanted—needed—to get Nelson out of there quickly but nothing about justice or law moves swiftly. Because Moonshines was within city limits, and because Billy and I were involved, both the Branson city police and the sheriff's department were called. After some debate it was decided to give the arrests for assault and for interference to our department. It took forty-five minutes to get the pair taken away. Johnny Middleton had disappeared.

After leaving Nelson with Billy I disappeared as well. I needed a little privacy to make a phone call. When I got back Billy was on the patio holding a guitar and standing at a microphone. It seemed he had a second job. When did he have the time? Checking the tune of his guitar, he strummed a few chords and smiled sheepishly at the small crowd. He saw me looking and he looked back. We had never seen each other in quite this light. Strange what a difference a dress and a guitar can make.

Billy kept picking a bit, without the smile now, but he kept looking at me. There had been no chance to thank him for the backup. If anything, though, I needed to thank him for the night he'd spent watching over me. All of a sudden I felt stupid for running out on him that morning. Running was becoming an ugly habit with me.

Billy looked different than he had the last time I had seen him, but I couldn't set my mind on any one thing. It was the guitar, I decided. That and the fact that I'd been shamefully slinking away and he'd been standing in the fog. With no words, he stopped tuning and started playing. It was an old John Denver tune, "Annie's Song." When he began to sing the change was amazing, like finding out the old horse you had ridden for years was a talking unicorn that recited Keats.

"He wanted me to tell you that he stayed at the river as long as he could." Nelson nodded toward Billy as he stepped up beside me. "And he said that the only people that came around today were some kids that he ran off and a couple of bikers that kept riding around."

The kids would be Carrie Owens, Danny Barnes, and cronies—I was sure of it. The bikers had to be Nightriders. Looking to make sure they'd run Clare off or for something else?

Was Leech one of them?

"Thanks," I told Nelson. "How about if we get out of here and get some real food?" For some reason Billy's singing was making me nervous. It was the first I had heard it but I had the feeling that I should have known.

"That sounds good," Nelson said, then he started clapping at the end of Billy's song. "Also, Billy said to tell you he would call you later. He's pretty good."

Despite my efforts to get us out of there, Nelson insisted on hearing a little more of the music.

It was just Billy and a guitar playing the kind of country rock that made the seventies so mellow. He had played songs by the Ozark Mountain Daredevils, Marshall Tucker, and the Eagles before I got us started for the door. Distance soothed my feelings about the music and Billy. As we walked into the parking lot I could hear him singing about making love in a Chevy van. Nelson and I were both laughing and singing the chorus when I pulled out of the lot and passed a white sedan with government plates.

When the laughing and the mood settled into the curves of the road, I asked Nelson, "What was going on back there?"

"What do you mean?" He lobbed the question back a little too casually. "You were the one in the middle of it," he said.

"They want you to sell your share?"

"I told you about that."

"Yeah. And you told me it was that Middleton guy trying to buy you out. You didn't say anything about the goon squad."

"It was as much a surprise to me as it was to you," he said, looking out the window.

"Was it?" I asked.

He looked at me and smiled. "Don't let them spoil our night. Where are we going?"

My call had been to Uncle Orson. He had steaks on the grill when we got to the dock. Alongside the meat were ears of bicolor corn that he had pulled from his own garden and soaked in butter before dropping on the grill. We caught him tossing a salad and cutting up yellow squash that he would coat with more butter and parsley before briefly grilling. The old guy was no chef but he was a heck of a cook. He'd be the first to tell you, though, he was number two to his brother.

I noticed the calendar was not on the wall. That was the kind of man Uncle Orson was. Having the calendar up would have been a form of pressure, an expectation to be the famous guy. Uncle Orson treated Nelson like an honored guest who he had known all his life. That's to say, like family. We had beers in our hands before getting to the dock, but I took Nelson's away. Orson noticed.

"You gonna let her treat you that way?" my uncle asked him.

"I have to," Nelson answered. "I just watched her take down an armed guy that probably had a hundred-fifty pounds on her."

"Nelson just needs to get some food in him before he has any beer." I said. "He hasn't had anything all day and it's kind of my fault that our dinner was messed up."

"Nothing about that was your fault," Nelson said. "It was that idiot Middleton and the goons he keeps getting into bed with."

"You knew about those guys?" I asked.

Nelson shook his head slowly before looking at me. "The place Johnny had before. He got out because he had owed money to some of those types. Might even have been those same guys. But he told me that was all over."

"And it should be all over for tonight, at least," Orson said as he pushed through the screen door bearing a platter of steaks and roasted corn. "The meat has to rest. I saw that on a cooking show. I just put the squash on the grill. Give it about two minutes a side and we'll be feasting."

There was a lot more I wanted to ask. It wasn't the time for those questions, though. It was time to eat. We sat around the old picnic table passing salad and jokes. Nelson finished less than half of the filet side on his T-bone. Vegetables must have been easier to manage. They were almost gone from his plate. He was too polite to tell me to stop the mother-henning. When I got up for a moment he'd gotten hold of a beer. I think it was more for his ego than the desire to drink. The level in the bottle never went lower than the neck.

"Desert Storm left you with a long-term reminder, didn't it?"

Orson asked Nelson when all of us had stopped eating and my uncle was on this fourth beer.

To be fair, if Nelson were not there I would have been keeping pace with Orson's drinking. As it was, I hadn't yet finished my second beer. And to be honest, I wasn't feeling the need to drink more. It was a surprising feeling and something I had almost forgotten possible. I excused myself and went out the screen door and walked toward the far end of the dock. I didn't really want to hear what was coming. But I didn't want to go too far away, either.

"Is it that obvious?" Nelson asked in return.

I couldn't see him but I pictured Uncle Orson leaning across the table. I did hear his half whisper that was supposed to make it man-talk and just between the two of them. "Like tits in a whorehouse," he said. "I've had a lot of friends go through the same things. Agent Orange. At the VFW I meet younger guys who have issues from the spent uranium used in tank shells or were exposed to sarin gas when we bombed that munitions plant."

The talk faded behind me as I went out to the edge of the dock and watched the water. Some late fishermen were coming in and there were a few going out to run jugs or trotlines. From where I stood it was easy to believe that the world was wrapped up in a comforting blanket of warm darkness. Across the water, in a piled snag of fallen trees, a bass hit at something on the surface, splashing loudly. I let the world surround me and my thoughts slip away. After a few minutes, it occurred to me that, even in the darkness, I was looking at the colors. The moon was yellow and haloed in a lighter shade that misted out into a blue tint. Where the light hit the water it reflected back and added its own green cast. Under the tin-roof canopy the old dock was painted variously in white, red, and pale blue. From every surface hung nets and minnow buckets, floats and oars. In the slips were the boats themselves in every shade, many shining with the glitter under the clear coat on fiberglass.

I realized slowly that I was looking for the dust of another place and waiting for the burning sense of loss that went with it. I was waiting to bleed and expecting the clatter of AK-47s.

"You should come back in," Uncle Orson said from behind me. I hadn't heard him come up. "He's not looking too good."

Nelson.

I led Orson back into the shop. Nelson was doing his best to look wide awake and strong, but he was failing miserably. He had gone pale. Sweat had beaded on his brow and over the crown of his head, making the pale skin look like a fish's underbelly.

"I'm sorry," Nelson said. "I'm not trying to be a pain in the ass."

Before I could say anything Uncle Orson moved around me and put a huge hand on Nelson's shoulder and told him, "None of that crap. What do you need?"

"I'm sorry," Nelson said again. "I think I just need to get home and rest."

He appeared to be as weak as a kitten with polio and he wouldn't look at me.

Shame.

Nelson didn't want me to see this. He didn't want to be like this in front of me. I understood the feeling; at least part of me did. Another part wanted to shout at him for being foolish. None of that changed the fact that I didn't know how to deal with the situation. I was afraid he would have to be carried to the truck. If nothing else, he would need help getting in and what then? How would I get him from the truck into his house? I had already realized that I would carry him if I had to. It didn't bother me—in fact, I wanted to help him—but I wanted to do it without making him feel like less of a man.

Again, Orson came to the rescue.

He asked, "Would you stay here with me? I was wanting to see if you'd go fishing with me in the morning. We'd need to get up pretty early."

Just like that, I knew that Nelson had been adopted. Nelson himself was looking pretty skeptical. I could tell he was ready to put up a fight when the case was helped by my phone ringing. It was Billy. There was another problem at Moonshines.

It was quickly decided that Nelson would stay with Uncle Orson. I would retrieve anything he needed from home once things were settled at the restaurant. That way the guys could be guys and Nelson wouldn't have to let me see him at his worst.

Johnny Middleton had returned to Moonshines and had gotten into a fight with a biker wearing an Ozarks Nightriders cut. It had started in the bar and moved as Middleton had retreated out onto the patio. Billy had come off the bandstand when things got too noisy but Middleton refused to make an issue of it, even to the point of allowing the biker to remain at the restaurant. That was when things got weird. Witnesses said, a little later, Middleton and another biker were in the parking lot when someone fired a shot. They said that it was the biker that pushed Middleton out of the way.

This time I was on duty. I changed out of the skirt and into pants and jacket in the houseboat. Once at the restaurant, I put on and adjusted my kit: cuffs, telescoping baton, tac light, pepper spray, and my service weapon. When I got inside, Billy was on break, drinking a soda at the bar with a couple of young women telling him how talented he was. He had about the biggest grin I'd ever seen.

"Pardon us, ladies," I said, taking the troubadour by the arm. "Sheriff's department business." I walked him out to the patio railing over the water. Standing right in front of him, I saw what was different. He had gotten a haircut. It wasn't the usual, cheap hack job, either.

"Really, Hurricane?" he said. "You show up now?" There was something in his tone too. Probably it was showing up then because it was the first time we were alone. Why it was showing up at all was eluding me.

"Hey, you called me," I told him.

"Yeah. Things have settled down a bit, though. City cops were the first to respond for all the good it did. No one can find Middleton or the biker. Since it involved one of the Nightriders, the sheriff said to let you know when I called it in." He wasn't looking at me. I followed his gaze and caught sight of one of the girls who had been with him. She was smiling and waving at him like bait happy to be on the hook. The attitude made more sense. He was mad because I had pulled him away from the skank buffet.

"Catch you at a bad time?" I asked.

He looked at me then. It was an odd look. It made me feel like I had forgotten a promise and Billy was waiting for me to say something about it. Then he let it drop and said, "A couple of songs and I get more attention than I ever got for being a cop."

"Is that the kind of attention you want?"

"Do you want to know about the bikers or not?" He shot his question right back at me as if I had stuck my finger in a wound.

I could have asked him what the problem was. Instead I asked, "Bikers? More than one?"

He nodded. A little bit of the light went out of his eyes. "The one that argued with Johnny Middleton, the mean one; he acts like a boss and he smells like a run-out horse. After they fought, another guy came in. He was wearing the same colors and the boss guy gave him a hard time. He was the one who was outside with Middleton."

"Did you get a good look at them?" I asked.

He nodded and I pulled out the printed sheets I'd collected on the Nightriders membership. He identified Cotton Lambert as the second biker. He couldn't ID the greasy "boss" guy. I didn't have a picture of him, but there was no doubt in my mind it was Leech.

"There's something else, though," he said. "I've been hearing talk about someone dealing meth here."

"Here? As in within this establishment?"

"That's what I've been hearing," he said. "And that does seem to fit the biker lifestyle."

Billy looked eager to get back to the musician's life so I let him go. That seemed to annoy him even further. I didn't have time to worry about what was going on with him.

Johnny Middleton needed to answer some questions, but he was still missing. I stuck around and pressed the staff for a while, but Middleton never showed and no one admitted to knowing where he was. A few of them did say they had seen the bikers around but didn't want to talk about it. They acted vaguely scared, although if it was of their boss or his friends I couldn't sort out.

After half an hour I left, making a pass through the parking lot to look for white sedans before getting onto the road.

Nelson's cabin was dark when I got there. So dark it was almost a negative, like a house-shaped black hole on a cliff. The headlights of my truck swept over the garage doors and surrounding trees showing nothing as I pulled in to park. Once outside the truck, though, I had the feeling that something was wrong. Some people claim to feel danger like a sixth sense. I don't: With me, it's more of a mental registering in the lizard brain that the monkey brain missed something.

It was there at the corner of the house, a slight glint of chrome. Then the cherry of a cigarette glowed with an inhalation. As I reached for my weapon I caught a smell on the breeze. It was old sweat and beer, an unwashed animal smell that managed to mix threat and testosterone.

I responded with both fight and flight, stepping away from the scent coming from behind me and turning to raise my weapon at the same time. The blow that was aimed at the center of my skull whipped through my hair, grazing the back of my head. It was a graze like a freight train sideswiping a car. Stars exploded behind my eyes. By the time I had gotten turned, bringing my automatic up, the blunt object had reached the limit of its swing and returned. The strike on my weapon jolted up my hand and arm like a hot spark of Tesla's best. I dropped the automatic, but had the sense to get my arms up as soon as it fell from my fingers.

Another blow hit my left forearm close to the elbow and went off to my side. That gave me a moment. I brought my left arm around and down, following the club and trapping the attacking arm under it. At the same time I pulled and extended my baton. As I raised it, I put my left foot forward between the assailant's legs, forcing his left knee into the open. I brought the baton down as hard as I could on the outside of the exposed knee.

"Motherfu—" He couldn't even finish the expletive as he rolled to the asphalt in pain.

I would have had him. I *did* have him, until the other man—the smoker hiding by the bikes—hit me with a body block in the ribs. That hurt, but it was the impact of my temple with the rocker panel of my truck that put me down. At that point I'm not sure which of us was luckier that the bikers ran for the motorcycles and roared away. I was hurting but pissed off enough to put up a lot more fight.

I knew who they were, though not enough for a jury. Smells and being sure are not as well accepted as a good look at a face. But I knew well enough for me. They just had to be tracked down.

And I will track them down.

The smart thing would have been to get up and call in. I stayed down and didn't call anyone. It had already been a wild night. The last thing I wanted was to fill out a report and department protocol would have required me to be checked over at the hospital. My one concession to smart thinking was to secure my weapon.

After lingering on the driveway, leaning against the tire of my truck for a while—I had no idea how long—I managed to get myself up and to the house. There was a broken pane of glass in a door that led into a back mudroom. In there was the circuit-breaker box standing open with the main breaker pulled. That was much more ominous than I had thought. It was an ambush.

Why?

I went to the garage and got a couple of boards that I wedged between the wall and the washing machine and across the base of the door. It would hold the mudroom door until the glass could be repaired.

Upstairs I tried not to snoop as I grabbed a few bits of clothing and shoved meds into a shopping bag.

There are so many.

In the bathroom, I took Nelson's razor and toothbrush but only after I looked at myself in the mirror. I was a mess—in more ways than showed in my reflection. The bruises were starting to show up, burning in from angry red to purple and green. The worst was just below the left elbow where I had been hit by the pipe or whatever it had been. That could be hidden, though. The one turning into a shiner around my right eye may as well have been a neon sign. It hurt too, right up on my temple and around the orbital bone where I had gotten to know my truck, face-first. If it was a contest, the blue ribbon for pain would go to the knot throbbing higher by the minute on the back of my skull.

I chewed up a handful of aspirin and washed them down with water from my cupped hand at the bathroom sink. Then I looked at myself again. That time I didn't see the bruises or the rat's nest of hair on my head. There were two women staring back at me from the mirror. One was the same angry woman who had to face a squad that refused to obey her orders while under fire. They believed that I had abused the system to harm the careers of the men I accused of rape. Individually, they were almost reasonable. Collectively, they believed a woman in the military was a dyke or a whore and either way deserved anything that happened to her. That woman had chambered a round in her .9-millimeter automatic and aimed it into the eye of the loudest-talking noncom. She was very, very angry. The other woman in the mirror was the one who had not undressed for a man in more than ten years. She was so very afraid.

Both women were there, but it was the scared woman who I felt was in the most danger. There was a lot to like about Nelson Solomon and a lot of risk.

"Don't be a pussy," I told the reflection. Then I went downstairs.

On a whim I stopped by the easel and painting supplies in the main room. There was a smaller version of the painting kit that had been impounded along with Solomon's truck. I took it with me.

It might make him feel better.

Chapter 10

Uncle Orson was waiting for me when I got back to the dock. It made me feel a bit like a kid sneaking home after curfew. At least it did until he offered me a beer. Dad had never offered me a beer when I came home late.

I took the bottle and sat beside him at the table. "What do you want to talk about?" I asked as I twisted the cap off.

"Who says I want to talk?"

I gave him a who're-you-kidding look that he ignored, instead taking a long drink. After a long drink of my own I settled into the chair and allowed the day to fall away.

"You know what you're doing?" Uncle Orson asked.

"Nope," I answered.

"Just checking."

I nodded and we both took drinks.

"He seems like a good guy."

"I think so," I agreed.

"Just be careful."

"Of what?"

Uncle Orson looked from me to his beer. He pursed his lips a little and took a stab at peeling the label. When the paper wouldn't come up he looked back at me and said, "Everything."

"Yeah," was all I had in me to say. There were some questions rattling around my brain as well that I wasn't sure how to approach. When Uncle Orson tilted up his bottle and sucked it dry it made me wonder if this was the best time. When he grabbed another one I wondered how long I might have to wait for a better time. "I want to ask you a question," I told him as soon as the bottle left his lips.

"Ask away," he said.

I didn't. I still had to think about it and wonder if it was wise to question such things. While I was thinking, Uncle Orson was drinking with one eye on me. Once his bottle was half empty he set it down, then slid it aside. He reached across the table and took my bottle from my hands and slid it to the side as well. There was nothing between us then. It was his way of saying I had his full attention.

I still didn't say anything.

Uncle Orson nodded knowingly, then said, "Okay, maybe I understand. You see, when a man likes a woman in a special way he wants to do things with her—"

"Uncle Orson." I couldn't help myself. I laughed and pulled my beer over and took a drink. Then I said, "It's nothing about *that*."

"Oh, thank God," he said, pulling over his own beer. "Because that was a bluff. I had no follow-up. You know I beat the ladies off with a stick, but I try not to talk to them."

"I know. It shows."

He was grinning as he brought the beer to his lips. After a big drink he wiped his mouth with the back of his hand and grinned again. "So, spit it out," he said.

That time I did. I asked him, "Did you arrange to have a man killed?"

His grin faded and his eyes focused like two cameras on my face. It wasn't a hard look, just attentive. The surprising thing was that he didn't look surprised.

"One of the men that I had—the problem with—in Iraq."

"He's dead?"

I nodded and looked at my beer.

"How do you know?"

"I heard about it a long time ago. I had been kind of keeping tabs on him. The other one left the Army and I don't know anything about him."

"That's all?"

I told him about Reach and how he had popped up and accused me of killing Rice. I told him about the night Reach had followed me. It told him everything I knew while staring at a beer bottle.

"Why are you asking me?"

"You're the only one I know that could . . ."

He kind of laughed. It was a little tired-sounding snort. "But I probably couldn't, you know. I've been a killer and I'll stand up and fight anyone that needs it. What you're asking about is something else." His beer found its way to his mouth and he swallowed the last of it in a gulp. When the bottle was finished Uncle Orson looked back at me and said, "Your father's the bad one in this family."

"What?"

"He's the one you should be asking, but I wouldn't, because you probably won't like the answer and some questions are best left unasked."

"But—he couldn't."

Uncle Orson looked over at the cooler and seemed to consider another beer. I could see him wanting it, then I could see him corralling the need. "You're probably right," he said and the pronouncement sounded half sad and half prideful. "When we were younger men . . . Well, there was a time I would have put nothing past him. Now, we're the old guys. Hell, I run a bait shop." He gestured around like I might have somehow missed the fact we were in a bait shop. "And your dad . . ."

"He's a consultant."

Uncle Orson smiled carefully and nodded, touching a finger to his nose. Then he stood and went upstairs to bed without another word.

I sat there for a few minutes longer while I finished my beer. The more I thought about it the sillier it seemed. My father was the spit-and-polish soldier who loved parades and visited the wall in D.C. The talk had lifted a weight from my heart, though. I believed Uncle Orson when he said that he hadn't had anything to do with killing Rice. Daddy obviously knew something, but I believed that he didn't know the whole story. Even if he was the kind of man who could make a killing happen in another country, he didn't know about Rice until recently.

I need to go to bed.

For a second there I thought about—wished that—Nelson was in my bed waiting. But the houseboat was empty. Uncle Orson had put Nelson up in the apartment, probably making sure that I didn't disturb him. Or making sure that my night was as frustrating as possible.

I woke the next morning to the undulations of the lake and the sound of my phone. It felt early and I was tempted to ignore the call, but it was work. The phone was in the pocket of my jacket and I climbed out of bed to get it. Everything hurt.

It was Sheriff Benson calling. "I know it's early," he said without a greeting. "But I'd like you to come in and have a little talk."

"About last night?" I asked him.

"About a lot of things," he said. "As soon as you can get here."

I cleaned up quickly, pulling on a pair of the old jeans I kept on the boat and a shirt that I left untucked. When I got to the door of the shop there was a note waiting.

Me and the painter went fishing. Trout for dinner. Make your own breakfast.

It was signed simply *Uncle*.

Nelson must have been stronger this morning. I hadn't seen him after I came in last night.

Usually weekend mornings were the busy time at the dock. I was surprised that Uncle Orson would give that up. At the same time, I wasn't. Not for the first time I wished I was a better daughter and niece and person in general. Then I went to the truck and headed in to see what kind of music I was facing.

As I was pulling up to the sheriff's department there was a white sedan pulling away. That suggested to me the kind of tune I would be expected to dance to.

The sheriff was in casual clothes, jeans and a pair of hand-stitched Mexican boots. The boots were up on his desk looking carefree, but his face didn't match his posture.

"Close the door," he said.

I did. Then I decided to beat the punch and turned to him, saying, "There's a lot you don't know—that Reach didn't tell you."

"He told me enough, goddamn it. Enough to explain a lot. Hell, I always thought you were gay."

The profanity didn't surprise me. The blunt statement about being gay stunned me. Sheriff Benson was the kind of man who fell into casual cursing whenever he got flustered or angry. But always in private and always within bounds. This was already going beyond his usual bounds.

The shock must have shown on my face because he put his feet down and tried to physically wave it away with his hands. They looked like he was shooing flies.

"I know. I know," he said. "I'm not supposed to say that kind of thing and I'm sure as hell not supposed to say it to someone that works for me. But honestly, I never cared and I wish it was true after hearing what that son of a bitch has been telling me."

"You should let me explain—"

He waved me off again. "You know he was here again this morning? Stirring the pot."

"I need to tell you—"

"*He* told me. The son of a two-dollar whore stood right there, and told me that you, one of my officers, had conspired to kill a superior officer while serving in the U.S. Army."

"I—" I choked. Tears were welling in my eyes and the words I needed were caught in my chest and pressing against my heart.

"Of course I understand why *you* didn't tell me. He told me about the charges you filed. And he said that when the Army could find no basis to proceed with criminal charges, you made waves." As if the word was not enough, the sheriff undulated his hands to show waves. "*He said* you were angry and talking to journalists and lawyers and doing everything to make the Army look bad. Then, *he says*, you had the bastard killed.

"And I said 'good.' I told the motherfucker, 'justice is justice,' and 'I have a daughter,' and 'if he didn't have any charges to file, get the hell out of my county.'"

"What . . . ?" I was confused by the tirade, and it was slow coming to me that his anger was directed at Major Reach, not at me.

"That's why I wanted to talk to you today. That man is here as part of an ongoing investigation. He came to see me as a 'courtesy visit,' to let me know that one of my officers is a suspect."

"I'm sorry about that," was all I was able to say.

"*You're* sorry? Goddamn it," he said. Then he added, "God*damn* it. I apologize about my language but, son of a bitch and God help me, I told the major, I hoped you *did* kill the man that did that to you. And *I'm* sorry. I'm sorry that ever happened."

He was too. I could see it in his eyes and in the tension of his body. He hadn't asked me in to tell me that I was fired or under investigation. He called me in because he thought I should know he had been made party to my secrets. He was trying to say he was behind me, but what he had learned had wounded him. The sheriff was hiding behind anger and language. I could understand that.

As shocked as he might have been by what Reach had told him, I think he was more shocked when I came around the desk and hugged him. I got tears and snot on his shoulder, but he just stood there and accepted it. I couldn't see his face. I was sure it was red with embarrassment. The world needs more men like Sheriff Chuck Benson.

When I stopped crying, he told me I didn't have to tell him anything. He only wanted me to know, he was behind me all the way. Then he asked where I got the shiner.

We talked for about an hour more. I told him about the biker connection to Angela Briscoe and the follow-up work I'd done to find Leech. He knew most of it because I'd copied him on all the e-mail correspondence with the feds. Then I told him about my suspicions that the kids, Danny Barnes and Carrie Owens, knew more than they were telling me. I also shared my opinion that something inappropriate might be going on at Carrie Owens's home. After that, I told him about keeping Billy out at the crime scene and followed up with the developments on the entirely new and confusing case of whiskey, bikers, and fine artists. I closed with a rundown of the previous night. I had to admit that I was at Moonshines with Nelson Solomon and that I'd taken him to my uncle's and that led to why I was at his home and fighting bikers at almost midnight.

The sheriff seemed actually glad that Nelson was with me last night. He didn't say so, but I think he was happy to believe I wasn't gay. He did get a little annoyed about overtime for Billy staying out at the river where Angela had been killed.

I told him that Billy had volunteered and was on his own time.

He asked if I thought he was the kind of boss who would expect his officers to work without pay. He wouldn't do that to Billy or anyone else, he said, but it was his decision, not mine.

It was a fair complaint.

Early morning had become simply morning, so I decided to get back into work. I checked e-mail and voice messages, deleting the one from Reach without bothering to listen. As far as Angela Briscoe went, bikers and Leech had taken up most of my attention. I couldn't shake the feeling that the Barnes kid and Carrie Owens had more to share if I could shake it loose. I'd made calls to both homes and, while I was tracking down bikers, talked with Lloyd Barnes, Danny's father. It was a waste of time. He barely knew his son's age, let alone cared what he was doing as long as he "didn't get trapped by some little bimbo."

Carrie was the key, I'd decided. I'd gone back to her house looking for her mother or father. Nothing. Each time, I left a card in the door with a note to please call. Each time I went back, my card was gone. I'd called and left messages that had never been returned. Now, sitting on my desk, were sheets on the parents that I'd requested to be pulled. They didn't paint a pretty picture. Deputies had been called to the residence a dozen times. Carrie had a juvenile file that was mostly vandalism. Because of issues at home and because she'd gotten herself into the system, the court had assigned a caseworker. She'd be able to tell me a lot more than what was in the files. That was another round of calling, leaving a message and following up with e-mail.

Even when there is a murder investigation there is other work to be taken care of. I went through the piles and returned the calls I'd been putting off. An hour later I was starved. Uncle Orson did say breakfast was my responsibility.

I left the building feeling both better and worse than when I'd gone in. It was a weird emotional confusion that I didn't bother trying to work out. As much as I hated my life being put on display, the sheriff was behind me, and I'd actually gotten quite a bit of work done. So far the day was a win.

When I pulled up to one of my favorite cafés, there was a familiar truck parked in front. I decided to join Clare Bolin and see what the special was.

Clare was indeed having the special: three eggs, country ham, what would probably total half-a-dozen potatoes' worth of hash browns, along with biscuits covered in sausage gravy, and coffee, black and strong. I would not have wanted to be his heart. I chose just a short stack instead. We talked a while and I learned quite a bit about his illegal hobby. The one thing I learned that seemed to have real meaning was that Clare was not the only one being muscled. All of the other guys he knew who were making and selling had been visited by one of the Nightriders. Unfortunately, what I didn't learn was why anyone would want to cut in on such small operators.

I enlisted his help in making a survey of local producers, people he knew and the people they knew. It put me in the ethical dilemma of making a promise not to use the information against anyone whose name showed up. Knowing that I was promising on the sheriff's behalf, as well as my own, doubled my ethical issues.

When I left the café, Clare was still sitting there working on the biscuits and pouring down another steaming mug of coffee. Behind Clare's truck was the white sedan. Major Reach was crossing the street with a smug look on his dark face.

"What is your problem with me?" I asked even before he had finished crossing the street. I didn't quite yell.

"I'm just a man doing my job," he answered and, I thought, doubling the level of smug.

"We've been over the you-doing-your-job thing," I said.

"Nice eye."

"Yeah. Real police work is hands-on."

"Oh, I'm taking a good, hard look at your hands-on work, Hurricane. Don't you worry."

A city sidewalk is not the best place for a confrontation, especially if you're a public official, but I was past caring. Framed in the window of the Taneycomo Café for a full audience, I stood toe to toe with Major John Reach and told him, "If I thought you the least bit competent, or believed you had the slightest integrity, I might worry. But if you were those things you wouldn't be here, would you?"

Reach leaned in even closer and put his gaze even with mine. "Former Lieutenant Williams," he said. His voice was as narrow and focused as his eyes. "You shamed the United States Army and yourself. You brought charges against superior officers without proof or witnesses, a court-martial offence, and when you lost, you took the law into your own hands. You will spend the rest of your life worrying."

"Is everything okay here?" It was Clare asking from behind Reach's shoulder. "You need help, Hurricane?"

Reach turned quickly and said, "What's a fat-ass redneck going to do to help? Huh? She needs you to shut up and keep walking, fat man. And so do I."

God bless him, Clarence Bolin just smiled. He gave a friendly nod to the insignia on the major's collar and said, "I wore that uniform too. In sixty-five, when some whites were still angry about sharing bunks and meals with blacks. I was at Ia Drang and I didn't care that the man I pulled off the field was a black kid from Philly any more than I cared that the guy who pulled me out was another black kid from Mississippi. I wore the uniform with guys who had it a hell of a lot harder than you and they made it look better than you ever could."

Clare turned away from us without waiting for a response and then crossed the street to his truck and climbed in. Once behind the wheel he rolled the window down and yelled, "Hey Major." With a wide grin spreading over his face, he gave Reach the middle-finger salute and backed the lifted truck up over the hood of the white sedan.

"Are you going to do something about that?" Reach yelled at me as Clare drove away, still flipping the bird.

"Sorry," I said. "I didn't catch the license number."

When they left the pavement, my tires raised a cloud of dust that billowed and swirled behind the truck, then into my open window when I slowed down. I had called the dock with no answer, so I went with another whim and drove out to where Angela had been killed. Pulled off into the grass not far from where I had first seen Clare was Danny Barnes's car.

It was only the two of them, Carrie and Danny. For good reason. They were on the ground right where Angela had been lying. Carrie's shirt was open and her loose bra was up around her throat. Danny was kneeling between her legs with his pants open. There was something in his hand and he flicked it away. They were a pair of white panties.

For the past several years, brown has been the refuge color for my rage. Soft, bled-out colors, all from Iraq, have followed my inner turmoil projecting themselves out into the world with my anger, hatred, and pain. At that place and moment everything was different. Red— thick, rich, red spurted at the edges of my vision like the rush of arterial spray into strong wind.

A hurricane.

White, thin, and filmy as the young girl's panties, flitted like a sheer banner to which I reacted with rage.

The two colors swirled in the dark chamber behind my eyes. They didn't mix. They whipped by, filling my vision with streaks of blood and delicate fabric.

Then there was the screaming as Carrie was crying and pleading. The impact of each blow triggered more anger, driving my lust for the kill up my weapon and into my arms, communicating red and white into my heart. I can't remember pulling my automatic, but I had. It fit in my hand as comforting as the rage that had settled in my chest.

A hand gripped my arm and pulled. Someone screamed at my ear. It didn't match my violence. It was not the screaming of rage but of fear. More. Terror.

The words came to me as if shouted from a great distance and into the wind.

"Please."

I struck again.

"Please," she said. Carrie. She was pleading. She was begging me. "Stop. Don't hurt him anymore."

My voice swam up through fluid, a river of blood and white satin. I barely heard it say, "He won't hurt you again."

"He didn't," she cried. "He wasn't hurting me. I let him. Please."

When I broke the surface of the river I felt the colors, like physical currents flowing away, down my shoulders and off my body. I held Danny by the collar and my weapon in my hand. Both were bloody.

"Please. We were just fooling around."

The sheriff held my service weapon dangling from a finger in the trigger guard as the ambulance pulled away. All lights and the siren were on.

"Tell me again," he said.

I did. From the moment I had pulled up to the moment I had called in for EMTs and backup was laid out like a series of film frames whose sum were so much more devastating than any individual image. The sound of my own voice was hollow. But even the cotton batting I seemed to be hearing through allowed the shame into my ears.

I told him how I had found the two in the woods and right on top of the still bloody leaves where Angela Briscoe had been murdered. I told him also of the girl's bare breasts and disheveled clothing, Danny's open pants and the panties, tossed aside. My belief that Carrie Owens was being raped and would be murdered, just as Angela had, sounded foolish to me in the retelling. By the third time I related the story it sounded like lunacy.

Sheriff Benson asked if I was all right. He spoke in the same kind of voice I imagined him using to speak to the Briscoe family.

I nodded. I was tired of talking. But there was still something left unsaid. I could feel it in the sheriff's posture. A weight that he despaired of hanging on me. Was I primed by experience to expect rape when there was none? Was my judgment impaired? Was I dangerous?

The weight remained on his shoulders and the questions stayed unasked. I was grateful for that. Officially, though, he had to place me on suspension.

When everyone had gone, I stayed there standing in the dirt road leaning against the fender of my truck. It should have been one of those moments of evaluation and reevaluation, what my grandparents had called "a come to Jesus moment." It might even have been. If it was, I didn't remember it. When I leaned up against the truck it was late morning and the next time I looked up it was afternoon. The sun had shifted in the sky and shadows had begun to appear like rot under the day. I had the feeling that my thoughts had been deep and memories had played over bare nerves, but that was it. A feeling.

Since I couldn't conjure the memories I decided to kill the feeling.

The tailgate of the truck made a perfect spot to sit and sip from the jar of Clare's whiskey. I wish I could say I sipped.

Once again, time disappeared. When it returned it was carried on the soft, almost silent, tread of the sheriff's road tires, not the ground-gnawing rubber of Humvees. He stopped but remained in the SUV as my father got out. When Dad had my keys in hand he waved and the sheriff went the way he had come.

The jar beside me was well on the way to half gone. Sun and shadows had shifted again. My father poured the whiskey out onto the road and then sat beside me, allowing more time to pass while I cried. Then he drove me back to the dock, taking a very long way around and going slow while I slept.

The day had shifted into early evening by the time we got back to the dock. I was all cried out but still drunk and sleepy. We pulled up and parked well away from the dock gate so as not to disturb Nelson, who was seated on a kitchen chair in the middle of the parking lot painting. He smiled at me and rose when I melted out of the truck, but sat again when my father held up his hand and took me under his arm. Half guiding and half shoving, he got me onto the dock, through the shop, and onto the houseboat without a word. Once he had me in the bunk he removed my boots and covered me.

"Thank you, Daddy," I said. "I love you."

"I love you too, candy corn." The nickname always made me

smile. He had called me that one Halloween, saying I was the sweetest and silliest thing. Then he said, "I'm sorry about everything, but we'll make it right."

The next I knew, it was dark. Not completely: It was the point of the evening where the day had given way, but the night was not yet strong enough to hold the world on its own. Uncle Orson used to say, If the day was a pig, this time was the curl. I always liked the thought that the birth of night could be the curly tail of a pig going over a fence.

Outside the boat's cabin, coming from the picnic table inside the shop, were voices and the sound of a meal. They sounded happy. I opened a window and sat very still in the darkness beside it to listen. It was a bad idea. Not only the sounds came through but the smell of the fish they had cooked.

The simple and sane thing would have been to bolt outside and throw up into the lake that was only feet from the door. I went to the sink and banged my head on the cabinet in the process. At least no one got to witness that bit of indignity.

That pig's tail slipped beyond the horizon, leaving true night behind as I put myself back into bed and drifted away again. In the night I woke and heard my father and Nelson talking. I only heard voices and not words, but the conversation was friendly—warm, even. Nelson was a hard man not to like and my father was quick to take to people. I knew only that they were sitting outside under the dock's awning, talking. It had to be about me. I felt vaguely ashamed as I went back into sleep.

The next time I awoke it was because Nelson was in the room with me. He was trying to be quiet but he was coughing. When I sat up he said, "I brought you some water."

I took it but didn't say anything. Sips, just enough to wet my mouth were all I allowed myself. He offered aspirin and a wet cloth for my head, but I declined. Before he left I was out again.

The dreams came after that. Desaturated in color, flowing and unpredictable in movement, images churned like old movies projected onto a quick-moving river. Behind the wall I bled and watched the dust come. First like snakes, excellent in their animal camouflage, looking like the burnished earth and slithering one at a time, searching me out. Then many at once, so many they joined into a tide of misty dirt to cover me. At times I watched myself in the grave as dust piled up, both covering and filling me, until my bleeding was dust into dust. Other times I watched, a third-person omnipotent viewer, as the living dust came to me-but-not-me. I was Angela Briscoe, motionless and accepting. I was also Carrie Owens in displaced underthings, pulling the rain of dirt onto myself, participating in my own burial.

Again, I awoke and I cried. My father was there. He had brought in a lawn chair and sat beside my bed. Another cycle of sleep and dreaming to awake and cry followed to find Nelson sitting in the chair. He was there the next time too, painting on his small easel in full daylight. If I was grateful for anything, it was that he didn't try to make me talk. His presence was an invitation, not a demand. For a little while I watched him paint. Every so often he took his gaze from the art board to look at me. At one point I had the horrifying thought that he was painting me sweating and mouth breathing—looking like the creature from the booze lagoon.

Without saying anything to Nelson I flipped over, turning my back on him. He continued working without a pause. I hoped that meant I wasn't the subject. The sound of his work soothed me then, little scrapes on the board, the small clatter brushes made when dropped in the tray, quiet movements.

Finally, I slept and fell into true darkness. Dreams, and all consciousness, were left at shallower depths. When I awoke that time the light was either fading in or fading out. Out, I decided, only because it was still hot. I was alone and I smelled like a weekend drunk tank. I actually had to look to be sure I hadn't wet myself. No, but the sheets were soaked with my sweat. Worse was the taste of death and moldy peanut butter in my mouth.

Where had that come from?

Two times I brushed my teeth, then I stripped and remade the bed with fresh sheets. After that I brushed my teeth again before stepping into the boat's small shower. Soap and water made me feel two steps closer to life. Even when the water turned from warm to cold it felt glorious. My teeth got one more vigorous brushing. I scrubbed the top layer of skin off my tongue and the roof of my mouth. By the time I had brushed my teeth enough to face the world, the world was hiding its face from me. Most of two days had been lost. I stepped out into the cooling air to see if I had lost anything else.

Nelson was sitting alone in the shop. Dishes had been cleared

from the table and he had his easel set up, painting a picture of the
dock at twilight. Everything was there: the colors, more than I had
ever noticed. A fading sky was bruised purple. Still water seemed to
move, green on green. Strung around the edge of the dock were the
bare bulbs. They outshone the nascent stars. It reminded me of that
painting of the diner by Edward Hopper, only without threat in the
darkness. Nelson's painting was all about joy.

"Hi," he said as soon as I came through the screen door.

"I'm sorry," I answered.

"Don't be," he shot right back. "Sit with me. How would you feel
if I said I missed you?"

"What do you mean?" I asked, sitting. I looked at the painting,
not at him.

"Your father and uncle went out. I think they wanted to 'give us
room.'"

"Hmm . . . very considerate of them."

"Wasn't it? I won't ask if you want a beer." I could hear the smile
in his voice. Just to be sure, however, he turned and winked. From
behind the easel and art board he pushed a dripping glass of ice
water. "Here. Best thing for you."

"Why did you ask me how I would feel if you said you missed me?"

I took the glass and drank every drop, then sucked on ice until it
disappeared down my throat.

Nelson watched me and dabbed away at the painting. When I set the
glass down and began to breathe again he said, "Because I missed you.
And because I don't want my missing you to be a burden. And . . . well
. . . I don't want—" He stuck his brush into some white, then some blue.
I almost said something about a mistake, then he ran the brush over a
bit of dock and the colors streaked together—mixed without mixing.
It looked right but I didn't understand how.

That seems to sum up a lot of things for me.

He let his hand come down to the tabletop. It rested there like it
was thinking of its next move. I covered it with mine. As soon as they
touched he turned, ready to speak, ready to tell me what he didn't
want.

I kissed him.

As we kissed I held on to that hand and squeezed. I wanted it to
know I was there. When the kiss broke I thought he might try to talk
again, so I shut him up. That second kiss was more about heat and

hunger and I pressed my tongue into his mouth, tasting him and giving myself to be tasted.

I took my hand from his and put it behind his head and pulled him tightly to me. We let the kiss fade slowly and I released him at the same rate.

A breeze, cool and clean, smelling of rain, trickled through the screens. For the first time I noticed the falling pressure. Rain was coming.

"Come with me," I told Nelson.

Outside we stood beside the water and watched the sky creep with muddy clouds coming from the southwest. They were heavy and dark, flashing with silent lighting. Under our feet the smooth water trembled like skin that had gone untouched too long. I kissed him again.

For a long time we stayed embraced within the building wind. Our kisses were wet with desire. The penetration of his tongue in my mouth was becoming a teasing mockery of the true act.

Air, moist and quick, eddied around us and my skin puckered with gooseflesh from the cool motion. Nelson wrapped me tighter in his arms. In the crowding sky an anvil of dark cloud stacked higher and higher. Fingers of electricity clawed through it and for the first time we heard the thunder. I bit Nelson's lip and his hands responded on my back, tracking my spine and then digging in at the top of my hips.

I put my hands on his face and held on and sucked the air of his breath from his open mouth, swallowing him into me. With my hands, I then pushed him back, severing the kiss. I could feel the regret in his hands as they traveled up from my hips to my waist.

"I want this," I said and my desire was punctuated by another flash and rolling rumble.

Nelson opened his eyes wider and pulled a sharp breath from the wind. Then I saw something replace the understanding in his eyes. On my waist, his grip became even softer. A gentleman to the end, he said, "I think you might still be a little drunk."

"Maybe," I said and then I smiled. "But I'm not *that* drunk." I released his face and pulled open the front of my shirt. For the first time in forever I wasn't thinking about scars as soon as my skin uncovered. My bra was thin spandex; it showed the dark shape of my nipples standing out from the breasts. I wanted them touched, needed to feel his mouth on them. I grabbed his hand, still gently holding my waist, and brought it up.

I felt like the clouds above us, heavy with rain and charged with electricity. There was a moment, a beautiful moment without fear or reservation. I let my head fall against Nelson's, cherishing the feel of his intimate touch. Only a moment. Then the wind carried dust and dead leaves, brown decay and fear.

"I'm sorry," I told him. Seemingly on its own, my hand pushed his off my breast and I pulled the front of my shirt together.

As I clutched the fabric, tight as a wet knot, at my chest and pressed it to my sternum, Nelson let his hands fall to his sides. He stepped behind me and pressed his chest against my back. With his lips in my hair, he whispered, "Don't be sorry. We'll give what we can."

I was relieved. But—I touched the crescent scar at my left eye.

After that I was angry. Lightning broke through the clouds to reach out for the tall trees atop the bluffs on the far side of the lake. That was how the anger felt inside me. It was energy, branching out and touching everything. It flashed and it burned, leaving me charged but immobile. Anger at myself and at the Army, at the men who hurt me, at the violence I had set loose against Danny, all branches. But that night, there was a new branch. I was pissed at myself for feeling relieved. I was hiding from life at every turn and now I felt relief to let it pass.

No more.

I released my shirt front and took Nelson by the hand. I pulled him toward the houseboat. Once inside he started to say something. "Shhh," I said.

Digging through a drawer in the dark produced a book of matches that I used to light three glass-globed storm candles. All the light in the world was in motion. The candle flames flickered. Lightning flashed. The outside dock lights rocked in the wind and scattered reflections over the rough water.

I dropped my shirt to the floor.

Nelson put his hands on my bare shoulders. He was shaking.

"I don't know if I can," he said so softly that, at first, I thought it was the wind. "I don't know . . . I'm not sure I can. If I'm able."

In the shadows and candlelight I couldn't see the color on his face, but I could honestly feel the heat of his blush. For the first time I realized that it wasn't only my own fear I was challenging.

"I'm not sure I can, either," I told him. "But I want to try. Do you?" His hands trembled but they didn't leave my skin. Nelson didn't speak but I could feel his answer. I don't know from where—maybe it was from him, maybe I was still a little drunk—but for the first time in over ten years I found the courage to say, "Touch me."

He found the courage to do so.

Chapter 11

Later, we talked in the darkness with the raw honesty of new lovers. For me it was mostly confession. For Nelson it was a strange kind of stage setting. He kept trying to thread the needle between plans for life and plans for death. The carefulness with which he spoke of the future said to me that his statement about not dying may have been more wish than promise. I didn't have the courage to ask.

Maybe the future is best without promises.

I told him everything that had brought me to this place. He couldn't ever know me without knowing about the assault and everything that came after. My bloody experience in the field hospital and waking with the unit commanding officer beside my bed. The CO didn't ask about insurgents that had taken and done this to me—he told me about them. When I told him it was men under his command who had done these things, he told me that I was confused.

I told Nelson all about the horrible convalescence in a military hospital in Germany. Army personnel, some of them lawyers, some just bureaucrats, visited me daily with sad faces and offers. If I accepted their truth and signed their papers I would be given an early but honorable discharge and stateside treatment. When I asked why I hadn't been interviewed by the Criminal Investigations Division they always said they didn't know anything about it.

It was a nurse who finally understood what was happening. She had seen it before. She called CID. Captain John Reach was the investigator that showed up. He took detailed notes, said the usual sympathetic things, and disappeared for a week. When he came back he said his investigation was complete, there was no evidence of the assault and no charges would be filed. Then he warned me.

Most people who never run up against the peculiarities of military law are astonished to learn that it is a crime in the service to accuse any superior officer of illegal action without bulletproof evidence. Nelson had been a marine and knew the code. Like most service people, though, he had never seen it in action. I had accused two men, both superior in rank to me, of rape. The only evidence I could give was my absolute knowledge of who had done it.

That was where the real honesty began. I admitted to Nelson, and myself for the first time, my own complicity in what happened. I had accepted my fate. I bought the Army line that the chain of command was sacred and over all else; it was the Army itself, the institution that I loved, which needed to be protected. After everything, I refused to resign. Then I was sent back to active duty with my company. Both of my assailants had been promoted and I had a new reputation within the command. It took another month for me to understand that there was no going back.

I would never fit into my unit again and probably nowhere else in the Army. So I talked to a reporter. I filed official reports with everyone I could reach. The institution responded with charges of its own and threats of a court-martial. I heard later that I was saved only by the intercession of a member of Congress. It was something I never expected or understood. I was saved, but my career was dead. Even after that I had tried to stick it out. Then came the patrol where my men all explained to me how they felt and, under fire, refused my orders. I'd almost had to shoot the corporal to regain control. It was over. My resignation was accepted without resistance.

I wasn't even supposed to have been in combat situations. Officially women weren't allowed in battle, but the wars on terror were different kinds of wars. There were no front lines and no facing armies. Everything was mixed up with civilians and militia groups, and women in the American military were under fire. No one wanted to hear about their successes or their failures. They just wanted the problems we presented to go away.

Nelson made the comment that at least it was over and behind me. That's when I told him about the reappearance of Reach in my life and the accusation that I was somehow responsible for the killing of one of the men that had raped me.

He said he wouldn't judge me if I was. I laughed, truly grateful for that statement.

Nelson told me his story. The contrast was stunning. Not because his experiences in Kuwait and Iraq were so different. Living and fighting within the artificial night created by a thousand oil-well fires had left its mark on him just as indelible as those on my skin and, ultimately, more dire. The contrast was that his story was all after war. Even dealing with the cancer in his lung, which was small-cell and aggressive, he had hope that his story was still ahead of him.

I hope so too.

When the talk slowed and the rain had become a steady drizzling, I turned my body into Nelson's and cuddled onto his lap. I kissed him while I pulled his hand down between my open legs. Then I told him, "Do it again, please."

He laughed and the warmth in his voice was joy in my ears when he said, "Anything for you."

The next day was full of light and humidity. Moisture rose from the ground, giving the day a steam-heat texture. Every breath was like sucking through a wet blanket. Nelson said it was good for landscapes, that water droplets colored the air and made the heat ripple as it rose. He spent the morning painting on the top deck of the houseboat and only came down long enough for breakfast. I don't think he was really hungry—he barely touched food—but I could tell he liked the company. We smiled at each other like kids with our first crushes. It all felt so good and, since I was on suspension already, I called and cancelled my next appointment with the therapist. *That* was a liberating feeling.

Dad and Uncle Orson tried to ignore us but I know they were laughing about it when we couldn't hear. The pair of them had argued that morning in the parking lot. It wasn't the usual kind of argument I'd seen between them a million times. This one was real. The fact they'd felt the need to sequester the conflict out in the parking lot, out of my earshot, said a lot as well.

It passed quickly, though. Afterwards, they went to the grocery store, still bickering. But I had the feeling that something big had been left unresolved. Something about me. When they came back, they carried enough food for a dozen breakfasts and then cooked it all.

We had grits and French toast, bacon and ham, eggs both scrambled and fried, and biscuits. Everything was slathered in real butter and enough grease to clog even my uncle's sewer-pipe arteries. It was delicious and the best time—with the exception of the past night—that I'd had in years.

We had an entire day like that. The night was another thing of beauty and secrets. Nelson and I barely slept. But nothing good ever lasts.

The goodness ended just before noon the next day with the rumble of loud pipes. Eight motorcycles, some carrying two riders, came slowly down the road and aimed right for the dock. As soon as I saw them coming I grabbed the ancient Colt .45 that Uncle Orson kept under the counter and stuck it into my belt at the small of my back. "Call 9-1-1," I said. Dad followed me. Nelson was on top of the houseboat and I would have shouted to him to stay there if I didn't know he would ignore me. I went to the end of the dock ramp and waited.

Two of the riders were those I had encountered before: Cotton Lambert and, leading the pack, Leech. I'd suspected he was the one who had jumped me in Nelson's driveway, but seeing him, I was sure. He was wearing a shiny-new metal brace over the knee I'd hit with my baton. Riding on the back of his bike was a woman. Even with glassy eyes and a bad dye job she looked more like a housewife than a biker girl.

Almost in unison the bikes died but no one got off.

"I want to talk to the painter." It was Leech talking.

"You're under arrest for assaulting a sheriff's detective. The person you need to talk to is your lawyer," I told him.

The whole group laughed like I'd told a joke. Looking at their numbers, I guessed I had.

"You ain't no cop no more," he said.

"Where do you get your information?"

"Shit, lady, everyone knows about that. You beat up a little kid. Tough cop."

"Tough enough," I said. "How's your knee?"

"Fuck you," he said but without much spirit. "Tell the painter it's time to sell out and get out."

"Sheriff's department has already been called. They're on their way," I told him.

He spit his derision on the asphalt. "Lady, you local Barneys don't worry me none. We're making this county ours and there ain't nothing you can do about it."

He started his bike and the others roared to life right after. Without another word they circled and left. I could hear their pipes long after they were gone. As I was following the sound I caught sight of another generic-looking sedan parked in the lot. A rental car with Major Reach sitting behind the wheel. He was looking my way.

It never rains but it pours. I took a deep breath and glanced behind me. Dad was there just a few feet away. He looked ready to chew barbed wire.

"Did anyone call 9-1-1?" I asked.

Dad didn't answer. He was staring across the lot at Reach, who must have stared back because my father spit into the lake. I had never see that man spit in my life. The gesture was so malevolent and intentional it made me wonder how well I knew my father after all.

Behind him, the shop's screen door flapped open. Uncle Orson and Nelson both stepped out. Uncle Orson was holding a cut-down double-barreled shotgun, Nelson a fifty-year-old J. C. Higgins .22 revolver. They were both grinning like demons, just a little disappointed they didn't get to shoot anyone.

"What do you think?" Uncle Orson asked.

Of course not.

"What's a Barney?" Nelson asked.

"Barney Fife, deputy of Mayberry," I heard Uncle Orson answer.

I'd turned and taken a couple of steps to go out and talk with Reach, when I had a thought. Sure enough, Dad was right behind me. "Wait here," I told him. He didn't even look at me. "Please?"

That time he looked. He nodded his assent, but I could tell he didn't like it.

"Nice car," I said as soon as I got close enough for Reach to hear.

"I'll send a bill for the other one. Uncle Sam doesn't like holes in the accounting."

"You can just drop it off out there." I pointed to the center of the lake. "That's where all the junk mail goes."

"You're funny," he said in a way that suggested that he didn't really think so.

"What do you want, Reach?"

"Major Reach, United States Army. A full twenty years. Don't you forget it."

"That's the beauty of being out. Your rank doesn't mean squat to me. I get to save my respect for real soldiers, not just any piece of polished brass that shows up. Now you're taking up my day. What do you want?"

"You need to come in and have a sit-down. There are a lot of questions you need to answer."

I laughed. I'd learned a lot in the last several years. "Kiss my ass," I told him.

"You can be compelled," he said.

"That's the thing. I can be compelled if there's evidence or just cause. But you're no Mr. Nice Guy and you've never been subtle. If you had the authority to compel anything we wouldn't be here talking. You're firing blanks in the dark, hoping to scare me. I don't scare as easy as I used to."

His eyes narrowed and I could see the muscles in his jaw knot up and release like he was trying to crack nuts with his teeth. I was right and he knew it too.

"There is new evidence," he finally said. "It seems that Homeland put Sala Bayoumi into special rendition. He's being questioned out of country and he's using a lot of familiar names. Yours is definitely on the list."

"I thought you said *evidence*," I said.

"The evidence is a wire transfer from a U.S. Intelligence account to Bayoumi before Rice was killed."

I looked over the top of the car into the houses and greenery sloping up and away from the lake. It was hard for me not to see the sand whipping over mud walls and feel the blood dripping from me again. Hard, but not the impossibility I had come to believe it to be.

"You better rethink that one, Reach. It's going to blow up in your face."

"Would you consider yourself a credible, uninvolved source?"

"No game on this, and you can check it out. I never had access to any funds while I was in and I sure haven't had access since. Looking for an intelligence op that would authorize killing of a serving Army officer is above your pay grade."

I expected some kind of comeback or new accusation. Instead, Reach looked past me. When I turned, there was my father. He was looking just as hard at Reach.

I turned around and started walking back to the dock.

"Hey, Hurricane," Reach called.

Without answering I stopped and looked back.

"The other guy, Captain Ahrens. You remember, he was a lieutenant when you knew him. Did you know that he's been married three times? Seems every time he finds true love his wife gets a mysterious package that contains the entire written file on your case. All your statements. Your description of his ring and how you said you knew who he was. Funny thing how they all believed it. Poor son of a bitch can't see his kids, can't have a marriage, he can't even hold a job. What do you think of that?"

"Karma," I said. "She's a bitch."

"Yeah," he agreed. "Karma just can't seem to let this one go." He started the car and did a wide turn passing between me and the dock to go out the same way the bikes had.

As soon as he passed, I ran to my phone and called Darlene. This was the best chance we'd had to catch Leech. By the time units responded, the road was empty.

Chapter 12

After the intrusion of the Nightriders, the afternoon was quiet. Heat broiled down out of the pure blue sky. The temperature seemed to be racing past the slow creep of the sun. Almost no one came into the shop or onto the dock to take their boats out. The lake was a glossy green plane, like old glass with just enough ripple to give it some character.

Three of us were hot and sweating in the un–air-conditioned bait shop. But Nelson was looking like he'd been steamed and rung out. His clothes were wet and sticking to his bony frame. Water ran in constant beads down his face and into his shirt. Despite that, he was standing straighter and, I thought, breathing better. Everything about him was signaling that turn he'd told me about. He was smiling when he asked if he could take us all to one of the music shows on the Branson strip.

Dad and Uncle Orson looked at me like it was my decision. I made it.

Nelson asked me to take him to his house for appropriate clothes and I found myself telling him we would only go out if he took a nap. The other two men in the room were suddenly very interested in the view out the window. They were no help to him when Nelson tried to tell me he was fine and didn't need to be treated like an invalid.

He took a nap.

It's funny how power can go to your head. I told the other two to dig out some clothes of their own. No jeans tonight. No one argued. Dad said he would have to go home for clothes and to make some calls he'd been putting off. Uncle Orson gave him a look, but Dad gave it right back. I didn't worry about it. They had probably been arguing about my life. They'd get over it.

It was good to have something to do. Downtime is nice but my head was full of strings. None of them seemed to lead anywhere, but every one of them wanted pulling. I probably should have been thinking about what I had done to the Barnes kid and the possible consequences. Or maybe I should have been thinking about what I was getting myself into with Nelson. That was a knotted rat's nest of strings it would take an army of therapists to straighten out. The truth was that none of the obvious things had my attention. As I got into the truck for the trip over to Nelson's house it was something new bothering me. Like a splinter it had gotten under my skin without my even noticing, but once there it kept nagging.

The biker, Leech, had said something. "Sell out and get out." It didn't mean anything to me at the time, but it bothered me later and was still working on me as I drove. These guys had been trying to get rid of Nelson. Maybe they were just not very bright or maybe they thought he knew what it was all about, but something got lost in translation. They wanted him gone. And they wanted him to sell out something before going.

Other people, the creep and his muscle from Moonshines, were trying to get him to sell out too. His own partner seemed to want a deal made. Nelson had said Middleton wanted to buy him out but seemed to be trying to fix Figorelli up with the deal. The easy thing would have been to ask Nelson. Or it should have been. I had the feeling he was holding back from me almost as much as from them. I decided to make a little detour to Moonshines before heading over to Nelson's. It was time to have an off-the-record conversation with Mr. Middleton.

That turned out to be harder than expected. I got to Moonshines and they were busy with an afternoon crowd. Everyone working wanted to know where Johnny Middleton was too. They were just too busy to look for him.

I found him at the far end of the parking lot in the only shade available. The car was a Jaguar, but it had apparently lost a lot of its resale value. The engine was off and the windows were up. Flies were already crawling along the edges of the door and window glass. I didn't open the door. There was no point. Heads don't hang like that unless the person attached to it is dead.

I called it in, then I called the sheriff at home. Even without a closer look I could tell that he had been shot at least two times. There were bloody red blooms at his temple and in the center of his expensive white shirt. A quick look around the ground showed no brass casings, but that didn't mean a lot. They could be inside the car or the killer could have used a revolver. The other option had to be considered: There would be none because the killer had taken them with him. I was betting that there would be casings in the car along with the small-caliber weapon that killed Middleton.

Television and movies have muddied a lot of water for cops. People now think that there is a magic DNA machine in every department that tells us the killer the same day. They think we can pull prints off of anything and enhance video too. They think miracles are routine and never imagine the hard work or man-hours that go into every major case. At the same time everyone knows now that Mob killers use .22s and shoot in the head. Every night of the week they get a little crime lesson that includes gems like *use an untraceable weapon and drop it at the scene so you won't be caught with it.*

Most citizens would be amazed how hard it is to keep a weapon untraceable. And the thing about .22s: TV will tell you it's so the low-power bullet goes in the skull and bounces around without coming out the other side—the truth is it's mostly about noise. Like when you shoot someone in a car with the windows up. Even in the full light of day, in a public parking lot, a .22 or .25 fired within a running car would be swallowed up in the usual noise of traffic, wind, talk.

Deputies arrived within a few minutes. The sheriff was there in about fifteen. He brought my shield and weapon.

"I was going to wait another day," he said. "Thought you could use some time to ponder on what had happened."

"But?"

"But—since you were involving yourself in an investigation and dragged *this* into our yard—I figured it would be better to have you back on duty. And by the way, if anyone asks: I was out at your place and gave you these things an hour ago."

"Okay, I understand," I said, not entirely sure I did. "What about what I did to the kid?"

"I have it on good authority there won't be any charges coming from that. And your record will show that you were overly enthusiastic in your apprehension of a suspect, rather than that you used wildly excessive force on some kids getting dirty in the woods."

"What good authority?"

"My authority. And the DA's. Barnes had Angela Briscoe's crucifix in his pocket." He let that sink in for a moment before he said, "We also followed up on your request for time and location of the speeding ticket he got the day of the killing. It was given that afternoon, less than a mile from where you found Angela."

"Circumstantial," I said.

"Lethal-injection circumstantial," he said right back.

"Death penalty for a juvenile?"

"That shit's not up to me, thank God. And speaking of penalty . . ."

"What?" I asked. He stood there looking at me like he had bad news that he enjoyed delivering. He did.

"I've added a mandatory additional six months to your therapy requirements. It's written up and put in your file."

"Sheriff, that's—"

"Don't say it. Not another word because I promise that you will regret it." Sheriff Benson, an honest man, stared straight into my eyes with a look that said nothing will ever be plainer than this. "It's bullshit. I bet that was what you were gonna say. It's what I would have said. And it is. But it's the kind of bullshit that is keeping you on the job—cause, God's honest truth, girl—you have a problem. I'm on your side fighting it, but if you ain't doing the work it will eat you alive and I will cut you loose. Do you have any more to say about it?"

"No, sir," I answered.

"Good. This is your scene and your investigation. Get to it."

"Sheriff?" I said before he could walk off. "There is something I wanted to ask you."

He waited and I thought carefully.

"Major Reach suggested to you that maybe I killed the man who hurt me in Iraq. You told me how you felt but didn't say if you believed I did it."

"Is that what you're asking me? Do I believe you killed that man?" I nodded, watching him watch me. He didn't look away. Then he said, "No. I don't believe you killed him. But I do believe you could."

Somehow that made me feel like my own violence was a punch line to the bloody scene I had been given to investigate.

* * *

We'd gotten the car door open and I was right about the weapon. It was a .25 automatic, the kind of gun ladies were supposed to keep in their purses in bad neighborhoods. This particular example was old and the grip was only metal frame covered with tape. There was a casing partially ejected so the gun had jammed after only two shots. Two were enough. When everything obvious was photographed and then collected I released the body to the coroner's office and told a deputy to get the car towed and secured.

I went back into Moonshines to talk to the employees. No one could give me a time that Middleton had left the building, but several mentioned a group of bikers that rolled into the parking lot and left just as quickly. That was troubling. One or two hanging out and trying to push meth was a concern, but a normal one. A bunch of them at the scene of another murder was something else. Clare had seen bikers around where Angela had been found. I saw Leech on Angela's street the next day. Cotton Lambert had beaten Nelson and tried to run him off. Twice, some of the Nightriders had been at Nelson's house. Then they'd come to the dock, warning Nelson away again.

There were links that just weren't clear yet. But how did Danny Barnes's killing Angela Briscoe fit in? Did it fit in at all?

I spent another hour taking notes and sketching in my pad. At one point, flipping through pages, I noticed one of my sketches of the Leech image with the arrow points. That was something else that was puzzling. Why all the graffiti about a greasy biker? I wanted to find out more about it but there was a fresh case at hand. When I had everything down and noted and timed, I sent a deputy looking for Byron Figorelli.

Johnny Middleton's murder looked like textbook Mob work. That didn't mean a thing because the whole point of having a textbook style is to send a message. Mob hits only looked like Mob hits when someone wanted them to. That someone may or may not be Mob. Again, this was thanks to the *Godfather* movies and that *Sopranos* show.

With that in mind, the only people around who fit the mobster description were the guys I had put in the can Saturday night. No one had mentioned them today, but they were my first choice for this.

Imagine my surprise when Byron Figorelli and Jimmy Cardo, the man Billy had stunned when we arrested them, came rolling up into the parking lot in an RV the size of some homes.

It took about two minutes to ascertain that they'd been clowning it up in go-karts and at the batting cages, getting a lot of attention from management all day long.

Once again I had to note that my life was never easy.

As soon as the scene was cleared and I had talked to everyone at Moonshines, I started home. If I hadn't seen a billboard for the Oak Ridge Boys, the show we were going to, I would have gone all the way back. Almost four hours after I had left the dock I finally pulled into Nelson's drive.

I was careful this time, going slow and checking every spot someone could hide. Before going in I walked the perimeter and checked the doors and windows. Inside, everything was the same and secure as well. Before going to his bedroom I stood for a few minutes in the middle of the great room with the view and the art in progress. It was a good room and fit the man.

It would be impossible not to know I was falling for Nelson. It was just as impossible not to picture myself here, with him, maybe in winter with snow on the ground and a fire in the woodstove. A month ago—no, less than a week ago, even—that thought would have probably given me a panic attack. I could not have imagined—this—any of this, my feelings, desires, plans for a future.

Things—*life*—seemed different in just the last few days. It was so strange to think that I had spent years worried about men. I had feared them and their intentions and believed all of them capable and ready to do the kind of things to me that had been done in that other life. Standing there in Nelson's house, for the first time I began to see the men who were actually in my life. They were so much more than the shadows I was running from. So many good men surrounded me that I wondered then how it was I had only seen the bad.

The rack of paintings beside the work space drew me. I knelt beside it and flipped through the canvases and art boards. It was a catalog of the Ozarks, colors and places that I thought lived only in my mind. Streaks of paint, built-up and shifted, pushed by brush and knife all conspired to present the world the way I had always thought of it. Beautiful.

Nelson's tools were there, scattered but clean and ready. I held his brushes and smelled the rag that rested by the easel. It smelled of the oils and thinners he used. It smelled like his hands after he worked.

To one side, there was a small end table with a drawer that stood open. Inside the drawer was a small case. It would have been so easy to write it off as just another box of paint. I couldn't do that. It was obviously new. Everything else was worn and used. Then there was the texture to it. The box was dead, dull plastic. It had a utility that clashed with the wood and animal bristle all around it. Most of all I couldn't ignore it because I had seen its kind so many times before.

I opened the case and pulled the revolver from its perfect vacuum-formed cradle.

Sometimes we stumble across parts of other people's lives that we know are secret, even if they are not well hidden. We seem to have a sense about these things and touching them imparts an instant guilt that is greater than the action. It's the knowing, not the finding. And we can never unknow.

The revolver had never been fired. It was loaded with only two cartridges.

Only two?

With sudden clarity I knew that two was one too many.

I looked back in the drawer and found the receipt and the box of shells. The paperwork was dated about a month prior. There was something else. Stuffed to the back of the drawer where they had been shoved aside like a horrible joke were a pamphlet for a hospice and another that was titled *End-of-Life Options*.

I put it all back just the way I had found it and went upstairs to gather Nelson's clothes.

We made it to the Oak Ridge Boys show just in time. Everyone but me looked rested, ready for a night on the town. I wore my other pretty dress but felt like a sack of potatoes wearing heels. There was too much to think about. While the Boys were singing about Elvira, I was doing a mental inventory and craving a drink. At least the craving kept me awake.

After the show I got my drink, but it was only beer and I was careful. If I had been alone I would have gotten into Uncle Orson's behind-the-counter-special reserve. I drank my one beer while we had an impromptu fish fry for a late dinner. Dad dredged catfish filets in cornmeal with salt and lemon pepper, paprika, cumin, rosemary, and sage.

That's his mild recipe. When I'm not around he'll usually add cayenne and probably some other things I don't want to know about. While he dredged, Uncle Orson manned the outdoor fry pot. Nelson and I cut red potatoes and roasted them while we blanched some asparagus then sautéed it in olive oil with garlic and melted Parmesan cheese over it in the covered skillet.

It was another feast and it should have been joyous, but I kept watching Nelson's plate.

"You're not eating as well as last night," I said even as I told myself not to.

"I'm doing okay," he said. "I'm loving the fish."

"You've only had one bite."

"I'm pacing myself."

"Only one bit of potato." I said it like an accusation and I suppose it was.

"But an entire stalk of asparagus," he said through an embarrassed smile. "If we're keeping count."

I shut up. But it was difficult. I knew he wasn't trying to starve himself, but it still felt like that and pissed me off. While we were cleaning up he asked if I would take him to get his truck in the morning. He said he had things to do in Springfield.

The whole keeping-my-mouth-shut thing fell apart there. I tried to sound casual when I asked what things.

He didn't look at me when he said, "Doctors' appointments."

The multiple wasn't lost on me. "Want me to come along?" I asked, still trying to keep it a casual offer.

Nelson shook his head and then he put on a smiling mask of good feelings. "You'll be busy tomorrow with important things," he said. "I'll be fine."

"You don't have any idea what's important," I said. I had spoken quietly but it felt like shouting. The look on Nelson's face said the same thing. He was confused and hurt by my self-serving and selfish little one-line tantrum. I left him standing there and went outside. My footsteps were just heavy enough to keep him from following.

On my way out I grabbed another beer and went to the top deck of the houseboat. That spot that had become Nelson's unofficial work space. It was high with a wonderful view of the lake and a perfect place for brooding. I was feeling sorry for myself, not him. He didn't invite sorrow and that made me wonder if I was bringing it into his life.

No one came up to talk to me. I could feel them giving me space and being kind about it. That pissed me off too. I wanted someone to poke their head up so I could chew it off. My therapist said that when I share my anger I'm really trying to share my pain. Sometimes I fantasized about shooting her between the eyes.

The night was so clear in the sky that it was hard to tell where the lake ended and the horizon began. Stars reflected in the still lake shimmered and broke in the small waves before reforming. As open and lonely as it was, I had never heard quiet in an Ozarks summer night. Sound crowded in from every direction. Cicadas buzzed constantly. Frogs, both lake and tree, were chirping as well. It was a comfort.

Somewhere in the water a fish broke the surface and splashed. The sound was loud even within the millions of night calls going on. It rolled over the surface of the water and I could imagine it being carried down the lake and well into Arkansas.

I climbed down the little aluminum ladder and paused at the window into the cabin. Nelson was inside sleeping. My lonely vigil up top had been longer than I thought. For a couple of minutes I watched him. Half of me wanted him to wake and see me. The other half wanted him to keep sleeping. That part cherished the anger I still felt and wanted to milk it a while longer.

I needed another beer or something stronger, so I went into the dark shop.

"I wondered how long it would be," my father said. He was sitting at the table with a beer open in front of him.

"Were you so sure I would come in here?" I asked. Even to me my voice sounded petulant and pushy.

"Yep."

"How?"

He studied me from the shadows. I couldn't see his face exactly; just the outline, but it was enough. I knew for a certainty that whatever he said to me was going to be perfectly reasonable, not unkind, but would sting. It would also be completely true. His hand reached forward to grip the neck of the sweating beer bottle. He held it between his thumb and two fingers and swirled the last quarter of the liquid around. Then he drank it all, turning the bottle up and finishing with a satisfied sigh.

"This is where the beer is," he said. Quite reasonable. Quite true.

"Yes," was all I could say.

"This was the last one." The bottle hit the tabletop with a hard *thunk.* "I couldn't drink them all. I had to pour some out. Your uncle's going to be a little put out with me, but what else is new?"

"Why would you do that?"

"You have to ask?"

I didn't, but I wasn't in the mood for admissions.

"You have a problem," he said. "It's not insurmountable and it's not the end of the world, but it has to be addressed before it consumes you."

"You think I'm a drunk?" I asked. It was both a question and an accusation.

"No," he answered, reasonable and not unkind. "I think you have a million reasons to drink. If you deal with them you won't need to drink anymore." He smiled and then said, "Then you can drink for fun. Like me."

"You think it's that easy?"

"Nothing's easy." He was still smiling.

"I've got a therapist, you know. I don't need another. It's her job to deal with my problems."

"No," he said, dropping the smile. "It's your job. Have you been working at it as hard as you could?"

I didn't say anything back. What could I say? I didn't like therapy. I liked hitting people and getting drunk. At least sometimes I thought I did.

Then he asked, "Can you handle the burden you're adding on?"

My cheeks flushed with heat and my eyes brimmed with tears. I didn't like where this was going at all but I was afraid of walking away.

What I finally ended up saying was, "That's none of your business."

Dad smiled and said, "It is. Of course it is. You will never be none of my business."

What he said made me think of the Briscoe family. Longing and loss, love violently truncated. I wondered: If I could see my father's eyes, how much would they look like David Briscoe's? All these years I had denied him the chance to know his daughter's pain. Sharing always has a bit of the selfish to it, but I couldn't see if it was more selfish to share the truth with him or to keep it from him.

It didn't matter because that was not the time. Nelson was the elephant standing in our room.

"I'm sorry," I said.

"I know."

Finally, with a deep preparatory breath, I told him, "I don't know what to do."

He pulled out the chair beside him, making room for me. I sat down and all the words fell from my mouth like they had been teetering on my teeth, waiting for me to stop balancing them. I gave him a synopsis of the past couple of days: the murder, the whiskey, meeting Nelson, beating the boy. All of it came spilling out and when it was finished pouring and it was just talk—the talk was all about Nelson.

When I told him about the gun I had found, I ran out of words and energy. I ended up saying, "I don't know how I feel." I'm pretty sure Dad heard the lie in my voice. Then I said, "I don't know what to do." And we both knew that was the truth.

"Do about what?" he asked. Dad was all about precision. "How you feel or how your feelings are going to hurt you?"

"It already hurts."

"Oh, honey, the hurt hasn't even started. This—" He gestured around the darkness with a hand showing nothing and everything. "All of this—is the sweet hurt. A life well lived hurts like hell. That's why I don't believe in that kind of afterlife. Who needs it?"

"If this is the sweet stuff I'm not sure I can handle anything more."

"That's the choice you have to make, isn't it?"

"What do you think I should do?"

"I think you ought to like him. A lot. I think you should help him and be kind and care. . . ."

"But?"

"But he's hurt waiting to happen. If you can't take it, it's not fair to him to keep it going. Is it? He damn sure can't take it. Maybe that's the question. Which one of you is the strong one?"

"A relationship where I'm the strong one? That's hard to imagine."

"You're strong, sweetheart. You're just like your mother. It would be so much easier if she was here for you to talk to. She didn't know her strength, either."

"You never talk about her."

"The end was one of those hard hurts. Something that takes your wind and leaves you gasping. It's hard to talk about even the good stuff without feeling some of the hurt again."

"What if you didn't have to go through it? What if you knew about the breast cancer when you met her?"

"What-ifs are just that—what if? But I'll tell you, if I knew—I would have made all the time we had even better."

I kissed my dad on the cheek and hugged him hard. It reminded me how badly I wanted to kiss Nelson.

"Good night," I said and headed for the houseboat. Dad didn't say anything, but when I got to the door I heard the hiss of a beer bottle opening. "I thought you said they were gone?"

"I lied. Dads are allowed."

"Hey, I thought you said we were going to handle my problems?"

"We are. You only really have the one. Everything else is just part of it."

"And what's that, Dr. Freud?"

"Fear, sweetheart. You are afraid. That's what I've been telling you. Life is kind of an angry bitch. She fights you every step for every piece of joy in your life. Being afraid of the hits she gives won't make her hit any less or any less hard. It just makes you miss the joy."

Nelson was sound asleep when I got back in the cabin. Even with the lake below us and a cool breeze sneaking through the windows, it was hot inside. He was sleeping shirtless and without covers. Boxers only. I decided to take life by the balls, but in only the most loving of ways. He woke smiling and we stayed close and naked the rest of the night.

Chapter 13

Wednesday came early to the dock. Nelson was up before the sun and painting when the first light bruised the east. Uncle Orson was up and banging around doing chores he had put off with guests. Dad helped him by netting out the dead minnows from the live-bait well and spreading coffee grounds over the two worm beds. Uncle Orson replaced missing bumpers on some of the boat slips. That sounds like it might be quiet but it involved nailing sections of old tire to deck planks. At least I wasn't hungover.

As much as I love my time on the houseboat and dock, the bathroom is a real limiting factor, especially on a workday. I slipped out and went home long enough to shower and dress for work. I came back to the dock, kissed Dad and Uncle Orson good-bye, and then took Nelson to get his truck out of impound. We agreed to have dinner together at his place. I would be there at six.

My morning was paperwork. I had to fill out reports and time logs. There were routine cases and dead-end investigations to be summarized and filed. All of the busywork was to keep my hands occupied and allow my mind to process. I always seemed to think best when I had two tasks: one routine or done by rote, the other purely mental. If I'm not thinking about thinking, my brain will sort things out on its own.

There was a line, I was sure, that lead between Byron Figorelli and the bikers and it somehow passed through Nelson, Johnny Middleton, and finally, Angela. That line was written in whiskey somehow or another.

I made a call to the agent in charge of liquor control for the Missouri Department of Public Safety in the southwest district. Voice mail. After that I called the City of Branson Finance Department to get information about Moonshines. I got a live person but she had to take a message. A few calls later and I gave up and turned to e-mail. When I had contacted everyone on my list I made my summary report for the sheriff—longhand on a legal pad—and left it on his desk.

I needed to talk to someone face-to-face if not voice-to-voice, and one person I could be reasonably sure of finding was Byron Figorelli. It was a good idea and it worked—almost.

When I arrived at the parking lot to Moonshines, the big RV was taking up most of the back end. I parked out front but stayed in the car. At the RV's door was a man wearing a cowboy hat and a black suit with rhinestones and cow-skull appliques. There was something about him that made me think I'd seen him before. I just couldn't remember where.

The man in the suit had a look of restrained anger. He had one foot on the asphalt and the other up on the RV's step, but he wasn't going anywhere. He was standing firm and giving Figorelli a talking-to, punctuating his remarks with a long finger. I knew from experience that Byron Figorelli didn't take that kind of interaction well. This time he was taking it and keeping quiet. A couple of times he tried to open his mouth but the other man just kept talking and pointing. When it was over, the shiny cowboy went to a car and drove away quickly. When I approached the door of the RV, Figorelli and Cardo were just coming out and locking the door behind them.

"Who's your fancy friend?" I asked.

"Hey, look who it is," Figorelli said, nudging Jimmy Cardo, who still had the key in the lock. "It's the dyke with the big stick."

Cardo smiled without mirth. It was an expression meant to insult and it worked. But I kept my cool.

"No answer for me, then?" I tried again.

"What can I say." He shrugged his huge shoulders. "You're just not asking very interesting questions."

"Interesting, huh? Would it be interesting to talk some more about Johnny Middleton?"

"He was a drug-addicted redneck creep that thought he was somebody. What's interesting about that?"

"Is that all?"

"No." Figorelli held out his hand and Cardo gave him the key. He pocketed it, then said, "Johnny was a one-hundred-percent douche bag. You want to know anything more?"

"You always do business with douche bags?"

"I do business with money. Not people. Johnny's problem was he couldn't stick to the money at hand. He always kept trying to reach into another pot."

"I can see how that could be a bad habit."

"Fuckin' A."

"Is that what got him killed?"

Figorelli looked right into my eyes for the first time. Cardo stared from over his shoulder, still smiling that lifeless show of crooked teeth.

"You asking me if that was what got him dead, or if *I* killed him for it? Because me and Cardo here were enjoying the local highlife all day long. But you know that."

"Some people kill with the gun and some with the word. Maybe that's why you took advantage of the local highlife, *such as it is*. So everyone would know where you were when Johnny got popped."

"You seen too many movies, Detective. Are we through here? I've got some things need taking care of."

"I'm sure whatever it is can wait for one more question. What's Leech mean to you?"

"Leech?" He repeated the word without understanding. "What the fuck is *leech*? Another redneck delicacy?" He laughed as much at me as at what he'd said. It was meaningless to him.

"Listen," he said. "There's no hard feelings here. You come on by Moonshines and it's all on me. And tell your boyfriend, I'll be talking to him. We got business to settle."

"He told you *no*. Seems to me it's pretty settled."

"Things change," he said. "We're partners now that Johnny bought it. Maybe now he's ready to let go. He can just retire and paint. Leave work to the regular slobs like me."

I couldn't tell if he was telling me something or just talking to hear himself. I did latch on to one word, though. "Partners?"

"See, you don't know everything, do you? I bet your boyfriend don't, either. Johnny borrowed money from me. He secured it with his share of Moonshines. Funny thing is—Johnny didn't tell boyfriend about me. He sure didn't tell me about boyfriend. Things have a way of coming out in the wash, know what I mean? You ask me, a guy like that—he's just looking for what he got."

"You're a class act, Figorelli. I don't care who says different."

"Class, huh? Like this whole state—peckerwoods, crappy music, and bikers. That's where Johnny had problems. Why aren't you hassling those shitbirds?"

I didn't answer. I left him standing there staring at me as I walked away.

After rattling the cage with Figorelli, I decided to check on another cage. Our jail is run by a 300-pound former deputy who seemed to care less with every pound he added. His name, Donald Duques, condemned him at an early age to be known only as "Duck." He was friendly to me in some bizarre, old-school way that seemed to assume that no observation or comment was off-limits. It took me a while to understand how to handle him. Turns out, he likes it mean and feisty right back, so . . .

"What's up, Duck?" I asked at his wire-mesh cage.

"What's got up you, Hurricane?" he said, winking. Even that little movement made his chins wiggle. "Someone good, I hope."

"You know I'm just waiting for you to lose enough weight so we can find things."

"Oh, funny girl. You be careful what you go looking for. It's liable to be more than you can handle. Now, what you wantin' in my jail?"

"Besides you?"

"Even an old man's got his dreams."

"Figorelli or that other guy, Cardo," I reminded him. "Visitors? Phone calls?"

"Figorelli made one call after processing. Then they both settled in to wait. They acted like it was a party. Met with a lawyer couple of hours later. Guy in a shiny suit. It wasn't much of a party after that. They made bail at arraignment the next morning. Cash. Never heard a peep out of them otherwise."

I nodded and worked through the timing in my head. A couple of hours after they got here someone shot at Middleton and missed. No better alibi than being in custody. "Anything at all strike you as strange?"

"What do I know from strange when it comes to the lowlifes? Most of them only talk about freedom to live the way they want, but keep doing the things that put them inside. You ask me, half the world has some kind of defective gene."

"Okay. Thanks for your insights into the human condition. Do you have the kid?" I asked. "Barnes?"

"Juvenile segregation and suicide watch. He just sits there staring at the wall and marking it up."

"Marking? With what?"

"Either he had a coin we didn't catch when we searched him or he found one in the cell. He was using it to scratch things in the paint. As if this place needed more decoration."

"I want to talk to him."

Duck looked me over like I was an attractive mule who had just asked him to dance. He seemed to be weighing the pros and cons.

"It's your case, but you know a kid with no parents and no lawyer—anything he says won't make it into court."

"I know the drill," I told him. "I'm going to talk to him, not question."

"Explain the difference and you could be his lawyer too. But there's the other thing."

"The other thing?"

"They say you went all God's vengeance on the kid. Not that he didn't deserve it. Still, I ain't lettin' you in the cell with him and I'm not putting him in an interview room alone with you. Other than that, it's your case—go on and fuck it up."

Duck was an ass but he wasn't wrong. Keeping the kid out of my reach was just good sense that protected me, Danny, and Duck. He was right about the interview as well. Anything Danny said to me could not be used. Even though he'd been Mirandized, he was a juvenile. Parents or his lawyer had to be in the room if I wanted information that could be used against him. But that wasn't what I wanted.

"Hello, Danny," I said from just beyond his cell door.

"I don't have to talk to you," he said instantly. His tone was surly and defensive and he practically spit the words out.

"No, you don't," I answered. "But I thought I'd try."

"Try what?"

"Just talking, Danny."

"You had no right to hit me like that. Sneaky bitch. I coulda kicked your ass if you didn't sneak up on me."

I already wanted to pull him out and give him another beating. Instead I said, "Threatening people, especially cops, isn't the way to help your case, is it?"

I waited for an answer but he just pushed his shoulder deeper into the corner and stared at the painted brick. The area above his wall-mounted bed was scratched with fresh marks. Danny worked hard while he had his coin. He had written Carrie's name several times over and in different ways. The only thing featured more prominently was the name, Leech. In places the right angle and arrows were incorporated into the name and in others it stood alone like clock hands, eternally frozen fifteen minutes apart.

"Has Carrie been to see you?"

"Of course not. I'll never see her again until she gets away from her mother. You made sure of that."

"What do you mean, *gets away*?" I asked.

"When she's eighteen. Then she can walk out of there and never look back. Then she'll come be with me."

"Be with you? In jail?"

"I won't go to jail."

I wasn't sure if the fact that he was already in a jail was lost on him or if he was clear-thinking enough to mean he would not go to prison.

"Why are you sure you won't go to jail?"

"You don't know anything. When I'm out of here I'm going to sue you and the cops. You'll be sorry and I'll be rich and you won't be talking down to me anymore."

"Danny, I'm sorry if you think I'm talking down to you. I don't mean to. I'm just trying to understand."

"You can't understand. Not yet. You will, though, when I get what's coming to me."

"What's coming to you, Danny?"

"Everything I want," he said, growling with energy now. For the first time he came out of the corner and off the bed. His eyes were jittery in his head like he didn't know where to look or maybe he saw something I couldn't. Something moving. Danny stood at the door to his cell with his hands at his sides and his face knotted in concentration. "I get everything. And I get Carrie. Rewards come to the ones who serve the best and that's us. We did everything and we get everything. When she has the baby then you'll see."

It would be easy to say the kid's train had skipped the tracks. There were a couple of bits of information to follow up on, though. Was Carrie Owens pregnant? And who was it he thought he was serving?

I didn't get the answers from him. I didn't get any more from him at all that time. Danny stood still in front of his door and just darted his eyes at the rest of my questions. I didn't get the feeling that he was mentally troubled. It just gave the impression that he was being a smart-ass, acting crazy.

After my time in the jail I wanted to be outside. Since none of my calls had panned out, I decided to check up on Clare. He wasn't at his home but I had an idea of where to find him that I wanted to check out. Friday, while Nelson was being tended to by the EMTs, I had wandered to the cliff over which he had been painting. I had seen a bit of white smoke curling up from under a canopy of oak, walnut, and hawthorn. It was a clean white smoke, seasoned wood. The fact that there was smoke at all suggested to me it was a new fire, not yet hot enough for full combustion. At the time I didn't think a lot about it, but it struck me that Clare would have to build up his new still camp after being run off.

It took a little prowling around but I found him about where I expected to. The new camp was more compact than the last and the spring it was alongside was smaller, but even clearer, if possible. Driving up, I caught Clare building up a new compost bin.

"You're the only environmentally conscious moonshiner I've ever heard of, Clare," I said as I got out of the SUV.

"We're not all toothless bumpkins with no worldview."

"Worldview?" I asked. "I think you're one up on me."

"I come from a long line of farmers. My granddaddy went bust in the Dust Bowl days. Most of that was because the land was used in ignorance. All those old guys learned from their mistakes and built the land back up."

"So your worldview is hillbilly hippie? How does that set with tax evasion and unregulated production of controlled substances?"

"Did you know I was a teacher?" I must have looked surprised because he laughed to see the expression. "Yep. High school history for twenty years. Before that, I was a *different* kind of teacher." Both the tone of his voice and look on his face said there was a story there.

He shrugged them off and asked, "Wanna know another secret? Most of my life I've voted Democrat."

It was my turn to laugh and Clare joined in. As far as I knew, no Democrat had won an office in Taney County in the last fifty years.

"I'd appreciate it if you didn't let that get around," he said. "I *am* what you call a fiscal conservative, but since I take some social liberties of my own I would hate to take them from anyone else."

"Okay," I said. "You're a renaissance man. Are you trying to make a point?"

"I am. Taxes should be paid, but not as a means to control individuals and benefit industries. Regulations are important because industries put profit and shareholders above the resources they should be stewarding. I'm a good steward and I run a homegrown business that hurts no one and helps those I do business with."

"You like to give the same kinds of lectures as my uncle."

"Orson's a good man, but I'm not just flapping my gums. There's something about that distillery restaurant."

"Moonshines?"

"Yeah. The way I understood it they had to jump through lots of hoops to get licenses."

"Well, the liquor industry is heavily regulated."

"That's the thing. This place is outside of the industry. I said *lots of hoops* but I didn't say difficult ones. Something is rotten with that place because the kind of people who would shut me down in a second don't look twice at a place like that."

"Rotten?"

"As Denmark," he said.

"What about other moonshiners? Are they getting the same pressure to stop?"

"Almost everyone I know has stopped. Or, like me, they moved deeper into the woods to cook and it's mostly about the cooking. The doing what you want and waving the big screw-you at everyone else. Hardly anyone is selling."

"Why's that?"

"Beats me," he said, shrugging. He put a hand on the side of his compost bin to check the sturdiness. It held. "But there are two possibilities as I see it. Either the people who buy are scared to do it, or they're getting it at a better price."

I thought of Byron Figorelli. "There's another option," I said. "They could be scared and taking the price they're given."

Clare shook his head and looked out over his camp. "That's the old days. And stuff like that is about the money. I made a profit of about seven grand last year. Most of the guys I know do a lot less. It's just not worth it."

Maybe he was right but it bore looking into. When I got my information back from the e-mails and phone messages from that morning I would have more to go on. One thing for certain: Figorelli was in it for the money. So where's the money coming from?

After leaving Clare I went up the road to Carrie Owens's home. That was when I walked face-first into the connection I'd been looking for. The door opened quickly, forcing out a wash of air. It carried a heavy smell of cigarettes and sour beer. For the first time I was face-to-face with Carrie's mother. She was the same woman I'd seen on the back of Leech's bike.

Mrs. Owens wasn't happy to see me. "Go away," she said as soon as she saw me. "I don't want to talk to you."

I was stunned. I stood there with my mouth hanging open for a moment, waiting for more tumblers to fall into place. They didn't. Nothing magically opened up to show me the whole story. I finally managed to shut my mouth and say, "I have some questions."

"I don't care," she said and tried to close the door. I put my hand up and held it open.

"We can do it here and friendly, or we can go in and make it official."

"What do you even want from me?"

"May I step inside?" I asked, trying to sound reasonable about it. She said, "No."

"What's Leech's name?"

It was her turn to stand openmouthed. Her surprise was not at all what I'd expected.

"Leech," she said as a statement, not a question.

"Yes," I said. "I want his name and how to find him."

"Leech," she said again.

"Yeah, Leech," I said back, getting a little exasperated. "I need his name."

"Are you a crazy woman?"

"What?" She surprised me a second time.

"Leech is just some made-up kid thing. There ain't no other name."

I didn't let my mouth gape that time but it was an effort. I'd made so many assumptions based on a name carved on some trees. It was like Danny and Carrie had seen me coming.

"The biker," I said. Her eyes got large and she looked past me, glancing each way up the street.

"How do you know? Who's been talking about me?"

"I saw you. You were on the back of his bike at my dock."

She stared blankly. She didn't remember and I believed it. She'd looked like she was on something at the time.

"What's *his* name?" I asked.

"Riley. Riley Pruitt," she said. As easy as that.

If I hadn't spent all that time chasing an imaginary Leech, I probably would have had him by now. I pulled out my notebook and wrote the name down, then asked, "Where can I find Mr. Pruitt?"

"How the hell should I know? He shows up when he shows." She craned her neck, trying to see the length of the street around me.

I couldn't tell if she was trying to see if the neighbors were watching or if she was expecting someone. "Is he on his way here?"

Like a kid caught peeking at something she shouldn't, Mrs. Owens pulled her head back and centered her gaze at about my collarbone. "What do you want? We're good people." Then she looked me in the eyes, a slow thought blooming in her face. "This is just between us, isn't it? It doesn't have to be public?"

"It depends—"

"I have a husband."

"I know."

"It's not like you think. Everything is over. You know, all but the paperwork. But I have a chance with Riley."

"Right now, I think you might be more concerned about your daughter."

"She can stay with her dad. This ain't about her. It's about me."

"Ma'am, I don't think you understand."

"No, that's not a good idea, is it?"

She wasn't really listening to me. There was some kind of selfish dialogue playing in her head, making plans and excuses.

"*Ma'am,*" I said, firm as a smack. "I need to talk to Riley Pruitt about the murder of Angela Briscoe. You need to help me find him."

"No," she said. "No. You got Danny. You got the little bastard that's been around my girl. Who knows what all he's done. But you got him. He's the one."

"I still need to talk to Pruitt."

"This can't be happening."

"And I need to talk to Carrie, too."

"What?" That brought a new focus to her eyes. "What for?"

"She lied to me. She's involved with Danny Barnes."

"Leave her out of it," she said with a fire building under her words.

"I can't do that, ma'am."

"We'll hire a lawyer," she threatened. "Don't think we won't." That point she emphasized with a bony finger pointed right at my chest.

"Ma'am, I don't believe your daughter is accused of any crime," I tried to tell her.

"People—good people—good names get dragged through the papers and that stink don't come off once it sticks to your family. People don't know, but they think they do."

"Mrs. Owens, no one is saying anything about your family." I tried hard to sound calm and reassuring.

She stopped for a moment and looked at me like I had just appeared before her in a flash of light. Then she put her fingers—thin with big, red knuckles—up to smooth her tousled hair. "Why would they?" she asked quietly. The smoothing became a kind of nervous tugging. "What's there to say about a good family?"

"It would really help if I could talk with Carrie, ma'am."

Mrs. Owens hissed at me like you would to shoo a cat, then she said, "We don't need your talk. We are private people. Private stays in family."

"Ma'am—"

"You go," she hissed again.

I tried to give her another card and ask her to call, but she shoved it back and told me to stay out of her family's life. Not out of her daughter's life, out of her family's life. Under the circumstances it wasn't an odd choice of words and certainly not strange for the woman hissing her distrust at me, but still . . .

I thought about it as I walked back toward the parked SUV. When I glanced back I saw Carrie looking out a window at me. Her face was carved and motionless. When I smiled and raised my hand to wave, she lifted her middle finger, flipping me off without the smallest trace of feeling.

I used the radio in the unit to call into Darlene. I requested a family services visit to the Owens home and I asked for a unit to park out front for the rest of the day and keep an eye out for Riley Pruitt. I also requested a search of the system for Pruitt so it would be waiting when I got into the office. Once off the radio, I called the sheriff's cell. He didn't pick up, so I left a message telling him about the situation. Then I called back and told him that I thought there was something more going on with Danny and Carrie.

Once I was finished, I considered taking Mrs. Owens in for a more formal interrogation. It only took a second to talk myself out of it. Honestly, I didn't think I would learn anything more. Besides, the last thing I wanted was to further disturb what little home life Carrie had. The image of the boat Nelson had painted flashed in my mind. It floated, untethered, in a confused light. I understood it a little better.

Dave Briscoe came out of his house before I started the SUV. His face was as hard and lifeless as Carrie's had been, but in a different way. Her face was a mask hiding feelings. His was feeling carved in place.

"We heard about what you did," he said. "We appreciate you getting him."

If he had it in him to wink, I think he would have. What I did, in his book, was to beat the kid that hurt his daughter. How could I say to him that it wasn't about his daughter? It was my own weakness.

The last thing Dave Briscoe cared about was my weakness or my guilt. He pointed over at the Owens's house and said, "We used to let that girl come over and stay with Angela because we felt sorry for her. We even took her to church."

"Why did you feel sorry for her?" I asked even though I was sure I knew.

"That family. The mother's a hair-trigger lunatic and the father is one of those sad sacks who never seem to get it right but always thinks he knows the answers. He has someone to blame for everything you can bring up."

"I don't guess he was home."

"He's never home. His job is something about oil-well equipment. He travels a lot to sell it or fix it, I don't know. But it was better before affirmative action, he'll let you know that. To hear him tell it, no white, Christian man ever got a fair shake."

"I wonder if you know his feelings about discipline."

Briscoe looked at me. His face remained hard and still, but his eyes flashed a trace of feeling before he said, "No, I don't exactly. But I've always had my suspicions."

Chapter 14

The sheriff called back late that night and agreed with my decision not to pull Carrie's mother in. He chatted distractedly for a bit about the cases. We were in agreement that the overlap between Angela Briscoe and bootlegging was a bizarre coincidence. He kept on talking long after he'd exhausted his purpose and I was about to ask him what was wrong. Before I could, he said, "You cancelled a therapy appointment."

"Yes," I admitted.

"I made a new one for you. Tomorrow morning."

"But—"

"Same time, same place," he said. "Be there or don't sign back in."

What could I say to that?

Therapy day. For the first time I was almost looking forward to it. Not because I needed help. What I needed was a break from a case and a life that seemed to have imploded on me.

I had spent the night before with Nelson on the houseboat. I had gotten closer and wanted more, but there had come a moment that teetered between bliss and terror. I had seen in his eyes and the soft look in his face what he was going to say.

It should have been a warm moment. A hot one, even, when the passion spilled over from joy. What I felt was a cold wind. Nelson had the word *love* on his lips and I stopped him with a kiss. One of us had to be sane. His feelings were the result of desperation more than of me. It was a sad thought and maybe not very generous to either one of us. Love at first sight happens in movies and when people are thrust into extraordinary circumstances. Those circumstances are usually intense and short-lived. So are the feelings.

I covered his mouth with mine and pushed my tongue inside, forcing another kind of heat into the passion. My own desperation.

It worked. I kept his mouth too busy to speak until he was exhausted and drifting off on the pillow beside me. Yes, I had used sex to distract and manipulate. Yes, as I went to sleep beside him, I felt pretty good about it. Nelson wouldn't complain. I worried about the morning, though.

As it happened, there was no reason to worry. The sheriff had lied. Maybe not a lie, but he was wrong, at least. Darlene called to let me know that my appointment wasn't at the same time. Since I was being fit in, it was in the late afternoon, not the morning. That gave me an excuse to get in and to work, avoiding the possibility of a declaration of love over breakfast. It turned out it wouldn't have mattered. Nelson said he had another appointment with his lawyer and was seeing a new doctor in the afternoon. At that point the whole thing turned around on me. Ignoring the sheriff's threat, I offered to skip my therapy session to go with him to the doctor. It was Nelson who squirmed out.

So I got what I wanted, which was not the therapy but time to plow through documents about Moonshines and the growing pile of arrest sheets on the Ozarks Nightriders. On top of that pile was Riley Pruitt. He'd done time for distribution—mostly meth—interstate trafficking of controlled substances, extortion, weapons charges, and domestic violence. It turned out that he was the founding member of the Nightriders.

To finish things at the desk, I made a call and followed up with e-mail to the Branson police department requesting to be copied on all material relating to the shooting at Moonshines. The city detective sent a few pages right away and promised more when he had them typed out. I took what he had and went to find the witnesses and ask some of my own questions.

The interviews were useless. The witnesses had seen Cotton Lambert push Middleton aside and heard the shot. No one admitted to seeing the shooter.

It was quick work, so afterward I stopped at the county courthouse. Since I had not yet gotten the materials I'd requested on Moonshines and the arrangement they had to distill whiskey, I thought I'd do some digging of my own. It only took a few minutes to understand why I'd not gotten a quick response. There were hundreds of pages. That was just the county. There had to be similar bundles registered with the City of Branson and the State of Missouri.

I filled the rest of the workday with the normal grind of investigation. I read until I was bleary eyed. With each page I alternately cursed lawyers and wished I had one to guide me. I was grateful to stop and start the trip up to Springfield and my appointment.

Driving there was great, just what I needed: Clean, rushing air thick with the scent of summer growth combined with the smooth speed of the truck and the oldies station to take me on a ride that was more unknowing my problems than forgetting them.

The problem with rides is that they always come to an end. Sometimes that end brings you to a smug, humorless woman with a lot of letters after her name who flicks her high heels and purses her perfectly colored lips as if to tell you how a real woman should look while she dissects and orders your life into neat rows of scribbles on her notepad. Not that her amazing shoes and expensive skirts have ever made me feel less than happy with my jeans and boots lifestyle.

She always asks me why I think violence will solve my problems. I always tell her it doesn't, it solves other people's. That day though, she didn't ask me about anything at first. She told me that she had been notified by the sheriff about my additional requirements. Everyone knew what happened to bring that about, I imagined, so I didn't volunteer anything.

"You seem more annoyed than usual to be here," she said.

"No more. No less," I said.

"Tell me about your week." That was how she often started and just as often ended. I hated the question and the implication that there were telling events secreted away in my life in the week since I had last seen her. All my problems were obvious, even to me. And they all happened years ago. All she ever wanted to talk about was now.

That time I let her have it. I spilled everything. Without holding back, I put it all out there and every word carried me a little deeper into my anger. By anyone's standards I figured it was a pretty eventful week. Honestly, it was chafing me a little that she wasn't acting the least bit impressed. At the end of outlining my week I was pretty heated. If life were a Warner Bros. cartoon, my head would have turned into a thermometer that went up and up until the mercury boiled, then burst.

"So that's my life since we last talked," I said with a bit of the dramatic to punctuate my thoughts on the subject. "That's what I had going on and pulling me six different directions. Seven, if you count having to come here to spill it all to you."

"You're angry."

"Is it any wonder? Every time I get a little peace, every time I feel like I'm close to dealing with the problems in my life, someone or something brings it all back. I can't escape."

"Do you want to?"

"That's why I'm here, isn't it?"

"You're here because the sheriff's department required it."

"All of a sudden you have a sense of humor?" I asked.

"All of a sudden you don't?"

I swear the corner of her perfectly red lips flicked up into a smile.

"You're pushing," I said. "Why? Why today?"

She pointed her nose back down into the notebook and read to me, *"Every time I feel like I'm close to dealing with the problems in my life, someone or something brings it all back."* Then she turned her face back up to me and finished. *"I can't escape."*

It felt like an accusation even though she read it with the kind of feeling usually reserved for stock quotes. I didn't know how to respond or even if I should, so I sat there looking at her, waiting for the other immaculate high heel to drop.

She waited too, but she was better at it or at least not feeling put on the spot. Either way, it was me who broke and asked, "What are you trying to say? Because I know you're saying something."

That time she didn't look into the book to repeat the words. She kept her gaze locked on me. *"Every time I feel like I'm close to dealing with the problems in my life..."* She waited again and I squirmed. Then she asked me, "Have you ever really dealt with anything in your life?"

"What the hell?" I said. "Of course I do. You know I do. It's why I'm here. It's why—everything. I deal with it every day. I *live* with it every day."

"See that's the thing," she said in that infuriating, quiet voice. "I don't think you do. I don't think you deal with it and I know you don't live with it."

"Kiss my ass," I said in a quiet voice of my own. I don't think she heard me.

"You live it. Not *with* it. There is a big difference."

"What would you know about it?"

"Enough to know when someone is lying to herself and loving the lie."

I crossed my arms in front of my chest and gave her the kind of look that warns most people off. She set aside the notebook and gazed back at me with the kind of look that I think was intended to draw me in. She gave up first.

"You told me all about your week. All the events and people and transitions, fear, violence, romance—it's been like a movie and then you complain about how all that has gotten in the way of dealing with your life."

The arms in front of my chest felt heavy.

"Your life." She said it in a way that I could hear the period and the dismissal of it at the same time. "You've made your whole life one episode. You wallow in it. You wrap yourself up in it like a blanket that you hide under when the storms come. Maybe you do that because if you live in that pain, nothing will ever hurt like that again."

"Yeah, thanks, Oprah," I said, but my arms were no longer crossed and I wasn't feeling quite so righteous in my anger. "So why are you telling me this now?"

"Don't be silly," she said. "I've told you a hundred times. What's different now?"

"I don't know."

"Maybe this time you have another life worth living. Something worth giving up the pain for."

I hated her. I hated that woman and her perfect clothes, her perfect makeup, and quiet voice. I hated her so much that morning that I didn't go see Dad or go to breakfast. I just drove. With the windows down and hot wind in my hair I traveled through green landscapes and broken roads to find moments of yesterdays—the time before. What I really hated her for was planting the seed that made me feel guilty for feeling so bad. Ever since the moment two men dragged me from a tent and spent the night, then morning, raping me and carving my skin, I have hated, and blamed, and feared, and cried, and lived in that shadow. I knew what she was saying. I just rejected it. Or I wanted to reject it.

Rice and Ahrens did those things to me.

They had created the pain and the harm.

The shadow after it—

Could the shadow of dust-choked winds be something I did?

I drove and I hated and I cried.

When I didn't call in or show up, Darlene called me. I told her I wasn't coming in. I didn't give a reason or ask if it would be a problem, nor did I say *thank you* when she marked me down as having called in sick. I simply crawled deeper inward and drove.

So many roads and thoughts passed under the tires of my truck that I lost track of everything but the soothing motion. I didn't want to eat but I did want to drink. Because of that, I kept going. If I stopped for gas or food I would end up drunk and fired or dead. Maybe more crying. That thought was worse than any of the others. I was cried out and angered out.

Numb.

Numb was good. Feeling was tiring. Thinking was worse. Hours and miles melded into an undefinable passage that took me nowhere and gave nothing back. It simply passed. Shadows lengthened and I noticed in the same way I noticed road signs that warned of curves ahead. Under the trees, dark solidified much quicker than it did in the sky, but all was dark before I noticed.

The road ahead was so black that it was as if I existed only within the reach of my headlights. Anything beyond their reach was void. It was almost a comfort. My window was still open and the wind, with occasional cool fingers, blew over my face, even sliding up my sleeve and billowing under my shirt. It was a little like being touched by an old lover eager to reacquaint himself with my body. I didn't want to think about love or lovers, I told myself. I didn't want to think anymore. It was good just to exist in my bubble of light flying through the void of night.

Occasionally an animal, an opossum or raccoon, would be caught at the edge of my lights. When it happened their eyes would reflect back, unblinking green questions I ignored.

I didn't want it. I didn't search it out. Still, the desert and dust came into my bubble and drew me away into its. Darkness became light like a negative of a photograph. Moving foliage swirled into clouds of razor-edged grit. The moment. My eternal moment.

All my color bleeding away.

Did I cry when they ripped the clothes from me? Did I beg? I couldn't recall, but I believed I must have. Afterward, in the back of a Humvee, the corpsman's eyes were wide with fear and embarrassment. He had never worked on a woman before and certainly never one so intimately harmed. He looked all of nineteen.

Working as quickly as he could, he followed the lines of cuts on my body and filled them with hemostatic powder. When he cut my pants off and spread my naked legs to pack those wounds, his eyes rimmed with tears. While he touched me and bound the lacerations that could be bound, he talked. Mostly he said everything would be all right. He said it like a mantra more for himself than me.

"It'll be all right."

"We'll take care of you."

"Don't worry, we'll get you to the field hospital and they'll take good care of you."

"Everything will be all right."

He wouldn't look me in the eyes.

Outside, the thick, hard rubber of the Humvee's tires roared loudly on cratered asphalt. The machine itself groaned and squeaked almost as loudly. It was strong but unhappy with the loads it carried.

So many of the bad things in life come from the actions we choose. Genetics or environment—take your pick—seem to prime some of us for becoming the victims of our own destructive natures. Fate. I don't believe in it. Whenever fate rears its ugly head you can be sure that there is some bit of unpredictable, random circumstance that had been looking for an accomplice. Every life has its own roulette. *Fortunada* spins her great wheel of chance, every number a land mine of vicious delight. She celebrates the mayhem.

Fortune and personal failings, God's gamble with every life.

As I was coming back to myself, back from the brown void to the dark road, I thought I had come through. The day that had thumbed its nose at me was passing. I was whole and sober. There was a man who would be waiting for me and I was ready to put my mark on the *win* column. I could have if I'd been able to go straight to Nelson.

Headlights appeared behind me. *Appeared*, because they came around a bend and I noticed them for the first time. There was no saying how long they had been following.

Following.

I didn't know how, but I knew it. I knew it like I knew the desire for whiskey.

I drove and I watched. Proving to myself with each careful matching of pace and distance that I was being tracked. It didn't make me afraid, simply wary. And it made me want to drink. It wouldn't be the bikers because a single car was not their style. It could be Figorelli or one of his goons, but that kind of criminal doesn't usually get personal with cops. Most likely it was Reach.

I drove some more, working things through my head and only vaguely aware of running my finger over the scar around my left eye. No conclusions. No chance I was taking whoever it was to Nelson's house, either. More than I wanted answers or conclusions, I wanted to drink. Recognizing the desire in myself always made me ashamed. Not because I wanted to drink, but because I wanted to drink to be drunk. Drinking turned me into a different person. Before I take the first sip I always believe that person will be happy or at least not feel as bad as I do. I'm always wrong but that never changes the belief.

The car behind me was an excuse. I took the long way but I headed for Shep's bar.

Fortunada spun her wheel. My phone rang. It was a number and area code I didn't know. I should have let it go to voice mail, but I picked up. On the other end was a drunken voice that asked, "Lieutenant Williams?"

Every hair on my spine stood on end and I felt cold. "Who's this?" I asked.

"It *is* you." The voice sounded surprised.

"Who are you?" I used my command voice.

"Why won't you let me have my life?"

"What?"

"It was a long time ago," the voice said and I knew. "Why do I have to keep paying?"

"Ahrens," I said.

"I want my life back," said Michael Ahrens, the man who had cut a slice of skin out of me to take a prize of pubic hair. He was also the same man that shoved his fist and cadet ring inside me.

"I want my life back too," I said. "All of it."

He was crying; blubbering, really. In the background I could hear the noise of a public place, probably a bar. I had been drunk-dialed by one of the men that raped and left me for dead ten years ago.

"Make it stop," he pleaded.

I had imagined something like this a million times. All those times it felt good. In truth it felt something much less. People have always said revenge is best served cold, but this was not my revenge. The taste for it was gone; all the savory flavor I had anticipated, frigid and bland. I'm not the kind for a cold revenge, I realized. If I were to have it and have any feeling about it, the act would have to come while my blood was still hot.

"I can't make it stop," I told him. "I'm not doing it."

"You're lying," he yelled through the phone. In my mind I saw patrons of the bar stop what they were doing and stare at him like in a movie. "You're lying," he yelled again. "What am I supposed to do?"

"Live with it," I said and closed the connection.

It had been a day of rolling peaks and troughs, high waves that I usually smooth out with a few drinks. One would think the sound of drunkenness in Ahrens's voice would push that aside. I didn't want to be like him in any way. Even so, I couldn't help wondering how many times I had been that drunk and that desperate.

The car followed me to the liquor store. After that I stopped noticing it.

Chapter 15

That night I didn't go back to Nelson's place. I didn't go to the houseboat, either. I went home to Iraq. Isn't it funny how all the things you run hardest from are always waiting for you at the bottom of the bottle you reach for like life itself?

I went to Iraq but drove, once again, to the place where I had found Angela. The silence and the pain of the place drew me. The sense that nothing was over made me want to stay.

Nothing is ever over.

Down in the valley, at the lake level, cool air settled. Night mist formed on the upper layers of air, making wispy clouds that spread over the land. In places it could be as if you were a giant with your feet on the ground and your head in clouds. Driving with your window open, each layer licked across you as you followed the hills down toward the water. Where I was sitting I could see mist that formed on a ridge, white and ghost like in the moonlight. As it cooled it flowed over the edge and into the deeper valley where I was. It was just like dust in eddies flowing over a wall.

She was right. I hated thinking that. The therapist was saying the same things my father was saying. I was afraid and for some reason I couldn't walk away from the moment that put the fear into me.

But I can drink.

I did drink. That night, though, I didn't cry. I sat in the darkness, under a hot, starry sky watching mist creep in on silent feet, but I was seeing only cold dust and dirty daylight.

Watching colors bleed.

I didn't cry. I was looking my pain in the face and I wouldn't let it see me cry.

The whiskey that I had picked up was cheap but good enough. I never saw the car drive up. One moment I was alone, the next, lights washed over me glaring like an accusation. Between them and me stepped Major John Reach.

He opened the truck door and I didn't quite fall out.

"You're a disgrace," he said.

"Fuck you," was my answer.

"A cop, drunk and driving. A cop with a history. They'll take your badge."

"You want my badge?" I asked. "You can have it if you're man enough to take it." I grinned the challenge at him. "I don't think you can handle a real badge, though. It comes with responsibilities."

"You're a good example of that."

"You don't deserve to carry any kind of badge."

"You want to talk about deserving? I bet I wouldn't be the first to say that you deserved—"

I never heard the end of that thought. Not in Reach's words. I heard something else. It was probably not what he was going to say. It could have been a case of my whiskey putting words in his mouth. We'll never know. Things got fast and hazy after that.

First contact was a slap and a lot more than that. My hand was open but it didn't strike his face. The palm smacked hard against his ear. The impact and air pressure stunned, then disoriented him. Reach dropped to one knee with a hand held to the side of his face. I'm sure he thought it was over. What sane person would continue the assault?

What sane person would have started it?

He was vulnerable. I took advantage. With my hand on the back of his head I pulled him forward at the same time I kicked my knee up. His nose broke and gushed. I watched the blood spray, fanning out in the harsh beams of his headlights. It fell red. It splashed brown and fading into the dirt and gravel.

I put my foot on his throat and I added weight. It may or may not have been John Reach I was seeing myself kill. I don't remember and I don't think he'd say. I know I talked to him.

Someone.

I said a lot of things that I can't recall. The only part I do remember after I put my boot on his neck was pouring out what was left in my bottle all over his face and body. That is a clear memory because I recall thinking how lucky it was that I bought two bottles.

I must have let him go because I know I watched him drive away—fast, with me yelling behind him, "You better go find a cop."

After that I remember the sound of the empty bottle breaking. It wasn't loud because I had thrown it a long way. Then I heard the tiny *snip* sound of the tax seal breaking as I opened the other bottle.

At that point I wasn't a cop anymore. I had thrown that away just like everything else. If I hadn't been who I was—If I hadn't gotten that call—If I hadn't gotten drunk—If Reach hadn't goaded me—If—If—If—If the goddess of fortune had a kind bone in her skinny body—I slept in the truck and dreamed of my therapist in perfect heels spinning the great wheel of chance and looking at me with that smug smile that said it was all my fault.

When I woke, I drank. Then I slept again. It must have happened several times because the bottle kept getting lower.

Twice in one night a car seemed to appear from nowhere. That time there were no lights in my face, though. It was parked close. I could clearly hear the ticking of the engine as it cooled. It was Billy's car. He didn't get out. I imagined him in there sucking his soda as I drained my bottle.

We all have our crutches.

At another time either the car went away again or I did. Either way it was gone from sight or notice, leaving a vacancy behind that was more real than the thing itself. The moon shifted and stars cycled in their slow path, shining flakes of diamond dust that told me that everything was like everything else. Still, I drank without crying.

When the car returned it was no longer Billy's cruiser. It was a Humvee. Idling hot with all doors open, it waited. Scoured olive with hulking, deep tread tires that were blacker than drunken confessions, it was the only thing in the world with daylight on it. Everything else was under the blanket of night.

Just as sure as I knew the whiskey had brought it, I knew I could go to the Humvee, get inside, and return to the moment in which it always waited for me. In the vehicle and the moment it represented, there would be a young man inside with kind eyes and hands that were embarrassed by my body always willing to fight for my life.

He always waits.

Without my noticing, the Humvee became a county cruiser again. Billy Blevins was standing beside my open window looking at me.

He has kind eyes.

I think he touched my face. I'm pretty sure he took away my bottle. That night, though, he didn't say anything. At least he didn't say anything that I heard.

The next time I opened my eyes the night mist had melted away and the morning fog was just rising. On the eastern horizon the sky was pink. Happy and hopeful. It kind of ticked me off to see it. I was alone in the quiet world and the only evidence that I had not been alone the entire night was the absence of the bottle I had cradled so lovingly.

Billy.

He had done more for me than take my bottle. I found out later that Reach had indeed gone and found a cop. Deputy Calvin Walker didn't like me much, but when Reach told his story—reeking of cheap whiskey—Calvin called Billy to see if he knew anything. Whatever Billy said made Reach sound more like a stalker than an Army investigator. Reach wasn't arrested exactly. After a quick patch-up, he was given the choice of sleeping in the iron-bar hotel with or without an arrest on his record.

I had my job and a hangover to celebrate.

We're not a big enough department to have detectives work only one case at a time. I don't guess any sheriff's departments are. Luxury is not a big part of law enforcement. After I returned home and cleaned up, Darlene called to check that I was available for duty. She asked it like she knew a secret and didn't want to upset me by being too direct. It made me wonder what exactly she knew.

Who else knew?

When I said I was on my way into the office she directed me to meet one of the rangers in the Mark Twain National Forest instead.

It wasn't a completely unusual assignment but ordinarily a deputy would get transport duty. Was I being treated gently today or was I being kept busy and out of the way? Maybe it was me being paranoid. I looked at myself in the truck's mirror and decided that today was a good day to keep my head down and do what I was told.

The national forest land was on the northeast corner of the county: As far as I could go and remain in the county. The rangers had caught a pot grower. I was to take custody of the prisoner and "coordinate." That means sign papers and shake hands.

I didn't have any problem with a nice, long drive over there. Time to think.

More time to think, I corrected myself, not sure if that was really a good idea.

It was one of those days that started hot and took a quick drop into hell. Hot enough that even I rolled the windows up and ran the air conditioner full blast. Closed windows made me dread the drive back. The people we transport are not known for hygiene. At least they were mostly quiet. The people that like to act the badass also act the most childish when they're caught. And they tend to hate any kind of authority so we worry more about being spit upon than having our ear chewed off.

I was in for something different.

My prisoner was a perfect example of life in the Ozarks. Almost all white and conservative, the region has a long history of frontier freedom. It's a tradition that has attracted all kinds of people who like to be left alone. We get more than our share of end-of-the-world and coming-race-war militia types, building compounds and getting ready for their beloved Armageddon. At the same time, we get lots of live-off-the-land, worship-the-goddess wannabe hippies as well. The biggest problem with both of those kinds is that they don't want to work for anyone, but everyone needs money. Almost invariably they turn to marijuana.

Twenty some odd years ago—my prisoner wasn't sure—his parents, John Light and Amber Wilson, parked a trailer on the edge of the Mark Twain National Forest. They stood under the trees and stars, clothed only in a few flowers and declared themselves married. John ran off after a few months leaving Amber to give birth to, and raise the son she named Moon. Moon Light.

Moon grew marijuana on public land. He was usually careful about it but early that morning, probably about the time I was waking in my truck, he had walked into one of his crops and right into the hands of U.S. Forest Service Rangers.

Moon told me the whole story as I was taking him to the county lockup. Three times I reminded him that anything he said to me could be used against him in his trial.

"What's it matter?" he asked. "They already got me."

"Sure," I told him. "But there's caught and there's stupid. Don't just hand them matches to burn you with."

"I guess you're right, but I figured they'd catch me long before this. Heck, I been growing since I was ten. My daddy run off. Did I tell you that? He run off and I had to take care of Mama."

"*Moon*," I all but shouted his name. "Every time you talk you dig your hole deeper. If you have to talk, do it about something other than your farming so I don't have to testify." He was a hard guy not to feel sorry for. In a way, he reminded me of a young Clarence Bolin. If Clare was ever that skinny and lonely for someone to talk to.

"Okay," he said. "But do you really think they'll jail me? I mean, it was just a little pot."

"It was a lot of pot and it was a commercial operation on federal lands." Moon's mention of jail reminded me of my earlier discussion with Danny. "Do you know the difference between jail and prison, Moon?"

He laughed, hard and loud, then said, "No. I don't know that one. Do you know why the chicken crossed the road?"

"What? Everyone knows—"

"To show the possum that it can be done."

He laughed and at exactly that time I passed an opossum carcass lying in the middle of the road. I laughed right along with him. It was true: Opossums never seemed to make it across a road without being squashed.

"Moon." He was still laughing. This time I did shout, "Moon." He stopped and looked up at my eyes reflected in the rearview mirror. "I wasn't trying to tell you a joke. Jail is more of a short-term thing, usually a year or less in a county or city facility. Prison is the big time. Real bad guys and hard time with the kind of people that will knock your teeth out so they can rape your mouth. That's what you're looking at. I don't think it's the kind of place for you, okay?" He nodded at me and for the first time looked scared. "Stop telling me things about growing pot. Think of it like this: Every word is evidence and when they ask me I have to tell them the truth."

"It's just pot," he said quietly as if he was trying to convince himself. "It's not like the meth."

"What did you say?"

"You told me not to talk about things." Moon's gaze was turned down to the floor now. He looked like a chastened child.

"I did say that. However, if it's not your meth it's important that you tell me."

He kept his head down and mumbled, but I could make out the words, "It's not mine." I waited for his need to talk to return but he kept staring at the floor. Probably he was seeing a future that he had never believed could happen to him.

"It's important, Moon. You need to tell me about the meth. This is the kind of thing that could help you."

"You mean snitch," he said. It was an accusation for both of us.

"Listen, you might think the people who make the meth are your friends—"

Moon shook his head vigorously. "*They* are the bad guys."

"Bad guys talk about snitches. They call people names like that to try to control them. They try to make it sound like you owe them something, but you don't. They would dime you in a second to help themselves. You need to help yourself now, Moon."

"How?" he asked, again looking into my reflection.

I smiled at him. "Tell me this: What kind of people are cooking meth?"

"The bikers."

That was what I wanted to hear. Truth be told, Moon probably would have answered all my questions there in the car. That would have helped me, but not him, and I really didn't want to see what prison would do to him.

"Let me make a call," I told him.

Sometimes being in law enforcement means straddling uncomfortable fences. You make deals with demons to get the goods on devils. Sometimes you get a deal you can feel good about. The problem was that I didn't trust Moon to make his own deal. The only way I was going to feel good about how he was treated was to cross a line or two. My call was to a friend. A lawyer friend, named Noble Daniels.

Generally it is frowned upon for cops to give legal advice to suspects. Just another reason the sheriff would have to put me out of his department when my crap pile gets too high. The thing is, if it gets these bikers, takes meth off the streets, and shuts down a lab, I'm okay with saving the state the cost of incarcerating Moon. And saving Moon the cost of his humanity. If I didn't prime the well, though,

the state would take the bikers and Moon and make no distinction between them.

My friend Daniels would help Moon make the best deal possible.
If it turned out that he didn't have much to offer, Daniels would still
do his best for him. Sometimes that's all you can ask.

"You're not a bad guy, are you?" I asked Moon as soon as I hung
up the phone. "And it was just pot, right?"

Moon never stopped talking all the way back to Forsyth. He was
actually a likable guy. Despite that, I was never so happy to hand
someone over to Duck. There was one thing to be taken away from
Moon's ceaseless chatter, though. With him, there was no way to ignore my status as a cop. And if I really took a look at that status I'd
have to say I was coming up short. In fact, I would have had to say
that lately many of my actions were coming down on the wrong side
of the line. Worse, the only problems I'd been paying attention to
were my own. Maybe what I needed were fewer long, contemplative
drives and more putting my ass to work. So that's what I did.

Since I was already in the jail, I decided to try again with Danny
Barnes. As soon as I stepped in front of his cell he started yelling.
"It's your fault," and "You'll get what you deserve."

I took it. He ran out of rage after only a minute.

When he was only screaming with his eyes I asked, "What's my
fault?"

"Look at me," he said. "Where I am. What's happening to Carrie.
All of it. All your fault."

"What's happening to Carrie?"

Danny tried to sneer but it looked like rigor mortis. "What do you
care?"

"I care," I told him. "If something bad is happening, I can help."

"We had help until you showed up."

"I don't understand, Danny. What kind of help?"

"We had Leech."

Suddenly the rigor twitched and Danny darted his eyes at something only he could see. I couldn't tell if he was faking.

"Leech? How did you have Leech, Danny? Is he even real?"

"We had Leech. And he had us."

"But you don't anymore?"

"That just shows what you know."

"I don't know, Danny. Help me to understand. It might help you too."

"You'll never understand. And if Carrie gets a baby we'll have Leech forever."

"Is that what's happening to Carrie? Is she pregnant?"

"It's all your fault," he said quietly. Then he screamed it. "All your fault. Your fault, you bitch. You fucking bitch. I hate you." He kept screaming, this time adding venom and vulgarities until Duck came and pulled me back down the hall.

When I made it to my desk there was a voice-mail response to one of the calls I'd made. I called right back and had the luck of connecting with Detective Deveraux of the New Orleans Police Department.

"They call him Figgs. Member of the Marciano family," he said as soon as I asked him about Byron Figorelli.

"Marciano?" I asked.

"Yeah, like the old fighter. They claim to be related. Who knows?"

"What can you tell me about him?"

"I can tell you he's a fuckup dancin' on his last dime. Probably worse than I heard if he's up there with you. These guys travel for business only when things are real good or when they are real bad. The family business is in liquor, moving it quiet-like, under-the-table sales . . . They force bars to buy product with fake tax seals, then squeeze 'em for protection. Figgs got involved with two things that put him on the hook. First was the wrong guy's wife. Second was some idea to sell legal booze in restaurants. Turns out, trying to do things legal gets a lot of unwanted attention. City, parish, and state jumped on that bandwagon. I don't know how much money it cost to get the family out, but Figgs has got to find a way to make good."

"I guess that's what he's doing up here," I said.

"That and waiting for Joey D to cool off."

"Who's Joey D?"

"Joseph Dio Marciano. It was his wife Figgs tapped. Like they say in the previews for those movies, *This time it's personal.*"

He laughed at his own joke. We talked a little longer but there wasn't much more to tell. There didn't need to be. It all fit. Unfortunately, this part of an investigation is like doing a jigsaw puzzle upside-down—all the pieces fit but you have to show the picture to prove it.

After that call I filled in my case logs and time sheets, added up mileage, and wrote my longhand report for the sheriff.

There was a reason for focusing on the busywork. Guilt is one of those emotions that feeds on itself. With every bite it gets a little heavier. I had not seen or called Nelson since early the day before. That made me feel guilty, so I put off calling and tried not to think about it. Not thinking about it meant that I hadn't even asked him about his medical appointment. That left me feeling really guilty, which forced me to deal with paperwork rather than face my failure as a human being. Another night spent drinking added to the load, so I hesitated about that. No wonder they say confession is good for the soul. Even better is when all is forgiven without the confession.

Nelson called me. He wasn't angry or complaining. He said he would be caught up for a while but not to worry. He added that he wanted to see me that evening if I could. Okay, it was a cheap way to get out from under the guilt, but I was more than willing to let him lessen the load.

Nelson lightens my load.

It was a good thought. And true. As soon as I hung up the phone, my day was better. My attitude was certainly better. Sitting there at an ancient, gray metal government desk I realized for the first time that my life was better with Nelson Solomon in it. More confusing maybe, but better.

It was late afternoon and I was feeling good—really good, actually. I couldn't say why; wouldn't say why. Maybe the load was lighter but it wasn't gone. Besides, it wasn't just Nelson. Maybe the answer was in work.

In forgiveness?

Or in giving myself the chance to be happy. It was probably in a lot of things or maybe there weren't any answers. Anyway, I was ready for a weekend and for doing it sober. I'd turned a corner, I decided. I was shutting the door on self-pity and saying the big up-yours to therapists everywhere. It felt great. So great, in fact, that I stopped and bought wine and flowers.

Most of the time I had spent with Nelson had been beer and lake time. We needed something different. Not completely different, it turned out. My next stop was to fill up the truck. Down the street there was a big station, the kind with twenty pumps and an attached store that supplied quick groceries and kept the fishermen in beer and ice. As I was pumping my gas I noticed a few guys were crowding around the back of a pickup the next pump over. The owner had pulled out a stringer of fish and was showing off his catch. Not a good idea. On the far side of the lot, at a diesel pump, Mike Resnick was filling up his big green 4x4 with the Missouri Conservation Department logo on the door.

That gave me an idea and a momentary pang of abuse-of-authority guilt, but I got over it. After capping my tank I wandered over to the guys checking out the fish. The proud fisherman had an almost full stringer of six rainbow trout.

"That's a nice catch," I said as I stepped into the middle of the men.

"Thanks," the one holding them said. "Best day I've had in a long time."

"Just you?" I asked him, looking around at the other men.

"Yep. Just me. Wife has me working all weekend so I called in sick to work. It was all worth it."

"Well," I said, looking the stringer over. "I think ten bucks will be worth it too."

"What do you mean?"

"Five a fish. I'll take those two." The pair I pointed out were nice fish, almost two feet long, but I left him the largest.

"What makes you think I'm going to sell you my fish, lady?"

I showed my badge and he no longer looked so confident.

"You're over your limit. Only four trout per person. And I'm assuming you have a valid trout stamp."

The onlookers started fading away and the fisherman tried one last stand.

"So what," he said. "You ain't no game warden."

"He is." I waved over and caught Mike's eye. He waved back. When I turned back to the fisherman I held up a ten-dollar bill and asked, "What's the over-limit fine these days?"

He handed over the fish and I put them in the back of the truck while I went inside and bought a Styrofoam cooler and a couple of bags of ice. One layer of ice, then the fish, another layer of ice, then two bottles of Pinot gris.

After that I stopped and picked up some fresh rosemary and thyme, a couple of lemons, some wild rice, and broccoli. Dinner was planned. It amazed me how happy I was to think of making dinner for Nelson as I drove away.

* * *

Nelson wasn't home when I got there, but it was for the best. His kitchen was a mess. Not that he was a slob, but it hadn't been used in quite a while. The counters and table were layered in dust and the refrigerator was mostly stocked with condiments and limp celery. There were a few cups of yogurt that were past their expiration too. Even the pots and pans were grimy with dust. I split the flowers into two small vases I found and started cooking, cleaning what I needed as I went. Since the day was beginning to cool I set the table on the deck.

When he got home, Nelson looked tired and drawn like he had been through a mangle then tossed over a line. He perked up when he saw the flowers, then looked at me like he had a secret.

I put a glass of wine in his hand and kissed him. He kissed back with a strength that surprised and impressed me.

We both have a lighter load tonight.

I smiled and thought about asking, but didn't. If there was some kind of spell happening I didn't want it to break. "I set the table outside," I told him. "Would you rather stay inside? It's still hot."

He took a sip and a deep breath, then said, "No. I like all the outside I can get." Once we sat at the table he told me, "I missed you last night."

I caught myself touching the scar at my eye. The reflex of a bad habit—what did I have to worry about at that moment? I dropped my hand away, then said, "It was a busy time. I had a lot to do. And to think about. My week was spent with possible gangsters, a possible rapist, a moonshiner, a pot farmer, and one trout poacher. It's been exciting and in the case of the poacher, pretty delicious, if you ask me. None of that was what I was thinking about." I opened my mouth to say more, then closed it. I touched the scar again before asking him, "Two whole days without me around. What did you do?"

"About the same," he said. "Instead of criminals, I spent the day with doctors and lawyers. You know, the other criminals." He laughed then. Harder than the joke warranted but it was genuine, warm, and lively. It sounded good.

We ate our dinner. Nelson even ate all of his fish. As the sun set, we watched the sky shade to a brilliant red that burned even deeper on the underside of the clouds as it got lower on the horizon. It was an easy time with hands held gently. I told Nelson the joke that Moon had told me and then shared Moon's life story. We laughed again and wished him well.

"It really does sound like you did a little good today. Can't ask for much more than that," Nelson said as the tail of the pig went over the fence.

"To days well spent," I said and lifted my glass. We touched the stemware and took sips, looking at each other. "I know about the gun," I said. It was done without thought or plan. Words I didn't even know were there fell from my mouth, exposing my worry and my snooping. Nelson looked confused at first, then he glanced through the window toward his work space and he knew what gun I meant.

Then I said, "Things aren't that bad."

"For a long time I thought they were. I was expecting to be stuck in a bed with a morphine drip and sad-faced strangers watching me disappear into nothing. I'd decided not to let that happen."

"And now?"

The thought, the knowledge of his mortality, lay there between us. It was another carcass, the deadweight of loss like a hole in the future.

"Don't use the gun," I said. My voice was quiet and pleading. I would have begged.

"I'm making other plans," he said quietly.

"What plans?"

He sat the wineglass down. "This," he said. The kiss was like feeling the sunrise all over my skin. All the weight that had ever been on my shoulders went away. There was no guilt, no worry, and no plan. Not only did he open my mouth, but he put a hand at the back of my neck and pulled me in tighter by the hair. It wasn't force or violence in any sense; it was—wonderful. With his other arm he wrapped me and brought my body in tight against his.

His kiss had more fire than it ever had before. He was not just taking pleasure, he was devouring. It was like he was stealing away bits of me with his mouth to hide them away from the world.

When he started to undress me I pulled back. It wasn't just that we were still outside on the deck that had me putting the brakes on. I was less concerned with what a distant stranger might see than what I knew for sure Nelson would see. There was too much light left in the evening and I still wasn't showing my scars in full daylight. Fear or vanity? It didn't matter. Nelson didn't push. He did let me return the favor and undress him as I urged him back into the darkness of the house.

We only made it as far as the couch.

We had been there, on the couch, for a couple of hours. Air-conditioning did nothing to cool the heat we were generating. Both of us were covered in sweat. It didn't help that the couch was leather. It didn't hurt, either. He was naked. I still had my shirt and bra on. Nelson wasn't complaining. He had risen for me a second time and was close to his release. I was lying under him watching his face as he urged both of us toward the fulfillment we were craving. I made it first. When my eyes widened and my mouth opened to gasp at the moist air he looked at me with pride. It was what he wanted and perfectly all right with me. Then his rhythm caught, went out of step, his brow furrowed and eyes glazed. He pulled back slowly but I wrapped both legs around his hips and pulled him into me.

"Don't hold back," I said. "I'm ready." I kissed him hard, sucking his tongue into my mouth and biting gently. He moaned. His body shook slightly. I took my mouth from his and pulled him down onto me. I whispered into his ear: "Now. I want it all."

He gave all he had as deeply as it was possible and I sighed with pleasure.

That was when the phone rang. It was the sheriff.

Chapter 16

It was a strange feeling. The last thing I wanted to do was to get up from that couch and go out into the night to face another example of the worst people could be. But I went with a light heart. I went singing along to the radio, and I'm not afraid to admit it, dancing a little in the truck seat as I drove.

There was a part of me that knew that nothing had changed. There was another part that was convinced that everything had changed. Either I was psychotic or there was another reason. I wasn't so giddy yet that I would think about that other reason. For now, I would just enjoy the ride.

The drive to the call out was a quick one. When I got there the nightmare of the scene sucked my feet right back to the ground. Almost every car in the department was on-site. Lights—spot and strobe—were raking at the night like digging a hole that kept collapsing overhead. You couldn't see it but as soon as I got close I could smell the remains of gunsmoke.

When I rolled up, Byron Figorelli and Jimmy Cardo were standing with deputies in front of the RV. It was parked in the same spot I'd last seen it, in the back of the Moonshines parking lot. That RV was a drivable behemoth, the kind of mobile living space that cost ten times what most of the houses in the county cost. It was also shot to hell.

The sheriff was getting out of his car as I pulled up. He saw me and sent a deputy over before I even had the engine shut off. The deputy told me they were called out on a report of multiple gunshots about forty minutes earlier. When they arrived the RV was ventilated end to end with multiple calibers of bullets and double-aught buckshot. The witness who called it in said they saw several men on motorcycles pull into the parking lot and leave in a hurry after the shooting stopped.

I thanked the deputy and went to have a talk with Figorelli.

"Used to be a nice place you have here," I said as I approached.

"You really are a funny girl. Must be open-dyke night at the comedy club, huh?" He laughed at his own joke. Cardo joined in with his dead-fish smile and unreadable eyes.

"Is this thing insured?" I asked Figorelli.

"You bet your pretty ass it is."

"Then keep a civil tongue in your mouth or I'll write a report that says you got drunk and shot it up yourself."

"You can't do that."

"What? Only scumbags like you two can screw the system and walk away laughing? I'm in no mood."

"You're in no mood? Look at this RV. A million-two this thing cost."

"Why'd they do it?"

"How the hell should I know? This whole state is the armpit of the country and you ask me where the stink is coming from?"

"Do you know these bikers? Have any dealings with them?"

"I seen 'em around, hanging with Johnny some. First him, now us. Why don't you do your job?"

I was about to say something to that when a man I had never seen came up to talk to Figorelli.

"Boss, I called the motorist-assist the insurance company said to. They're on their way."

"Who are you?" I asked.

"That's my driver," Figorelli answered.

"Did I ask you?" I turned and called over a deputy. It was Calvin Walker, the man to whom Reach had reported me. As he approached I wondered what I would have to deal with, but Calvin said nothing. "Take this guy's statement," I told him still with a bit of trepidation. "Get his IDs and commercial driver's license checked and run him for priors." It wasn't until he had taken the driver away that I relaxed and turned back to Figorelli. "So your driver wasn't in jail with you. He have an alibi for the times when Middleton was shot at and the day he was killed?" I asked.

"He don't need one," Figorelli answered.

"Not yet," I said.

The mechanics of investigation labored on, almost mindless. *Who* was known to a degree, even if not by actual name or location. *Why* was the real question dangling. *Why* is the making sense, the glue that would hold together the different people and the different crimes. There are a lot more whys in life than whos.

I continued talking and trading insults with Figorelli, enough to know that he didn't know how to get to the Nightriders any more than I did. I could tell by the threats. They were all bombast and wind, nothing even vaguely specific or suggesting a plan. He spoke on and on, using the phrases "When I find them" and "Those guys are gonna wish they were never born." It was my experience that a guy like Figorelli, when faced with a known enemy, would have either said nothing or something simple. Saying, *I'll take care of it* carries a lot more weight with these guys than any threat.

Even though I doubted I would need them anymore, I told Figorelli and Cardo to stick around, then I told Calvin to make sure they did. I went to talk to the driver and asked him as much about Johnny Middleton as tonight. Most of his answers were "I don't know." While we talked, I looked over the parking lot. It wasn't very full but the perimeter was lined with people looking on and taking in the activity. There were a few talking with deputies; either they thought they saw something important or their car was hit by stray fire.

Past the edges of milling people I saw a man. He was dressed like Porter Wagoner on steroids with sequins on his Western-cut jacket and a big Stetson. It was the same man I had seen talking to Middleton in the bar the night I got into it with Figorelli. And the same one I'd seen talking to Figorelli on the steps of the RV. I was sure he was also the lawyer that had bailed Figorelli and Cardo out of jail. I still hadn't seen his face but, even in Branson, there were not that many men dressed to star in a country music show. It was too much of a coincidence not to ask questions so I tried to catch him. By the time I got to the scene tape he was nowhere to be found.

As I was searching faces and checking out moving cars, Billy pulled into the lot and came over. "I'm out giving tickets when all the cool stuff happens," he said.

"How come you're not playing the patio tonight?"

He nodded over at Figorelli. "The new management decided that my services were no longer required. They said they were going to put in a zydeco band. I think they didn't want a cop around. I figured I'd volunteer for some overtime."

"New management? That didn't take long."

"The way I heard it, they came in around noon the day after Middleton was found dead. After announcing it to the staff the first thing Figorelli did was take the mountain oysters off the menu." He laughed. "At least the only people he fired were me and the distiller."

"The distiller? Isn't that they guy that makes the whiskey?"

"I guess they have their own guy coming in."

"Now that's interesting," I said.

All things are like clocks, I guess. They run down. Even the big, violent events run to a halt. It took a couple of more hours but that scene dwindled down to nothing with the removal of the RV. I played a little trick on Figorelli. The tow truck his driver had called showed up, but I directed the operator to take the land yacht to impound. Not only was it not going to be repaired for a while but the tow bill was coming out of his insurance.

I left the scene grinning and settling back into my original mood. If I had been in one of my bad or drinking moods I might have missed what happened next. Because I was going straight back to Nelson's house—and his bed—I got caught up in an accident.

In the center of the road was the carcass of a deer. To the side, across a ditch and smashed into a wall of rock, was a pickup truck. Milling around that were four kids, too many kids for the cab of the truck. I wasn't the first cop on the scene. Billy was there and he was working over the body of someone in the ditch. As soon as my lights came on he looked up and waved me over.

I took a moment to call in, just in case Billy had not had the chance. I renewed the request for an ambulance and traffic support.

In the ditch was another girl. Three boys and two girls. It was obvious what had happened. The kids had all piled in the truck, girls on laps and everyone having a good time. Too good to be careful and probably too fast to see the deer until it was too late.

I forced the standing kids to back away and get off the road. Then I knelt beside Billy. He was up to his elbows in the girl's blood. She was young and pretty with dark hair, Hispanic or Native American looking. Most of her shirt and her bra had been cut off but Billy left part of the shirt to preserve the girl's modesty. I thought even more of him for that.

"Hold right here," he ordered as soon as I was down. He didn't wait for questions or for me to hesitate; he took my hand and put it under the girl's arm, then wrapped my fingers around where he wanted them. "Squeeze tight," he said. "Hard, like you're trying to pinch it off."

When he moved his hands I noticed for the first time the one-and-a-half-inch diameter branch protruding from both sides of her arm and the ragged hole it had cut going through.

I glanced up and saw the remains of a scrub tree bent over the hood of the truck and sticking into the cab. When I looked back down, Billy was digging into a large medical case. It was the kind you see with EMTs, not the usual pack our deputies carry.

He worked quickly without looking at me or giving any further instructions. I began to wonder if anyone could work quickly enough. My hands were getting bloody from the arterial pulse that still pumped from under my fingers. I squeezed harder and with both hands.

Billy turned on a small but bright LED flashlight, then shoved the butt end into his mouth, smearing blood from his hands to his face. Using his head to aim, he put the beam on the still-flowing gash.

I don't know why he bothered; he worked mostly by feel. Pulling gauze pads, he packed them into the wound. After that, he brought out a pair of hemostats. I felt something moving before I saw what he was doing. His fingers were in the girl's arm, under the skin and muscle, feeling for the artery.

I became aware that he had begun talking. Not to me, to the girl. But they were words I had heard before.

Mostly he said everything would be all right. He said it like it was a prayer as much for himself as for her.

"It'll be all right."

"We'll take care of you."

"Don't worry."

"Everything will be all right."

He never looked at the girl's face. He was talking through her wounds, focusing, forcing kindness into a brutal business.

"Move your grip up higher," he said. He had to say it again before I came back to time and place. "Here," he said, pointing with the flashlight, "in the armpit as high as you can, as tight as you can."

I shifted my grip and I felt his fingers follow under the skin.

"You're going to be fine," he spoke softly. "We'll take care of you." Then a little louder: "Hah." Under mine, his fingers pinched and pulled at the artery. He threaded in the hemostats and clamped the pulsing flow down.

When it was done, Billy smiled at me.

He has kind eyes.

"I didn't know you had EMT training," I said.

"Army medic," he answered before turning back to bind the wound more.

Nelson was still on the couch when I returned. He was also still naked. But he had covered himself with an afghan. The big windows let in the light of the moon and stars almost like a lens with Nelson at the focal point. There were spots of blood on his cover from where he had been coughing.

Seeing his blood put a sour charge in the bottom of my gut; the feeling of tequila on an empty stomach. He was getting better. Stronger. I could tell. He was healing. We were both healing, I hoped. But . . .

I sat on the floor beside him and put my head into his shoulder. Sleep might have come. Instead, Nelson's hand slipped into my hair.

"Welcome home," he said in a sleepy voice.

Home. The word gave me a feeling not quite equal parts delight and panic. I wasn't sure which was greater at the moment.

"Busy night?" he asked.

I nodded, knowing he could feel the motion.

"Did you do any good?"

"Yes," I said. "There was a girl in an accident. Billy saved her life. I bet he saved her arm too. He was amazing. I didn't even know until tonight that he was a medic in the service."

"Army?"

I nodded again.

"The Marines call the Navy corpsmen *doc*. They're the best people in the world. The bravest."

"I've known Billy for years. How come I didn't know that about him?"

"Does he know everything about you?"

"What?" I raised my head and looked at Nelson's face in the pale light. "What do you mean?"

"Have you told him what happened to you in the Army? A lot of us have things we don't talk about from those times. I think every corpsman pays a price for the people he helps. If Billy had wanted you to know about that part of his life he would have told you."

"I only found out because he helped that girl." I turned my back to Nelson and looked out the windows at the night beyond.

"He's a deputy now, not an EMT. He's trying to leave something behind."

"You think that's it?"

"That or he's carrying something around that he doesn't want anyone to see."

I nodded at that, then said, "Secrets are hard." The hand that had stayed in my hair pulled away. Its absence felt like a sudden silence. Behind me Nelson shifted up on the couch and drew in a breath to speak. Before he could, I said, "I'm a drunk."

The breath in his chest came out in a long wind. I started talking and I didn't stop until I had told him all the events of the last couple of days.

"You really broke his nose?" he asked when I got quiet.

"I almost did a lot worse."

"But you didn't."

"Next time I might. I almost used him for revenge against the whole Army."

"I know you know it," he said. "But you really need to understand it—feel it. The Army's not your enemy. Just a few assholes in it."

"I know."

"That's pretty much life, isn't it? Something wonderful except for a few assholes."

I smiled. Nelson's arm wrapped around my shoulder, pulling me back against him. I put my head against his chest. Then his hand cupped my breast. It felt good.

"I have a proposal," he said.

"I bet you do," I told him and I was laughing a little. "But we're both too tired."

He pulled his arm away then brought it back. In his hand was a small box. "No. I have a proposal." Quicker than I would have thought possible Nelson sat up, then dropped to the floor beside me. At first I thought he had fallen but he was getting on one knee. Naked and wrapped up in a red, white, and blue basket-weave afghan, he asked me to marry him.

"I know it's quick. And it seems impulsive, maybe even foolish, but I have never been more sure of anything in my life."

I didn't answer. He opened the box and revealed a ring with a stone as large as my badge. When I continued not to answer, Nelson said, "But you're obviously not so sure . . ." There was a touch of humor in his voice as if he was not surprised at my silence. He put the box, still open, on the coffee table. "I'll just set this here and let you think." Then he stood and pulled the cover around himself, watching me.

Finally he stepped back and said, "You have a lot of thinking to do, I can see." The humor had gone from his voice. "It's late and we're both tired." He stepped farther back. "I'll be in bed if you want to come up and talk."

To my shame I let him go without a word. Everything felt so heavy.

Chapter 17

Once again I was driving deserted roads in the smallest hours of the morning. I told myself I didn't know what I was looking for. That might have been half true. I didn't know specifically but I knew I was looking for some place to put my fear and anger. That was the surprising part. I was angry. Nelson had asked me to marry him and I was angry. The confusion I felt at that added more fuel until my spine felt like a column of steam ready to burst from my ears.

After several silent miles, fire caught my attention. Big yellow flames that danced like gypsies in the darkness. Color. Life. Rage. I could almost hear the clattering spin of *fortunada*'s wheel.

The flames I saw were coming from a familiar bit of woods. Only a couple of days before I had been there talking to Clare. It was his camp on fire.

Hitting the gas and my emergency lights at the same time, I rushed to the break in the trees and fencing that I knew would open onto a rutted dirt track. As I drove I tried to call in for support but I couldn't keep control and dial at the same time, so the phone got tossed. Off the main road and onto the rough trail I pushed my truck faster than I should have. Rocks heaved up from the annual freeze-and-thaw cycles filled each rut. Some were big enough to crack open an oil pan. Many were sharp enough to cut through the sidewall of a tire.

As I got closer the road became visible, twin depressions of clay and stone meandering in a long arc around a copse of old trees. The fire ahead backlit the oaks and scrub brush. Before I got to the final turn, other lights, headlights, came on. Their beams were blue and white straight-edge beacons both cutting through and made crisply visible by the smoke. Light was followed by noise as motorcycles, many with open pipes, howled into life. As I passed around the last screen of trees the bikes were screaming right at me.

Law-enforcement personnel are discouraged from using our vehicles as a weapon except in cases of stopping another fleeing vehicle. That's to say car-on-car. In no case would it be considered proper to use my truck as a battering ram against a motorcycle. In these instances, where it is a cop's word versus a running arsonist wanted for questioning in a shooting—well, they'll take my word that he hit me.

I twisted my wheel and darted the truck headlong into the two lead bikes. One of them was clipped and shot spinning into the grass. The other hit slightly inboard of my driver's-side headlight and was flung up into the windshield. It was Cotton Lambert.

He rolled off the hood of the truck and into the dark grass before I could get stopped. By the time I did stop and get out, he was back on his feet.

I'd like to say I was worried that they had harmed Clare. I'd like to say I believed that the Ozarks Nightriders and Cotton Lambert in particular had done more than property damage to an illegal moonshine operation to which I had turned a blind eye. I'd like to—I can't. I wasn't thinking about any of that. I was thinking of dust and brown wind that crawls over your skin and embeds itself in open wounds.

Cotton took a swing at me. That was all I wanted and less than I needed. I had come out of my truck with my automatic holstered and my baton in my hand. That was the same as saying, "Let's dance."

Cotton's punch was a rocket aimed right at the left side of my face. To meet it I raised my left fist and caught my wrist at his elbow and pressed out at the same time as I stepped in with my left foot at 45 degrees. By the book. As I turned his arm out I opened my hand and let it slide down until I closed my fingers on his wrist. That's when I brought my baton down from my right shoulder onto his bicep. He was lucky. I had a choice of his bicep or his elbow. Following through, I released his arm and held the baton with two hands sliding my right in a little to allow the butt to protrude. I pulled back, twisting with my hips to add power and drove the butt up into his abdomen.

In my head the blood was rushing like rivers of anger. I heard every rapid beat of my heart thrumming like a dynamo and I felt good. Honestly, I wanted more. If Cotton had had any sense he would have gone down and stayed there. He didn't. Bent double, he charged, lifting me off my feet and slamming my back against the truck. I brought the baton down on his back, butt first, a small steel fist going hard into the meat between the spine and the shoulder blade.

When he let me go I raised up for another strike, this one falling on the left trapezius as hard as I could bring it. He screamed, clutching at the impact point. His body was shocked by the pain, his back arched and his legs locked straight. I took advantage and kicked my heel into the inside of his right leg. He was down, screaming through his pain, and no more threat to me. But he still managed to call me a name. It was one short, ugly, hateful word that I won't tolerate. And I've been called a bitch more times than can be counted.

I broke his jaw.

Everyone else was gone. It was just me and Cotton out there: Him under the headlights and me under the stars. The other bike that I had hit had been able to get away. At least I couldn't find it. I couldn't find Clare, either. It was just the still that had been hurt. The flames were from a mixture of gasoline and alcohol. I wondered what Clare would think of the awful liquids that were running into the small stream beside his camp.

I was shaking and light-headed when I dug the phone out of the seat to call in. It was the effect of so much adrenaline draining from the blood, but I suddenly felt as weak as moth's breath.

While I waited for the other units, the EMTs, and fire department, I had a lot of time to simply be with what I had done. Cotton was silent on the ground. I had done that. I was justified. I felt justified—at first. Standing there as a witness after the fact, I wasn't so sure. The darkness was a black, silky depth pushed out by flames on the ground and embraced by stars overhead. There was no dust. The blood wasn't mine.

When Cotton stirred, I stood over him and said, "Now, maybe we can have a conversation."

His answer was a hateful glare.

I tried again. Because I'm a calm and patient professional, I spoke slow and clear, trying to keep the situation calm. "You kept Middleton from being shot, Cotton. Who did the shooting?"

He said something I couldn't understand. It had slipped my mind that he'd taken a baton to the jaw.

"Say it again," I told him. "Slowly."

He said it with his middle finger.

I pinched the bridge of my nose. Criminals are exasperating. I thought about cuffing him and just going back to sit in my car to wait. Instead, I asked another question.

"Did you do anything to the girl?"

There was no mistaking the confusion in his eyes.

"The still you busted up tonight. It used to be over by Bear Creek. There was a girl killed there."

He nodded. He knew about Angela.

"Was she part of this?"

Cotton shook his head.

"Did Riley Pruitt have anything to do with it?"

His answer that time was to try to get up and, I assume, somehow get away. I kicked his legs out from under him. I was cinching the cuffs down when the first units began arriving.

Work, both the routine of it and the puzzle, would provide a distance from Nelson that I needed. Not all that I *needed*, but at least I could think about what he was asking. Forget the fact that the sun was not yet up and I hadn't slept. The previous night I had not really slept, either. Passed out drunk in your truck is not exactly beauty sleep. As my tires bumped up from grass back onto asphalt I decided to turn toward home rather than back to Nelson's place.

The question—proposal—was hanging there in front of me demanding the kind of attention that I wasn't sure I had to give. I tried to ignore the thought that after I had run out like that he might no longer be asking. Discussion always helped me think things through. Uncle Orson was usually my go-to guy but there were some subtleties of emotion for which he was not the best sounding board. So, as I drove unlighted roads that snaked through dark woods between sheer rock walls and equally sheer drops, I called Dad. The fact that the landscape I was threading my truck through was not unlike the emotional world I needed to navigate was sticking in my mind as the phone rang.

"I wondered when you would call," Dad said instead of *hello*. He was wide awake.

"He talked to you?"

"For a long time. I helped him pick out the ring."

I said something to that, a word I rarely use and never to my father.

"What was that?" he asked and the smile in his voice suggested to me that he knew exactly what I had said. For just a moment I thought that my ideal father would have pretended not to hear that, but we never get the ideal, do we? He didn't wait for me to say. He asked, "Did you accept it?"

When I didn't answer with words he said, "I told him you might not right away."

"What? Why?"

"You tell me. You didn't take it, did you? You didn't call to give me good news; you called to be coaxed."

"No. I didn't," I said. "I called to talk. I wanted your opinion and your thoughts and . . . Why would you say to Nelson that I might not marry him?"

"For the same reason that you didn't tell him you would. Doubts."

"You doubt my feelings? You're the one that told me—"

"I don't doubt your feelings at all. You do that. But this isn't exactly about honest feeling, is it? How long have you known him? How much is feeling and how much is time? I told him too; I wasn't sure there was time for your feelings to catch up to his needs. My doubt is that you could make the decision before it was too late."

I had to swerve to miss an opossum that was standing his ground in the middle of the road and hissing at the headlights of my truck. Once around the angry creature I told my father, "I can't believe you would say that to me, or to him. I know my own mind." My voice was a bit shriller than I wanted it to be.

It was quiet on his end of the line for a long time before he said, "We're not talking about your mind, sweetheart." His voice remained calm and steady. "We're talking about your heart. And I think you've been afraid for so long you hate the thought of giving it up. The fear you're comfortable with is a shield you hold up between you and your own life."

"You don't know anything about my fear." When I said it I didn't recognize the voice. I thought I was angry but it sounded quiet and like I was about to cry. For some reason I wondered if it was how Angela Briscoe's voice sounded at the end.

"I know all about the pain you live with," he said, "and the fear."

"Orson promised—"

"He didn't tell me. He didn't have to. Respect for a loved one's privacy only goes so far. It goes until it's more important to know the secrets than it is to keep them. You learned that when you looked in that box and found Nelson's gun."

"Dad, I don't understand . . . I'm confused by all of this . . ."

"Katrina, do you want to marry him?"

"I don't know. We're just getting to know each other. I know it's too soon, but I'm afraid of losing him."

"Everyone loses. Life is full of losing. Your problem is that you've convinced yourself that you can't lose what you didn't have. Today you're finding out how wrong you were."

"I don't know what that means."

"You've spent ten years with a hole in your life. If you don't put someone in it, you're going to fall in and never get out."

"Daddy?" I was crying then. I was confused and kind of angry. I wanted to talk to Nelson but I didn't know how.

"Trying not to get hurt is no way to live."

"You sound like the therapist," I said. It was supposed to be a thumbed nose at both of them. The gesture didn't really come through in the words, so I hung up.

After the sun was well up I came out of my place cleaner, if not rested. Coffee was on my mind. There was a boring sedan parked in the drive and Major Reach leaning against my truck.

Checking out the bandages, I said, "Nice face."

"Fuck you," he shot right back.

"You tell your buddies a girl did that to you?"

"No. I told *your* buddies. Cops stick together, don't they? Just like you complain about soldiers."

"In case you missed it, I was a soldier too."

"Not in my book," he said, trying to put a sneer into it. It didn't work with the nose.

"What do you want, Reach?"

"Just wanted to let you know that the messages got through," he answered. "All of them."

"What messages?"

"*What messages*, she asks." He rolled his eyes. "You're good. But I think you got into a hurry."

"I don't know what you're talking about. Now do you mind? I have a real job to do."

"I know all about the way you do your job. Seen it firsthand. Do you bring anyone in without busting them up first?"

That brought a burn to my cheeks.

"Do you see me up on charges?" That sounded weak even to me.

"I know you're in therapy. Mandated by your department." He arched his eyebrows in mock surprise. "What's that tell us?"

"It tells us you had better be careful whose truck you choose to lean on. Now get out of my way."

"Two messages yesterday. One telling me that Bayoumi died in custody. Just like that—died. Homeland is closing its investigation. It could have been a weird coincidence; people die sometimes. I could have bought it. Until I got another message, an official message from my CO, telling me to halt any investigations involving you. Unless I have new, *specific* evidence of a crime or conspiracy. Suddenly it's not a coincidence anymore, is it?"

"I wouldn't know," I told him. "I wasn't involved."

"So, is your vendetta over?"

"Vendetta?" I asked, and when I did I got up close to him. Dangerously close. I could see him tense up, ready to defend himself. "All I ever wanted was the justice I was due."

"You got your justice. A full investigation—"

"I got you. And I got people like you following rules. Rules that are there to protect the Army, not the soldier."

"You accused superior officers of crimes in a combat zone. They had alibis."

"They had friends." I was yelling in his face now. My hands were clenched hard at my side, and I had to consciously tell myself to keep them off my weapon. "The same friends that spread rumors and bile about every woman on base."

"I did my job and I'm doing it now."

"Maybe you did your job," I said, getting my voice under control and quiet. "But you failed everyone who needed something more from you."

"This isn't over," he said. His voice was flat and overcontrolled.

"Believe me, I know it's not over. I got a message last night too. A call from Ahrens."

Reach smiled slightly. Just enough.

"You did it," I accused. "You gave him my phone number."

"Not at all," Reach answered. I could read the lie in his eyes and on his lips. "However . . . Contact with another party of the investigation—hostile contact, I can assume, given your history. Maybe that can be considered evidence of a conspiracy. What do you think?"

"I think I'm getting in this truck and driving away. If your ass is still on the fender when I do, I'm not responsible for the kind of ride you get."

He tried to look mean but when I started the truck he jumped. After that he kept a cautious gaze on me as he went to his car. I don't think he trusted me.

Why can't a day ever start well and stay that way?

It's a bad habit, I know. Like a poker player's tell, touching the scar around my eye displays my agitation. My therapist calls it self-soothing, like I'm a baby sucking my thumb. That made me madder than it should have, I guess since it was hard to argue with. As I drove that morning I was working it pretty hard.

There were a lot of things that I could be worried about. Even beyond the obvious personal turmoil, there were two people who I had beaten pretty badly, Reach trying to pin me to some bizarre revenge conspiracy, bikers lighting up the county like a free-fire zone, and RV gangsters taking over a club. Anyone would think I'd be glad to have an obvious and clean suspect in Angela Briscoe's murder. I wasn't. It didn't feel right in a strange way. It was like solving an empty puzzle box. You did everything right but there should be something more. Everything else was turning out to be about greed, money. I really didn't have any doubt that the case tying Figorelli to Riley Pruitt and the bikers would come together. They were a bunch of checkers players trying to compete in chess. The truth would come out in paperwork or a witness and then, with a little pressure, someone would talk.

Because things weren't fitting for me—in so many ways—I didn't go into the sheriff's office. I went back out to the scene of Angela's murder.

This time there was even more crime-scene tape and even more damage to it. After Danny's arrest and the details of what he and Carrie were doing out here got out, news crews and the curious had been all over the scene. It always worked that way. If I was there to look at evidence, I would have been pissed. I wasn't, though I wanted to be there to think.

Like everything else, wanting wasn't enough to make it happen. Nothing was clear and my thoughts were as tangled as the roots and branches I walked between. Not only was I not getting any answers, I couldn't even work up good questions.

Wandering beyond the place of Angela's death I came to the edge of the creek and looked down at the water. It was higher and faster than the last time I had looked. For a long time I just stood and watched the silver ripples running over rocks and eddying into the contours of the bank. There weren't any answers there, either. As I watched, though, the sound changed. That's not true. It didn't change: It was added to by voices. From somewhere downstream there were people talking and laughing. It was soft enough to blend in with the sound of the water and if I had been looking for it I would have missed it.

Following slowly, I stayed on the thin trail along the creek's edge, but kept my eyes watching inland. Kids. There were two young teens, a boy and a girl behind a catalpa tree. On first sighting them, I thought they were talking or making out under the tree. When I went off-trail and circled closer. I saw that she was watching him carve something into the soft wood bark with a large folding knife.

It was impossible, at least for me, to remain stealthy for long in the thick undergrowth and they saw me coming. As soon as they did the pair bolted, laughing as they went. I didn't try to chase them. I did go to the tree to see what they were inscribing. The tree had evidently been used as a message post for years. Old scars cut into the surface read *Class of '68* and almost every year since. There was a ragged and overgrown, *RD+MF*. I wondered who they were and how things went. The only fresh carving was a large L with arrows at the tips and the letters *e-e-c*. It looked like I had interrupted them before they could carve the entire word: Leech.

Again, that name had fooled me and slipped past my attention. Once I understood that Carrie had sent me on a goose chase, telling me Pruitt was Leech, I had all but dismissed it. My assumption had been that it was something made up by Carrie and Danny with meaning only to them. I had believed it was just another aspect of the secret game they were playing. Now it seemed that they weren't alone in the game.

Chapter 18

Billy was waiting when I got back to the road. His truck was parked next to mine, his arm out the open window and his head tilted back in sleep.

"I guess that answers my question," I said once I got close.

"What question?" he asked without either opening his eyes or sounding surprised.

"I was going to ask when you slept. Between working overtime, playing songs in a bar, and fishing, I didn't see how you managed."

He held up a huge plastic drink cup with the letters *XXXL* silk-screened on the side. For emphasis, he shook the cup, sloshing the liquid and ice inside. "Liquid energy," he said.

"My God, I've never seen a drink cup that big. What is that, a gallon of soda?"

"I wish. What are you doing out here?"

"Trying to make some pieces fit," I said. "What happened with the girl? And why aren't you at home sleeping?"

"She's going to be fine. There'll be a scar but she'll keep her arm. If she does the physical therapy it should work okay too."

"Nothing fun about PT," I said.

"I'm not at home because I'm still working," Billy went on. "Sheriff had me over by the national forest keeping an eye on some things. And I'm here, looking for you." He took another long drink from the cup.

"What kind of things?"

"That's what you want to know? Not why I'm looking for you?"

"Whichever you think I most need to know, then," I told him.

Billy sort of half-smiled around his straw. It looked like he was stalling. "Before I tell you," he finally said, "I want you to know that people talk; things get around."

That's a sentence that can never sound good. I guess he *had* been stalling. "Spit it out," I told him.

"I don't know what your relationship is with the painter," he said in a way that told me he knew exactly what it was. "But I thought you might like to know there was a 9-1-1 from his house a while ago." Before I could react or move he added, "It's over. He's fine. The call said there were motorcycles in his driveway making lots of noise. When the cruiser got there it was quiet. I just thought you should know." I didn't say anything. Billy looked at my face and nodded. "I thought as much," he said.

"I'm going to marry him," I said instantly, wondering why I had.

"That was quick."

"You have no idea."

Billy nodded again and took a drink. Once he finished, he nodded his head, indicating the woods where Angela had been, then said, "So, did you learn anything new?"

I heard him but I didn't really *hear* him. I put my hand in my pocket and pulled my cell phone. "I'd better call him," I said.

"Has he called you?"

"What?"

"Check your log. See if he called."

I looked. Then I shook my head.

"If he hasn't called you, he won't want you to call and check up on him. Unless you want him to know you're keeping tabs."

It made a kind of sense. A man's sense, I guessed. "You're not as dumb as they say," I told him.

"I'll have you know I'm regarded far and wide for my wisdom."

"Wisdom? That's what they're calling it now?"

"Wisdom and good looks. It's a package."

I put away my phone and pulled my keys, ready to get back to work. I was also thinking that I'd call Nelson anyway, but do it on the road. Before I went though I asked, "Why didn't I know you were a medic until last night?"

Billy hid most of his face behind the big cup. It didn't cover the bit of smile that reached his eyes. After the drink he asked me, "Why would you have known?"

"We're friends."

He laughed.

"What's so funny?"

"You," he answered straight back. "You are. Friends—" He laughed again, then sucked at the soda.

"What's so funny about that?"

"What do you know about me? You didn't know about the medic thing and you didn't know I played at Moonshines. Tell me something you *do* know."

I was blank. I asked, "What do you know about me?"

"A lot more than you've said, believe me."

I did.

"Truth is," Billy went on, "you play your cards a little close to have real friends."

"That's not true—"

"Who do you trust completely in this world?"

My father and my uncle. I thought it but didn't say it.

"Whoever comes to mind, I bet you knew them before you were deployed," he said as if he didn't really expect an answer.

"Are you trying to be a jerk?"

"Nope," he said. "I'm trying to be your friend."

I swear it was my intention to touch the scar beside my eye. Somehow I ended up pushing back my hair. When I caught myself I was completely self-conscious. I changed the subject. "While you were sitting here being wise and handsome, did you happen to see a couple of kids running out of the trees?"

"Yeah. They got in a car and left. I didn't pay much attention. Something up?"

"No. They were carving in a tree. I wanted to ask them about it."

"Carving what?"

"Leech," I said. "It's all over in there and I wanted to know about it."

Billy sloshed the liquid around in his huge cup like he was making sure he had enough left for what he needed to do. Satisfied, he looked at me and began to recite.

"Leech waits in the woods to give his gifts,

"He lingers and waits with arrow and knives,

"To take what's his by hard sacrifice

"Unburdening lovers, killers and lost lives."

He grinned at me after his little poem, then took a long, last pull, emptying his huge soda with a loud gurgle.

He was right. I knew nothing about him or, I suspected, any of the other people around me. "The hell . . . ?" I said.

For the next half an hour Billy told me the story of Leech.

It had begun as an anthropology project by a student at Missouri State University in Springfield. He had created a monster, a semi-human creature, eight feet tall with gangly limbs. Its hands were arrow points that pierced the bodies of victims and pulled them into the mouth, which was a gaping maw of knife-like teeth. It had no other face, just the bloody red knives within the wide mouth. Leech was said to have supernatural powers and would grant followers freedom from pain and suffering if the gifts they brought were good enough.

The idea of the project had been to show how quickly folklore and word-of-mouth culture could spread in the digital age. Once the creature was defined, the student posted stories about it online, along with blurry photos created by art students. In just a short time the stories and pictures, put up on two local web sites—one for paranormal investigations and the other focused on cryptozoology—had migrated and taken on a life of their own. In less than a year there were a dozen web sites dedicated to Leech with reported sightings and new photos. The most amazing developments were the addition of thousands of stories, poems, and songs by teenagers actively engaged in spreading the new mythology.

When he finished telling me what he knew, Billy rattled the ice in the bottom of his cup and sucked at the meltwater. "Time for a refill," he said.

"How did you know all this?" I asked him. "Leech? I've never even heard of it until I saw the word carved on the trees."

"I read," he said with a smile. "But don't feel bad. Kids—middle-school, high-school—think of it as their culture. They like to keep it that way."

Billy went off, either to refill his cup or empty his bladder. I called Nelson as soon as he was gone. We talked as I drove. I tried not to ask him about the 9-1-1 call, but failed. As soon as the words were out of my mouth I realized that Billy had been right. Nelson didn't want me checking up on him. I could feel it even on the phone, although he only said, "Everything is fine."

Neither of us said anything about the proposal.

I was headed in to the sheriff's department but decided to take a swing by the hospital first.

Cotton Lambert looked like hell. His eyes were blackened and his jaw wired and swollen. He didn't want to talk to me. It was a reasonable feeling, I thought. His room was barren. All his personal effects were logged and taken. There were no flowers or cards, not even a get-well balloon. There was nothing to look at in the room but him. So I sat and looked at him while he glared at me.

"Do yourself a favor," I finally said. "Get out from under this. Your boys are cooking meth. We're going to take them down. And we're going to get the lot of you for shooting up that RV. Depending on how it plays out it could be a reckless-endangerment charge or it could be attempted murder. You don't have to be a part of any of that."

He ignored me pretty well, staring at blank walls while I hit him with questions. Not answering wasn't the same as giving me nothing. His eyes and his body reacted when I asked about the connection between the Nightriders and Moonshines. When I asked if they had an arrangement with Middleton to crush the local bootleggers, his surly look told me *yes*. When I asked again about the man who shot at Middleton, he looked away without any of the attitude. He was afraid of someone.

It went on like that for most of an hour, me asking questions and him reacting without words. In the end I asked one more time about Riley Pruitt and his involvement with Angela Briscoe.

Through his tightly-bound jaw he said, "*Uck ooo.*"

I believe I understood. Talking to some people is like a cat trying to cover his poop on the linoleum—a pointless waste of time. That's the job a lot of the time. He was afraid of something, probably Pruitt. I'd either need more leverage or he'd have to get more scared before he'd talk. I decided to let him stew, then try again later.

Once outside the door, I had to track down the deputy assigned to keep track of Cotton. He was drinking a soda and eating doughnuts at the nurses' station. It was Calvin, the same man I had put on Figorelli's driver the other night.

"Hey Hurricane," he said when he saw me coming. "You come to finish the job on our guy? He can still walk, you know." Calvin laughed at his own joke and sprayed crumbs as he did. Then he looked at the nurse he had been talking with when I came up. "This is the detective I told you about, Hurricane. She lives up to the name too."

The nurse's eyes widened when she looked at me like she expected me do something strange and terrible.

Would smacking Calvin upside the head be very terrible?

"Has anyone been in to see him?" I asked after Calvin had stuffed the last of the doughnut into his mouth.

"Not since I got here," he said around the fried artery clog.

"Why are you here? I thought you were on nights."

"Switched," he said, then started pouring soda into his still-full mouth. I left before the expected gastric explosion.

Walking out the doors of the hospital I caught a flash of turquoise and silver coming from the parking lot. It was the man I had seen at Moonshines wearing the Grand Ole Opry styles. Today, despite the heat, he was wearing a black polyester Western suit with appliques of cactus and wagon wheels. His tie was actually a kerchief with a huge turquoise stone set into hand-tooled silver. He wore matching bracelets and rings. Even the tips of his boots were dressed with silver toe caps. I stopped at the head of the stairs and waited for him.

"Hello there," I said as he took the last few steps.

"Howdy do," he answered while touching the brim of his Stetson. I noticed that he was still wearing the cold-weather felt rather than a summer straw.

He would have kept walking if I didn't ask, "Mind if I ask you a couple of questions?"

His motions put me in mind of a bird when he cocked his head my way and looked out from under the hat. "Well, they ain't no harm nor no law against askin'," he said in an accent as thick as the piney woods that it evoked. The smile he gave looked practiced. Like he wasn't sure why it was done, just that it should be done. All in all, the man gave an unwholesome impression up close, like meeting a buzzard fresh from eating a rotting carcass. Then he pulled off the Stetson and wiped his brow with a black handkerchief that looked like silk. Out from under the shade of the hat his face took on a new cast. His eyes didn't quite match in color; one dark brown, the other a light green. And the brim of the hat had taken focus from the protrusion of his nose. That crooked hook of cartilage completed the buzzard look.

While he wiped his brow, then replaced the hat, his smile held. I knew there was nothing casual about it. It would hold until he decided to change expression.

"Who are you?" I asked.

"Well ma'am, who are you? I was always taught, the person askin' makes hisself know to the person approached. That's manners, you see."

"I *do* see," I said. "I'm Katrina Williams."

"That is a lovely name, Miss Williams," he said as he reseated the hat and began walking past me again. "You have a wonderful day, ma'am."

"You didn't tell me your name."

With a hand on the door handle he stopped and then turned back to look at me. The eyes were hard to focus on, like one was much farther distant than the other. "No, ma'am, I didn't."

"Sir, I'm a detective with the Taney County Sheriff's Department. I'm asking your name."

"Ma'am, the fact that you did not disclose your position put our meeting on a social level. On a social level, I may choose to talk with you or not to, as I wish. Am I not correct?"

"Yes, sir. But—"

"Do you wish to officially take me in and hold me for questioning?"

"No, sir. I—"

"Am I being detained under suspicion?"

"No, sir."

"Y'all have a very good day, Detective." He went through the doors, removing his hat again as he did. As the door closed the glare on the glass made it seem as if he disappeared into another world, one like this one but different in ways that could only be understood by following him through.

He was smarter than his down-home accent suggested. It was probably as much a conscious affectation as the rest of him, a package wrapped up in Dollywood. Mr. Homey-as-Grits was playing a game. He wanted everyone underestimating him from the start. He could only be a lawyer.

Chapter 19

Even in a sheriff's department the weekends can be quiet. Not because there is less crime, but because all the support staff are weekday employees. The building is quieter. You'd think it would be easier to work. Quiet is not always what you need, though. It reminded me of how everyone was telling me my life looked—partially occupied.

I sat at my desk and looked around the place. Half the lights were off. Gloomy and quiet was not a good combination. It had a real *Walking Dead* feel. Sheriff Benson was in his office. That was a surprise. So was the closed door.

Without exchanging words with anyone I went to my desk and did an Internet search for Leech.

Billy was right. It had taken on a life of its own. There were dozens of pages that claimed to have documented proof that Leech was wandering the Ozarks. There were others that shared stories about the creature. Some of them read as breathless secrets from young people telling the kinds of stories that were once shared only around campfires. Some, however, were first-person narratives about personal encounters. Those were the most disturbing because the line between fantasy and reality seemed to not exist for the writers. They believed—or desperately wanted you to believe—they had seen Leech. Within that group were the truly scary accounts of those that said they had worshiped, even sacrificed, to Leech.

All of the writers on those sites were young. You could tell by both the nature of the writing and the references they used to video games, music, and movies. All of their own pop culture seemed to be mixed up in a strange gumbo that blended everything until the pieces no longer had separateness. The songs they listened to, the games of high-definition murder, were all stories upon which they fed and that some seemed to actually believe. Leech was just another part of a scary world.

Closing the browser on Leech, I was left feeling a little disturbed. Imagine peeking in the neighbor's window and catching them dressed in Nazi uniforms, engaged in bondage games with little people and farm animals. The world is a much stranger place than sometimes I give it credit for.

"Howdy there, Hurricane," the sheriff said. He was leaning up against my doorframe. I smiled to see him but it wasn't returned. He hadn't come to talk with me; rather to me.

He peppered me with questions. Why was I going into the jail to talk with Danny Barnes? Didn't I have enough sense to stay away from Danny Barnes? Will *we* need to talk about Danny Barnes again? That sort of thing. I told him that I wasn't satisfied with how that case was stacking up.

He shrugged and said, "There is rarely any satisfaction to putting a kid in jail." Then he said I could follow up but not to engage Barnes any further.

Fair enough. I had plenty of other anvils to juggle. I did something then that I had never done before. I asked him about his wife. I'd heard someone say that she had been ill. If Billy had not gotten me to thinking about how I keep everything close, I would never have thought to ask.

"We dodged a bullet there," he said. "The biopsy was positive, but we caught it early."

A hot blush crept up my throat into my face. The rest of me felt cold but I started sweating. I had thought it was a gallbladder thing. At the same time I was glad I hadn't been specific in my question and ashamed of myself for not knowing.

"There'll be a lumpectomy. Coulda been a lot worse. We thought at first she was going to lose the . . ." He pointed to his own chest, just below the badge, and circled his finger around. The man that could shout profanity as well as any sailor couldn't say the word *breast*. At least not in this situation. I nodded to say I understood. He nodded back before saying, "We're grateful."

"I understand, sir. My mother . . ."

I didn't finish but he knew what I meant. He simply nodded

again. His eyes, though, looked at me like I was the most important person in the world for that moment. Then he was gone.

A few minutes later I saw people I didn't know passing through the brackish hall. They went straight back to the sheriff's office. After a while Billy went by with a couple of other deputies. He waved but didn't stop. They all went into the sheriff's office and closed the door behind them.

Between reevaluating my whole life and who I thought I was, I kept drilling deeper into Leech. There had been other kids who had been caught doing crimes in his name. Two in Arkansas had stolen money and tried to offer it up by stapling cash to trees in a wooded area. There were three instances of kids sacrificing animals, two cats and one dog. Comparing that kind of desperation and confusion to the turmoil in my own life began to make me feel downright small. The one thing I found in common among the kids described was abuse at home.

Were Carrie and Danny both victims of abuse? And was Angela Briscoe their idea of a sacrifice?

Wondering and thinking, there but for the grace . . . I was lost in someone else's problems for a change when I heard a knock on my door. The noise made me jump.

"Cat walk over your grave?" It was my friend and Moon's lawyer, Noble Daniels, standing at the door, asking. I must have looked confused because he clarified, "It's something my father used to say when someone was startled. It was because a cat walked over their grave. Never understood it, though. Did the cat walk over the place your grave would be or did it walk over your grave in the future and you felt it now? Strange man, my father."

"Working on a Saturday?" I asked. "Strange kind of lawyer."

"It was my destiny to be so. Did I ever tell you I was named after the lawyer in *True Grit*? My father again. Thought it would ensure I was a lawyer or 'defender of truth,' as he liked to put it. Sometimes I wish I was the 'litigator of big corporations' instead."

"What truth are you defending around here?"

"Working some things out for your pal," he answered. "The one who won't ever shut up."

"What?"

"Can you waterboard someone to make them *stop* talking?"

"I guess you're talking about Moon," I said.

"*Moon Light*, you mean," he answered. "The man with a motor-mouth and the sense God gave a turnip."

"You talk about all your clients that way?"

"Yeah, I do. I'm a criminal-defense attorney. My clients are not the Mensa crowd but this guy—" Noble let out a long breath that sounded like frustration escaping. "You were right about this one. If I wasn't there to control him, he would have sent himself up for ten years then brought the angry bikers in with him."

"You like him, don't you?"

"His name is *Moon Light*—how can you dislike that? Besides, he grows pot to support his mother. Five years from now his crop will probably be legal and he'll be a forward-thinking entrepreneur. Any-way, the deal is good. He'll be kicked loose Monday, charged only with growing for personal use. He'll lose the operation, of course, but there'll be no jail time."

"Deal?" I asked. Noble stood there looking at me a little too quiet and a little too long to feel comfortable. "Noble?"

"Guess they didn't tell you."

"I guess not."

"Moon gave up the location for the meth lab. It's on federal land. He put names to faces and even laid out a schedule. Your office is coordinating with the Forestry Service investigators and DEA. It's going to be a big deal. One of your guys has been on the place since this morning, confirming the location and logging activity."

Ten seconds later I was at the sheriff's door. He wasn't alone. There were a couple of suits there along with two of our detectives taking up the chairs, and Billy and two other deputies were standing to the side. I realized then that Billy must have been the one sur-veilling the lab. That was what he had been doing before he found me this morning. And that explained why he didn't just come right out and tell me where he had been. He saw me at the same time as the sher-iff. Billy was the only one in the room who looked pleased to see me.

Sheriff Benson held up his finger at me, then went on talking to the suits. Once he finished his point, he stood slowly, excused him-self and then came to me out in the hall, closing the door behind him.

"Because it's not your case," he said.

I opened my mouth to speak and he put up his finger again.

"*And*—you are not invited because you already put one of the suspects in the hospital. And. *And*—I know you want to be involved. I know it overlaps. And I know you got the initial information. *But.* This is a big deal, for the department and the county. It requires co-ordination with federal authorities who have asked that you not be involved."

"What? Why?"

"They weren't real specific. It might be that you have a reputa-tion. Do you want to ask what kind of reputation?"

I didn't.

"Or it might be that your friend the major got to them. One of the feds mentioned 'past history.'"

My finger was tracing the shape of the scar on my face as my mind was filling in blanks with hard-edged expletives. There wasn't time to curse or even snarl, otherwise the suits in the other room would have gotten a firsthand experience of my *reputation*. Before I could dig my grave any deeper, Darlene was at my side, reaching be-tween me and the sheriff to hand him a note. Without a word she was off again.

Sheriff Benson read the short lines on the little pink memo page then looked up at me and said, "Cotton Lambert's dead. He was shot in his hospital room."

The sheriff turned away from me to stick his head into the office and cut his meeting off. He told Billy to "Stop sucking that damn soda pop and get on the job." Then he turned back to me and said, "Stay away from this."

I needed to tell him that I had been there. It was important to be clear about timelines and what I had seen. But that was when the two feds came filing out of the office. They had both heard the sheriff telling me to stay away. They were smirking like they had read my name and number on the wall of a gas station bathroom.

Reach had gotten to them.

It is amazing how small the law-enforcement community can be. You encounter the same people when jurisdictions cross and agencies overlap. Like a small town—or worse, like a small high school—it only takes a few words to mark you in certain ways. And like the big, alpha, macho men they were, the feds were more than willing to believe the worst about a woman. Especially when that worst comes packaged in sneering innuendo and delivered by another male authority figure. I was suddenly thinking of what Billy had said to me that morning: *people talk, things get around.* Yeah, I was the poster child for that.

I opened my mouth to say something. Before that I hadn't bothered to think what I would say, so no telling what would have come out if Billy had not rattled the ice in his big soda cup. The feds walked out without the benefit of the piece of my mind they needed.

Billy stopped in the hall beside me. He looked one way to see the sheriff headed for his car. He looked the other way to watch the feds going off to the visitors' lot. With the cup in his hand he gestured at the backs of the suit jackets. "You know," he said, "some people are jerks. They don't mean to be, they just are. But they aren't enemies till you make them that way."

"What're you trying to say, Billy?" I left the edge in my voice so he would know that friends only goes so far.

"I'm trying to say that sometimes we have power we don't even realize."

"I want to chew nails and you're talking in riddles."

"The power to make enemies. And not to make them."

There is a lot to be said about having friends. Unfortunately, there is so much more to be said about being your own worst enemy that sucks the power out of so much self-understanding and New Age in-touch Zen bullshit or whatever Billy was finding in his soda.

"Don't you have to take a leak and get a refill?" I asked him. As I walked away I could feel him watching me and I wondered what he was thinking.

The real question was: What was I thinking? I wasn't. I was acting on my impulse to get the two feds out in the parking lot and—what? Nothing good. It was habit or it was a get-them-before-they-get-me instinct. Anyway I could look at it, confrontation was my first goal.

My only goal?

Maybe I'm learning. Maybe I'm growing. For once in my life I did the better thing and walked away. Both of the men were staring at me.

They expected me to make a scene.

"Good luck with everything," I said with a smile as I walked past their car. Then I waved and I smiled again as I went the long way around the building to my truck. I felt proud of myself.

* * *

A sane woman would have gone to Nelson's place and had a talk, maybe got herself proposed to again. If not that, then at least engaged in some joyous physicality. It'd been a long time since I was accused of sanity.

I went looking for Clare Bolin. I didn't find him by phone or by driving to the usual places. *His* usual places, that is. I found him at one of mine. His truck was in the lot in front of Uncle Orson's dock.

Being Saturday and a perfect day for fishing, the shop and dock slips were busy. Men were tinkering with their boats, pulling out or pulling in. Two men were cleaning their catch at the sinks mounted right on the railing. They used the hand pumps to bring lake water up and carry the scales and guts right back down with it. Unheeding of all the activity, Orson and Clare were sitting at the table eating chicken just off the grill and drinking clear whiskey from mason jars.

"Have a drink," Clare said, sliding one of half-a-dozen sealed jars across the table.

I don't know how my face looked at the moment but it must have been saying something. Uncle Orson reached out and slid the jar back with the others, then said, "I think Katrina is keeping a better eye on what she drinks these days." He grabbed an orange soda from the cooler and opened it with a rusty church key that had been dangling from the same string for longer than I'd been alive. "Isn't that right," he said, sliding the bottle across the tabletop.

"Close enough to right," I answered. I took a long drink.

"So are you going to marry him?" Uncle Orson asked while I had the bottle tilted up and my head back.

When I lowered the soda from my mouth I turned the bottle away and touched the back of my hand to my lips.

"So?"

"That's good," I said in the way of pointedly not answering. Then I looked to Clare. "I've been looking for you," I said.

"Don't bother," he said. "I'm out of the business."

"That's why I was looking."

"Did you know that Clare isn't just another bootlegger?" Orson chimed in. "He's certified."

"Certified?" I asked and I'm sure my eyebrow made a Vulcan arch as I did.

"Told you I was a teacher. Gotta do something with those summers off. I took classes in distilling and brewing. Lotta good they did me."

"Have you found out anything more about what's been going on?"

He shook his head. "Not really. Only thing I hear is about that restaurant place and I already told you what I think about it."

"What have you been hearing?" I asked.

"They're making over quota. That's all I know. I talked to Gabe Hoener. He was the master distiller there before he got fired."

"Over quota? Wouldn't that be a good thing? Why'd he get fired?"

"Not like that," Clare said. "Over state quotas. For in-house, they're only licensed to produce so much for onsite sales and enough to keep a gift shop going. They can distribute locally to wholesalers but the agreements say the distribution has to be less than fifty percent of total production. Gabe got fired for pointing that out."

"How much more are they making?"

"He said they could do a thousand gallons a month if they wanted to."

"That sounds like a lot."

"That place is lucky to sell one gallon a month," he said before taking a sip from his jar.

I took a drink from my soda, then asked, "So where's it all go?"

Clare shrugged. The motion seemed both an answer and a resignation. I finished my orange soda.

Uncle Orson tilted his head toward the screen door and followed the motion. I went with him outside to stand beside the grill. He picked up a pair of tongs and poked around at the chicken and brats. To the side was a pile of burgers keeping warm in a foil pan.

"So? You're not answering my question?" He added the brats and a couple of chicken breasts to the warming tray.

"Would you wrap up a couple of those burgers for me? I'll take them home to Nelson."

"Home?" he asked.

"Burgers," I said.

"You know, not answering is a kind of answer."

"You know what's an even better answer?"

"What?"

"Hamburgers. With cheese. And a frosty mug of shut-the-hell-up."

"I tell you," he said. "There's no love to be had around here."

"That's not true," I told him and put my hand on his arm and waited for him to look me in the eyes. "I love your burgers."

"You get your sense of humor from your father. He was never funny, either."

"I called him early this morning. I kind of thought he might be here."

"Nope. Not today. He's busy with work. Like it would kill him to retire."

I reached to the overhead shelf and lifted the brick that kept the stack of paper plates from blowing away. I pulled a couple out and reset the brick. "How busy can he be?"

On his side of the shelf Orson pulled down buns and put them on the plates. "Who knows with him? He went to Washington, I think. He wasn't very clear. There's a mess between Homeland Security and DoD involving an investigation into stolen weapons. For some reason they need an old man to take care of it. Must have been important. He sounded worried."

"He doesn't get worried," I said, opening and laying out the buns while Orson slipped the dripping patties onto them.

"No. He just never lets you see him worried." He hung the tongs on their hook and closed the lid on the grill before turning to face me straight on. "You know, we're not going to be around forever," he said.

I covered the plates with plastic wrap and concentrated on what I was doing.

"You understand what I'm saying?" he asked.

"I know what you're saying but I don't really want to think about it right now."

"There's never a good time for those thoughts. But maybe you need to spare some for the idea that someday you might have to take care of your dad instead of the other way around."

"Not him," I said, finally looking up. "And not you. Both of you are like rocks. You're always going to be here."

"Rocks used to be mountains," he said. "All of us pass."

"Is there something you're trying to tell me?" I asked. "Something specific?"

"Just that time has a way of running away with us all and maybe your daddy would retire, take things easier, if he felt a little more secure about you."

"That's a vote of confidence. Are you wanting me to marry Nelson so I'll be secure?"

"No. That's just so you'll be happy. I want you to be secure so your father can get on to his happiness."

I stacked the plates up and gestured with them. "Well, I'll be sure and let you know. Thanks for the burgers."

"Don't go away mad," he said. "And tell Nelson, *hey.*"

I did kind of want to be mad but it wasn't in me. It had drained out through the day. He was right, anyway. Not that being right had ever stopped my anger. I had realized, though, that I wanted to talk to Nelson; I wanted to share the thoughts I was having with him.

When I went back into the shop, Clare was no longer at the table. He was behind the counter, helping a bemused-looking man decide between mealworms and salmon eggs. At the same time he was discreetly slipping a jar of whiskey into a bag. It looked like having Clare around would help Uncle Orson's sales, if nothing else.

Nelson had been at the inside of the house like a tornado in a trailer park. There were boxes everywhere. Most were stout cardboard from the supermarket, but many were crates, wooden structures strong enough to carry gold bars. They held paintings in twos and threes. On the table were stacks of paper laid out in ordered rows, each pile bearing red tabs poking out every which way. They were all legal documents and the tabs were those little sticker things that point out the places one needs to sign.

Remaining untouched in the corner was the big easel and a work in progress. Beside that was the little stand with the single drawer. It was open and empty. I looked around through the jumble for the case with the revolver.

Packed away?

The sliding door to the deck stood open, letting fresh air and an equally welcome break from the heat into the room. Thinking I'd find Nelson out there, I followed the breeze. He wasn't there but he'd left something behind. A cigar butt and a Zippo lighter engraved with the Marine Corps globe and anchor.

A cigar? Is he kidding?

From behind me I heard the wet spit of a pull tab being opened. Nelson was standing there in old desert camo pants and no shirt. He was grinning like a Cheshire cat that had just won the lottery.

"Are you crazy?" I asked, pointing at the cigar stub, then to the beer in his hand.

His answer was to reach out his free hand and pull me into a kiss. I didn't want a kiss. I wanted an answer, but . . .

He tasted of beer and faintly of cigar. His skin was wet with sweat and smelled musky. He'd tried to cover it with—*was that Old Spice?* Altogether it was about as manly and wonderful a mixture as I could imagine. I kissed him back—hard.

When the kiss broke, I pulled back and looked at him. I knew I wanted to be angry with him for abusing himself but I couldn't. He really did look better than I had ever seen him. The bones that had shown through were maybe slightly less defined. On his head was a definite and prickly shadow of new growth. The real change was in his eyes. There was a lively fire to them that made me think of joys I'd never imagined.

"Crazy about you," he said.

There's something about a man with a stupid line when he doesn't know it's stupid. I kissed him again and decided not to nag about the cigar.

"You brought hamburgers," he said, pointing at them on the table as he led me back inside.

"And you brought lawyers."

"Don't worry," Nelson said after turning to wink at me. "It's not a prenup."

"Like you have anything I want," I teased.

"That's not true," he hit back earnestly. "You like that painting." He pointed to one securely crated away.

"I've already got that one on a coffee cup."

"You're breaking my heart."

"And who said I was going to marry you?"

"Like you have options." He grabbed up one of the burgers and pulled the plastic wrap away before burying his teeth in, chomping away almost half.

"You're in good spirits," I said. "Mean. But good."

"I feel good." He spoke and smiled while chewing. Then he used the beer to wash down the food. "I mean it. Good. Like I haven't felt in a long time, good."

"And all this?" I pointed to the piles and mess around us.

He'd taken another bite and was smiling around it. When he forced it down he said, "I'm making room."

"For what?"

He sat the remainder of the burger down right on top of a stack of papers. The look in his eyes was not as happy as it had been.

"I've been going through them too. Thinking and remembering. They need to be someplace more suited to long-term storage."

Nelson hadn't answered my question, but I didn't push. I was caught up in what he *did* say. It was easy for me to think of the thoughts and memories he spoke of as physical objects. They were boxes, some wrapped and secret, some worn from opening so many times. The contents were all treasures, even if some were sad. They were sitting, piled around us; the accumulation of a life. It was how I felt often. Like I lived with boxes labeled *Never Forget* or *Never Remember. Things That Were. Things That Might Have Been.*

"I know you think you're getting better—"

"I *am* better," he said.

After a long, thoughtful time I said, "I can't watch you die."

"That's not what I want. I want you to watch me live."

"What if these are just a few good days?"

"What if?" he said like it was a curse. "You can't live a life worried about all the what-ifs, because that's all there are. What if something good happens? What if something bad happens? News flash, Katrina Williams: They will happen. They have happened and will continue happening. I can make you a promise, though."

"What?"

"No matter what if—I promise that cancer won't kill me."

"How can you promise that?"

"Because this is my life—this is our life—and I'm bigger than cancer."

He smiled. It was so warm and confident it could not be doubted, but still . . . I flashed on an earlier thought I'd had on the deck: *There's something about a man who believes his own foolish lines.*

"I don't know . . . I don't know if I'm capable . . . I'm afraid I can't be here with you. For you."

"It's not for me, Katrina." He smiled like he had a secret thought, then he said, "Katrina. My own hurricane. You are a wild bluster. You blew into my life and changed everything."

That was the first time I was proud to be called Hurricane.

"I'm not so selfish to have asked you to marry me if it was for my sake," he said. "It's not for me, it's for you."

"I don't understand."

"You know the difference between you and me?"

I shook my head.

"I've been fighting to live. I think you've been fighting . . ." He thought about it. Then he shrugged weakly like he was giving up the search for the words he needed and said simply, "not to."

It was like being slapped.

"You think I want to die?"

This time it was his turn to shake his head. "Not wanting to die is not the same as wanting to live. Really live."

I wanted a reason to strike out at him. I wanted to conjure the anger again and shout, to scream how wrong he was.

But he wasn't. The real shame is that, until the last few days, everyone had seen it but me. At least I saw it then. I kissed him and told him that I loved him. Then I told him I would marry him.

Chapter 20

Islept in Nelson's bed for the first time that night. We were naked and close, whispering words that disappeared in the dark. Meaningless sound, endearments, and soft breath that held back, at least for me, the smallest worry. All the world melted away in our lovemaking. Nelson had opened not just the sliding door but most of the windows as well. The night carried clean heat and ripples of chill that washed the atmosphere of the house.

Everything about the night brought my skin to life. Everything made me smile. At one point, I had a secret thought.

The wheel spun in my favor.

I didn't say it out loud. Nelson would have thought me crazy. I wasn't so sure myself. Did insanity feel like happiness? Was it simply insane to be happy in this world?

When we were spent and tangled in stillness, I quietly said, "I'll never fall asleep." Then we were both out.

I didn't dream. That's to say, I didn't dream so I could see. My dreams were only feelings of warmth and safety within the void. I awoke with the creeping sunrise. My mouth was hot and dry. It felt like a monkey had been sleeping within it and smelled like it too.

It didn't matter and I couldn't wait. I woke Nelson. It wasn't easy but I got him to open his eyes and look at me. I asked him, "Do you still promise?"

"I promise."

Then I kissed him with my monkey mouth.

Sunday was like a cauldron into which we both dropped words and feelings, memories and expectations creating a spell of good feelings. We never left the house. I helped Nelson crate more of his work and I told him everything about Leech. The open, breezy windows of the house were like a single Cinerama screen on the world around us. Above, the sky was the color of old jeans with tufts of tangled white thread wearing through. Below, the rippled lake was catching sun on one angle and sky on another. Filling everything between sky and water were the trees. From far away there were only greens, but closer . . . reds and oranges mixed with yellow flipped at the tip of a branch that barely broke the frame of the window. A large white oak had begun turning.

From famine to feast, as they say. When I made it into the office Monday, my in-box was stuffed with responses from the previous week's calls and e-mails. There were notes from Family Services and multiple e-mails with attachments from the City of Branson, county, and state liquor-control agencies. The documents concerning Moonshines I forwarded to the sheriff and to the district attorney. I would go through them for information to connect dots between people but I was not qualified to make judgments about the legalities of the contracts. That would be someone else's job.

It was Carrie who I was most interested in. I had an e-mail confirming there was a file on her and the family with the Missouri Department of Social Services. That was basically all it said. That wasn't news to me. When I called, the social worker assigned to her case wouldn't talk to me on the phone. I gave my badge number and asked her to call me back at the sheriff's department number but she said no. She would not talk to me without meeting in person first. Some people are too good at their job. I had to go into Branson to meet her at the county office.

Marion Combs, of the Missouri Department of Social Services, was a sharp woman of about fifty. Blonde, but the color was fading away. She didn't dye it and something about that made her seem both tougher and warmer. Her eyes were blue and had a way about them that said little gets past. Immediately I knew she took her job and the kids assigned to her seriously.

"You look like someone who had a good weekend," she said as soon as I had introduced myself. Then she laughed at the look on my face. "Don't mind me. I get used to reading faces because almost everyone I meet in my job is hiding something. Like your job, I guess."

"At least in my job if they lie I get to beat it out of them," I said as I sat beside her piled desk.

Marion laughed again, then pointed a sharp, pink nail at me. "You have a reputation for such things, *Hurricane*."

"I have a tough time getting away from that."

"Don't try," she said. "There are much worse things to be known for than being a tough cop. Chuck hasn't fired you yet, has he?"

"Sheriff Benson? No ma'am, he hasn't, but I think at times it crosses his mind."

"I can call him Chuck. He was my beau once upon a time." Her smile was like an old photograph. It told the story of a lost moment. Then it faded and she asked, "You know why he won't?" I shook my head but Marion wasn't waiting for me. She went right on answering her own question. "Because you're the one cop in the county that everyone knows and is afraid of."

"I'm not sure that's such a good thing," I said.

"It is," she stated with complete certitude. Turning to paw through file folders on her desk, Marion shifted to the task at hand. "Now remind me: Which of my kids were you needing to know about?"

"Carrie Owens," I said.

She stopped digging and leaned back in her chair. "I don't need the file to talk about her. Wouldn't do much good. Almost nothing in it. Nothing on the lines, that is. Hers is sort of a between-the-lines kind of case, you know what I mean? What's she done? What do you need to know?"

"Abuse?"

"That's—between the lines. But I believe so. If I could prove it or if she would speak up, I'd have her out of that house."

"I actually think she might be counting on someone else to get her out."

"Who?"

Marion's blue eyes grew wide as I told her what I knew about Leech. When I finished, she went back to the piles on her desk and grabbed a thick file. From that she pulled a sheet of notebook paper with *Leech* scrawled over it in thick, scratchy letterings all made with different pens. She turned it over and on the back there was the same little verse that Billy had quoted to me. Below that, in a neat, girlish cursive unlike the bold strokes on the other side, were three lines.

I would give you anything,
I would give you anyone,
For you to give me a real family.

I liked Marion and meeting her had kept my mood up even after learning what I had about Carrie. Truthfully, though, my joy was buoyed by more than the new friendship. I had fallen for Nelson like a schoolgirl and was enjoying the drop. It was hard to focus on work and the things I needed to do. I wanted to check in on Clare and to make an appearance at Moonshines. I hadn't done anything on the investigation into the great RV shoot-out. Not that there was a lot of investigation needed. I was pretty certain who had done it; it was bringing them in and finding a witness to speak up that was the trick. That probably wouldn't happen now that the feds were involved and looking at the Nightriders for their own purposes.

Dad used to tell me: Line your problems up, largest to smallest. Then he went on to tell me that largest didn't always mean biggest. Sometimes the largest problem is a little thing that's important. So I went to Carrie Owens's home again wondering if, this time, I would get inside the front door.

I needn't have worried. Doors were not the issue. As soon as I pulled onto the street I could see a knot of people on one side watching the three on the other. Carrie, her mother, and a large man who looked like a Neanderthal with a cheap suit and cheaper haircut were in the yard yelling—make that *screaming*—at each other. The Neanderthal had to be the errant dad come home.

No one paid any attention to me as I pulled up, then got out of the SUV.

"I hate you," Carrie wailed in a cracking voice. "I hate everything about you. I just want to be left alone."

Her parents were ignoring her cries, too involved with venting their rage on each other.

"You make her like this," the mother shrieked. "You love her too much and coddle her, you make her a baby just like your little pet and you set her against me. How can I live with her when you're gone? You're always gone."

The father was flailing his arms like the words coming at him from both sides were physical blows that had to be deflected. He didn't scream, he bellowed. "I earn a living and I love my daughter. I'm a good father. What's wrong with that?"

"You love her more than me, that's what's wrong with it. You're wrong. Your love is wrong. Everything is wrong about you."

Carrie was still standing but she looked limp and crumpled. Over and over she said, "I hate you," but her screams had withered into wet sobs.

I thought the worst was over. They all looked wounded and spent. I should have been able to step in and talk, get them all separated and cooling down. This might have been the perfect time to get some truth, but it didn't happen that way.

Mr. Owens heard the shift in his daughter's voice from anger to despair. He turned to it and reached out to her. At the same time, several things happened and I had no way of telling what started the other or if there was some kind of emotional spontaneous combustion that flared from the smoldering heat.

Mrs. Owens darted forward with a voice that sounded like she had been gargling glass and snarled, "Don't touch her."

Carrie's voice exploded into a knife-edged wail as she screamed, "No."

The father didn't yell anymore: He swung out with fists that looked to be as large and hard as frozen turkeys. Carrie fell to the ground, pushed rather than punched, but still hit hard. Mrs. Owens caught the back swing of knobby knuckles against her temple and went down even harder.

I didn't talk then. I jumped in and hit the big man in the small of the back with my lowered shoulder. He shrugged me off and kept his feet. I almost fell but managed to keep my feet. It would have been better if I had fallen. Owens caught me by the hair, then pulled me in front of him while pushing my head down at the same time. Then his huge right hand smashed against my ear.

The blow was glancing but I heard the fireworks bursting in my head. When he struck, he released my hair. Either he thought I was done or he realized I was not his wife. It gave me the moment I needed to bring my weapon out and step back into a two-armed stance. My head was spinning. I needed the footing of the stance just to keep from falling. If I had to pull the trigger there was no telling what I might have hit. Probably nothing I aimed at. Luckily, I didn't have to find out.

Mr. Owens froze when the pistol was pointed at his chest. And when I commanded him to get on the ground, he did so. That was when I noticed the silence. Carrie, her mother, and her father on the ground were all looking at me like I was William Shatner beamed down among them.

I was grateful for the quiet. Once Mr. Owens was cuffed I left him there and called for transport and a deputy to take statements. I wouldn't be able to write anything until I saw fewer than five of everything. I also asked Darlene to call Marion Combs to tell her that I had arrested Mr. Owens and that Carrie probably needed some help. I didn't say that what I had heard confirmed our suspicions, but I was feeling pretty sure—with her father in jail—Carrie might feel better about talking to someone.

I was high on adrenaline and self-congratulation. One from the violence and the other from getting an abusive parent away from a child. The high dulled the grinding pain at my temple and carried me back to the sheriff's office with a song in my heart. Other people have MP3 players. I had personal playlists of songs locked in my head to fit most any mood I'd ever been in. Songs—like magic bookmarks on my emotions popping into focus like old friends to say: Remember this feeling. For a long, black period it had seemed to fail me. I was noticing more and more that it was cropping up again. As I drove with my windows down and a hand out in the hot wind I realized that the song in my head was "Mr. Blue Sky" by ELO. That had always been my happy, proud, and pleased-with-myself song. I thought I had lost it.

When I pulled into the parking lot I was still high on myself and the music of Jeff Lynne. If I hadn't have been so high I might have been paying more attention. Moon was just outside the doors of the jail talking with someone I couldn't really see and didn't really want to. There were other things on my mind. The two men were talking and Moon was shaking his head. My assumption was that the other man was also freshly released and asking for either money or a ride. I parked the SUV and sat for a moment with my head tilted back and my eyes closed. It felt good to just feel good for a minute. When I accepted the real world again and opened my eyes Moon was walking away alone. The man he had been talking to was leaving the lot in a hurry. Even through the tinted windows on his car I caught the flash of silver jewelry and a wide-toothed grin. The same man I had seen outside the hospital and at Moonshines.

Even through my good mood that nagged at me. Perhaps I should have listened.

Inside the station I sat at my desk and stayed there for only a few minutes. Nothing, not the grinding ache in the side of my head or the good feeling of putting Owens away, could keep my mind off of the previous day. Is it any surprise that phone calls and paperwork couldn't hold my attention?

I checked out and went to get some lunch. Since we had eaten the greasy burgers and delivery pizza all weekend I sacrificed and picked up a couple of salads and went to share with Nelson.

Sometimes sacrifice has its rewards.

Nelson didn't want food. When I came into the house he was working at the easel. He and the painting were both bathed in sunlight. The smile that crossed his face when I came in was brighter, though. Then it changed into a smile that had a touch of the night in it.

After putting down his brushes he wiped his hands off on a stained cloth, then his shirt. The shirt was almost a palette of its own, smeared and blotted with bright reminders of the images he had captured.

As I set the food on the table he caught me and pulled my shoulders around. It was a gentle demand. But still demanding. His warm hands—still smelling of paint and oil, smelling of him—embraced my face. Then they pulled me into a kiss. The kind of kiss most of us dream of coming home to. At once, as if the moment were choreographed, his tongue slipped into my mouth and his thumb brushed the scar beside my eye. I accepted both completely and it was as if the scar were being erased in the wetness of the kiss.

His hands, his mouth, his eyes—even his skin—seemed to be hungry for contact as he touched me. Not touched: He enveloped me like a microbe I had learned about in biology class long ago. It fed by engulfing prey and simply making the smaller creature part of it. That was how Nelson was making me feel.

And I was responding. So help me, I was just as hungry and didn't know until he had shown me what I needed.

At my desk again, I smiled through my paperwork. Between sexy daydreams I even managed to write out a very long, detailed synopsis of everything I had been working on. Within it I drew both connections and conclusions between the various elements. I gave special attention to Mr. Owens. I suggested further investigation into the murder of Angela Briscoe and gave my opinion that Carrie Owens had put Danny Barnes up to the murder in some kind of weird pact to gain favor from Leech. Responsibility, I ultimately laid at her father's feet.

On a separate couple of pages, I recounted my visit to the hospital and subsequent encounter with the man dressed like a square-dance pimp. Then I noted seeing him talking with Moon here at the jail.

The man had a definite connection to all the different groups that were somehow connected to meth, whiskey, and murder. I had seen him at Moonshines on that first night and the night that the RV was shot up. He had shown up at the hospital where Cotton was being treated, then murdered.

I made a note to check up on Moon.

The sheriff was not in the office and Darlene told me there was a planning session with the feds. We were all hitting the Ozarks Night-riders meth lab early Tuesday morning. *We* being the DEA, the Forestry Service, and the Sheriff's Department. *We* except for me.

I was excluded.

I felt excluded and angry about it. Honestly, though, it was a confusing kind of anger. Maybe the anger came from the confusion—I didn't know. What I did know was that I had put myself here. It doesn't sound like much of a revelation, but it was. After more than ten years of blaming events and other people I could finally say most of the mess in my life was my doing. It only took years, gallons of beer and whiskey, everyone I knew telling me the obvious, and falling in love.

Who's counting?

They say that it's never too late to start trying to repair your life. I called a florist and sent flowers to Emily Benson, the sheriff's wife.

My day was over. I packed it in, putting my notes in my files, turning in my logs, and dropping my legal pads on Sheriff Benson's desk. There were still some things I wanted to look further into, so I printed some of the material sent to me in response to e-mails. It all dealt with liquor-control regulations and the concessions made by all parties to allow a distillery restaurant under state, county, and city regulations. There was a lot of it. Apparently, there had been many promises made and even more stipulations put on those promises. It was a complex deal that involved taxes and tax incentives, zoning, and sales controls on all liquor produced. I thought I would go over it tonight looking for some reason behind the death of Johnny Middleton.

After another handful of aspirin for the throbbing Owens had given me, I went home to pick up a few things. On the way I called Daddy. He didn't answer. I called Uncle Orson on the shop line and Clare picked up.

"Sounds like you have a new summer job," I told him.

"Just helping out," he said. "And selling some—"

"Really, Clare. The less I know, the better."

"Worms," he finished. Then he hollered across the room and into the phone: "Orson. It's the Hurricane."

"Don't call me that," I said but I was speaking to the air.

The phone rattled on the far end, sounding like it had been thrown and dropped, then Uncle Orson was on the line.

"Hey kid."

"Have you talked to Daddy?" I asked.

"Nope."

"He's not picking up. Do you think he's all right?"

"I think he's just busy," he said. Then his tone changed to conspiratorial as he asked, "You have something to tell him?"

At first I tried to sigh it away like he was being silly, but Orson didn't let up. He didn't talk, either. Silence spoke his expectation.

I said, "Yes," and I was amazed to hear the joy in my voice.

"Don't tell me," Orson jumped in. "Not officially. I'll wait until after you tell your dad. He'll be pretty happy, though, I'm telling you."

"Thanks, Uncle Orson, I'm glad. We'll come see you soon."

After hanging up the cell I rolled the windows down and listened to the tires on the road and the songs in my head. I should have been listening for the next spin of fortune's wheel.

There was something that I had read in a book about a girl with cancer. She talked about patients having that last good day. The final day when they feel good and strong and the world holds promise. After that comes a final fall into one long, final tomorrow. The thing about the last good day, she wrote, was you never knew until the long tomorrow that the good day had been lived.

Chapter 21

All the way back to Nelson's place I was still singing cheerful songs. The last couple of miles, though, the thoughts behind the tunes began to turn decidedly naughty.

I hope he has the strength for more of what we had for lunch.

Those thoughts were derailed by the sight of a strange car in the drive. It was sleek, black, and expensive looking. As soon as I stepped out of the truck I could hear loud voices coming through the open windows. Nelson sounded angry. Byron Figorelli sounded desperate.

"You got no idea what kind of shit storm is coming down the pipe on this," Figorelli said.

"I'm ready for it," Nelson told him. "No. Screw that. I want it. I want your best shot because I'm ready to dance."

"You ain't ready for this, you stupid fuck. Nobody is. You're messing with money and people that don't give it up. Worse than that, you're putting me in the middle. Same place you put Johnny."

That's when I walked in.

"Is that a threat?" I asked as soon as the door was open.

Figorelli looked like he was going to spit a bad taste from his mouth. He looked at me, then he looked back at Nelson.

"You can fuckin' bet this ain't over," he said, then jabbed his fat finger like he was marking something in the air between them. "It's just gettin' started." He turned back to me and took a calming breath as he ran his hand over his fading hair. "Only punks make threats. I ain't no punk."

"Which one of us are you trying to convince?" I asked him.

"You're kind of a tough broad, ain't you? But I asked around. It wasn't always that way."

It took a moment for his meaning to sink in. Nelson understood instantly. He rushed forward with his arms out like he was going to grab Figorelli by the neck.

"You son of—" It was as far as he got. With surprising speed Figorelli turned, using his bulk and his powerful arm to punch into Nelson's gut. It made an awful sound like a locomotive hitting a cow. Nelson went down in a pained outrush of breath and a spray of fresh, red blood.

Seemingly at the same time, as if he had expected it, my weapon came out and Figorelli's hands went up.

"Just let one of your chins wiggle," I said. "Give me an excuse."

He smiled. "You think I'd still be here if I ever gave a cop an excuse?"

We stayed like that for too long, gazes locked, listening to Nelson gasping, his lungs clawing for breath on the floor. Finally I twitched the gun in my hands. pointing toward the door.

"Get out of here," I told Figorelli.

"Aren't you going to tell me that we'll finish this later?" he asked, already moving.

"Wouldn't that be a threat?"

He didn't answer and I didn't wait to get on the floor beside Nelson. His breath was coming back and he was using it in a kind of wheezing laugh.

"I don't know what you have to laugh about," I said.

"I—" he said then gasped some air. "I—" Gasp. Laugh. "I—I keep—I keep getting my ass . . . kicked."

"Yes," I agreed. "That's funny stuff."

I wet a cloth in the kitchen and cleaned up the spots of blood on Nelson's face. There was more than I would have expected.

"What's the story with the blood?" I asked. "You said you were getting better."

"A little better every day but not overnight," he said, watching my face as I cleaned his. "What a woman."

"Don't think I can be distracted that easily. What was all that about, anyway?"

"Same shit, different day."

"I think you were purposely trying to antagonize him. These people can be dangerous."

"You're dangerous," he said.

That stopped me and I really looked hard into his eyes when I asked, "What's that mean?"

"You do things to my heart."

There was no holding back the laugh. I don't guess his feelings were too hurt because he joined in and pulled me down onto the floor with him. He tried to kiss me but I was laughing too hard and pushed his face away.

"See?" he said. "Now you're breaking my heart."

"There's nothing wrong with your heart," I told him as I got to my feet and offered my hand to help him up. "It's your head I'm not so sure about."

Once on his feet, Nelson took a moment to straighten out and stretch, then he said, "I have something for you." He pointed at the big easel in the corner.

There was a small painting there. It was a colorful forest scene with dapples of sunlight through green leaves and shadowed trunks. It would have been lovely except for the figure in the center. Nelson had painted a black and ragged-looking Leech who appeared to be striding through the wood with an evil purpose.

"Why?" was all I could say.

"I thought it might help you reach the girl. The one you told me about. If you give it to her—"

I cut him off with a kiss. It was warm and loving. I was grateful for his thoughtfulness, and the fact he'd taken an interest in someone who was important to me but he'd never met. After that, I kissed him again, with something a little more than gratitude. As soon as my motivation shifted, so did his.

It was just another way he was so much like a new man. The change made me determined to be a new kind of woman to go right along with him. That was how I ended up naked and on the couch again.

In so many ways, even with words, we said, "I love you."

We slept well.

I slept well. For the first time in so very long I dreamed of summer and color. There was no fear or fading away. Once in the night I woke. Something had changed. Sleep, for any veteran who's been in combat zones, was like that. You sleep through anything routine, but the slightest change will bring you bolting upright. It's like perimeter watch or hunting: You let your eyes lose focus and see only movement.

It was Nelson's breathing that had changed. As I waited in the dark beside him, it caught again, sounding wet and rough for a moment, then evened. All was right with my world and I closed my eyes, finally understanding some of the lessons my father had tried to give me about being happy.

Choose it, he'd said so many times. *Choose to be happy.*

I could hear myself telling him, *It's not that easy.*

You're right, he would say. *Easy is sitting around feeling sad and sorry for yourself. Happy takes work. Did I raise a lazy girl?*

I drifted off again with Nelson's breathing and Daddy's wise words in my head.

The next time I awoke the sun was up and the alarm on my phone was sounding. Nelson was already gone. When I shut off my phone I noticed that the case was gone from his pillow. On the pillow were still wet red-brown stains where blood had soaked through.

His breathing.

We needed to have a long, hard talk about his health. I had been meaning to but avoiding it at the same time. Trying to run toward happiness and away from the darkness at the same time. It was true that at first I was hiding my head in the warm embrace of ignorance, but yesterday was like a miracle. He was the man you saw in his eyes. Maybe I just didn't want to curse the light and blow out the candle.

Nelson came into the room with coffee and a grin. Nothing else, though. He was still completely naked.

"Morning," he said with the kind of cocky smile that speaks of the best kind of pride you can see in a lover's face.

I wasn't buying it.

"There was blood on your pillow. You were trying to hide it."

The smile flickered but he put it into the coffee before it collapsed entirely. When he looked back up it wasn't quite a smile anymore. "Yes," he said. "That'll still happen for a bit."

"We haven't talked—"

"There's no reason to. Don't I look better to you? Stronger. Wasn't I feeling better last night?"

Cocky.

He won me over, but not back into bed. He did come into the shower with me. I had to kick him out when he asked if he could do the shaving. I would have never gotten to work.

Nelson's painting of Leech was wrapped in butcher paper and tied with a string. There is no appropriate festive wrapping paper for a present that is meant to break the ice and get a girl to talk about her friend's murder. I carried it with me as I walked up to the Owens house. If Carrie was looking out the windows I wanted her to see it, maybe get curious.

When I had followed up with Marion after arresting Carrie's father, I was surprised to learn that the girl would remain in the home. Marion said the mother would fight any action, and with the dad out of the house, she'd win. I don't envy a social worker her job.

Carrie opened the door before I knocked. She pulled it back just enough to push her face through. The rest of her was draped in a cartoon-character bathrobe that was much too small and all but falling apart. Her legs were bare. On the one foot I could see was a fuzzy animal slipper.

"You can't be here when my mom's gone," she said.

"Where is your mother?" I asked.

"With lawyers. What's that?" She nodded at the package in my hand.

"Something for you," I told her. "A present."

"For me?" Carrie thrust her arm through the gap in the door to reach for the picture. When she did, the unbelted robe fell open. Under it was only a pair of stretched and ragged princess panties that should have been considered outgrown years ago.

"Cover yourself up," I said.

Carrie looked at me like I had shouted. She pulled her arm back and clutched the robe for a moment before she tried defiance. "What's it matter?" she asked. "You're a girl." She let the robe open again, then placed her hands on the jutting bones of her small hips. "Mama says boys are the problem. They always want something. If it's just girls it's fine."

"It's rude," I told her before pushing past into the dim house. "People don't need to see you naked. It's about respect."

"Well, what if I don't respect you?"

"Self-respect, Carrie. It's about respecting yourself."

I refused to look at her as long as she was trying to shock me with skin. She tried to hold her ground but I could feel her staring at the gift in my hands. While she worked through things I looked around the front room of the house. It was tidy in a way, but dirty. Like a junk store that took care to arrange odd bits of furniture then never dusted or vacuumed the merchandise. It smelled of mold and moist rot.

"You can't be in here without my mama home," Carrie said.

When I looked at her the robe was no longer wide open but it wasn't closed. I shot her a hard look and turned away again.

"Even a cop?" I asked. "Would she really mind you talking to me?"

"Mama hates cops. She says they're just snoops looking in on other people's business." She pulled the robe tight. "What's in the package?"

That time I smiled when I looked her over. Then I sat on the edge of a chair and said, "First, come here."

"We're not supposed to sit in here. It's for company, but we don't have company. Ever."

"Is that your father's rule?"

Carrie shook her head. "Mama's rules. They're all her rules. What are you doing?"

I had untied the cotton string that wrapped the package and held it out to check the length.

"Come here," I said. She came and stood right at my feet. I put the string around her waist and tied it like a belt for her robe. "There. Isn't that better?" She shrugged with her eyes locked on the open package in my lap. "Okay, time for the present."

I lifted the painting from the paper and turned the front around with a little flourish. Carrie's face lit with the kind of awe usually reserved for miracles. Without making a sound her lips formed the name Leech.

She took the picture in her hands, staring at it as if she could fall in, then said, "He's beautiful."

I was ready to tell her about who painted it and why. I thought it would make asking some questions easier. But . . . what she said stuck in my mind.

He's so beautiful.

Not the painting. Leech himself.

The phrase, along with the reverential look on Carrie's face, set off alarms in my brain.

This was a bad idea.

There was something wrong about her reaction. It gave me the feeling that I had just tried to put out a small fire with napalm.

That was when the door opened and Mrs. Owens came in.

"What are you doing here?" she asked, huffing and dragging out the word *you*, until it sounded like *heyew*. The combined effects of accent, cigarettes, and liquor did nothing to hide the hate in her voice.

Carrie was frozen in place for no more than a heartbeat, then she ran. Without looking back she disappeared into the gloom of the house. I heard her feet moving on stairs, then silence.

It felt wrong. All of it in so many ways. Somehow I had made things worse. I knew that as surely as I knew the pattern of my own scars. It was the feeling you get when you take the last wrong turn in a place where your skin color marks you as either threat or target. A storm-cloud feeling.

I stood. Mrs. Owens came away from the door, leaving it open behind her. She got up in my face close enough that I could smell the booze on her breath. She wasn't drunk, though. I didn't think so, anyway. That judgment could have been colored by my own guilt about drinking and control. It would have been easier if she was obviously drunk. I would have had reason to take Carrie. I would have called Marion and gotten her there.

"What were you trying to do to my daughter?" Mrs. Owens's question dripped with disgust at its own accusation.

It was a shocking suggestion. Another wrong heaped on the pile of what I was feeling at the moment.

"I just needed to ask Carrie some questions—"

"My lawyer says you can't without me or him there."

"That's right, but—"

"Get out."

"Ma'am—"

"Get out," she said again in a voice that had gone painfully flat.

Wrong. Wrong. Wrong.

"Her daddy's gone," she said, pointing at Carrie. "And my Riley won't come around. You've ruined it all. Get out."

I left. With me I took the feeling of spiders dancing on my skin. A thousand tiny legs tapping out a Morse-code warning. My only defense for leaving was that I didn't understand.

Chapter 22

I called Marion and she said she would visit Carrie and her mother that afternoon to check on things. It wasn't perfect but it was better than nothing. While we talked I tried to explain my feelings. There were no words. There should be. There should be a word for certainty of danger without reason or genuine knowledge. *Faith* came to mind, but it didn't fit. I didn't just have faith that I had blundered and made a bad situation worse. I knew the way you know the threat of a snarling dog.

I did everything I legally could and I did it right. After I talked with Marion, who was the girl's advocate and caseworker, I went to the station and had a talk with the sheriff. He didn't complain or tell me I was being foolish. A unit was parked at the end of the street in the same spot where I had first encountered Carrie and Danny. Then he thanked me for the flowers.

"She liked them?" I asked.

"She loved them," he said. "Wildflowers are her favorite. Getting them meant a lot." His eyes welled and reddened. His big hands were shaking slightly.

"Something's happened," I said. "The lumpectomy?"

"It's small," he said. "We caught it early, we thought. We—I—I goddamn well thought it was going to be fine. Early is good, you think. Small is the motherfucking best case, isn't it?"

I nodded mutely. He watched me for a moment then looked away.

"She was having headaches. Everyone has headaches and all she's going through, who the hell wouldn't have headaches?" He kept looking out the window as he spoke. "Shit."

After a long silence, I said, "Sheriff . . ."

"Shit," he said again. "Shit. Shit. Shit. Goddamn, motherfuck."

He turned and looked right at me and continued. "Son of a cocksucking bitch, Hurricane. Headaches. Why would you think anything about that when she had breast cancer? She was dizzy too. We thought it was stress. Bad sleep. Bad thoughts.

"Did I ever tell you how glad she was you joined the department? She barely knew you but she was proud of you just the same. She loved that we had a woman we could call Hurricane. 'That girl kicks ass,' she'd always tell me. 'She's a keeper.' Hell, if you were to run against me, I think she'd vote for you."

I tried to smile. I said, "Thank you," then wondered why. There was no knowing what to say.

"It's in her brain," he said, all the fire having gone out of his voice. "Breast cancer in her goddamn brain. How does that happen? How does any of this even happen? No one deserves this." He rose from his chair and shoved it aside as he went to a box of tissues he kept on the windowsill. They were there for hard conversations with loved ones. He probably thought he'd never need them for himself. "It wasn't supposed to be like this."

I took the precaution of locking the office door before I embraced him. He cried as I held him tightly with nothing to say that could ease his pain.

When he had finally fallen quiet I suggested that he should go be with his wife. He wouldn't, not with the biker bust in the morning. "It's too big," he said. "Too messy with too many jurisdictions. Complicated is dangerous."

So I went.

"Detective Katrina 'Hurricane' Williams," Emily Benson said as soon as I appeared in the doorway of her hospital room. The flowers I had sent were on the nightstand beside the bed. They were not alone. There was a river of flowers, cards, and balloons running along the room's windows. Emily herself looked as lively as the festive display that hemmed her in.

She was smiling and wearing a pink gown as bright as her eyes. I smiled back, so relieved not to see a frail, suffering woman.

"You look like you saw a ghost," she said. "Or maybe you expected to."

"The sheriff is pretty worried."

"I know he is. In here you can call him Chuck. Sit. Talk with me."

"How are you?"

"About anything but that," she jumped in.

So we spent the afternoon talking. Technically, I was on duty. If anyone really needed me they'd call, I rationalized. Since no one did . . .

She was easy to talk with and aware of everything that went on within the department. When she heard about my handwritten reports to her husband she said, "We'll put a stop to that. It's just because he likes you. I *can* count on you not to try and steal my husband, can't I?"

"No promises," I said.

Emily laughed hard. It was like the cackle of the good witch.

Telling her about my morning eased my mind more. Not because she offered any profound advice. It was more because she was a good person to talk to. And talking about my encounter with Carrie and her mother actually created a bit of distance from the moment. It was easier to believe my fears were foolish chatting about them with someone who was doing so well with their own worries.

When I left, I promised to visit again and often. The day was over. I called in and checked myself out.

I went home to Nelson's place and, for the first time, put on the ring that he had given me. I would have been happy staying in. Actually, I would have preferred it, but we went to Moonshines again. Nelson said he needed to check in and talk with a lawyer about how Middleton's death impacted the partnership. There was something about it that he left unsaid, though. Worries or thoughts that he kept out of words showed on his face. It had something to do with why Figorelli had come to see him, I was sure. Nelson denied it.

Walking into the place, I noticed a genuine difference. There were all the same things in the same place but the feeling had changed. For one thing there were fewer people and a lot less noise. The Wild West party atmosphere was gone, replaced by a kind of police-state vibe. It was what I imagined a Mob club might have felt like in the 1940s— *Have all the fun you want, but we have ways of making sure you color inside our lines.*

Without a word the hostess took us into the restaurant. As we passed the bar I noticed a knot of men at a table. They were all thick-necked and black-suited like a funeral director's mafia. In the center of them was Byron Figorelli. He saw me looking and he stared right back. I couldn't hear but I saw him saying something and smirking at his own sense of humor. Everyone at the table turned and looked at us, then shared a laugh at our backs. Nelson seemed not to notice and I held my tongue. The hostess took us back to the same secluded table we had before.

Again, without our having asked, a platter of assorted appetizers came to the table. It was followed by the appearance of Figorelli. He was shadowed by Jimmy Cardo and the other four men in black.

"I see you got the appetizers. I wanted you to give them a try. A peace offering for things over and done with, know what I mean? I fired the yokel tried to pass off cow nuts as food."

"Bull," Nelson said.

"The fuck?" Figorelli shot back. His face went in two directions like he wasn't sure if he'd been insulted, but he hoped that he had been.

"Bull nuts. Cows don't have nuts. A cow is female."

Figorelli stared for a moment, his mouth open and his eyes narrowed. Then he decided to laugh. It was a mocking bray that triggered lifeless smiles in the other men.

"You're all right," Figorelli said to Nelson. "An' I want you to know I have forgotten all about our earlier encounter."

"Very kind of you," Nelson said flatly.

"Damn straight," Figorelli responded, not catching the tone at all. "No hard feelins. I understand a man wantin' to hang onto things. I don't let go so easy myself, but when it comes to gettin' mine . . . well, then I can be a patient man."

"What are you trying to say?" Nelson asked.

"What? I'm being too subtle? I'm just trying to be respectful with the good lady present." Figorelli nodded at me but his eyes stayed on Nelson. He was enjoying his position and whatever secret he thought he had. Looking at him I could see him as a child holding other kids in the dirt for the joy of hearing them scream *uncle*.

"No need to be prissy on my part," I told him. "Nothing about a man like you can shock me."

"Hey, that's good," he said, shifting his gaze my way for the first time. It was just for a moment, then his eyes targeted right back on Nelson. "Maybe the cow has the balls after all."

Even at the edge of my vision I could see a new tension form in Nelson's shoulders. At the same time, his hands flexed against the edge of the table. He would have stood and taken a swing at Figorelli in the next moment if I hadn't have put my hand on his shoulder. I didn't do it so much for Nelson. It was more for my job. The goons behind Figorelli were ready and eager for Nelson to make a move. I would have killed at least one of them. This time I hadn't left my weapon in the truck.

"Stop trying to show off your dick," I told Figorelli. "If it was all that big you wouldn't need four low-rent goombahs to stand around and give you reassurance."

Color bloomed in his jowls, darkening into a red deposit under his eyes. The false smiles on the four other men turned into straight lines of icy anticipation.

"Nice." All the life was in Figorelli's face now. His voice had gone as lively as rigor mortis. "You kiss your mother with that mouth?"

With my hand still on Nelson's shoulder I rose from my seat and looked down into Figorelli's face. "Believe me," I said, my voice as cold and hard-edged as his. "You don't want to compare which one of us shames their mother more."

The red on his face turned a deep, boiling scarlet. I think something would have happened then if we hadn't been interrupted.

"Well, ain't this a pretty picture?" It was the man in the sequin suit sidling up between the four sour-faced men in black.

"*Pretty* don't cover everything," Figorelli said, keeping his stare locked on me.

My hand was pushed off by Nelson as he stood slowly. He was the Marine he had once been: strong, straight, and angry. He moved sideways, injecting himself between me and Figorelli, then leaning down to get his face close to the other man's.

"We're a long way from pretty right now, you little pissant son of a bitch. If you want to trade insults or work it out some other way, let's you and me go dance outside."

I had to admit, even then, in the middle of the situation, I was proud of Nelson. There is something to be said about someone who won't back down even if he knows the fight won't be fair or go their way.

Figorelli broke first, though. He laughed softly without amusement. "Look at us," he said. "This isn't what I wanted. An' there ain't no reason for it, after all. Is there, Bodie?"

"None a'tall," said the man in the shiny suit.

"Excuse my manners," Figorelli went on, "This is Bodie Dauterive.

He's a lawyer helping me out on some business affairs. He was just filling me in on some new developments before you arrived."

"Indeed I was," Dauterive said, lifting the Stetson he had been holding down by his knee to cover his heart and satin-embroidered cactus. He did not offer his hand. "The lady deputy and I have met, although there were no introductions."

"Sheriff's detective," Nelson corrected him and I thought he sounded proud to say so.

"Detective." Dauterive nodded to me.

"And these are some other associates of mine from down home," Figorelli said, gesturing to the black suits. "You know Jimmy Cardo." Cardo didn't react at all to the acknowledgement. "Then there is Charlie Castellano, Dean Morelli, and Sal Rubio." The men were like statues almost posing for us.

"No one really cares," Nelson said. "I got a call from Mr. Dauterive here asking me to talk with him about Johnny's estate and the partnership. Now that I see he's your lawyer, I don't imagine that we have much to talk about."

"See, that's the thing," Figorelli said. "You don't. Or you won't much longer, will you?" He let that hang there a moment, then went on. "Johnny had contracts with us just like he did with you. An' funny thing about contracts. They can take care of so many little problems. His had a—whaddaya call it?" He looked at Dauterive.

"A buyout clause," Dauterive said.

"A buyout clause," Figorelli echoed.

"In this-here case, the clause compels the sale of shares to the partners in the event of death. We have exercised those rights and acquired all of Johnny Middleton's share."

"I imagine I had some rights to exercise if I wanted to. Why wasn't I offered the chance to purchase shares?"

"Well, now . . ." Dauterive looked like he found something distasteful. "See, we considered the point kind of . . . well . . . moot, bein' the best word, I'm guessin'. Considering your condition and all."

"And what do you know about his condition?" I asked, letting the anger rise in my voice.

"Everything we need to know," Figorelli said. "What is it? Couple of months at best?"

It couldn't be true, but hearing it spit out like that—bald-faced and hateful—was like pornography in kindergarten. It was Nelson's turn to place a hand on me, gripping my upper arm. Until he had, I was unaware of reaching for my weapon.

"Truth is we'll have all your shares in just a couple of months and all we have to do is wait. Unless you want a little play-around money before you kick off? We can still make a deal." Figorelli kept talking, kept trying to pull me out. I realized he wanted a scene for some reason. I realized as well, he was close to getting more than he wanted.

"That's what you're hoping for? That I'll just keel over and you get what you want?" Nelson almost laughed. It started as a half-smile, the kind that hides its meaning, then opened up ready to give sound to the expression. What came out never really matured into a laugh, though. It was a cough of dismissal, deep and full of irony. He covered his mouth with a napkin that came away wet with blood. All the men lined up against him looked at the red stain and saw weakness.

"I've got news for you," Nelson said to them, tossing the napkin down without looking at it. "You think I'm hard to deal with, wait until you have to talk to my wife."

"You have no wife, Mr. Solomon," Dauterive said. "You have been checked out pretty good, if I do say so."

Nelson grinned. I smiled. "Gentleman," he said, "First, maybe I don't plan on dying to fit your convenience. Second, please meet my fiancée, Miss Katrina Williams."

I lifted my left hand to show off the diamond sparkling there. No one was smiling.

"Understand—as soon as we're married," Nelson went on, "Katrina becomes my heir and executor of the trust into which all my assets will be tucked away."

I was as surprised as they were.

Figorelli said, "It won't matter. She'll have to sell." But I could tell a little of the air had gone out of his tires. He wasn't nearly as sure as he wanted to be.

Nelson looked over at Dauterive and said, "I have my own lawyer, Mr. Dauterive."

"He can't do that, can he?" Figorelli asked.

Dauterive said, "Yes. He can transfer or sell his shares before his death."

There was no reason to include the phrase *before his death*, yet it was spoken with obvious meaning. It wasn't a threat so much as pointing out a timeline. He was telling either Figorelli or Nelson that this wasn't over. I wasn't sure which.

"But you told me that he had to offer them to the partners before he could sell them," Figorelli said. He clearly had not caught the same meaning that I had.

"But he's not selling them, Byron. He's putting them into trust to provide for his wife." Dauterive looked from his client to Nelson, then said, "It is a rightly good move." It sounded like a compliment but this time his eyes showed that the words had real threat. They set the hairs on my body upright and sizzling.

"Ah believe we should leave these people to their dinner now, don't you?" He spoke to Figorelli, even putting a hand on his elbow to urge him away from the table, but there were two other things I noticed about Dauterive at that moment. His accent seemed to thin out when he wanted it to. And it was to him, not Figorelli, to which the four background men looked to at that moment. The one who had been introduced as Sal Rubio, a squat, bald man with eyes like a rheumy pig, nodded so slightly it might have been just a tic. Then he looked at me. He was the last to wander from our table.

They didn't go quickly but it was still a sudden silence. The tension that seeped from my body told me how ready I had been for violence.

Ready for violence or wanting it?

Not all of the tension left me. There was still one thing about the encounter bothering me.

"Do they know something about your health that I don't?" I asked Nelson.

He looked down before looking at me. On the table was the napkin spotted with his blood. Nelson turned it over as if hiding the evidence denied it. It was a guilty move. When he looked at me I asked the question again.

"They think they know something," he said. "Things were bad. For a long time they were very bad, you know that."

"And now?"

"I was weak. I was wasted and dying. Now I'm living."

"That's not an answer."

"I don't have any answers."

"Are you better? Are you going to keep getting better? What is your doctor telling you?"

"Look at me," he said.

I did. Even standing there in the faded light of Moonshines he stood straighter and filled out his pants more than when I had first met him. Reaching to touch his face, which had lost some of its angles, I let my hand stroke behind his ear and felt the new hair.

"Do I look like a sick man?"

He was right. What he looked like was a man who had been sick but was mending rather than a man who was sliding toward his death.

"I want to talk to your doctor," I said.

"Don't trust me?" Nelson asked, smiling.

"You're not telling me something."

He smiled again. It was easy and quick like a silk sheet pulled over a naked body. Then he relaxed into it and said, "You're right. I was going to wait until I got you into bed again to ask, but I want to marry you tomorrow."

"Tomorrow?" The word came right through my ears and splashed the back of my mind. He wasn't playing or bluffing.

Am I?

"First thing," he said. "Let's get out of here and tell your family. They'll want to be there."

"Yes," I said, just then making my decision. "Yes they will."

We left Moonshines laughing and holding hands and for the second time without tasting any food. As we passed the bar I noticed Figorelli sitting alone in a dark corner. He saw us but made no acknowledgement.

I didn't waste another thought on the man. As soon as we were outside of Moonshines I called Uncle Orson to let him know that we were on our way.

Chapter 23

By the time we pulled up at the dock, the smell of steaks over hot coals was coming through our open windows. In the parking lot were two other vehicles that I recognized. Clare's truck was close to the water and made obvious by the glare of the dock's strings of bare bulbs. Nestled into shadow, trying hard not to be obvious, was Major Reach and his rented car. Still watching.

Once out of the truck we started up the bobbing plank walkway hand in hand. At the gate, I stopped, then turned my body to block Nelson. With a quick smile I wrapped an arm around his shoulders and put one hand on the back of his head. It was good to feel the new fuzz on his scalp as I pulled him in for a deep kiss. I don't think he felt it when I lifted my hand and held a single finger up in Reach's direction.

There was no way to see if the major got the message. I was pretty sure he did. Sometimes you feel it when communication is clear. For too long I had been letting him do all the communicating. It was time my message got through. At first it had worried me when he came around with the suggestion that I was somehow taking revenge for what had happened to me. Then it had bothered me that all of this was still going on so many years later. Reach had a bug up his ass about me and most of it was personal. He took a lot of heat when things got messy. As soon as my case became high-profile someone had to get put down. It's the Army way. I understand pissed off. I live with my own anger every day. I was tired of dealing with his.

After the kiss, I disentangled myself from Nelson and asked him to go on inside and make sure my steak had some pink in it. Uncle Orson would just char them all if you didn't keep an eye on him.

As I walked back to the shore, the dome light on Reach's car came on and he stepped out to wait for me.

"This is the last time we'll get to talk for a while, I guess," he said as I approached.

"You won't hear me complaining about it."

"I don't imagine I will, but there's one thing I want you to think about."

"Don't bother," I said. "I have plenty of things to think about without adding your crap on top. In fact, that's what I came here to tell you. I'm finished. I'm walking away from the bad memories and from you. Rape and betrayal are what happened to me. They aren't me anymore."

"As far as the Army is concerned, none of that happened."

A breeze passed over us and I felt the grit of fine sand on my skin. Even if it wasn't there, I saw wisps of dust dancing over us and rolling up into the turquoise twilight. Darkness was falling quickly. I touched the scar at my eye.

When I was a girl and had problems with other kids at school—I had little patience with their teasing—my father would tell me about the goat. He said everyone has a goat inside and anytime it gets away from us we get upset and angry. But some people, he told me, always want your goat because it makes them feel better about themselves to have yours. So whenever someone was trying to push me into something he would remind me to watch my goat and never let anyone get it.

Reach had gotten my goat.

"As far as I'm concerned you and men like you are the worst part of the Army. You hide behind respect and tradition and use the need of the nation to justify what can't be justified."

"Are you about to lose your shit again? Getting drunk and getting violent—is that all you have left?"

If I could have growled I would have. "You haven't seen me violent. Yet."

I think he believed me. He eased back a little and said, "We're alike in a lot of ways, Hurricane."

"Bullshit."

"It's true. We both wanted to serve our country—"

"You serve yourself. You had a responsibility to your country to serve justice, even if it hurt the Army."

"Hurt the Army?" He looked incredulous at the idea. "What about hurting soldiers? How do you justify that?" His last question was booming with power and self-righteousness.

"Rice and Ahrens?" I asked. Where Reach had gotten loud I got quiet and I leaned in close so he would be sure to hear. "They weren't soldiers. They were like you. Criminals in uniform and the real shame of the military."

Reach squared his shoulders and tried to pull himself straighter, ready to say something back, but I didn't let him. "And before you try to put another one of your lies at my feet—get this—I never did anything to those men. My hands are clean."

"I know you didn't," Reach said, then quietly relaxed against his car like he had suddenly won something from me.

"What?"

"I know you didn't arrange for Rice to be killed or for Ahrens to be run out of every job and relationship he didn't screw up for himself. I know, beyond any shadow of a doubt, you had nothing to do with the death of Sala Bayoumi."

"Then why are you still here trying to be a splinter in my ass?"

"Because even though you didn't do them, they were done in your name."

I stopped and thought about that. Who could and would take that kind of action for me? I'd asked the question before. Uncle Orson denied that he could do such a thing. I fingered the scar and closed my eyes for a moment. Everything I was seeing was turning to dust and the dust was sucking the color of the night into itself. Behind my eyelids there was darkness, but it began to fill with the roaring sound of Humvees and thick, knobby tires on broken pavement. When I heard the first pops of AK fire I opened my eyes again.

There is someone else.

"Fuck you," was all I could say.

"Oh, that's right. You're getting it now. Daddy is the dangerous one, isn't he?"

"That's not possible," I said. The refutation was frail and without power.

"Daddy was spec ops in Vietnam. Bet you didn't even know that. Phoenix program—know what that was? Identification and elimination of civilian supporters of the Vietcong. That's some heavy stuff there. Extralegal stuff, operating as they did in Cambodia and Laos.

Those were the men responsible for the helicopter interrogations. You know, take up two that won't talk and throw one out. The other guy always spilled his guts. They got a lot of solid intel."

"You're just making things up now," I said. I was looking at Reach but I was seeing Daddy and his face was blowing into dust.

"Who still works for the intelligence community? *Consulting*, they call it now. Who has access to Congress and military contractors? Whose name came up when it turned out Sala Bayoumi was involved in black-market weapons supplied to insurgents? Turns out nothing much is beyond Daddy's reach. Not even a prisoner in the custody of Homeland Security."

I closed my eyes again and was instantly within the turmoil of wind and dust. I could feel my wounds again as if they were fresh and bleeding out the heat and color of my body into the desiccated soil of a land that hated me. The pain was an echoing that passed through me and through all the moments of my body since then. For the first time since it had happened to me I saw the faces of the men who had inflicted themselves on me. They had faces and names, histories of their own. It was all gone to me, though. They were that moment. They were what they had done and they would never be other.

Blood dripped from me. Tiny red splashes in dead, brown earth. I could see myself. For once I was not trapped in the pain and horror. I was outside. I was my father. I was watching my child suffer because of the people he believed in.

Rage.

I opened my eyes and let it all drop from me.

I understand.

Trying to keep it all from my father had made it worse for him. It was my fault in a way.

When I opened my eyes Reach was there, staring at me like he had just delivered the best news in the world.

"Why are you telling me this now?" I asked him. "Why even come here? You've tortured me for two weeks. Why?"

"It wasn't your name that came up when Homeland talked with Bayoumi. It was your father's. But he's a careful man. We put surveillance on his phone and computer before I put a little pressure on his baby girl. Then he wasn't so careful."

"Do you have him? Is he in custody? Is that why he doesn't answer his phone?"

When I asked the questions, Reach studied my face. Hard. He must have seen something that satisfied him because he nodded before he smiled a snake's smile. "That's all I needed to know," he said.

"What?"

"You don't know where he is."

"Do you?"

"We will," he answered. "Soon."

If the last time he'd gotten my goat, this time Reach snatched the whole herd. I think it was what he wanted. It was probably what I wanted too.

When he moved away from the car I raised my right hand in a fist. It wasn't subtle. He saw it coming, but that was what I wanted. Reach raised one hand to block my strike and the other to take his own swing at me. Instead of completing my punch, though, I absorbed his block and raised my left under his cocked arm. Both of his arms were up and blocked. When I pushed, his stance opened. With my right knee I put a hard shot right into his groin.

Reach hadn't expected that but he had expected something. When he doubled over, rather than grabbing his battered bits, he pulled a 9-mil from behind his back. There was no time for me to go for my weapon. I didn't need to.

Three shots cracked like thunder in a clear sky. Two bullets hit the car close behind Reach. One struck the rearview mirror and the other, the .22, punctured the fender with a tinny *plink*. The third shot fired had been a shotgun blast. When I turned I saw Clare just bringing the pump-action 12-gauge to level after firing it into the air. Between us were Uncle Orson with a rifle and Nelson with the .22 revolver. My own army.

Reach froze except for his hands. Those he opened. The gun, he let dangle from the trigger guard until I took it from him.

"Get in your car," I told him.

Once he was seated behind the wheel I dropped the magazine and ejected the chambered round before tossing everything in the backseat. I leaned down to the window so my face was level with his. It was my turn to smile. I turned it on big and bright and I leaned in closer to whisper. "Come around me or my family again, we won't just talk. The Ozarks can be a dangerous place where the bodies are never found."

Sure, Reach could file charges. He could bring in feds to handle it, even. But he wouldn't. If it didn't serve the job at hand he couldn't be bothered. He was a tool in a machine. I walked away feeling so much better. I had gotten my goat back.

Uncle Orson's table was spread with smoking steaks and vegetables pulled from the garden that day. Butter was melting into sloppy golden pools within huge russet potatoes. Beside each plate except one was a sweating bottle of beer. Before I sat down I traded the orange soda at my place for a beer. Uncle Orson didn't say anything but I got a look.

I filled everyone in on what Reach had said about Daddy.

"He'll be all right," Orson said, passing around the plate with the T-bones. "Don't worry about your father. I know for a fact that he has ways of handling problems."

"You know more than that, don't you?" I asked.

"I know what I need to know. So do you. Anything more and we become something he needs to worry about."

Nelson groaned loudly. For an instant I thought something horrible had happened. Then he smiled while chewing. "This is amazing." He didn't say it, so much as moan it. "I was so hungry."

That was when my mouth started to water and I realized how hungry I was as well. As I dug in, Nelson laughed at me. I returned the laughter and moaned into my own bite of grilled beef.

"Ohhh, this *is* amazing," I said. "The best ever."

"Clare made a marinade," Orson said.

Clare nodded but didn't say anything; his mouth was full. At that point everyone's mouth was full. For a couple of minutes the weight was gone. There was no talking. It was a good feeling—a surrender feeling. Eating wonderful food with people you love and trust—family—has a way of leveling out the world. It brings your problems down and your joys up. Outside was full night. The tail of the pig had already gone over the fence. It was happening a little earlier each night. Water moved slowly under the dock. Cool air let itself in through the screens. It carried the scent of home—water filled with fish and woods full of juniper.

Life. I felt like it had become a beautiful picture with something deeper behind it. Like one of Nelson's paintings.

"Nelson and I are getting married tomorrow," I said.

Everyone stopped. The three of them looked at me as if I had said *the CIA is telling me to kill the pope.*

"Tomorrow?" Uncle Orson asked. It was a nudge as much as a question. I could hear the sadness in his voice. The suggestion it carried—that I was not thinking of my father—bothered me.

Daddy would be the first to understand.

"Wouldn't you rather wait until we know about your father?" Nelson asked.

"No. We don't know how long that'll take. I'm tired of putting my life into pockets and waiting for the right time to live."

"Courthouse opens at eight in the morning," Clare said. "You both have to be there with ID to get the license. Judge Shea will do it, but he acts like you're pulling his teeth since his wife left him. That was twenty years ago. I can officiate if you want."

Nelson and I were both flat-faced stunned at the suggestion. Uncle Orson just cut a big slice of baked potato and pushed it into his mouth, skin and all. Once he swallowed he said, "Keep your mouths open like that you'll let the flies in. Clarence was a preacher before he was a teacher."

That opened our mouths even wider.

"Assemblies of God," Clarence Bolin, moonshiner and closet Democrat, said.

Things got loud again slowly—laughing, talking, and eating. No one tried to talk me out of the wedding or of doing it tomorrow. In fact, Nelson seemed to be buoyed by the thought. He was talking more. Joking loudly and laughing. When the food was gone he was the first to start clearing the table. Clare joined in and the pair of them went to work. Apparently, they had some unspoken plan to cut me away to let Uncle Orson have a talk.

"Come outside with me a minute, would you?" he asked me. Without waiting for an answer he sauntered out to stand against the railing. He flicked a switch that turned on an underwater light he had suspended below the dock. As I stepped up to the rail, Orson started dropping bits of bread into the water. He handed me half a roll. Minnows and sunfish came to the dropped crumbs as if they'd been waiting for the feast.

"Daddy will understand my decision," I said, hoping to cut off the discussion.

"Of course he will," my uncle answered. "He'd be the first to tell you, never put off today . . ."

"Then why the outside talk?"

"Nelson," he said, flaking and dropping more crumbs. "I'm wondering about Nelson."

I pinched off larger pieces and tossed them farther, watching the sunfish race to each impact in the water. "What about Nelson?" I asked. "You like him."

"Yeah, I do. I like him a lot. Now, I'm wondering if you understand what you're getting into?"

"You mean his health? You knew about that. You and Daddy have practically been pushing me at him since we met."

"It was different then."

"Then?" My voice got a little loud and a little edgy. I brought it down to say, "What *then*? It's only been a few days. Do you mean now that he's getting better?"

My uncle tossed crumbs and wouldn't look at me.

"He is getting better," I said.

"I've seen it before. All the old vets have."

"What are you talking about?"

"All the energy. The new liveliness. Appetite. Hell, even new hair."

"Those are all good things," I said. Even to me it sounded a little like pleading.

"Those meds are horrible things to live with. Worse to die with. A lot of guys stop. Either they give up or the drugs aren't working."

I threw what was left of my bread into the water. This time the fish scattered from the splash before cautiously returning to nibble.

"Any way you want it," Uncle Orson said, "I'm behind you. Your dad is too. He'll be there if he can. If he can't—he'll be there for you later."

My phone rang.

Chapter 24

Carrie Owens was missing.

Since the afternoon, while I was talking with Emily Benson, Carrie had been out of her house. Marion had gotten there to find the mother drunk and still drinking. When she wouldn't produce her daughter, Marion had searched for herself. She found no sign of Carrie. After that, Marion called in the deputy stationed outside. The second search was more thorough, looking under beds and behind piles of dirty clothes and in the dark crannies of the basement. Carrie was not in the house.

They did find one thing, though. On the floor of Carrie's bedroom there was a wooden dowel with a rough, blunt end and a threaded end. It was the handle from a toilet plunger. The end without the threads was bloody.

Her mother denied beating Carrie with the stick but neither Marion nor the deputy believed her.

By the time I was called, the sheriff was there. He had the same kind of search building up as had been done for Angela Briscoe.

I pulled up in the same spit of gravel where I had spent so much time lately. The high beams and emergency lights of my truck rudely intruded on the night. They gamboled over and within the trees on one side. On the other they licked in straight lines across the rock walls. Nowhere did they do more than shimmer in the darkness, dispelling nothing. It didn't matter. I didn't need them. The path I was following had become very familiar recently.

Carrie was sitting cross-legged in the same stained and matted spot where Angela had been killed. She wore the same robe I had seen her in earlier. It was still tied with the string I had put around her waist. Her head was bowed and her shoulders slumped. She had her hands in her lap. They were covered by the painting of Leech I had given her.

"You're so stupid," she said without looking up. "You can't fix some things."

"I know," I told her quietly. "But the things you can't fix you can get away from. You can make changes."

"I tried."

"With Leech?"

She didn't say anything but her back was shaking. I didn't know if she was sobbing or laughing.

"That's why Danny did it, isn't it? For you. To get Leech to help you?"

"God, you're so stupid. You don't understand anything."

I crouched in the grass in front of Carrie and brushed her hair back to see her face.

Crying.

"I understand that home isn't a good place for you. We can change that, get you out of there."

"Go where? You put my dad in jail."

"He's there so he can't hurt you anymore. I know you're mad at your mom for not protecting you. We can get her some help too, but first we have to get you away so she can't hit you again. That's why you ran away today, isn't it? They found the stick she hit you with."

"You don't know nothing."

"Help me, Carrie. Make me understand."

"He was supposed to help me. I gave him what he wanted. Angela wasn't like me. She was a perfect little goodie with her perfect life."

Carrie was beginning to sound sleepy, speaking slower, slurring. I touched her face and she flinched. Her skin felt cold.

"We need to get you out of here and someplace warm."

"Angela was a virgin," she said. "I did her a favor."

"A favor? Letting Danny kill her?"

"Danny didn't kill her. I did."

I froze. Even this far into the trees some of the strobes of my lights came through. Flashes bit at trees and leaves in a random staccato that gave the woods the appearance of moving slowly inward.

"You?" I asked.

"I hit her with the rock. She thought we were playing. I needed a virgin to give to Leech. He wouldn't want me. So I gave him Angela. When that didn't work we tried to make a baby here to give him. You screwed that up. You hurt Danny and spoiled everything."

My head was spinning with the lights. The food I had eaten earlier was rising in my throat with a flush of heat. I wanted to get her parents here, in these woods where so much harm had been done and make them pay. I wanted to make them wish for Leech to come take them.

"How old . . ." I choked back the question and the bile in my mouth. Then I tried again. "When your father . . . When did it start, Carrie?"

"God, you're so stupid," she said. "So stupid. You don't understand anything. It was Mama. It was always Mama." Carrie raised her face to look at me and even in the darkness I could see she was pale. "She didn't hit me with the stick. She didn't *hit* me."

Carrie slumped backwards, falling to the grass. When she did the picture that had covered her hands flipped up and revealed the bleeding gashes up her forearms.

"I want my daddy," she whispered.

It was the blood that finally pulled me into action. I grabbed Carrie up in my arms and started running between the darkness and the flashes of light. At one point I tripped in the trail and fell. Carrie never left my arms. I tumbled and rolled over, clambering back to my feet and ran on without slowing.

At the truck, I pulled out my small first-aid kit, wishing I had Billy's. Then I wished that Billy himself were here. He would have been handling this so much better. I called in and got units on the way as soon as I had her wounds bound. Instantly she bled through all the gauze I had, so I pulled a blanket from behind the seat and cut it into strips to wrap her tighter and more thickly. As I was working, Carrie started convulsing and throwing up a frothy bile. It spilled down her face and into her hair as I turned her head to try and keep her from choking. Within the hot and sticky flow were small white chunks that, for some reason, I thought were teeth. It wasn't until I tried picking them up that I understood they were the remains of pills.

This was a serious attempt at suicide, not an attention-getting ploy. I could see why she thought she was out of options. All her pleas for help had been ignored or misunderstood. Worse, many had been directed at a fairy-tale character.

Carrie Owens died just shy of eleven p.m. I was in the waiting room still bloody and stinking and looking for someone to take it all out on. I tried telling myself I was past this, when my skin felt the grit of another land's soil. The calming pastels of hospital walls burnished out to dead brown and the hot wind carried the dust across my eyes again.

I cried.

I cried like I never had before, in wrenching sobs of pain and uncontrolled tears. No one wanted to be close to me. No one wanted to even look at me until Sheriff Benson arrived. He cried with me.

That should have been it. In a sane and compassionate world the night would have been done with us. We could have gone into the darkness to rage, or drink, or wail in private. The memory of two young girls deserved that, at least.

But there is nothing sane about the world we live in. There is no compassion in the spinning wheel of fate.

The sheriff's cell rang. He took a long moment to compose himself before answering. When he did, his face that was slack and wan, flushed red and turned to marble.

"I'm at the hospital now," he said to the caller. "I'll meet them here. Get everyone not on scene to my office and call in anyone not on duty."

I had enough presence of mind to turn to the water fountain and splash my face. When I turned back to listen, Sheriff Benson said "No" in a very certain tone. Then he added, "I'll call the feds after we talk with the witness."

Once he cut the line he looked at me and said, "Come on, Hurricane. Our work's not done yet."

I followed him out to where the ambulances brought in their passengers. Then we waited.

Billy was the first of our two deputies to be brought in. After him was Calvin. They each had skull fractures behind the right ear. Someone had hit them with something hard. They probably weren't trying to kill; they just didn't understand or didn't care that knocking someone out isn't like the movies.

I tried to talk to Billy but he was out with a tube down his throat.

Does he hear the roar of Humvee tires on bad roads?

Seeing Billy, the liveliest person I'd ever known, slack-faced with a matting of blood in his hair hit me like a wave of hot water. Rage and something else that I didn't want to think about washed all around me.

The EMTs cared nothing for my need to hold Billy's hand. They pulled him away, even pushing me aside to get him into the building. I had just enough sense left in my brain not to fight. I stood there in the night under the glowing red *Emergency* sign. The sheriff followed both of his men into the hospital.

When the next ambulance backed in I was still standing there alone with black thoughts and a feeling in my chest like a raw, open wound. Billy was my friend. In many ways he was barely even a friend. I had kept him at a distance that was comfortable to me.

Why am I so hurt to see him wounded?

I didn't like the question or anything it implied.

I love Nelson.

It was true but all of a sudden it felt so damnably complicated.

Even though time seemed to be moving slow against a strong current, there wasn't enough of it to smooth out or even understand the complications of my feelings. The shrieking beep of the ambulance backup warning stopped. Then the doors burst outward. They were pushed by a pair of big hands and followed by a flurry of white hair. Lawrence, the same EMT who had taken care of Nelson that first day, jumped down from the deck like a much younger man.

"You part of this mess, Hurricane?" he asked even as he pulled out the loaded gurney.

His partner came out with the back end and I got look at the passenger. It was Riley Pruitt. He had been burned, probably shot as well. Lying there, he wasn't near the monster Leech was. As soon as I saw him I understood the basics of what had happened. We had plans with the feds to hit the bikers first thing in the morning. Someone had beat us to it. Someone who didn't have any problem with taking down the cops doing surveillance.

"I am now," I told Lawrence as they started taking their patient away.

He winked at me and then grinned without humor. "Give 'em hell," he said and they were through the doors, rolling smoothly into the light.

I knew exactly who had done this and where to find them. I went to the truck and headed for Moonshines. I should have told the sheriff. At least I should have called in to dispatch and given my location and reason for going. There were a lot of things I should have done, but I went alone in anger, paying no attention to the dry brown dust of other nations that swirled at the edge of my vision.

I hadn't forgotten Carrie Owens or Billy but I had laid aside my grief for them in favor of the rage that served only me.

Selfish.

My truck, with high beams and emergency lights, looked like a low-flying UFO on dark roads as I raced to the bar.

Vengeance.

When I reached the parking lot I stepped out, leaving the lights on. I pulled my weapon and checked its readiness, then I made sure I had spare and loaded magazines. It was just a precaution but it would have been foolish not to be sure. When I walked through the door I had my telescoping baton in my hand, not a gun. More discreet, less provocation, and I liked the feel of it. It's a good thing I did because I gripped it tighter the farther I walked into Moonshines.

The lights were off except for some in the far back, probably the kitchen. Most of the light came from Branson's neon ambience and the clear, moonlit night. In an eerie echo of the dark woods where I found Carrie, my truck's emergency lights shot through and died quickly within the angles of the restaurant. In the murk I could hear movement in two directions. On one side the slight sound of a footstep came from deeper shadows. On the other side, the bar, was the louder sound of ice in a glass. It was the combination of darkness, tiny sounds, and the threat within both that finally calmed me. I wanted vengeance but that wouldn't happen if I got myself killed. It wasn't the fear of dying, though: It was the fear of failing that let me be careful. I'd failed enough for one night.

Without turning my back on the shadows I went around the corner into the bar. There was Byron Figorelli in a square of sodium vapor light that came in through a high window. The yellow light reflected off the bottles behind the bar and through the glass partition, casting a speckled sheen on the stainless-steel distilling tanks. It was beautiful in a weird sort of way, like a promise you choose to believe against all reason. Figorelli put a cigarette in his mouth, then lit it. When the lighter flared the promise was lost to the light. His hands

252 • *Robert E. Dunn*

were swollen and cracked with one finger turned at an angle from the others. They weren't as bloody as his face. His right eye was blown and red and seemed to look at something not there. His nose was crushed and turned toward the bloody right eye. Everywhere there was blood. He smiled.

"You want a drink?" he asked. The slurred mumble wasn't because he'd been drinking.

"Who did this?"

"I ain't no snitch. A lot of things maybe, but . . . Fuck it." He poured more whiskey into the highball glass.

"Are they still here?"

He took a sip, careful of the split lip and broken teeth, then said, "I don't know. But if I had to bet I'd say yes. I'm still kicking so someone is waiting to finish the job." Figorelli took another longer drink and I felt myself craving one as well. "You should get lost," he said after setting the glass down. It touched the bar almost silently and I was surprised by the fact that he was using a coaster. That seemed to be the most normal and the most out-of-place action in this entire exchange. He took a drag from the cigarette then another drink, setting the glass exactly in the center of the coaster.

"I can get you out of here," I told him.

"There's no gettin' out of what's coming. You think about it, you'll know I'm right."

Something creaked in the dining area.

"Come on," I said. "There are still lots of ways this can play. Help me get the bastards, then laugh in their face. Don't do that honor-among-scumbags crap."

Figorelli laughed at that despite the pain it caused him. "I like you," he said. "You got some brass balls, lady. Bigger than I ever had." He laughed again; this time it was pointed inward. After that he drained the last of the whiskey from his glass.

"This isn't the time to talk anatomy, Figgs. I think we should get out of here."

"You think I'm a son of a bitch, don't you? You think I'm just another fucking goombah. Maybe I am. But you think I'm like all the rest of 'em. I ain't."

There was another movement in the shadows. It could have been a rat, but I knew it wasn't. I squeezed my grip tighter, comforted by the feel of my weapon in my hand. As soon as I thought it I realized that the weapon was my baton, not my gun. Was I being watched? If I went for the automatic at the small of my back, would I make it? I took a deep breath and held still. There was a chance that the lack of a gun in my hand was the only thing keeping things quiet so far.

"You know why I'm in this fix?" Figorelli asked. "Because I'm not a complete son of a bitch. Because I'm soft. I didn't kill your boyfriend because I felt sorry for him."

In my chest my heart beat hard and something cold bloomed outward with it.

"What do you mean?"

"We had a deal, him and me. He wanted to die and I wanted his share. Like some kind of schmuck I wouldn't do it. Who knew I had a conscience?" Figorelli laughed again. This time it was more spitting in the face of life than introspection. "Hell, he was dying anyway. I thought that just once things would go easy."

"Then why'd you send the bikers after him?"

"That was all on Johnny. He wanted the painter's share too. He'd already fucked up and got desperate to keep Joey D's people away. He let the bikers sell meth for a cut then used them to cut out the locals cooking booze. It didn't matter. It never mattered. The Marciano family wanted this place, they were gettin' it." He was looking at me then, really looking. The light of confession or maybe the light of death was in his one good eye as he stared. In his hand was the empty drink and his cigarette smoldered, untouched in an ashtray. "You got any idea what it could be worth? Owning a still that's legal but pumping out gallons of extra booze that no one looks for. That's just the tip of the thing. No middlemen, no markup, no taxes."

He started shifting his left eye, casting his fractured gaze over my right shoulder. When I began to turn, Figorelli shook his head. It was a small movement, barely a tic, but combined with the fear in his eye it stopped me. I adjusted my grip on the baton and put my thumb on the button.

"Can you believe this fucking world? I did the right thing, maybe the one time in my life, and it goes to shit. But there's no figuring some people out. First your guy wants to die but he won't just lay down and let it happen. He don't give a good goddamn about this place but he won't let it go. Some people gotta go hard. Then he tells Dauterive about this trust thing. He coulda just spit in the guy's face and dared him to do something about it. If he ain't got a death wish now he's just fucking stupid. If he'd just died like he was supposed to, none of this would have happened. Now Dauterive is going to make sure it happens before things get in your hands. This thing can't stand up to probate court and audits."

"Wait," I said. "Dauterive is going to make sure what happens?"

"What the hell you think?" he asked me. At the same time he opened his good eye wide and nodded his head. I imagine my eyes widened too, both in alarm at what he had said and in anticipation of the blows to come.

From behind me, stealthy motion became a lunge. Someone was coming out of the shadows making a reach for the baton in my hand. Trying to disarm me was their mistake. A blow to the head or a shot in the back and everything would have been over.

I felt hands touch my arm and I turned with it, rolling my shoulder forward and pivoting. As my body came around I pressed the button, dropping the weighted end of the baton into full extension. The body behind me kept moving forward as I came around my pivot point, swinging my arm and baton. When I came full circle I added extra energy by snapping my wrist. The baton slammed into the back of a thick skull with a satisfying *crunch*. The attacker went down sprawling onto Figorelli, then rolling to the floor like a spilled drink.

"Fuckin' A," Figgs said, then poured himself another highball.

"Who's that?" I asked.

"It *was* Sal Rubio. I wouldn't lay odds it's anything more than a body after that crack. They call you Hurricane for a good reason, don't they?"

"What did you mean, Dauterive was going to make sure things happen?"

"I told you. He ain't the go-to-court kind of lawyer. He's more hands on, know what I mean?"

"They're going after Nelson for his share of this place?"

"Dauterive said, if the painter dies before the trust thing is all set up he can beat it."

"When?" I almost shouted at him.

Figorelli held up his mangled left hand and counted off on his twisted fingers as he spoke. "Tonight was about the bikers, me, and the painter. In that order."

Chapter 25

The further that night went the further I strayed from being a cop. Who I was or who I thought I was didn't matter placed up against the lives of people I cared about. Nelson was in danger so I left Byron Figorelli sitting in a dark bar with a man—possibly critically injured, possibly dead—at his feet. They were my responsibility and I walked—make that *ran*—away with barely a thought. Once in the truck and speeding down the road, I did call in to report and request medical care. Our entire department was involved with the scene at the Nightriders meth lab and clubhouse. I tried to reach the sheriff directly but he wasn't picking up. In the end I left messages telling who was at Moonshines and why. I also outlined as best I could who was responsible for the violence and where I expected to find them. Finally, I asked for help to meet me at Nelson's place. It was a faint hope, since anyone who could help was on the other side of the county.

My ass was hanging out in the wind every bit as much as when I had left Figorelli. I believed him when he said there was no getting away for him. I'd gotten Sal Rubio but someone else would be coming for Figorelli: if not tonight, sometime soon. I didn't care about either one of us.

From Moonshines to Nelson's place is, at a normal pace, a fifteen-minute drive. It takes that long only because of the little bit of Branson traffic and the dark, twisted Ozarks roads. That night I was flying wildly over blacktop intended for meandering. Still, in the way that time has of dilating in crisis, the trip seemed to take hours.

Within my little bubble of time I had a chance to think. Not feel, but actually think about my choices and life. It sounds strange to say after so many years of almost obsessively considering and reconsidering every moment of my life. But that obsession, I had been learning over the last couple of weeks, covered more than it revealed. All thoughts in times of crisis are prayers, silent wishes, bargains, or gifts of forgiveness to those we love. In my truck, running headlong toward violence—*hoping for violence*—I realized that I had never left the dirt of Iraq. My blood and life were still dripping from me and I was still praying silent thoughts of love to the people in my life.

There was no God in my prayers. That kind of faith had long ago withered from my heart. It didn't matter. Like humanity everywhere I offered bargains for the ones I loved. Since I didn't have God to call on I grabbed onto someone equally perfect and distant. My therapist. I offered the one thing I had that she kept trying to get me to give up: anger. I promised, if my father was safe, if Billy would live and be well, if I could save Nelson for no matter how long, I would turn away from the dun-colored dust of Iraq. I would never again look on the muddy blots of my blood or watch the wisps of brown grit crawl across the sky. I would forgive Rice and Ahrens—even Reach.

If.

With my mind so deep into itself I almost missed the turn into Nelson's drive. If I had, it would have changed everything. As it was, I turned headlong into the lights of an oncoming car, both of us stopping barely in time to keep from colliding. The quiet of relief lasted only a moment then, from the passenger side of the car, came a muzzle flash and the instant inward crashing of my windshield.

I didn't wait for a second shot. I slammed the gas pedal down, ramming the car, then forcing it back down the drive. The car fought back but my truck had both weight and torque on its side. I pushed it back through the smoke of its burning tires all the way back until it hit Nelson's truck by the garage door. In the glare of my headlights I saw tiny glitter flashes coming from the backseat.

Dauterive.

Cutting my wheel to the left I opened the angle and let the car shoot off into the shrubs while my truck blocked the entire drive. That also allowed me to come out my door with the truck between me and the car.

This time I came out with my 9-mil ready.

They were ready as well. Two more shots finished off my windshield and passenger-side window. I dropped to the ground and into the gap between asphalt and the truck body. The driver had come out of the car. He was standing half-covered by the open door and turned toward the front of my truck. He was probably thinking I would come around that way because of the greater cover offered by the engine. It would have been smart, but I never claimed to be smarter than the bad guys, only meaner. I fired two rounds at his exposed leg. One hit the tibia just inches below the knee joint. He went down screaming.

I didn't linger to gloat. I rolled back and onto my feet, then crouched behind the rear tire. As soon as I stopped, the screaming guy started firing blindly under the truck. He was carrying a revolver—six and out. As soon as the hammer hit an empty chamber I darted for the bushes at the back of the truck.

From where I was hidden I could see that both of the passenger-side doors of the car were open. I could hear the scraping of feet but could see no one. I had to stand.

As soon as I did I caught the glint of sequins from Dauterive's suit. The sparkle was moving. I took aim forward of the motion, at the gap between house, cars, and shrubs. It was the same spot from which I had been ambushed by the biker.

Nelson, duct-taped hand and mouth, was shoved into that gap. Right behind him was Dauterive. Before I could fire there was a shot and a whining slug passing so close to my face I felt the heat of it. The screaming guy—I saw then it was Charlie Castellano—had reloaded and almost taken my head off. He was unsteady on one foot and leaning against the car, but I couldn't let him have another chance. I double-tapped, two rounds, center mass and he was down for good.

As soon as I fired, I moved. Half-a-dozen rounds sliced through the bushes behind me. Dean Morelli was not as old-school as his buddy. No revolver for him; he had an automatic. And I was betting from the way he was shooting he had an extended magazine. We were obviously two different kinds of shooters. He went for volume. I was more of a careful-aim kind of girl. The thing about volume shooters, they tend to be more easily distracted.

Between the asphalt parking area and the shrubs were a line of ornamental stones. I picked one up. When I'd last moved, it was to my right, away from Castellano. Morelli would expect me to keep going that way so I tossed the stone into a big bush to my right while I kept low and went left back around the still-running car.

Another flurry of rounds tore into the bush where the stone had landed. Morelli figured it out by the time I got around the car and Nelson's truck. When I popped my head up he had turned and was almost ready. *Almost* wasn't enough. I killed my second man that night with another two-round tap to the heart.

That left me with one round in the chamber and four rounds left of my ten-round magazine. They were all reserved for Dauterive's sparkling shirt. He was armed as well. His pistol was aimed not at me but at Nelson, who was leaning against the corner of the house.

There was just enough light that I could see Nelson's eyes, but not enough to read them. There wasn't fear—I was sure of that—but neither was I getting relief. All I felt from him was sadness and I didn't understand.

"Perhaps we should talk, young lady," Dauterive said without a trace of his peckerwood accent.

"What's to talk about?" I asked him.

"The life of your fiancé," he answered slowly and carefully.

"There's no discussion. If you harm him any further, I'll kill you."

"That's a fine way for an officer of the law to speak."

"That's the wrong hope to hang your hat on," I told him. "The law and I have kind of been letting each other down lately."

"I see," he said and he looked to be thinking things over. "My situation here might seem a mite"—he thought about it for a second—"untenable. But I don't believe that you will allow any harm to come to this fine and talented man."

"Try me," I said. "If I let you take Nelson away, you'll kill him anyway. So that's not going to happen. If you shoot him, you die. If you put your weapon down, I'll arrest you, for what it's worth. You're a lawyer with money and connections: arrest sounds like your best bet."

"I've never been one to play the best bet." He smiled like he was the most charming man at a party full of pretty people.

I shrugged slightly and said, "Untenable."

The smile slithered off Dauterive's face, leaving only a cold void of a face. He said, "The man is dying already. Time ticking away. Let me be on out of here and you can have what time is left with no more pain. Just let me walk away. Tell me you will and I'll take your word. I'll put my weapon away and be gone."

Nelson pushed himself up from where he was leaning to stand

fully on his feet. Even from where I was I could hear the wet grunting of his effort. The change in posture brought him more into the light. I could see the blood on the front of his shirt and smearing out from under the tape over his mouth. He looked at me. His eyes, I could see then, had the tired weight of ages and loss. Standing straighter, almost to attention, he then turned to stare down Bodie Dauterive.

"If I gave my word," I said, "I'd be lying. I'm not sure how many lies I have left in me."

"What's he doing?" Dauterive asked me, ignoring what I'd told him.

"I think he's telling you to go to hell, Mr. Dauterive," I said.

"No. He's doing something."

I took a quick look again and saw that Nelson had indeed taken a step toward the gun. My first thought was to egg him on, to use it to put more pressure on Dauterive until I began to understand the look in Nelson's eyes. He wasn't looking at me. He wasn't really looking at Dauterive. His gaze was straight ahead but he was looking at something no one else could see.

It took a moment, but right then I put everything together. Nelson wanted to die fighting. So much of everything that had happened was just him trying to find a fight that would take his life. It took another moment to realize that the only way I could stop what was happening was to shoot Dauterive. Another moment of hesitation and Nelson was moving, rushing right at the gun pointed into his throat.

Dauterive could have dropped his weapon. He understood that at the same time I knew I could shoot him. In the last fraction of a second he looked at Nelson and back to me. His choice was as cold as his face.

We fired at almost the same instant. Bodie Dauterive put one bullet into Nelson and I put five into Dauterive.

It was a terrible wound but just a wound. Dauterive's shot went into Nelson's shoulder but like so many things, that is not like we imagine. From close range the slug all but tunneled through the muscle and bone, leaving a wide, bloody hole. An ambulance and Branson police sent by the sheriff's department arrived quickly after that, while I was still cursing Nelson for what he'd done.

Suicide.

So much of what we'd gone through was about Nelson trying to die without pulling the trigger himself. I wanted to be angry but I couldn't. What had I been doing with my life but killing myself slowly for the last ten years? Even sitting in the driveway, with Nelson bleeding onto me, I thought of Carrie Owens and the depth of her despair. I couldn't be angry. Anger doesn't fix anything. I'd learned that much.

So I decided to drop the anger and to make a commitment to life. Nelson's and mine.

Three days later, as soon as I could arrange things, we married in the hospital chapel. Clare officiated. It was a noisy affair. Daddy was there to give me away. He'd reappeared to show me a file marked *secret*. It was only a few pages from a much larger file, but it told an interesting story. It had begun with a coincidence. Just as Reach had charged, I had indeed been connected to Sala Bayoumi. I had bribed him all those years ago to keep an eye on Rice. That wasn't why he'd killed him. There was no clear reason for that. Rice just made himself an easy guy to hate. Maybe it caught up with him. The coincidence happened when my father met Bayoumi while he was working with the DoD, investigating how weapons intended for our tribal allies were being diverted to insurgents. Sala Bayoumi was playing both sides of the field. When he tried to get out by feeding information to Homeland while seeking asylum, he gave up my name and it caused an alert on my father's involvement. Reach had never reopened an investigation on me. My father was the target and Reach was using what he knew about me to apply pressure. A dozen intelligence agencies working in our longest-running wars and not a one shared information. Typical.

My father told me he had fixed his problems and that I now had a clean record with the Army. I don't get justice, but I'm no longer the punch line in a horrible joke. Sometimes you take what you can get. I didn't ask about the things Reach had said. Isn't that what they say: Don't ask questions you don't want the answers to? It was telling, though, that Reach retired from the Army right after that. My father was indeed the dangerous one in the family.

Nelson asked Uncle Orson to be his best man. They both wore their uniforms and looked amazing. Friends were there too. Sheriff Benson and his wife Emily attended and so did Billy. It was a wonderful day. You never know when the last one of those comes until it's past. Of course the flip side is true. You never know when the next day will be amazing.

I insisted that Nelson begin chemo again. Then radiation. That's to say, I pushed, I nagged, and I fought for the life he seemed too willing to give up. One night, sitting beside him, I got the courage to ask, "Why? Why did you want to die?"

I didn't expect an answer. He was weak and so tired but he told me, "I didn't want to die. I just didn't want this."

"This what?"

"How I am now. Before I met you . . ." His words faded and I thought perhaps he had fallen asleep or had simply shied from the thoughts behind his closed eyes. "Can you imagine?" he asked suddenly and in a stronger voice. "Can you imagine doing this alone?"

"No," I said. It was the truth. Going alone into the world of pain and fear was a terrible thought. I'd had my own glimpses.

"Then . . . then I couldn't imagine making you go through it with me. I wanted them to shoot me so you wouldn't have *this*—all of this hell in your life."

I didn't know what to say. I sat and held Nelson's hand and silently cried over it. It wasn't for me or him, either. All the tears spilling out of me at that moment were for time lost and chances set aside because of fear and doubt, the right way to act and the wrong thing to say, time spent hating and regretting instead of living. Then I wasn't so silent. My back was shaking and thick sobs pushed my mouth open. Tears rained from my eyes and watered the wasted skin on his hand still in my grip.

Nelson said, "You're blowing like a hurricane, you know."

I didn't laugh.

Then he said, "I love you, Katrina."

"I know," I told him. "I love you too. So much."

"But I love you more now than I did."

"What do you mean?"

"Before, I loved you enough to die for you. Now—" He jerked my hand with surprising strength. "Listen to me. Look at me, Katrina. This is important."

I looked him right in the eyes.

"*Now*—" he said. "Now, I love you enough to live for you."

That would be the perfect place to say everything was all right and the ending was happily ever after. That would be cheating all the days after of their meaning. It was work and it was scary but we got through it. When he got over the wall and got a glimpse of the world on the other side, he immediately asked for his tools to begin painting.

For my part, I tried—honestly tried—to keep the promises I'd made in prayer to my therapist. I found out it was not so easy to just let go of anger. It has a way of hiding in your personal shadows and hanging on. The therapist says it's a process, not an event or even a decision. I didn't hate going to see her so much anymore.

Even when you are in the middle of fighting for life, life itself has a way of ignoring you and going right on with its business. In the days that followed that awful night, Carrie Owens's father was released from jail and her mother arrested. Both Angela and Carrie had their funerals. The news did stories about them and Leech, then all were forgotten by those who didn't know them. Those who did would never be able to forget or understand.

There was a lot of blood but no bodies were found at Moonshines. Byron Figorelli and his buddy Jimmy Cardo turned up in a Louisiana bayou with a bullet hole each and hands wired behind their backs. I actually felt bad for Figorelli.

Things settled down. It was just life. I rarely touched the scar beside my eye and the dust of Iraq mostly stayed away. By then it was fall, but fall is really just the end of summer, that beautiful transition.

Robert E. Dunn is the author of the novels *The Red Highway, The Dead Ground,* and *Behind the Darkness,* as well as the novella *Motorman.* Before writing novels he spent more than twenty years as a film and video producer for both corporate and broadcast projects. A full-time fiction writer, he now resides in Kansas City with his daughters, an old truck, and an even older dog.

He can be found online at robertdunnauthor.blogspot.com or on Twitter at @WritingDead.